THE SILENT SHORE OF MEMORY

Other books by John C. Kerr:

Cardigan Bay
Hurricane Hole
A Rose in No Man's Land
Only a Khaki Shirt
Fell the Angels

THE SILENT SHORE OF MEMORY

A NOVEL BY

JOHN C. KERR

FORT WORTH, TEXAS

Copyright © 2015 by John C. Kerr

Library of Congress Cataloging-in-Publication Data

Kerr, John C., author.
 The silent shore of memory : a novel / by John C. Kerr.
     p. cm.
 Summary: «The silent shore of memory chronicles the life of James Barnhill from his days as a young Confederate soldier through the trials of Reconstruction in his native Texas and his later career as a lawyer and judge. Steeped in the history of the South, [the novel] explores the nuances of views on slavery and the dissolution of the Union, the complexity of race relations and race politics during the thirty years following the Civil War, and the powerful bonds of familial love and friendship»—Amazon.com.
 ISBN 978-0-87565-619-9 (alk. paper)
 1. Lawyers—Texas—Fiction. 2. Soldiers—Confederate States of America—Fiction. 3. Southern States—Race relations—Fiction. 4. Reconstruction (U.S. history, 1865-1877)—Texas—Fiction. I. Title.
 PS3611.E7635S56 2015
 813'.6—dc23
                                    2015026387

TCU Press
TCU Box 298300
Fort Worth, Texas 76129
817.257.7822
www.prs.tcu.edu
To order books: 1.800.826.8911

Cover and Text Design by Preston Thomas

This book is dedicated to
DAVID M. POTTER,
HISTORIAN OF THE SOUTH

And, when the stream
which overflowed the soul was passed away,
A consciousness remained that it had left,
Deposited upon the silent shore
Of memory, images and precious thoughts,
That shall not die, and cannot be destroyed.

WILLIAM WORDSWORTH,
The Churchyard Among the Mountains

CONTENTS

Prologue   1

PART ONE
WAR

Chapter One	4
Chapter Two	16
Chapter Three	28
Chapter Four	38
Chapter Five	51
Chapter Six	63
Chapter Seven	75
Chapter Eight	87
Chapter Nine	99

PART TWO
RECONSTRUCTION

Chapter Ten	114
Chapter Eleven	125
Chapter Twelve	136
Chapter Thirteen	146
Chapter Fourteen	158
Chapter Fifteen	168
Chapter Sixteen	179
Chapter Seventeen	190

PART THREE
THE PROMISE OF THE NEW SOUTH

Chapter Eighteen	204
Chapter Nineteen	216
Chapter Twenty	229
Chapter Twenty-one	241
Chapter Twenty-two	256
Chapter Twenty-three	268
Chapter Twenty-four	279
Chapter Twenty-five	292

Epilogue   302
About the Author   304

PROLOGUE

*The Big Thicket
East Texas
October 1915*

The old man reclined in his camp chair, stretching his hands behind his head, staring into the blazing fire as the wind sang in the boughs overhead. The flames cast shadows on the tents circling the campfire, ghostly white in the moonlight filtering through the canopy of pines. Massaging his left shoulder, the old man said, "Norther's on the way. I can feel it."

"That old wound, Judge?" asked a man in the shadows.

The old man nodded. "Only with a change in the weather."

"I'll be dad-gummed," said another from the darkness, raising his voice over the wind. "After all those years."

"Fifty-two, to be exact," said the judge.

A teenaged boy sitting cross-legged stared across the fire, mentally calculating the year the judge was wounded. He was intensely curious about his grandfather's war experiences, though the old man seldom, if ever, discussed them. "Well, Grandpa," he said encouragingly, "sitting around a fire like this, with the rifles stacked by the tents, must bring back memories."

The judge considered. In truth, the campfire by the canvas, the wind in the pines, the scent of woodsmoke and pinesap flooded him with other memories. Bear hunts in the Big Thicket, year after year in October, for almost forty years. Then he summoned a dim remembrance of a campground, an entire hillside illuminated by hundreds, perhaps thousands of flickering campfires, the soft murmur of men's low voices, someone in the distance singing a slow, sad ballad. Thinking of home. Of Mother. He closed his eyes and silently recited the verses:

> *I have seen Him in the watch fires of a hundred circling camps . . .*
> *They have builded Him an altar in the evening dews and damps . . .*
> *I can read His righteous sentence by the dim and flaring lamps . . .*

Wrong anthem, he considered, but the lyrics captured the scene perfectly. Well, he never cared for the other one. Even the name—Dixie—connoted all the things gone wrong.

His reverie was broken by the strains of a harmonica, the notes bent and slurred together. The judge opened his eyes. An old black man, his slouch hat pulled low over his eyes, shaped the notes with his hands. "Ohhh," he sang in a rich basso, "the old dogs sleep in the sunshine, yes they do. And the ol' men, they doze in they chairs."*

The judge smiled in the darkness. "Pass me the bottle," he whispered to the man beside him.

"Sing it, Old Kil," called out another.

"The ol' guns hang there a-rustin'," sang the black man, "while they dream about killin' the bears."

"Yes, sir," said the judge, pouring an inch of bourbon into his cup as the black man resumed playing the harmonica. "Dream about killing the bears is about all we can do nowadays."

"Kil's hounds will find us Old Bruin," said another man, hitherto silent. "If anyone can."

"It won't be long, Mr. Walker," said the judge, "before the last black bear in Texas is gone. Even in the thicket."

"Yep," agreed the man next to him. "Those rich oil and lumber men from Houston, with their fancy guides and dogs, have damned near wiped them out. Just like the longleaf pine."

Judge James Barnhill stared into the flames as he took a swallow of whiskey, savoring the warmth that spread through his frame as the breeze freshened. "I remember the days," he said, "when a man with some good hounds and a '73 Winchester could bring home two hundred bears in a season."

"C'mon, Grandpa," said the boy. "Tell us a story from the war. Tell us about the Texas Brigade's attack on Round Top." Another boy, sitting on the ground next to him, gave the old man an expectant look.

"Another time, Jimmy," said the judge, tossing back the last of his whiskey and running his sleeve across his mouth. "It's late and we'll have to be up mighty early if we have a chance of finding Old Bruin." With a yawn he struggled up from his chair, his shoulder throbbing and legs half asleep. "Time to hit the bedrolls before that norther blows in."

* As recounted by the late W. T. Block in "The Big Thicket Bear Hunters Club of Kountze."

PART ONE
WAR

CHAPTER ONE

JAMES BARNHILL AWAKENED IN THE COLD DAWN, staring up at whitewashed rafters with his head propped up on hard pillows, gritting his teeth at the stab of pain that radiated from his chest. The thin wool blanket did little for the chill that numbed his toes. Other men in the makeshift hospital were waking, some groaning softly, coughing, or reaching for a glass of water. With daylight the nurse should be coming with her hamper of warmed blankets, and the black orderly with fuel for the pot-bellied stove in the corner.

Closing his eyes, Barnhill thought back to the abandoned barn where they'd carried him after the battle. Darkness had come early on that mid-December afternoon, with the temperature falling below freezing. The barn overflowed with the wounded packed on litters like cordwood, amid eerie shadows from the kerosene lanterns hanging from the rafters, the close air reeking of manure, carbolic, and ether, and filled with the agonizing cries of men braving the surgeons' scalpels and saws. More a charnel house than a field hospital. He had no idea how long he'd lain there before he came to, though he distinctly remembered the moment he regained consciousness, wondering if he'd died and found his way to some strange purgatory, and then overcome with joy at the realization he was alive. For a time he couldn't remember what had happened, and then the image of his cousin Sam peering down at him came to mind, and he understood at once the reason for the terrible pain in his chest.

CHAPTER ONE

He should have been dead. Along with the thousands in blue or butternut uniforms scattered in the underbrush of the tangled hardwoods of the Virginia countryside. When at last he was carried to the crude operating table under the brightly burning lamps, fortified by a large swig of brandy, the surgeon, whose sleeves and apron were covered in bright blood, whistled through his teeth as he cut away Barnhill's jacket to examine the wound.

"Jesus, Mary, and Joseph," he muttered in a faint Irish brogue. "You're a mighty lucky lad. That ball nicked a brass button, but this is what saved you." With forceps he gently removed a blood-soaked miniature Bible and held it up to show the irregular hole made by the .58 caliber minié. Gasping with pain, Barnhill signaled his comprehension, uttering a silent prayer for his deliverance. Consciousness, thankfully, fled. Conserving the anesthesia for amputations, the surgeon quickly dislodged the bullet and the shreds of paper from Barnhill's chest, stitched and dressed the wound, and called for the next man.

Barnhill glanced at the bedside table, where a small glass jar held that minié ball. A ball that surely would have passed through his heart, ending his life at the age of twenty-four, had it not been for the Bible, inscribed by his mother, that he always kept inside his jacket. He considered how many men had died and no end in sight to the war. It made him angry, angry at the Yankee generals for sending tightly massed men across a mile of open ground under relentless fire, and angrier still at the politicians who were bent on subjugating the South at the point of a bayonet. He tried to sit up but was convulsed by pain and slumped back on the pillows. Closing his eyes, he heard the door open and the creaking wheels of a cart. Two nurses, in matching blue-striped dresses with starched white aprons and caps, maneuvered a wicker hamper between the long rows of iron beds. As expected, an elderly black man followed behind with an armful of firewood. As he tended the fire, the nurses moved among the wounded, dispensing blankets, pouring water, removing bedpans, and checking the men for fever.

When the nurse arrived at the foot of his bed, Barnhill sighed as she draped a warm blanket over his cold legs. "I don't suppose," he said, "you brought that newspaper I asked for?"

She placed a hand lightly on his brow. "Of course I did," she answered, "though it's several days old. I'll be back with it when I'm done with the others."

"Thank you, ma'am," said Barnhill with a pained smile. "And I could sure use a cup of coffee."

"There's no coffee," she said curtly as she knelt for a bedpan. "Thanks to the blockade."

No coffee, thought Barnhill. Water, chamomile tea, stale biscuits, and Virginia ham were all that were offered in the hospital, a converted Richmond girls' school overseen by a certain Mrs. Webb, society matron. When the nurse returned with the *Richmond Enquirer*, Barnhill's eyes were drawn to the date: December 16, 1862. "Nurse," he said as she moved away.

"Yes?"

"What day is it?"

"Why, it's the twenty-second. Not long till Christmas."

The twenty-second, thought Barnhill. Almost a week since he'd been wounded. He'd spent the night in the field hospital and the next day on the bone-rattling train to Richmond. He turned back to the newspaper. The right-hand column was devoted to the battle, under the headline "MAJOR VICTORY FOR LEE'S ARMY AT FREDERICKSBURG." The detailed account of the fighting on Jackson's front accorded with his own bird's-eye view. He closed his eyes, his thoughts returning to the battle. The day had dawned bitterly cold with dense, swirling fog where the Texas Brigade, part of Hood's Division, was encamped on a gentle, wooded hillside several miles from the wide Rappahannock River. He remembered listening to the sounds of the Federals plundering the nearby town—explosions, whoops, and shouts—while he and his fellow officers sat around a campfire with their breakfast of cornbread, bacon, and coffee. The army still had coffee. Disgusted by the Yankee depredations against innocent civilians, they'd debated where Burnside's Army of the Potomac would attack—to their left, where Lee had posted the bulk of Longstreet's Corps on the heights above town; in the center, defended by Hood's Division and Pickett's Division of Virginians; or on the right, the line held by Jackson's Corps concealed in the woods above the railroad embankment.

All through the morning Barnhill had stared into the dense fog, listening to the faint sounds that drifted across from the thousands of men and horses that had crossed the river on pontoons in the night. As the sun rose in the pale blue sky now visible overhead, the fog crept from the woodlands across open fields toward the river, like water slowly draining from a tub. From his vantage on a slight rise, Barnhill had been able to see that Stonewall Jackson's Corps, approximately half of General Lee's army, occupied the high ground to the east, concealed in dense woods behind the curving embankment of the Richmond, Fredericksburg and Potomac Railroad. The attacking Federals would have to cross almost a mile of open ground under the Confederates' well-sited artillery. The fog slowly lifted, exposing the steeples and rooftops of the town, until all that remained was a dense, whitish mass obscuring the river and enemy lines. And then, before straining Confederate eyes, it burnt entirely away and rose like a curtain on an immense spectacle: row upon row of neatly ordered bluecoats, bayonets glinting in the sun, regimental standards streaming, tens and tens of thousands of men massing for an attack. The sudden appearance of so vast a force had been greeted with complete silence, the most beautiful and the most terrible sight Barnhill had ever beheld.

Opening his eyes, Barnhill turned back to the account of the battle in the Richmond paper, describing the furious Federal bombardment followed by massed infantry—Meade's Pennsylvanians, he noted with interest—charging across at least a mile of open ground toward the men of A. P. Hill's division on the right of the Texas Brigade. Staring up at the rafters, Barnhill envisioned the spectacle: the puffs of white circling the orange muzzle flashes of the Union cannons seconds before the thundering reports reached his ears, the shell bursts creeping toward Hill's brigades concealed in the dense woods. For close to an hour the Union batteries had pounded the Confederate positions, killing dozens of horses and splintering treetops over the heads of men hugging the cold, wet earth. At last a low yell traveled down the Confederate lines, signaling the start of the Union advance, three long lines of bluecoats, each ten thousand men or more, advancing in the perfect order of a dress parade, pennants and standards flapping, in the lee of the unanswered cannonade tearing the Confederate ranks. And then, with a shout that could be heard above the crashing shells, the Confederate batteries opened, sweeping the densely massed infantry with enfilading cannon fire, halting the advance, causing the lines to buckle and fall back.

For a moment Barnhill had thought the battle over, but the Federals straightened and mended their lines, and, with a coolness and resolution that sent a tingle down Barnhill's spine, began again their slow, determined advance across a mile of open ground littered with hundreds of dead and dying men. They closed within four hundred yards of the railroad embankment when all at once the hidden Confederate infantry unleashed a volley from thousands of rifles that rolled up and down the lines, filling the treetops with a dense cloud of black powder. Under the storm of shells and minié balls, the bluecoats charged toward the center of Jackson's Corps, funneling in a solid mass across the railroad into a boggy neck of woodland the Confederates had carelessly left undefended.

Barnhill and the rest of his regiment had observed the battle raging to their right with fascination mixed with an odd sense of detachment. As the Union infantry surged into the woods, Barnhill heard the sound of hoofbeats and watched as John Bell Hood, the division commander, reined in his roan at the regimental command post. Sensing the imminent peril of Hill's Division, Hood shouted a command: "Send an officer at once to Hill to inquire if the general desires we mount a supporting attack!"

That officer was Barnhill, riding a coal-black stallion, accompanied by his cousin Sam on a chestnut mare. They recklessly plunged down a narrow trail blazed by the Texans days earlier, the air filled with the stench of cordite and black powder and the clatter of rifle fire that drowned out the hoofbeats. Barnhill turned the stallion to the right, reasoning he would find the general's headquarters in the rear, but the path was obstructed by downed trees and impenetrable underbrush. Turning back to his left, he was suddenly confronted by hundreds of men rushing toward them, clad in butternut and gray, in the pell-mell dash of full, panicked flight, many bleeding, most without weapons, fleeing to the rear. Shouting "This way!" to Sam, Barnhill cantered up the hillside, conscious of the *sssss* and *smack* of balls of lead singing in the air and striking the trees. To his left he could dimly see an advancing line of bluecoats. Spurring his horse, he reached a clearing, where he found a neat row of tents, muskets stacked, and the men reclining on rolled-up coats or bedrolls. Riding up to an officer, he called out: "Where would I find General Hill?"

"Damned if I know," the man had drawled. "This here's Orr's Rifles."

As Barnhill wheeled in the direction of the intensifying battle, aware that the Federals had poured thousands of men into the boggy woods and were driving the fleeing Confederates, another horseman rode into the clearing, a handsome man with a full black beard wearing the fine embroidered gray coat of a brigadier general. "Hold your fire!" the general shouted, his eyes ablaze. "It's our own men!" As the Federals rushed forward, the Confederates in the clearing bolted, dashing into the woods in full retreat. The dark-bearded general stared for a moment at the onrushing bluecoats and then was shot with a cry, falling from the saddle with one boot tangled in the stirrups.

Opening his eyes, Barnhill listened to the low voices of the nurses at the far end of the room and then turned back to the newspaper. Under the caption "General Gregg Slain" was the likeness of a handsome officer with a thick black beard—the same man, Barnhill was certain, he'd seen as he fell from his horse. He quickly read the newspaper account: "The attacking Federals advanced as far as the South Carolina regiment, whose gallant commander, General Maxcy Gregg, was mortally wounded, until repulsed by the brigades commanded by General Jubal Early." The rest of the article was devoted to Burnside's attack on the Confederate left, wave after wave of Federal infantry storming the high ground known as Marye's Heights. "The Union men," wrote the reporter, "pour out upon the plain in a stream which seems to come from an inexhaustible fountain. The meadows are black with them." Longstreet's brigades, sheltering behind a stone wall, had cut them to pieces. Tilting his head back on the hard pillow, Barnhill stared up at the ceiling, trying to piece together his jumbled memory. From the moment the general was shot from his horse, it all was a blur . . . thrown from his horse when the poor creature was shot through the neck, suddenly finding himself in the midst of a mass of onrushing men clad in butternut, screaming and firing their rifles as they charged the bluecoats. Grabbing a rifle from the hands of a fallen soldier, Barnhill had fired round after round, with Sam kneeling and firing beside him until, at last, the advancing Federals wavered, halted, and then rushed toward the safety of the railroad embankment. And then, with the sensation of a horse's kick to his chest, he was flung on his back. Gazing up at the bare winter branches, he could dimly see Sam's face, dimly hear his voice. . . . He kept staring at that face until all was blackness.

Barnhill slept. He awoke at the sound of hushed female voices. A number of well-dressed women stood in the doorway at the far end of the room. With the redoubtable Mrs. Webb leading the way, a delegation of wives of Confederate dignitaries passed slowly from bed to bed, dispensing home-baked Christmas treats and words of consolation. When the ladies reached the foot of his bed, Barnhill smiled pleasantly and brushed back his hair.

"This is the young man I was telling you about," said Mrs. Webb, a trim, middle-aged woman wearing a brocaded jacket above her hoop skirt with a shawl over her shoulders. The woman she addressed was strikingly attractive though not pretty, with dark hair parted in the middle and gathered at the nape of her long, slender neck, and wearing a green silk dress trimmed in lace with a cut no doubt copied from the latest Paris plates. "From Texas, I believe," added Mrs. Webb.

The attractive woman approached his bedside. "Hello," she said with a smile. "I'm Mary Chesnut. Why was a man from Texas fighting alongside the Eighth South Carolina?"

"Mrs. Chesnut's husband is Mr. James Chesnut," said Mrs. Webb proudly. "A senior aide to President Davis."

"And the senator from South Carolina," said Barnhill, "before secession, if I remember correctly."

"You do."

"I'm James Barnhill. Lieutenant with the Fifth Texas. Pleased to meet you, ma'am."

"The pleasure's mine. And so . . ."

"General Hood sent me to try to find General Hill . . ."

"Sam Hood?"

"Yes, ma'am," said Barnhill, though he was surprised to hear the general addressed by his nickname. "Our commanding officer."

"Such a fine man."

"At any rate, we got mixed up in the fighting in the woods—never did find General Hill—and the next thing I knew we were smack dab in the middle of these South Carolina boys."

"One of the other men," said Mrs. Webb, "informed us that you were present when General Gregg was mortally wounded."

Mrs. Chesnut sat lightly on the end of Barnhill's bed. "Maxcy Gregg was a dear friend," she explained.

"He rode into camp just as the Federals appeared. There were so many Yankees pouring out of the woods. The general tried to rally his men." Barnhill visualized the confused look on the man's face. "Very courageous, I assure you. And then he was shot from his horse."

"And what happened to you?" she gently asked.

"When the battle was over, I was standing there, taking it in, when I was hit by a Yankee sharpshooter." He tapped the bandage on his chest.

"It's a wonder you're alive."

Barnhill nodded.

"Well," said Mrs. Chesnut, rising from the bed, "please accept this small token of our thanks." She placed a package on the blanket. "Thank you, Lieutenant, for sharing your account with me. It will be a comfort to Mrs. Gregg."

Christmas dawned cold and wet, with low clouds and drizzle that beaded the windows. His wound healing, Barnhill was able to prop himself up on pillows, reclining against the iron bedstead. He surveyed the ward, some forty beds in two long rows, occupied by sleeping men with varying degrees of injury or illness, many with amputated limbs, others with portions of their faces, arms, or legs disfigured by steel splinters or the large-caliber ball thrown by a Springfield rifle. He lightly massaged the bandage on his chest, relieved that his wound was relatively minor, and gazed at the garlands of evergreen and holly fashioned by the nurses over the doors at both ends of the room. He reached for his handkerchief on the bedside table, unfolded it, and nibbled on the last of the cookies, brittle and crumbly with a dusting of sugar, just like the ones Hattie had baked every Christmas for as long as he could remember. Where was Hattie this Christmas morning? Undoubtedly in his mother's kitchen, preparing to roast the turkey, spanking her biscuit dough. His mother would be in the dining room, taking the good silver from the buffet, his sister Anna helping to set the table with the finest linens and china, those that had traveled all the way from Virginia when his father settled in Texas, among the earliest pioneers. His father's place at the head of the table would, however, be vacant. He had died suddenly, a month before Fort Sumter and the outbreak of the war, whose coming he had dreaded. Having fought alongside Sam Houston at San Jacinto to win Texas independence, his father believed passionately in the inherent right of men to declare themselves free of an oppressive government, and in the right of the states to dissolve the compact entered into in 1789. Yet in the will penned in his own hand a month before his death he had manumitted his slaves, field hands and house servants alike, bequeathing to the adults their simple quarters and enough land to make a crop.

With her husband dead, and only son far away in Virginia, Barnhill's poor mother had somehow learned to make do. At first she had feared that the freedmen would melt away, but they were as dependent on her continuing patronage as she was on their continuing labor, an unwritten, unspoken understanding of mutual obligation built on years of respect and fair treatment. Barnhill sighed deeply. Thoughts of home on Christmas morning filled him with a deep ache of longing. Perhaps, when he was stronger, he might obtain a furlough and make his way back. But what about his men, what about his young cousin Sam, whose mother, Aunt Beth, had pleaded with him not to enlist? Did Barnhill's mother even know he'd been wounded? He had written her, of course, but a letter might take many weeks to find its way to Texas. Barnhill looked up at the sound of the nurses. In addition to the black orderly with his armload of firewood, they were accompanied by the doctor, an erect man in a black frock coat with wire-rimmed spectacles and flowing white hair. He typically made his rounds after breakfast, but as it was Christmas morning he presumably was anxious to complete his duties and return home. The group passed slowly from bed to bed, the doctor speaking in a low voice, the nurses taking the men's pulses and inspecting the dressings for signs of suppuration. They halted at the bed opposite Barnhill, occupied by a boy, eighteen at most, whose groans had awakened Barnhill in the night.

"I don't care for the look of that bandage," Barnhill overheard the doctor saying.

"He's hot as blazes," commented a nurse with her hand on the boy's brow.

The doctor opened his bag, removed a long pair of scissors, and cut away the dressing on his forearm. "As I feared," he said. "Gangrenous. It'll have to come off."

"Nooo!" the boy wailed loudly, rousing all in the ward still sleeping. "Please, not that! I can't take it!"

"Hush," said a nurse, patting his shoulder. "You'll be all right."

"Send for an orderly," said the doctor, moving on to the next bed. Half an hour later, after the terrified boy had been wheeled off to surgery and the doctor had completed his rounds and bid the men a merry

Christmas, Barnhill sat on the side of his bed examining his chest in a mirror supplied by one of the nurses. The doctor had removed the dressing, pronounced him healing nicely, and instructed the nurses merely to sponge the undressed wound with disinfectant. Barnhill studied the bright pink scar and catgut stitches, just over his heart where the muscle had thickened from years of heavy lifting on the plantation. He handed the nurse the mirror and said, "You don't suppose I could have a robe and be up for a while?"

"It will do you good," she replied. "Help to build back your strength."

After donning a dark-blue cotton robe that hung loosely on his lanky frame, Barnhill slowly made his way out of the building, down a passageway where poinsettias adorned the windowsills, to a pentagonal solarium with an arrangement of wicker before a cheerful fire. One chair was occupied by an older patient with a long brown beard who scarcely looked up from his book as Barnhill approached. "Mornin'," said Barnhill, eliciting a brief glance and nod. Lowering himself into a chair, Barnhill audibly exhaled, worn out by the brief exertion. Absorbing the warmth from the fire, he gazed out the lace-covered windows onto the broad lawn and tall, leafless trees whose branches were black with rain. Substantial brick houses stood beyond an ivy-covered wall with a white church steeple in the distance. Inside the houses he imagined families were celebrating Christmas, preparing for the traditional feast, and in the church worshippers were singing the familiar carols, giving thanks for the coming of their Savior, and praying for peace and goodwill toward men. Listening to the crackling of the fire, he could faintly hear music somewhere in the building, men and women singing in unison, accompanied by a piano: "O come, all ye faithful . . ."

Barnhill must have dozed off, for when he opened his eyes the chair with the brooding, bearded man was vacant, and the only sounds were the hissing of the embers and a soft, muffled tap on the roof. The air outside was thick with snow, clinging to the crooks and crotches of the oaks and elms, spreading a powdery blanket over the lawn. Snow! On Christmas Day. A rare sight for Barnhill, a native Texan, that filled him with irrational happiness. He turned at the sound of creaking on the hardwood floor as a nurse wheeled a handsome officer into the solarium.

Wearing a fine gray uniform coat over his pajamas, the officer smiled at Barnhill and said, "Good day, sir. I see you've found this cheerful spot to watch the snow." The nurse parked the wheelchair between Barnhill and the fireplace.

"Nurse," said Barnhill, "where would I find the firebox?"

"Don't bother," she replied. "I'll send Tom with more wood. Will you be all right, Captain?" she asked deferentially.

"Of course," he replied, "though I'd be grateful for another cup of coffee."

Barnhill placed the officer's distinctive Virginia accent.

"Yes, sir," said the nurse with a slight bow.

"My name's Selden," said the captain, reaching out to give Barnhill an awkward handshake. "Edward Selden."

"James Barnhill, lieutenant with the Fifth Texas."

"Hood's Brigade," said the captain. "Regarded by General Lee as one of the finest." The observation elicited a curious look from Barnhill. "I serve on Lee's staff," said Selden in a matter-of-fact way. "Or did, before I was wounded. What happened to you?"

"Shot in the fighting on Jackson's front at Fredericksburg," said Barnhill.

"Jackson's front? Hood wasn't engaged."

"No, but I was sent to find General Hill and got caught in that melée in the woods. Wound up in the middle of Gregg's Carolinians."

"Too bad about Gregg."

Barnhill nodded. "I saw him fall."

"You're a Texian?"

"Born and raised. My father left Virginia to settle there in 1830."

"Whereabouts in Virginia?" asked Selden. "My home state."

"A plantation somewhere in the Tidewater."

"Do tell. My home is Sandy Point, outside New Kent on the Peninsula. We may be kin, brother Barnhill." Selden, who had bright blue eyes, blond hair, and a neatly trimmed mustache, launched into a lively account of his family's descent from the earliest colonists, their role in the Revolution, relation by marriage to the Lees, and large holdings of land and slaves in easternmost Virginia. The nurse, who was, in truth, Mrs. Webb's niece, returned with a lacquered tray and with something like a curtsy lowered it to serve Selden his coffee in a bone-china cup and saucer. "Thank you, ma'am," he said with a smile.

"You're welcome, Captain. Compliments of Mrs. Webb."

Barnhill shot her a reproachful look as she turned to go.

"Something the matter?" asked Selden.

"There's no coffee for the men in my ward," said Barnhill.

"Nurse," called out the captain. "We could use some Christmas cheer. Would you bring us two hot toddies on this snowy morn?"

Once they were settled with steaming mugs of bourbon, water, and brown sugar, in the warmth spreading from a replenished fire, Selden said, "Tell me, Barnhill. What brought your father from Virginia to the wild Texas frontier?"

"Abundant, cheap land. Rich soil to grow cotton." Barnhill sipped his drink with a satisfied smile.

"One of those great Gulf plantations one hears about?"

"We have some thousand acres in cultivation. In a good year, with the long season, yielding as much as six hundred bales."

"Very impressive," said Selden. "How many slaves for an operation of that size?"

"All told, about two hundred."

"And so you, like me, have taken up this cause to defend your livelihood. Now that Old Abe has declared his intention to emancipate the slaves, notwithstanding his previous denials."

"He can't emancipate my family's slaves," said Barnhill, sipping his toddy.

"How so?" said Selden with slightly raised eyebrows.

"They're already free. Manumitted by my father at his death just before the war broke out."

"Most unusual, if I may say so. Do you believe in this war, Barnhill?"

"My friends call me Jamie. Yes, Edward, I do, though it's a damned shame. Lincoln should have let us go in peace."

"Yes," said Selden with a dark look. "Instead they've invaded our country and destroyed our farms and towns. My home is no more. Put to the torch by McClellan."

Barnhill gazed at the proud young officer, obviously the scion of one of the first families of Virginia—FFVs as they were generally known—with his shattered leg. A wave of guilt passed over him for the homesickness and self-pity he'd indulged in. "I'm sorry," he said. "Is your family all right?"

Selden nodded. "Mother and Father are here in Richmond. They managed to get out with the silver and a few heirlooms. You'll have to come with me for a visit when you're feeling up to it."

CHAPTER TWO

JAMIE BARNHILL PACED SLOWLY, the wide planks creaking under the tread of his boots, savoring the musty smell of leather-bound volumes that filled the tall bookcases. He paused to study a collection of history and biography, selecting a handsome edition of Carlyle's *The French Revolution,* bound in scarlet morocco with a raised gilt spine. After examining the inscription on the flyleaf, he settled in an easy chair by the fireplace, which radiated warmth from a bed of glowing embers and a single crackling log. Barnhill glanced around the snug library, with its braided oval rug, old-fashioned clock on the mantelpiece, yellowed wallpaper, and burl walnut secretary. It reminded him slightly of his father's library, but seemed much older . . . Old Virginia, the Old Dominion his father had left for the Texas frontier.

He opened the volume in his lap, searching for his place. He had been reading Carlyle when the call to enlist had sounded in the settlement of San Augustine, near his home a few miles west of the Sabine River bordering Louisiana. His father had arrived there with the first settlers, acquiring several thousand acres of rich bottomland and timbered, rolling hills. He had sent for his wife Mary in Virginia, who arrived the following year to find a newly built homestead, no rough cabin hewn of logs, but a proper two-story house of milled lumber, with wide galleries above and below to catch the cooling breezes, a brick fireplace, and kitchen at the back. Along with the good silver, china, and linens, his father's large collection of books had made the journey from Virginia and filled the shelves of the library off the parlor, the finest in the county, if not the state. Barnhill thought back to that room where he had spent so many evenings reading by the light of an oil lamp—the wide cypress floorboards, his father's rolltop desk, and the cameo portraits of the grandparents in Virginia he'd never known. If he tried, he could almost hear the cicadas chorusing through the open window on a summer evening and the wind singing in the tall pines.

Leafing through the fine vellum, unable to find where he had left off so many months ago, Barnhill turned to the section Carlyle titled: "Terror—the Order of the Day." In the silence, he read with growing revulsion of the unremitting violence, of "death vomited in great floods" by guillotine and fusillade, the transformation of *Liberté, Egalité,* and *Fraternité* into the Reign of Terror in the year '93. Closing the volume with a sigh, he reflected that democracy, unchecked, could descend to anarchy more odious than the most oppressive autocracy. It was not surprising, then, that Bonaparte had been heir to Robespierre. Barnhill rose, stretched, and walked across the room to replace the volume on the shelf. It was fashionable, among educated officers and the Richmond social elite, to regard Abraham Lincoln as a latter-day Bonaparte, a vile tyrant sending armies of invasion into the South in flagrant violation of the Constitution. Clasping his hands behind his back, Barnhill resumed his pacing. Or suppressing a *rebellion,* as Lincoln would have it, in *defense* of the Constitution. Either way he looked at it, Barnhill was sickened by the terrible cost in bloodshed. Hospitals were overflowing with men, like so many in his ward, who would never again steer a plow or earn an honest day's wage.

"Pardon me, sir."

Barnhill stopped and glanced over his shoulder.

"I have your mail, sir," said a young private scarcely old enough to shave. He held out two envelopes.

Mail, thought Barnhill with a thump in his chest. The first in months. He accepted the envelopes with muttered thanks and stared at the familiar cursive—his mother's hand—as the young man walked quickly from the room. Slumping in the chair by the fire, he studied the tiny scrawl on the second envelope. He slit open the envelope from his mother and extracted several folded sheets of pale-blue stationery. Dated January 5, 1863, the letter began:

> My dearest son,
>
> It was with sadness mixed with great relief, and thanks to our Savior, that I read your account of the great battle at Fredericksburg, how you had been wounded and your life spared by the Bible at your breast. Oh my dear boy how I long to be near you, to nurse you back to strength and vitality.

Barnhill paused to brush a tear from the corner of his eye.

> But when I reflect that as soon as you are well they will send you back to your regiment, it is more than I can bear. Your father, were he living, would be so very proud, yet I am weak and pray only for your safe return. I fear that this war will crush us, that we are being taught a terrible lesson for our Pride and Arrogance.

Barnhill swallowed hard. Such sentiments were almost never voiced in the army or heard among civilians. Crossing one boot over the other, he turned to the next sheet:

> In my despair my spirits are lifted by the blacks, especially Hattie and Elijah, who attend to me with the greatest consideration. They are, in truth, a joyful people, trusting in God, going about their work without complaint, though I sense in them a deep contentment to be *free,* though nothing is spoken of it. In truth, I am grateful for their freedom, as I have nothing to fear from them, like so many slaveholding mistresses with menfolk away, nor concern that they might run away.

Barnhill put the letter aside and stared into the fire, reflecting that his father, in a final act of mercy or conscience just before the outbreak of the war, had unintentionally spared his mother and sister the anguish of so many Southern women, sharing their plantation homes with slaves who might rise up against them or melt away, seeking their freedom behind Union lines. He lowered his eyes to his mother's letter:

> As much as you were missed this sad Christmas season, our sorrow was nothing as compared to so many families

whose sons will never return. On Sunday last, Anna and I called on the Rev. and Mrs. Jones, though the roads were nigh impassable with rain and sleet. In their inconsolable grief, they speak of William, who fell at Shiloh, at evening prayers as though he were among the living and set a place for him at the table.

Barnhill quickly finished the letter, dejected by his mother's sadness and obvious loss of hope in the Confederate cause. Carefully refolding the sheets into the envelope, he turned to the other letter, from Kate, the first in months. He tapped the envelope on his palm, gazing in his mind's eye at her face, the lively green eyes, the auburn hair parted in the middle and gathered with a ribbon in the back, the dimples in her cheeks when she smiled. He had neglected to write, perhaps because their love affair seemed, after eighteen months' separation, little more than youthful flirtation and infatuation, which caused him a pang of remorse. "Dear Jamie," she began in neat handwriting so small he had to squint to read it:

Mama learned today at church that you'd been shot at Fredericksburg. How my heart aches. You haven't written, nor have I, but you have been constantly in my thoughts and prayers, especially since we learned about poor Theo. He was with Terry's Rangers at Shiloh and then fell ill with the measles and passed before we could arrange to bring him home.

Papa is beside himself with grief, sitting alone for hours. Life is dull here, with scarcely any boys or young men about, and not enough to eat, no coffee, nor chocolate. But what about you, my dear Jamie? Is your wound healed? Will you go back to your regiment?

Barnhill dropped the letter in his lap, thinking about Bill Jones and Kate's brother Ted, two of his best friends since boyhood, spending many a lazy summer afternoon fishing in the creek or at the swimming hole. Now they were both dead. Poor Kate, who, unlike his mother, had no servants to help with the chores or at her father's general store, with precious few goods on the shelves. He recalled how bitterly her father had denounced secession, that it would mean war, and war was "bad for business." And now his only son dead from measles.

How would he answer Kate? Lightly massaging his tender chest, he knew that the time was fast approaching to report back to the Fifth Texas. There was no sense of urgency, as the army was in winter quarters outside Fredericksburg. But a rumor was afoot that Lee intended to detach Longstreet's Corps and entrain them south of Richmond to meet the Yankee threat to the vital supply lines from coastal North Carolina. He expected to receive his orders any day.

Hearing commotion in the hallway, Barnhill quickly stuffed both letters into his waistcoat. He watched as Edward Selden awkwardly made his way, leaning heavily on a crutch and half-dragging his bad leg. As usual, he was dressed in a fine gray uniform with his face smoothly shaved and hair neatly parted and combed. "Reckoned I'd find you here, master Barnhill," he said with the Virginian's broad "a." "With your nose in some book."

Barnhill rose from his chair, took Selden's crutch, and helped him to sit on a horsehair sofa below a framed lithograph titled *The Old Mill*. "It's actually a right good library," said Barnhill. "Found Carlyle's *French Revolution*. I was reading it when the war broke out."

Selden gave him a queer look. "You're a most surprising frontiersman. More interested in book learnin' than bear huntin'."

"Unlike Virginia," said Barnhill as he settled back in his easy chair, "Texas is a young country, with not many folks about and hardly a school, apart from the itinerant Yankee schoolmarm. Reading's a fine way to pass the time if you're fortunate to have the books. But," —he paused to give Selden a smile—"I do enjoy tracking bears with a good set of hounds."

"You should try fox hunting," suggested Selden. "The sport of gentlemen."

"You get that leg mended, Edward, and we'll ride to the hounds, once this dad-blamed war's over."

"Speaking of the war, I have it on good authority that Longstreet has been given independent command. The politicians are scared the Yankees will land a force south of Richmond and cut the railroad."

"So it's true," said Barnhill. He was aware that Selden had confidants on General Lee's staff and trusted the invariable accuracy of his intelligence.

"I reckon I'll be joining the Texas Brigade when they break camp and move south."

"Yep," said Selden with a smile, "your malingering days are nearing an end."

"I wonder if Old Pete is suited to command an army," said Barnhill as he resumed pacing. "He's a damned fine general, as good on the defensive as anyone in the army, but he lacks Lee's cold nerves. Or Jackson's for that matter."

"I agree," said Selden with a nod. "But the Federals can land as many men as they please at Chesapeake, and we've no choice but to interpose a strong force between them and the capital. Without North Carolina pork and cornmeal, there's no way to provision the army."

Barnhill slumped in his chair, reached into his waistcoat for a cheroot, and lit it with a match struck on the sole of his boot. "I don't care for dividing the army," he said with a puff. "I'll tell you, brother, we were far outnumbered at Fredericksburg. And with Longstreet's Corps south of Richmond, if Hooker resumes the offensive . . ."

Selden dismissed the idea with a wave of his hand. "After the licking they took in December, I can't imagine the Federals mounting an offensive before spring." Following a lapse of silence in which both men appeared to be weighing the Confederate options, Selden said, "I say, Barnhill, we need to fix you up with a new uniform."

"I can get by with these," said Barnhill motioning to the light brown coat and trousers he'd purchased at a nearby clothier, "provided I can find a new campaign hat. You should see the rags that pass for uniforms among the Texas boys."

"That may be," said Selden. "But you'll need a proper uniform if you're going to accompany me to Mrs. Chesnut's."

"What?" Barnhill uncrossed his boots and hunched forward. "Mrs. Chesnut?"

"You've met, as I understand it. She keeps the finest table in Richmond and entertains the general staff and the top men in the government. I received an invitation for dinner on next Saturday. Why don't you come along and help me get around?"

"Why, I'd be honored," said Barnhill, taking another draw on his cigar.

"Very well," said Selden. "I know just the tailor to make you a new uniform." He pulled a slender watch from his fob pocket and snapped open the case. "Time to be going," he said, reaching for the crutch leaning against the wall, "if we don't want to be late for supper."

Barnhill stood before the mirror in the front hall examining himself in the light of an oil lamp. His tunic was of fine wool, the collar trimmed in gold, with yellow embroidery on the sleeves and a double row of shiny brass buttons. He adjusted the leather belt with its "CSA" buckle, imagining how a saber would look hanging from the loop. With polished boots that reached his knees and a brimmed hat, he was turned out as stylishly, he imagined, as any officer in the Army of Northern Virginia; a uniform, Edward Selden proudly informed him, sewn by the same Richmond tailor J. E. B. Stuart had chosen for the coat he'd presented to Stonewall Jackson as a gift before the Battle of Fredericksburg. Where Selden had found the money to pay for it Barnhill couldn't say, but in his genteel Virginia way, he had insisted, producing a large roll of Confederate banknotes.

At the sound of a closing door, Barnhill turned away from his reflection to observe Selden slowly making his way down the hall. "My, but you look splendid," said Selden. "That tailor did a fine job fitting your tall Texas frame." Barnhill, who stood several inches over six feet, nodded in agreement. "I'll wait here," said Selden, "if you'll look outside for our carriage."

The night was cold but clear, with innumerable stars glittering in the black sky as Barnhill stood calling to the coachman at the corner. He watched with curiosity as a lamplighter, his breath clouding before his face, ascended a ladder to put his flame to the gaslight. When the carriage pulled up, Barnhill spoke briefly to the driver and then returned for Selden, who handed the driver his crutch and allowed Barnhill to lift him up on the seat. Barnhill climbed in beside him and, swinging the door shut, leaned forward to give the driver the address. With a slap of the coach whip, they started forward amid creaking springs and clattering hooves. Barnhill gazed out at the substantial brick houses and commercial buildings dimly visible in the glow of the streetlamps, reflecting that Richmond was the first proper city he'd visited since leaving home. After a lapse of ten minutes, the driver brought the coach to a stop before an imposing residence.

Barnhill helped Selden down and then turned to study the impressive neoclassical dwelling with fluted columns flanking the partially open front door beneath a fanlight. He listened to the sounds of voices, laughter, and violins in the still night air. "As you've come along to look after *me*," said Selden, planting his crutch firmly on the flagstones, "why don't you lend me something to hang on to." Placing his arm around Selden's waist, Barnhill helped him to walk, slowly and painfully, to the entrance, where an elderly black man with a starched shirtfront stood at the door.

"Evenin', gentlemen," he said with a wide smile. "Allow me to take your hats."

The front hall and parlor were packed with senior military officers and distinguished-looking civilians, the men attired in uniform or black frock coats and the ladies in long gowns of varying colors with wide hoop skirts. Feeling utterly out of place, Barnhill leaned over to Selden, who was smiling with a confident air, and whispered, "It's *you*, brother, who needs to look after me. I feel like a tadpole in this big pond." Before Selden could reply, a number of ladies suspended their conversation to stare at the two handsome officers, one of them obviously severely wounded. A tall, dark-haired woman, wearing a low-cut gown with a pendant at her neck, stepped forward with a rustle of petticoats. Barnhill recognized Mary Chesnut from her visit to his hospital bedside before Christmas.

"Good evening, Edward," she said with a smile, extending her hand and allowing Selden to kiss it. "I see you've brought along your friend from Texas."

"Lieutenant James Barnhill," said Selden. "I believe you've met."

"Evening, ma'am," said Barnhill with a slight bow.

"It appears you've recovered nicely from your wound," said Mrs. Chesnut. Lightly placing a hand on Selden's arm, she added in a soft Carolina drawl, "The gentlemen are enjoying a libation in the parlor."

With the tall Barnhill close beside him, Selden made his way deliberately into the adjoining room, murmuring greetings to a number of senior officers and political figures, who greeted him as "Edward" or simply "Captain." Aware that Selden couldn't manage a drink while standing, Barnhill escorted him to an armchair in the corner. Helping him to sit, Barnhill leaned the crutch against the wall and turned to a Negro servant bearing a wide silver tray filled with glasses.

"What will it be?" asked Barnhill. "Champagne or brandy?"

"Brandy," replied Selden.

Barnhill took two crystal tumblers from the tray, handed one to Selden, and took a sip. "You know many of these folks?" he asked in an undertone.

"Oh, yes," said Selden. "There's Wade Hampton, talking with Senator Wigfall." He gestured to two distinguished-looking men by the fireplace. "Old friends from South Carolina."

"Wigfall's from Texas," objected Barnhill.

"He is now," said Selden. "And, if I'm not mistaken, here's your commanding officer."

Barnhill turned as a tall, leonine figure, wearing the uniform of a major general, with a long, tawny beard and deep-set eyes, entered the library. "I'll be," said Barnhill. "It's General Hood." Hood glanced around the room, spoke briefly to an officer at his elbow, and then, espying a tall, beautiful woman in the front hall, moved quickly in her direction.

"He's obviously more interested in Buck," said Selden with a smile, "than conversing with the men."

"Buck?"

"Buck Preston," said Selden. "A great South Carolina beauty, whom, according to gossip, the general's wooing."

Well, considered Barnhill with a nod, his hoped-for introduction to the general would have to wait. "Who is that fellow?" he quietly asked, looking in the direction of a tall man in an expensive-looking coat and crimson waistcoat with a glass in one hand and cigar in the other. Standing beneath the chandelier, his dark hair shone with what Barnhill regarded as an excess of bear grease.

"A certain Mr. Rutledge, I believe," replied Selden. "A wealthy Carolina planter, though I haven't made his acquaintance."

A short, stout man with his back to Selden and Barnhill was speaking to Rutledge in a loud voice, punctuating his comments with jabs of his forefinger. "What's needed, sir," he said, "is a decisive victory. Lee must take the offensive and drive the Union army from Virginia. We can't possibly expect to win a long war."

"I disagree," said Rutledge. "Lee must maintain his defensive position on the Rappahannock, and spare more men to fight Rosecrans in Tennessee...."

"Defensive," repeated the other man. "Fiddlesticks."

"We can ill afford," countered Rutledge, "another reckless toss of the dice like Sharpsburg, where the army suffered a near calamity. . . ."

"Beg pardon, sir," interrupted Selden from his chair. Both men turned toward Selden and the tall officer standing next to him. "Sharpsburg, sir," said Selden, "was a near calamity for the *Union* army."

Stepping forward, Rutledge took a puff on his cigar and, with an ingratiating smile, said, "I meant no disrespect, Captain . . ."

"Selden. And this is Lieutenant Barnhill, with the Fifth Texas."

"My pleasure," said Barnhill, reaching out to shake Rutledge's hand.

"Harrison Rutledge," returned the other with a slight bow. "May I introduce Mr. Magrath. Of North Carolina."

"The Fifth Texas," said Magrath with a pull on his goatee. "Your brigade was present at Sharpsburg, was it not?"

Before Barnhill could answer, Selden said, "Present? They saved the day for the South with their stand in the cornfield." Turning to Rutledge, he added, "And Sharpsburg is where I suffered my wound."

Rutledge pursed his lips and looked Selden in the eye. "I am sorry, sir," he said, "if I gave offense. None was intended."

"None was taken," replied Selden. "However, I strongly support the views of Mr. Magrath, whom I overheard. General Lee must take the offensive and whip the Federals once and for all."

Rutledge turned to Barnhill and said, "Do you have an opinion, sir?"

"I wholeheartedly agree. My men are in tatters, forced to forage off the countryside. Many have deserted. We cannot endure a long war, but must force the issue when the opportunity is presented."

The colloquy reached an abrupt end with the sounding of the dinner gong in the hands of the elderly black servant. "Come along, gentlemen," Mrs. Chesnut called out brightly. "Find your places."

Seated at the lower, in social rank, of two elegantly appointed tables, Barnhill passed the dinner in relative quiet, paired with a homely redhaired young woman he surmised had come to Richmond from the outlying countryside and was terrified to open her mouth amid the sophisticated banter. Barnhill nevertheless enjoyed the delectable fare: creamed oysters on toast points followed by roast duckling and corn pudding, and decanters of claret that made their way around the table. Best by far was the warm Sally Lunn with ice cream, the first he'd tasted since leaving home. Edward Selden sat at the far end of the table, handsome and self-assured despite his infirmities, shamelessly competing for the attentions of the beautiful Buck Preston with a plainly irritated General Hood. When the servants finally cleared the table, Mary Chesnut rose and announced that for those so inclined, music, cards, and port would be available in the drawing room. After many of her guests donned their warm coats and gloves and said their goodbyes, she took Mr. Chesnut by the arm and led him to the drawing room, where two card tables had been placed before the blazing hearth, each with a deck of cards and decanter of port. Miss Preston was at the spinet in the corner, against which an enraptured General Hood leaned an elbow, unable to take his mournful eyes from her perfectly oval face.

"The game will be four-hand casino," announced Mrs. Chesnut. "Mixed partners, of course. Edward, will you do me the honor?" Helping Selden to sit, Barnhill graciously accepted Mrs. Chesnut's suggestion to join the game—which he'd played often with his mother, father, and sister—partnering with a plump, rouged woman whose husband reclined sleepily on the sofa after an abundance of food and wine. The game went quickly, the players concentrating too much on snatching the updealt cards to notice the music, until Mr. Chesnut, an especially amiable man who contented himself with a book as his wife entertained the remaining guests, said, "I say, Buck. Do you know 'Lorena'?"

"Yes, cousin James," she replied, "though, as you well know, I can't sing."

"Surely," said Chesnut, "someone can sing to Buck's accompaniment?"

Taking a swallow of port, Barnhill pressed a napkin to his lips and said, "Pardon me, ladies, but I can oblige Mr. Chesnut."

"Well, I'll be hanged," said Selden with a smile.

Buck arranged the sheet music, played a chord, and then the introduction to the sentimental favorite. Standing behind her, with no sound but the hissing of the fire and the clear piano notes, Barnhill, in his rich baritone, sang:

> The years creep slowly by, Lorena,
> the snow is on the grass again;
> the sun's low down the sky, Lorena,
> the frost gleams where the flowers have been. . . .

When the final chord died away, there was not a dry eye in the room. "Thank you, sir," said Buck, looking up over her shoulder. "You have a beautiful voice."

"Here, here," said Selden, slapping a hand on his good knee, which led to a general round of applause.

"Very well done, Lieutenant," said General Hood. "I understand you're with the Fifth Texas."

"Yes, sir," said Barnhill.

"Barnhill," said Hood, stroking his long beard. "The only officer in the brigade wounded at Fredericksburg, as I recall from the reports."

Barnhill nodded. "I was sent to find General Hill."

Hood also nodded. "A close thing it was. Well, Lieutenant, we've been ordered south to Suffolk. Are you fit to report?"

"Yes, sir. Absolutely fit." Barnhill was conscious of Selden's approving glance.

"Very well," said Hood. "I'll see to your orders in the morning. And now I have a certain lady to escort to the Spotswood."

CHAPTER THREE

LOOKING BACK OVER THE SPAN OF YEARS that had dimmed so many memories, Barnhill would always remember a particular moment with remarkable clarity: the sound, like the growl of far-off thunder, that signaled the first clash of armies at Gettysburg. Marching with his men on a dust-choked roadside in the heat of a midsummer afternoon, Barnhill stopped to listen, staring at the towering cumulus clouds in the pale sky. It was artillery, not thunder, he was sure of it, many guns echoing across the gentle Pennsylvania hills.

"Hear that?" said the man marching beside him, a barefoot sergeant clad in tattered homespun whose dark beard was flecked with gray. "Sounds like we found the durned Yankees."

"Yep," said Barnhill as he fell back into step. He untied the kerchief from his neck and wiped the sweat from his face. Something was wrong. He was present at General Hood's headquarters just that morning when the courier galloped up with General Lee's orders to all division commanders: avoid a general engagement with the enemy until the army could be concentrated. From the sound of it, someone had disobeyed those orders. At two o'clock on the afternoon of July 1 the division had struck its tents, loaded its wagons, and set out on the Cashtown road for the town of Gettysburg, a march of some eight miles to the southeast, where the leading elements of A. P. Hill's Third Corps were believed to be situated. The Texas Brigade was in the vanguard, stretched out for miles on the narrow, undulating road over South Mountain, with Law's Brigade several miles to the west at New Guilford. After another hour's steady march, with the sound of the guns intensifying, the column came to an abrupt halt. As the weary men slumped down on their haversacks, Barnhill made his way to the head of the column, where he found Major Sellers astride his tall chestnut mare in a heated conversation with a captain from Allegheny Johnson's Division, a part of Ewell's Second Corps.

"I'm sorry, sir," said the captain, whose face was flushed with anger, "but you've been ordered to halt until our wagons have cleared the turnpike. . . ."

"And how long is the train?" demanded Sellers.

"Something like fourteen miles."

"Good God, man! We'll be here all night!"

"The orders are General Lee's," shot back the captain, who turned his horse with a jerk on the reins and cantered away.

Stretched out on the grass with his back against the fence rails, Barnhill absently watched the mule-drawn wagons creaking under their loads of flour, bacon, ammunition, and sundry supplies, one after another in what seemed an endless procession. Chewing a stalk of sweet alfalfa, listening to the hum of insects, he considered pulling off his boots, though he knew the difficulty he'd have getting them on again. With a yawn he closed his eyes and thought back to the regiment's winter quarters outside Suffolk on the banks of the Nansemond River, the neat rows of peaked tents, the men warming themselves by campfires on cold February nights, the sounds of banjo and fiddle, and the desultory skirmishing with the Federal gunboats that plied the wide river. Best of all, the frequent passes to nearby Richmond, which in that winter of '63 still brimmed with hope for the fledgling republic. Accompanying Edward Selden to many a dinner party or festive ball . . . so many pretty girls, the recollection of whom provoked a pang of guilt for his inattention to Kate back home. He thought of the regiment's march through Richmond on a sunny morning in May; the citizenry lining the sidewalks or gazing down from their balconies to catch a glimpse of the legendary fighting men of the Texas Brigade arrayed in butternut and buckskin, many with long Bowie knives in their belts, hurling playful taunts to any young men in the crowd. When they rounded the corner on a broad avenue, Barnhill's attention was drawn to a beautiful woman—Buck Preston—standing under a parasol beside Mary Chesnut, who stepped down from the sidewalk to give his hand a squeeze and his cheek a kiss with the words, "God speed, Lieutenant Barnhill."

He must have dozed, for when he looked up the last of the wagons had passed and his men were on their feet, shouldering their packs and muskets. When the march resumed at last the sun was sinking toward the horizon. Barnhill shook his head. Hours had been wasted waiting on the wagon train, and the army was scattered all over the countryside. Portions of Longstreet's First Corps were strung out as far as back as Chamberstown; Ewell was somewhere to the north; A.P. Hill's divisions were presumably in a scrap with the Federals at Gettysburg; and the whereabouts of Stuart's cavalry was an unsolved mystery. Even more troubling, Dick Ewell had just assumed command of Second Corps following the tragic death of Jackson after his great victory at Chancellorsville, and few believed that "Old Bald Head" would prove the equal of "Stonewall."

The advance was infuriatingly slow, covering at most one mile in an hour, with frequent halts as the infantry could travel no faster than the wagons barring their path. Night fell and the men marched on, singing for a while to relieve the tension that accompanied an approaching battle, and then to the sound of tramping feet and jangling gear. Though they'd had nothing to eat since noontime, they departed with bellies full from a large barbeque of fresh beef, smoked hams, and ample beer liberated from the bounty of the Pennsylvania Dutch countryside. Barnhill gazed sleepily at the stars in the black above the treetops and watched as the half-moon rose slowly in the east, silvering the ground at his feet, glinting on the gun barrels, casting strangely precise shadows. Rhythmically marching, the straps of his haversack digging into his shoulders, he tried to keep his drooping eyes on the man in front and then stumbled on a half-buried rock that jolted him awake. Most of the men, he surmised, drifted in and out of sleep as they marched, a knack they'd acquired while crisscrossing northern Virginia, Maryland, and Pennsylvania. Finally, at two hours past midnight, the men were granted a brief respite. Shedding haversacks, rifles, and cartridge belts, they were fast asleep as soon as they stretched out along the verge of the road. Awakened after two hours' slumber, the men fell into a swinging route step, covering the final miles in less than an hour and breasting a low hill just as the prismatic rays of the sun streamed over the horizon.

Shielding his eyes, Barnhill studied the ground: a long, gentle ridge, and beyond it, the town of Gettysburg, with neat rows of clapboard houses, church steeples, and an imposing brick building with a cupola at the center. To the east, a steep hill joined another ridge, higher in elevation than the first. In the weak morning light Barnhill could make out hundreds of tents and the smoke of countless campfires along the length of the distant ridge. As he took a pull on his canteen, Major Sellers rode up, dismounted, and touched his hand to the bill of his hat.

"Mornin', Jamie," he said with a pat on the mare's neck. Despite the major's laconic manner, Barnhill was conscious of the excitement in his eyes.

"Mornin', Harry," said Barnhill. "It appears we've found the whole damned Union army."

Sellers nodded. "Here," he said, reaching into his coat for a folded map. "Let's have a look." Kneeling, he spread out the map on the ground. "This," said Sellers, tracing a line, "is Seminary Ridge, just over yonder." Both men gazed at the nearby sloping ground, where large numbers of Confederate troops were visible in the early morning haze. "General Lee's headquarters, where we've been ordered to report. Just south of town is Cemetery Hill." Barnhill studied the map and then glanced at the low hill in the distance. "That high ground to the right," said Sellers, "is Cemetery Ridge. Extends about three miles south into the woods where those two tall hills stand." The major gestured with his gauntlet. Barnhill looked at the features on the map. Little Round Top and Round Top.

"There are three Union corps astride that ridge," said Sellers. "Holding the high ground on the left . . ."

"Cemetery Hill," said Barnhill.

Sellers nodded. "And all along the ridge opposite Hill's Corps. Ewell's Corps occupies the town and the ground to the north and northeast."

Barnhill stood up and dusted his hands on his trousers. "I don't like it," he said. "We're far outnumbered, and we don't have all our people up."

"Pickett's division is back at Chambersburg," said the major. "And God only knows where Stuart's troopers are."

"And the Federals are holding the high ground."

Sellers refolded his map and tucked it inside his jacket. "You reckon

Lee will dig in and wait for the Federals to attack?" he asked.

With a shake of his head Barnhill answered, "I doubt it."

Swinging back into the saddle, Sellers said, "We'll proceed to Lee's headquarters and wait for orders."

Despite their all-night march and lack of nourishment, the men of the Texas Brigade, battle-hardened veterans of Malvern Hill, Second Manassas, and Sharpsburg, were in fine fettle, with little banter or joking to relieve the nervous anticipation of the bloody fighting that almost certainly lay ahead. Reaching the sprawling encampment on Seminary Ridge, Major Sellers consulted briefly with his officers, ordered the men to fall out, and then joined General Hood at headquarters, a fieldstone farmhouse with a garden enclosed by a white picket fence. Hoping to see General Lee, whom he greatly venerated, Barnhill made his way to the farmhouse, where he settled for a glimpse of Traveller, Lee's famous dappled gray, tethered to the fence, and a brief look at General Longstreet—"Old Pete"—barrel-chested and grimly resolute with his long brown beard.

Before long the major emerged with orders to head south along the ridge, halting in a verdant meadow with a meandering brook, an ideal location to gather water and firewood for the commissary wagons. As the cooks lit the fires and set out their skillets and the men stretched out on the grass, one of the men—a German immigrant who, as a desk clerk at the Menger Hotel in San Antonio before the war, had been acquainted with Lee and Longstreet—ventured up the hillside in hopes of overhearing the conference taking place among the commanders. As the aromas of baking bread and frying bacon drifted among the resting soldiers, Private Hahn scurried down from the hillside.

"Might as well douse them cook fires," he breathlessly told Barnhill.

"Now, Ferdinand," said Barnhill, seated on the grass with crossed legs, "just what did you hear . . ."

"And pack up the chuck wagons. No time for a hot meal, no sir," said Hahn.

Barnhill gave the man a curious look and slowly rose to his feet, towering over the diminutive private.

"I heard 'em, sir," said Hahn. "Plain as day. General Lee took a look at that hill over there through his glasses"—Hahn pointed at Little Round Top—"and said the Federals have occupied that high ground. You, sir, he said, meanin' General Hood, your men will have to take it. Longstreet said, now, General, that's a mighty tall order, but General Lee said, we'll attack up the Emmitsburg Road, and hit the Union flank, and you, sir—meaning General Hood—must take that hill."

Barnhill stared for a moment at Hahn, glanced at Little Round Top in the hazy distance, and said, "Thank you, Ferdinand. Most interesting." Hearing loud hoofbeats, he looked over his shoulder as a courier galloped into camp and shouted, "Orders for Major Sellers!" With the other officers gathered around, the major quickly scanned the note and then said, "Order the men to fall in. Reissue ammunition, forty cartridges to a man. Tell the boys to grab something to eat before we march." Within the half hour, under a hot noonday sun, the three Texas regiments, joined by a regiment of Arkansas men, were on the move again, side-stepping McLaws's Georgians and, after a time-consuming march and countermarch to avoid detection by the Union signalmen on Little Round Top, finally taking up positions on the far right of the Confederate line. To the northeast, beyond the shallow depression of the Emmitsburg Road, was a peach orchard, the dense green crowns full of ripening fruit, and beyond the orchard, Cemetery Ridge, bristling with Federal infantry and artillery. In their front, rocky Little Round Top rose above the densely forested ground, perhaps a mile from the brigade's position. Farther to the right was the higher summit of Round Top. It was obvious to Barnhill within a moment of studying the ground that if either side could succeed in placing guns on that summit they could pour devastating artillery fire on troops below.

Passing among the men, Barnhill said little, aware that they preferred to devote the time before battle to silent contemplation; those who could write penning a final note to a loved one to entrust to a friend; others, if they could read, turning to a favorite passage in the Bible most carried; and some, especially warlike, taking a whetstone to their Bowie knives and bayonets. He found Sam Perkins seated on a tree stump with his head in his hands, as if weary or in prayer. Walking quietly up to him, Barnhill said, "Hello, cousin."

Raising his eyes at the familiar voice, Sam said, "Hello, Jamie."

Barnhill thought he detected a slight tremor in Sam's voice. "Are you ready?" he asked. "It's bound to be a hot one."

"I reckon," said Sam with a nod. "There's just one thing." He reached into his shirtfront for a folded envelope and handed it to Barnhill. "For Mother," he said softly. "In case something should happen."

With a brief glance at the envelope, Barnhill slipped it in his pocket, looked Sam in the eye and said, "Good luck. I'll try to look out for you. Remember to keep low and try to find some cover." Patting him on the shoulder, he moved to a clearing and slung down his pack. Dropping to a knee, he unpacked the fine gray coat trimmed in gold that Edward Selden had purchased for him in Richmond. He proudly shrugged it on, despite the heat, buttoned up the brass buttons, buckled his leather belt, and patted his holster with its Colt revolver. Well, he considered, he only lacked a saber to lead his men into battle in proper style, but a well-aimed Springfield with fixed bayonet was a far more practical choice of weapon. With the sun shining brightly on the regimental standards and a soft breeze rustling the boughs overhead, he checked the time—two o'clock—and wondered why the order to commence the attack had not been given. At that moment General Hood rode up on a fine black stallion—not his usual roan the men had christened "Jeff Davis"—and called for Major Sellers.

"Sir," said Sellers, giving the mounted general a quick salute.

"Take two of your best scouts," said Hood with a tug on his beard, "and send them up to the top of that tall hill. Determine if it's occupied by Federal troops."

"Yes, sir."

"And tell them to be quick about it."

Two lanky privates, frontiersmen with considerable Indian-fighting experience, were promptly dispatched on horseback, concealed by the woods, to the right and rear of the promontories known as Little Round Top and Round Top. Returning to the Texans' position at a gallop, they reported sighting large numbers of bluecoats on the crest of the smaller hill and in tight ranks on the rocky slopes leading up to it. But the tall hill was unoccupied.

"What about the ground to the rear of the smaller hill?" demanded Hood.

After pausing to spit out a stream of tobacco juice, one of the scouts wiped his mouth and said, "An open pasture where the Yankees have parked their wagons, sir."

"Is there a road to haul guns to the top of the big hill?"

"Not a road exactly, but a clearing we follered all the way up . . ."

"You can see the whole dang Yankee army," said the other. "With a couple o' good teams and drivers we could put a battery on that hill, Gen'l, and shoot the Yankees to kingdom come."

Hood silently stared at the lofty eminence above the dense woods, again stroked his long beard, and turned to Major Sellers. "Harry, send an officer to General Longstreet," he instructed. "Advise him that in my opinion it would be unwise to attack up the Emmitsburg Road, that I request permission to turn Little Round Top and attack the enemy in flank and rear. Tell him the tall hill is unoccupied."

"Yes, sir," said Sellers, turning immediately to his adjutant, whom he instructed to deliver the message on the fastest available mount. Barnhill straightened the front of his tunic and walked up to the major. Hood, sitting on his tall black horse, glanced briefly at Barnhill's fine uniform, smiled, and said, "Afternoon, Lieutenant."

"Afternoon, sir."

"Fine day for a battle," said Hood. "But it would be suicide to assault that smaller hill without seizing the tall one first." He paused at the sound of approaching hoofbeats and watched as the adjutant reined in a bay colt.

"Well?" said Hood.

"General Longstreet says General Lee's orders are to attack up the Emmitsburg Road."

"Major Sellers," said Hood angrily. "Go back to Longstreet and explain the situation yourself. We can flank the Federals holding that little hill! Tell him we can put guns on that big hill that can rake the whole Union line!"

It was not to be. To Hood's utter dismay, Longstreet turned a deaf ear, insisting the attack go forward as planned across the boulder-strewn ground forever remembered as Devil's Den.

At the command "Forward!" the brigade advanced from the tree line in columns of four, with the Fifth Texas on the far right of the line, next to Law's brigade of Alabamians, which was to lead the attack in echelon. Barnhill assumed his customary place at the head of Company B, next to his first sergeant, a redheaded Irishman named Dillon whose practice was to consume a half pint of whiskey before going into battle. As the Confederate shells shrieked overhead, crashing into the peach orchard a mile to the Texans' left, Dillon, his face flushed with alcohol and excitement, turned to Barnhill and said, "It's goin' to be hot work, Lieutenant, to take that little hill." Barnhill merely nodded, tightening his grip on the stock of his rifle, sweat dripping down his neck under his scratchy wool collar as they tramped across the dusty turnpike into an open field in plain view of the Federals on the ridge, walking as though in a trance, wondering *Will this be the moment, the chance to rout the Federal army once and for all and end the terrible war?* Puffs of smoke on the heights signaled the opening of the Federal bombardment, the first shell, solid shot, landing twenty yards in front of the column, showering the men with dust and dirt and bounding harmlessly over their heads. The next shell exploded within ten yards, severing one man's head in a fountain of blood and slicing another in two. Down the line the word was passed: "On the quick, but not the double quick!" and the men broke into a shuffling trot, lowering their heads as if facing a gale. Barnhill caught sight of General Hood on his fine black horse, perhaps two hundred yards to their left, waving his hat over his head, and faintly heard him shout, "Forward! Steady, forward!"

The men plunged ahead through the shower of grape and canister poured down from cannons on the heights. Glancing quickly over his shoulder, Barnhill saw Hood knocked from the saddle by a shell burst overhead. As the ground trembled with the nearly continuous Union and Confederate salvos, the regiment broke into a run, up the hillside toward a line of timber concealing the Yankee riflemen crouching behind a stone wall. Now a hail of minié balls mixed with the bursting shells, smacking into the trees and dropping men by the dozens, whose wails blended with the roar of the cannons and staccato cracks of the Springfields. Barnhill was dimly aware of the sergeant at his side, panting, cursing, and then screaming incoherently as he raced for the stone wall, firing his rifle from the hip and then plunging his bayonet into the chest of a startled Union private. Dozens of men in tattered butternut, many barefoot and hatless, leaped over the wall, some fighting with Bowie knives, others, like Barnhill, firing rapidly with revolvers at the backs of the fleeing bluecoats. Up the hill raced the Texans, splashing across a shallow stream, no longer in any sort of line, kneeling to bite off cartridges and ram them down their rifle bores, seeking cover behind trees and large rocks strewn along the hillside, pushing back the Federals to a second line of defense below the summit.

Pausing to catch his breath behind a tall pine, Barnhill looked back down the hillside littered with the bodies of dozens of his men. After a quick gulp from his canteen, he reloaded his rifle and rushed into a clearing filled with enormous boulders, some the size of a small house. The survivors of their furious charge were sheltering behind the boulders as the Federals continued to pour tremendous and continuous cannon fire from the ridge to their left, and from skirmishers on a rocky ledge below the crest of Little Round Top. The men leapt from boulder to boulder, fighting their way up the slope, firing round after round from the abandoned rifles all around them, many screaming wildly, a scene straight out of the *Inferno*, thought Barnhill as he watched with something like detachment. Their only chance, he knew in an instant, was a final charge up that terrible rocky ground to drive the Yankees holding the summit, seize the lone Federal battery, and turn it on the defenders. Looking around him, he counted some fifty uninjured men, among them his cousin Sam, crouched in the lee of a huge boulder. Taking a deep breath, Barnhill dashed from his hiding place, called out something to his men—he was never able to recall the words, though Sam always insisted it was "For the Lone Star State!"—and recklessly plunged up the hillside amid the sound of lead ricocheting off granite. Above, through the dense underbrush, he could just make out the blue of the Federals' coats. He stood, took aim, and fired. Then he was conscious of a tremendous impact spinning him around and hurling him backward. He fell hard on a smooth slab of rock, which quickly puddled with his dark red blood.

CHAPTER FOUR

THE GIRL STOOD QUIETLY IN THE DOORWAY, resting one hand on the jamb, trying to detect any movement or sound of distress from the three men on pallets on the parlor floor. Most of the furniture—the horsehair settee and heavy armchairs—had been carried out to the barn, and a water pitcher, roll of cotton wool, and bottle of Pond's witch hazel occupied the marble-top chest in place of her mother's Belleek tea service. She lifted a hand to her face at the slight smell of suppurating flesh, dried blood, and disinfectant in the dimly lit room, whose windows, like those in the rest of the house, were tightly shut to block out the stench of decomposing horse and human flesh. Perceiving the slightest twitch on the face of the man on the left—the tall one, whose dirty socks protruded from the blanket—she crept closer until she was standing over his rigid form. As she studied his ashen face with its dark shadow of beard, his eyes fluttered open and lips moved, though without a sound. Frightened, she took a step back. Something in his expression made her think he wanted to say something. She tentatively edged closer and bent down.

"Who are you, child?" he whispered.

Without a word she stood erect and then bolted from the room, almost falling in her haste to get away from the spectral figure. Bursting into the kitchen, she ran to her father's chair by the stove and threw herself into his arms, burying her face against his waistcoat.

"For heaven's sake," he said, lifting her chin to look at her. "What is it, Dora?"

"He . . . ah, the tall one, he . . ." She stopped to catch her breath.

"Yes, yes, what is it, child?"

"He *spoke,* Papa. He said something."

"Well, well," said Reverend Henry Bryan as his seven-year-old daughter slid from his lap. "Perhaps he'll live after all."

Holding a candle on a brass stand and a bundle of clean towels, the reverend entered the parlor. Placing the candle on the table in the corner, where it spread a circle of yellow light, he knelt down beside the tall soldier. After a quick appraisal of the others, one of whom was so pale and still that he was surely dead and the other breathing heavily in his sleep, Bryan, in a voice just above a whisper, said, "How are you, sir? You've been sleeping for days."

Barnhill gazed up at the man, noticing the stiff white collar above the lapels of his black frock and his long, severe face. He tried to speak but his throat was too dry for words. "Water," he managed to whisper. Rising, the parson walked to the table, poured a glass from the pitcher and held it to Barnhill's cracked lips. Too weak to lift his head from the pillow, he managed to swallow a few gulps.

Wincing from the intense pain throbbing at his shoulder, James Barnhill said, "Where am I?" After the moment on that fateful second of July when he raised the rifle to his shoulder and fired into the mass of blue on the ridge above him, he remembered nothing. Nothing of the solicitude of the New York men who, astonished by the bravery of the Confederate officer in the fine gray tunic, carried him, unconscious, to be laid among their own wounded, nor of the skill of their regimental surgeon who stanched the bleeding and dressed his wound. No memory whatever of the bouncing ambulance on the track down the hillside in the darkness to the Union field hospital where another surgeon from Boston insisted on operating, ignoring the entreaties of the orderlies to let the damned Rebel die. Spared any recollection of that awful night, Barnhill had drifted in and out of consciousness for two days, hovering near death in a dreamless sleep, while the bloodied armies had slipped away, abandoning the town to the dead and wounded.

"In Gettysburg," replied Bryan. "In my home."

"And you . . ." whispered Barnhill.

"Henry Bryan. Rector of our local Episcopal Church."

Barnhill swallowed. "I'm James Barnhill," he said in a somewhat stronger voice. "Lieutenant with the Fifth Texas."

"Texas. You're a long way from home, son."

Barnhill briefly studied the room in the dim candlelight: the heavy drapes drawn across the windows, striped wallpaper, and floral carpet mottled with dark bloodstains. "What am I doing here?" he asked. "And who are the others?" The man on the pallet next to him stirred with a loud groan.

"The army was leaving," said Bryan, "and they had no room for the men in the moribund ward. I volunteered to take three of you in . . ."

"To die," said Barnhill in a whisper.

"In all likelihood. A Union man and another, like you, from the South."

"Quiet, goddammit!" snarled the man lying next to Barnhill, separated only by inches. "Let a body have some peace!"

Reverend Bryan stood up with a frown. "Well," he said softly, "it appears that two of you may survive after all. I'll have Dora bring you some consommé with toast."

By the following day, Barnhill was strong enough to be moved, aided by Bryan and his black servant Jason to stand and slowly shuffle to the sunroom across the hall. He sat in a rocking chair, his left arm in a sling with his shoulder dressed in a bulky bandage, staring out the window at the open fields south of the town and the brooding Round Tops in the far distance. Squinting, he could make out groups of men scattered across the fields for miles, details gathering up the bloated corpses to bury them in shallow graves. The once pastoral valley between the sloping ridges had become the valley of the shadow of death. He had passed through that valley, Barnhill reflected with an involuntary tremor. He silently recited the verses: *I will fear no evil, for thou art with me . . . thou preparest a table before me in the presence of mine enemies . . . Surely goodness and mercy . . .*

"Easy, there!"

Barnhill turned to watch as the preacher and his black servant carried one of the other men into the room, borne on a wicker chair. The man's wrist had been shattered by a minié ball, resulting in the amputation of his arm below the elbow, and his right thigh was badly wounded by a shell splinter. The third man remained unconscious in the parlor, as still and pale as a cadaver. In the process of lowering the chair to the floor, Jason lost his grip, dropping the chair the last few inches with a thud.

"Ohhh," gasped the man in pain. "God*dammit*!" he shouted at Bryan. "Tell that nigger to be more careful!"

"Sir," replied Bryan coolly, "you are not to take the Lord's name, nor use *that* term, so long as you are a guest in this house." The wounded soldier stared back sullenly. "Is that understood?" demanded Bryan.

"Understood."

Barnhill studied the soldier's features. Matted, reddish-brown hair, dark, close-set eyes like a weasel's, and a week's growth of beard. From his accent and dirty blue trousers it was apparent he was from the North.

"Somethin' the matter, Reb?" he said with a leering grin.

Barnhill slowly exhaled. It was the first time he had come face to face with a Union soldier except at the point of a bayonet. "My name's Barnhill," he said. "And you are . . ."

"Jeremiah Wilson. Where 'bouts you from, Reb?"

Barnhill painfully rose to his feet and stood over the Union man, who seemed to shrink in the chair. "I'd advise you not to use that term," said Barnhill, flexing and unflexing his right fist.

"Oh, all right," said Wilson sourly.

"What's your regiment?" asked Barnhill.

"Seventh Michigan. Yours?"

"Fifth Texas." Barnhill slumped back in the rocking chair. "I don't suppose you could tell me what happened."

"Happened? How you got here?"

"No." Barnhill winced in pain. "The battle we fought."

"You got whipped is what happened."

"We were in the thick of the fighting for that little hill," said Barnhill, gesturing toward the distance. "I got a knock on the head when I fell and can't remember a thing."

"Next day the Rebs—sorry, Confederates—come on agin. Opened up with every goddam cannon they had and come right on across that pasture, damnedest sight I ever seen. We figured we was safe, bein' in the center of the line, but oh no, here they come, broad daylight, comin' at a run." Wilson paused to give his chin a contemplative scratch. "We poured it on with everything we had, muskets, grape, canister. They never had a chance."

Barnhill stared into the distance, at the heat waves rising from the plain and buzzards circling over the burial parties, trying to visualize the battle. It was a mile or more across that open ground. My God, what courage to make that charge. But why attack the center? In an instant he understood that the prospect of a decisive victory had been lost. He turned back to Wilson. "After our charge was turned back, what happened to the army?"

"Well, I didn't see a damn thing. Passed out from losin' so much blood. Next day, after I came to, the Rebel army pulled out in the pourin' rain and plumb got away. Truth was, mister, we warn't in any shape to go after 'em."

So the army, or what was left of it, escaped, considered Barnhill. No doubt intending to move south across the Potomac and fight another day. My God, there would be no end to it. He noticed the little girl in the doorway holding a tray with a blue pitcher and two glasses. "Hello," he said with a smile.

Returning the smile, she walked into the room, giving wide berth to Wilson, and stood before Barnhill's rocker. "Papa sent me with lemonade," she said.

"What's your name, child?" asked Barnhill.

"Dora, sir." She placed the tray on a bench, carefully poured a glass, and handed it to him.

"Don't you know better," growled Wilson, "to wait on a Northern man before serving a Rebel prisoner?" Without answering, Dora, whose straight blond hair was cut in the shape of a bowl, poured another glass and handed it to Wilson.

As Barnhill took a swallow of the cool, sweet beverage, he reflected on the fact that he was a captive behind Union lines. "Thank you, Dora," he said. "It's delicious. Did your mother make it?"

"No," she said quickly, looking down at her shoes. "I don't have a mother." After a moment she added, "She's gone to heaven."

"I'm sorry," said Barnhill, thankful that the Union soldier, for once, was holding his foul tongue. As Dora picked up the tray and turned to go, Barnhill said, "Tell your papa that, when he has a moment, I'd like a word with him."

CHAPTER FOUR

Despite the agonizing pain from the slightest movement of his arm, Barnhill rose from the rocker and slowly made his way to the front hall, where, exhausted by the exertion, he rested for a moment, leaning against the banister. Dora reappeared and, taking him by his good hand said, "Papa will see you now." He followed her to the preacher's study, pausing at the parlor door to look at the third soldier lying still on his pallet.

Reverend Bryan rose from his upholstered armchair as Barnhill and his child entered the book-lined study with a window that framed a view of the Lutheran seminary. "Have a seat, ah, Lieutenant . . ."

"Barnhill. Actually, I'd prefer to stand." He rested his good arm on the back of a chair.

"Go along, child," said Bryan, returning to his chair. Crossing his legs, he said, "I've asked our local physician, a member of my congregation, to look in on you and the others."

"Is the man in the parlor still . . ."

"He's breathing," said Bryan. "I managed to give him a little water mixed with broth when he woke up. Perhaps you could try to talk to him, as a fellow officer."

Barnhill nodded. "That's why I wanted to see you. What do you intend to do with us?"

"I suppose I could turn you over to the army," replied Bryan. "Though what would be the point of that?" It was evident he addressed the question to himself.

"You've been extremely kind," said Barnhill, "to take us in and care for us."

"I did no more than I would expect of any Christian. Besides, your, ah, comrade, is far too ill to be moved. Let's have a look at him." Bryan rose, took Barnhill by his good elbow, and helped him to the parlor. As they approached the man on the floor he opened his eyes and looked up at them. "You're awake, I see," said Bryan, kneeling to gently touch his forehead. In the light filtering through the drapes Barnhill could see that his pale face was handsome, with a light brown mustache and goatee. Bryan rose, poured a glass of water, and held it to the man's lips. "This is Lieutenant Barnhill," said Bryan. "With the Fifth Texas Regiment."

"Hood's Division," added Barnhill. "In Longstreet's Corps."

The man gazed for a moment at Barnhill and tried to speak. After another swallow of water, he softly said, "I'm Robert Maxwell. Twenty-sixth North Carolina, Pettigrew's Brigade. Hill's Corps. Where are we?"

"In Gettysburg," said Barnhill. "This kind gentleman was good enough to take us into his home. I'm afraid the army is back in Virginia by now."

Maxwell nodded, took a deep breath, and closed his eyes. "Thank you," he murmured.

Barnhill sat half-naked on the kitchen table, squeezing his right hand into a tight fist and closing his eyes as the doctor probed his wounded shoulder. "Whoever performed this operation," said the doctor, a plump, bespectacled man with thinning white hair, "was a very fine surgeon." Standing erect, he took a handkerchief from his pocket and polished his glasses. "Very fine indeed. No sign of infection and a nicely stitched incision, though you've lost a good deal of flesh and, I suspect, a portion of the humerus. Remarkable the damage a .58 caliber ball can do." He sponged the long, irregular wound with spirits and neatly bandaged it with cotton wool and linen. Turning to Bryan, who was watching from the corner with a grave expression, he said, "It's important to change the bandage daily. Now I should examine the other Confederate."

When the doctor returned to the kitchen Barnhill was still sitting on the table with his arm in a sling and shirt on his lap, unable to dress himself without the reverend's assistance. "I'm afraid your friend's prospects are very poor," said the doctor with a frown.

"Friend?" said Barnhill. "I don't know the man."

"Shot through the belly," continued the doctor with clinical dispassion as Reverend Bryan draped Barnhill's checked shirt over his wide shoulders. "Exit wound on his lower left side. No doubt serious damage to the internal organs. They opened him up, evidently managed to stop the internal bleeding, and left him to die. It's a wonder he's still with us." Barnhill nodded, thinking that his own chances of slipping away and finding his way back to the regiment would be far better if Robert Maxwell had perished on the battlefield.

"What about the Union man?" asked Bryan.

"I don't like the look of his leg," replied the doctor. "You should turn him over to the army surgeons. They may want to take it off." He snapped shut his black leather bag and turned to go.

"Thank you kindly, Frederick," said the reverend. "May I ask a personal consideration?"

"Of course."

"Let us leave this matter between the two of us," said Bryan. "In strict confidence, until I resolve the correct manner of dealing with these poor men."

"As you wish, Henry," said the doctor, donning his hat and letting himself out the kitchen door.

Propped up on several pillows, Robert Maxwell was able to look around the parlor in the illumination of a candle on the table in the corner, with Barnhill seated in a straight-back chair next to his pallet. The other pallets, with their bloody sheets, had been rolled up and taken to the barn to be burned, and a feeble attempt made to wash the bloodstains from the carpet. His hair neatly parted and color restored to his freshly shaved cheeks, Maxwell picked at his supper—a few string beans, sweet corn, and a slice of cold chicken. "Our brigade," said Maxwell, "formed the center of the Confederate line." As Barnhill listened raptly, he described the Confederate assault on the Union center on the third day of the battle that later generations would remember as Pickett's Charge. "Pickett's Virginians were to our right. By the time the two divisions converged, we were swept by enfilading artillery. Firing canister, at that close range."

"A frontal attack," said Barnhill with a grimace, "across a mile of open ground."

"They cut us to pieces," said Maxwell. "When we tried to advance beyond the road, massed infantry opened with a murderous volley. That's when I was hit. Tryin' to scramble over the fence." Little Dora entered the room and, with a diffident smile, asked permission to take his plate to the kitchen.

"It's a wonder," said Barnhill, lightly massaging his shoulder, "Lee was able to get away with what's left of the army. But as you were saying, your family home is on the water?"

"Albemarle Sound," said Maxwell, "at the mouth of the Chowan River. Across the sound from the Outer Banks, maybe fifty miles across. Nags Head. Where we spend the summer."

"I've never been around water," said Barnhill. "The ocean, that is."

Maxwell looked at him in the dim candlelight. "We should rectify that," he said after a moment. "If you'll take me home, I'll show you the prettiest stretch of sea and sand you'll ever set your eyes on." He winced from a stab of pain.

Barnhill studied the handsome young officer lying on the pallet, unable to stand, let alone walk, and thought about the distance from Pennsylvania to the North Carolina shoreline. "Take you home?" he said.

"If we stay here much longer," said Maxwell in a low voice, "the Yankees will find us, and God knows where we'll wind up."

"They're coming for Wilson. Any time now."

"Then we better skedaddle."

Barnhill shook his head with a smile. "Now how do you reckon we could . . ."

"Take a coach," said Maxwell. "With two horses. You'll drive, I'll ride."

"A coach? Horses?"

"Look in my satchel there," said Maxwell weakly.

Barnhill painfully rose and walked over to Maxwell's worn black leather case on the table. Unfastening the straps, he reached inside and found a bundle of letters and worn diary.

"Sewn into the lining," said Maxwell.

Barnhill opened his pocketknife, slit open the lining, and removed a heavy pouch. From its heft and feel he could tell it was filled with coins. "How much?" he asked, holding it up for Maxwell to see.

"Two hundred dollars," said Maxwell proudly. "In gold."

Barnhill tossed the pouch in the air and caught it with a clink, thinking that Maxwell was in no condition to travel. And yet it was only a matter of time before they were taken into custody by the Federal authorities. "How were you thinking we'd get through the Union lines?" he asked.

"At first I supposed we might slip across at night . . ."

"And get ourselves shot by the pickets."

Maxwell paused to rest. "We'll have to get paroles," he said quietly. "With the help of the reverend."

It just might be possible, considered Barnhill. In a little town like Gettysburg, overflowing with disabled soldiers, why not parole two badly wounded Confederates and send them south? And Maxwell's two hundred dollars was more than enough to buy horses, a coach, and food and lodging along the way. "You take it easy," said Barnhill as he slowly rose from the chair. "And I'll have a word with the preacher. But neither of us is strong enough to travel at the moment."

Barnhill stood on the porch, leaning against the post, and watched the ambulance disappear down the dusty track, transporting Jeremiah Wilson to the Union field hospital, as the afternoon sun broke through the darkening clouds. Wilson had cursed the orderlies when they lifted him on the stretcher, cursed Reverend Bryan for "sending him to his fate," and delivered a parting curse to "the Rebs and their goddam secesh" as he was loaded into the back of the ambulance. Reverend Bryan, deeply offended by Wilson's hate-filled profanity in the presence of his beloved child and humble black servant, was visibly relieved to see him go. As the days passed, Barnhill had gradually regained his strength and appetite, though he had no use of his left arm, which hung limply in a sling. Robert Maxwell's condition, miraculously, continued to improve, though it required two strong men to left him from the pallet and help him to the privy behind the house.

"Well, Lieutenant . . ."

Barnhill turned to look at Bryan, who was standing in the doorway in his frock coat and stiff collar with an unlit clay pipe in his hand. "Now that we are rid of the sergeant," he said, "what's to be done with you and young Maxwell?"

Barnhill responded with an appreciative smile for Bryan's many acts of kindness, concealing the two Confederates for weeks from the Union troops bivouacked in town. "Perhaps we could talk in your study," he suggested.

Bryan sat in his favorite chair by the bookcase with the long stem of the pipe clenched in his teeth. Taking a puff, he said, "Ever since the battle I've been unable to work. Two Sundays now I've apologized to my congregants, telling them I had no sermon to offer, and merely led them in prayer. What can one say in the face of such . . . such unspeakable violence?"

Barnhill nodded. "This is a terrible war," he said quietly. "I was hoping this battle would end it." He shook his head.

"What will you do?"

Barnhill took a deep breath and looked Bryan in the eye. "I'd like to ask your help in arranging to be paroled."

Taking another puff on his pipe, Bryan said, "I see. But where will you go?"

"Captain Maxwell is from North Carolina. He'd like to go home, and I'd like to take him."

"But surely, James, it's a terribly long journey, and in his condition? Besides, how would you manage . . ."

"We'll need a coach and two horses. We'll pay a fair price, of course."

"You astound me. But explain the parole to me."

"It's merely a prisoner's pledge not to take up arms, to return peacefully to the other side. If you could vouch for us, as men of honor . . ."

"Well, you're certainly that. Whom should I call upon?"

"I reckon there's a Union force still in town, with so many casualties. You should ask to see the provost marshal. You'll only need our names and regiments."

Bryan rubbed his chin as he drew on his pipe. "All right," he said. "I shall call on the gentleman this afternoon. But what if your request is denied?"

"Then I suppose we're at the mercy of the Union army."

Resting in the parlor, with Robert Maxwell recumbent on his pallet, Barnhill looked up at the sound of hoofbeats on the muddy ground outside. Shortly after the reverend departed, the skies had opened, a drenching rain with claps of thunder that rattled the windowpanes, causing Dora to hide under the kitchen table, as she had during the Confederate bombardment on the first afternoon of the battle. By the time Barnhill made his way to the front door, Bryan had dismounted, with rain pouring from the wide brim of his hat. Hitching his mare to the picket fence, he opened the gate and walked up on the porch, where Barnhill awaited him with a look of nervous expectation. Bryan slipped off his hat and stamped his muddy boots on the weathered floorboards.

"Any luck?" asked Barnhill.

"When I finally succeeded in locating the provost," said Bryan, "he turned out to be a rather uncouth individual, disposed to chewing tobacco and foul language, with a powerful dislike for, ah, enemy soldiers."

Barnhill's heart sank.

"However," Bryan continued, "when I explained the seriousness of your wounds and assured him that you are honorable gentlemen, whose word is your bond, he relented. On occasion," Bryan added with a self-deprecating smile, "being a man of the cloth has its advantages."

"I suspect," said Barnhill, "he has his hands full of badly wounded Confederates."

"No doubt," agreed Bryan. Reaching into his breast pocket, he produced two folded slips of paper. He opened one and handed it to Barnhill, who read the printed form aloud:

> Dated July 20th, I, the subscriber, a Prisoner of War,
> captured near Gettysburg, Pa., do give my parole of honor not
> to take up arms against the United States or to do any military
> duty whatever, or to give any information that may be
> prejudicial to the interests of the same, until regularly exchanged.

The form was signed by Major Roy Allen of Company A, Twentieth Maine, who had added in his own hand: *This parole is extended to the wounded in consideration of humanity to save a painful and tedious march to the rear.* Below his signature, the major had neatly printed Barnhill's name, rank, and regiment. "Thank the Lord," said Barnhill with an immense sigh.

Lying on a litter fashioned from a tarpaulin and two broomsticks, Robert Maxwell was borne by Reverend Bryan and his servant Jason out the front door, through the gate, and up into the back seat of the brougham, where he was made comfortable leaning against a pillow with a thin blanket over his lap. Jason returned with a battered valise containing a change of clothes, extra socks, and the two soldiers' few belongings—including the fine gray coat Barnhill was wearing when he was shot—and stowed it at the back of the coach. With Dora watching at the gate, both of her small hands holding onto the pickets, Barnhill climbed carefully up on the driver's seat.

"I'm sending you with a basket of nice ripe peaches," said Bryan, mopping his brow with a handkerchief in the morning heat, "and some biscuits and smoked ham. And a demijohn of spring water."

"I don't know where to begin to thank you," said Barnhill, who was clad in a checked shirt, twill trousers, and a farmer's straw hat.

"It was the least I could do," replied Bryan.

"Not many men would have shown such consideration to their enemy."

"I regard no man as my enemy, sir. Though, as you know, I am unalterably opposed to secession and slavery, I wish only for this war to be over."

"You have the letter I left for my mother?"

"I'll see that it's posted today."

Lifting the reins from the yoke, Barnhill gazed over the heads of the matched pair of grays, whose ears twitched in excitement, raised his hat for a last farewell, and started the horses with a click of his tongue. As they circled the drive, he turned back for a final look at the house, with Henry Bryan and Jason watching from the gate, and waved goodbye to Dora, who, he believed, brushed away a tear. Turning south onto the Emmitsburg Road, Barnhill drove across the broad plain between the ridgelines where so many had fallen and now lay in simple graves, marked with wooden crosses. After a quarter hour the road jogged to the left, passing the field where the Texas Brigade had begun its ill-fated charge. Barnhill halted the horses with a gentle tug and paused to gaze at the boulder-strewn hill with its skirt of trees. Little Round Top, where so many friends and comrades, perhaps his cousin Sam, would forever lie.

CHAPTER FIVE

"WHOAA," SAID BARNHILL, REINING IN THE HORSES, which responded with a nicker and toss of their charcoal manes. He gazed at the dense black smoke spiraling from the sawmill chimney on the heights overlooking the wide curve of the James River, and beyond the mill, the church spires, redbrick dwellings, and warehouses of the town. At the end of each day he'd cut a notch on the reins, which now numbered twelve. It seemed more like a month since he'd waved farewell to Reverend Bryan and turned the horses south toward Maryland. "Are you awake, Robert?" he called down to his passenger.

"Is it Lynchburg?" inquired Maxwell weakly.

"It is indeed," replied Barnhill. "We've finally made it." In preparation for the journey, Barnhill had spread open the reverend's atlas on the kitchen table and studied the maps of Pennsylvania, Maryland, and Virginia. Deciding to avoid Harper's Ferry, he chose a route through Hagerstown, crossing the Potomac at Williamsport, and thence southwest to Winchester and down the length of the Shenandoah Valley, traversing the Blue Ridge at Glasgow to reach the railhead at Lynchburg, whence they would entrain to Petersburg and on to North Carolina. The sojourn had very nearly ended almost as it began with their first encounter with Federal pickets at the Maryland line. A gruff Union sergeant, suspicious of paroles, relented only after forcing Maxwell from the coach, stripping off his shirt and examining his ugly, festering wound. After he added his signature to the paroles, they crossed the state line, arriving at sundown at a tavern beyond Emmitsburg. The Union officer commanding the garrison at Williamsport, after a cursory inspection of their documentation, exacted a gratuity of ten gold pieces before allowing them to board the ferry to cross the Potomac.

Their fortunes brightened as soon as they alighted on Virginia soil, turning away from the Federal forces to the east and passing into the broad Shenandoah, whose residents were eager to succor two badly wounded survivors of Gettysburg. The late-August fields were fallow or contained a few stands of ripening corn, but the families' gardens overflowed with beans, peas, squash, and plump tomatoes. To spare Robert the trial of long days on the washboard roads, Barnhill made frequent stops to rest and water the horses, usually finding accommodations for the night in a farmer's barn or tavern in town. One hot summer morning just south of Winchester, Barnhill halted the coach to watch in fascination a long line of blacks plodding along the dusty road, old and young, mostly barefoot, many of the younger women clutching infants, making their way north toward the Potomac, to freedom.

Though Robert Maxwell ate little and was too weak to stand without help, he was driven by an iron determination to return home. As they lay on straw and blankets in the faint moonlight shining through cracks in the roof of a barn, it was all he spoke of: Widewater, the proud Maxwell plantation on Albemarle Sound, hunting ducks and geese in the fall and winter, strolling the beaches at Nags Head in the summer. And of his sister Amelia—*oh yes, Jamie, you'll find her right good looking, and intelligent too, far more than I.* By flickering candlelight Barnhill read to him, stories from a worn volume of Sir Walter Scott and familiar passages of scripture from the Bible Reverend Bryan had entrusted to them as a parting gift.

Barnhill took off his straw hat, whose band was stained from nearly two weeks under the late summer sun, and ran his hand over his glistening brow. "I'll find a livery in town," he called down to Maxwell, "and see what this rig will fetch. Ought to suffice for our railroad fares." With a click of his tongue and slap of the reins, he started the coach forward, the springs groaning along the rutted, downhill road, rumbling across the trestle bridge over the river, intact despite two years of fighting in the Shenandoah that had bypassed Lynchburg, on the eastern slope of the

Blue Ridge. After locating the livery on the outskirts of town, Barnhill, whose injured left arm still hung limp in a sling, awkwardly climbed down and unhitched the weary horses to water at the trough. Leaving Robert reclining on the seat, he went in to dicker with the stableman over the price for a worn-out coach and two ill-used animals.

During the course of the journey southward, Barnhill had observed that progressively more Confederate dollars were required for the same quantity of goods. Hence, he reasoned, the asking price for the team and coach in Confederate currency should be far greater than their cost in gold. Slipping off his hat, he approached a gaunt, bearded man standing behind the counter. "Afternoon," began Barnhill.

"Afternoon," said the man, shifting a wad of tobacco in his cheek and squirting a stream of dark juice into the brass spittoon on the sawdust floor. Glancing at Barnhill's patched, checked shirt and coarse duck trousers, he said, "What happened to your arm?"

"Shot," replied Barnhill. "At Gettysburg."

"I don't see no uniform," said the man in hostile tone.

"Listen, mister," said Barnhill, "my friend and I have come a long way. I have a brougham and matched pair of grays for sale."

The man scratched his beard and spat again into the spittoon. "Gettysburg was a sorry affair," he commented in the same truculent tone. "Mebbe time for you Rebs to think about quittin'." Barnhill returned the hostile glare. "Or mebbe you fellers done already quit," said the man in a weak attempt at sarcasm.

Though the man was twice his age and a good six inches shorter, Barnhill knew he was no match for him with his useless left arm. "I don't want any trouble," he said. "Just a simple business proposition." He turned and started for the door.

"Hold it," said the man. Barnhill stopped and looked over his shoulder. "Lemme have a look at them animals. Horses are damned scarce in these parts thanks to the damned Rebel cavalry."

Barnhill stood, watching carefully as the stableman pried open the mare's jaw and examined her teeth. Following a similar evaluation of the other horse's mouth and inspection of all eight hooves, he turned to Barnhill and said, "Twenty dollars. Apiece."

"Fifty," said Barnhill. "That is, unless you're prepared to pay in gold."

This elicited a slight smile from the bearded man. He reached into a back pocket and produced a billfold from which he extracted a number of worn Confederate banknotes. "Forty dollars," he said, counting the money in his palm. "Fer each animal."

"And how much for the brougham?" Barnhill glanced at Maxwell, who was watching the negotiations through the round rear window with a bemused expression.

"Wheels need some fixin'," he said thoughtfully, "but the axle ain't sprung, and with a fresh coat of paint . . . Hmm. Another fifty bucks."

"I paid fifty for it in gold," said Barnhill.

"Well, then, seventy-five."

Barnhill rubbed his chin and then said, "All right." The stableman unexpectedly thrust out his hand and gave Barnhill a firm grip. After going inside for more money, he assisted Barnhill to help Maxwell down from the coach and into the back of a wagon hitched to a mule. Barnhill tossed in their worn carpetbag and climbed up on the seat next to the stableman, who'd agreed to carry them to the depot for the price of two dollars. They passed without speaking through the town, staring at the storefronts, the old men in rockers on their porches, their wives in sunbonnets, children and dogs in the dusty streets, but they saw no young men. Turning at the courthouse toward the depot, their reverie was broken by the shrill blast of a locomotive's whistle and the distinctive *chugs* of an approaching train.

"You fellers are danged lucky," said the driver as he snapped his whip by the mule's ears. "That 'ere train runs once a week if it runs atall."

Leaving Robert Maxwell to rest on the carpetbag on the congested sidewalk, Barnhill made his way through the vaulted depot to the line at the ticket counter, where a likeness of Jeff Davis and the Confederate stars and bars adorned an otherwise plain wall. He noted the time, 3:00 p.m., posted on a blackboard for the scheduled departure to Petersburg and Richmond. When his turn came, he dropped the leather pouch on the counter with a clink and said, "Two seats to Petersburg."

The clerk, wearing an eyeshade and armbands over his rolled-up sleeves, eyed Barnhill's arm in the sling and farmer's clothing. "All sold out," he said. "Just one carriage for passengers."

"We're Confederate officers," said Barnhill. "Returning from Gettysburg. We should have priority . . ."

"No matter," said the clerk.

"But here's my parole," said Barnhill, reaching into his pocket.

"Pardon me."

Both Barnhill and the clerk turned toward a Confederate officer wearing a blue-gray coat with yellow lapels, who appeared out of the crowd. "May I?" he asked, reaching a hand out to Barnhill, who offered him the folded paper. After a quick perusal he returned the parole to Barnhill and said, "Where's your uniform, Lieutenant?"

"Outside in the valise with my friend," he replied. "Though it's in no condition to be worn."

"And your friend?" asked the officer, an older major with a full gray beard.

"Captain Robert Maxwell, with the Twenty-sixth North Carolina. He's badly wounded, in far worse shape than me."

"These men have priority," said the major sternly to the clerk. "Make room for them. At half the posted fare, as you well know."

"Yes, sir," replied the clerk meekly, conscious of the hostile stares of the men and women gathered around the counter.

Barnhill sat on the wooden seat facing Robert Maxwell, observing the gangs on the platform loading hogsheads of tobacco, sacks of cornmeal, and milled lumber on the long line of flatbeds behind the single passenger car. A stout white man, the apparent supervisor, brandished a long crook, the sort used to herd sheep, and struck the backside of an older black man he perceived to be working too slowly. The man stumbled, winced in pain, and then responded with a brief, hateful glare. Barnhill turned away and looked at Maxwell, dozing in the afternoon heat, his handsome face resting on his hand against the window frame. He awoke with a start at the sound of the locomotive's whistle and motion of the train. Barnhill gazed out at the faces on the platform—farmers and mill owners sending their goods to market and town folk seeing relations off to the city—and watched as the sloping roof of the depot and cupola of the courthouse retreated into the hazy distance. The train gathered speed, lurching as it rounded a bend on the steep hillside with a plume of sooty black smoke from the locomotive filming the windows. Barnhill studied the fields and pastures, noting the dilapidated fence rails, emaciated livestock, and blackened timbers of a barn put to the torch; the general neglect of small farms with no one but women and old men to look after them. The other passengers—middle-aged men and women accompanied by a few children and black servants—dozed in the swaying carriage or were preoccupied with reading or knitting, paying scant attention to the visible toll on their country ravaged by the foraging of armies, plunder of horses and cattle . . . two years of pitiless war. Was it any wonder Virginians fought on? But what about the Northern soldiers, for the most part conscripts like Jeremiah Wilson, without the least concern for the plight of the slaves, taking at face value the politicians' pledge that the war wasn't being fought to free them—or was it? Had Jeremiah Wilson taken up arms to fight for a mere abstraction, literally sacrificing an arm and a leg for "Union"? Barnhill shook his head, trying to clear his mind of such oppressive ruminations.

His eyes fell on his sleeping companion. Robert appeared almost peaceful. Well, he was going home, an attraction so powerful it had brought him back from the edge of the grave and sustained him through weeks of arduous travel. Barnhill closed his eyes and visualized his own home, the fine whitewashed house on the hilltop, with double galleries and a red brick chimney, set amid a stand of tall pines. More than two years had elapsed since he passed through the front gate. He wondered if the letter he entrusted to Reverend Bryan had been delivered. He suspected someone had reported him dead; his cousin Sam, presuming Sam had survived, or some other survivor of his regiment. How his mother must have grieved. And poor Kate, no doubt devastated by the news. Barnhill imagined the scene: the mourners gathered in the parlor . . . Opening his eyes, he gripped the armrest and stared out the grimy window. What foolish, sentimental rot. By now his mother surely knew he was fine, though injured, and it wouldn't surprise him if Kate was sweet on someone else, if indeed there were any boys left in San Augustine County. He hadn't received a letter from Kate in months. Still, he ached for home and admitted to some resentment, or at least envy, of Robert Maxwell for his imminent reunion with his loved ones.

Over the gently rolling Piedmont, clad in the dark green of late summer, the train slowly rattled on, eliciting the curious stares of poor white farmers tending their burley tobacco and, farther to the east, where the land flattened and pines grew tall, of teams of black field hands, barefoot and in rags, at work with their hoes. It was, Barnhill reflected, a truly agrarian society, not the ideal praised by Jefferson, but rather one sustained by the labor of African slaves. The shadows lengthened, Barnhill's eyelids drooped, and then, with a jarring squeal of brakes and hiss of escaping steam, they passed beneath a pitched roof and came to a stop at the depot. In the waning daylight Barnhill read the sign under the eaves: Petersburg.

After waiting for the others to detrain, Barnhill helped Robert to his feet, and painfully gripping their bag in his left hand, supported Robert and slowly led him to the steps down to the platform. Unlike Lynchburg, the Petersburg station, illuminated by gaslights, was crowded with Confederate soldiers; troops shifting from Lee's army north of the capital to the Tennessee theater, and the local garrison guarding the trains delivering precious supplies. The commander of the latter, a captain armed with a revolver and saber, noticed the two men struggling to alight from the carriage. Quickly coming to their aid, the officer reached for the carpetbag and took Maxwell by an elbow, helping him down the steps.

"Much obliged, sir," said Barnhill, wincing from his throbbing shoulder.

The captain thoroughly examined Barnhill and Maxwell in the flickering gaslight. "Are you men . . ." he began.

"We're officers," replied Barnhill quickly. "Wounded at Gettysburg. We were paroled." He reached into his pocket for his papers.

"Gettysburg?" the captain said skeptically.

"Yes, sir," said Barnhill, handing him the document.

Quickly scanning it, the captain looked up at Barnhill and said, "Desertion is a crime."

"We're not deserters," said Barnhill hotly, reaching for the parole.

Refusing to release it, the captain said, "Then where is your uniform, Lieutenant?" Turning to a young private standing rigidly at attention, he said, "Place these men under arrest." As the private menacingly lowered his rifle, Robert Maxwell groaned loudly and collapsed on the platform.

"Oh my," cried an older woman standing nearby. "Call for a doctor!"

In the ensuing confusion, another officer appeared, wearing a fine gray uniform trimmed in gold braid and leaning on a cane. "I'll be hanged," he blurted out as he pushed through the crowd. "If it isn't Jamie

Barnhill." With the insignia of a colonel on his collar, Edward Selden approached the captain and said, "What seems to be the trouble?"

"Hello, Ed," said Barnhill with an appreciative smile.

"You know these men, sir?" asked the captain.

With a quick appraisal of Barnhill's wounded arm and the man slumped on the ground, Selden, pale with anger, replied, "Yes, Captain, I know this man. I have no doubt he and his comrade were wounded in battle. Order your men to send for an ambulance, on the double."

"Yes, sir," said the captain with a hasty salute.

Barnhill knelt down and brushed back Maxwell's hair, just able to tell, in the shadows, that he was unconscious but breathing. Looking up at Selden, he said, "Well, brother, you're a sight for sore eyes."

"Let's get this man to a doctor," said Selden, "and then you can tell me your tale."

Seated at a corner table in the dimly lit tavern, Selden poured whiskey, looked Barnhill in the eye, and raised his glass. "To the cause," he said before taking a sip.

"It was damned good fortune you happened along when you did," said Barnhill, savoring a swallow of bourbon. "That captain was about to put us in irons."

"Bastard," said Selden. "Garrison soldier. I'll see to it he's transferred to the front. So you and this other fellow . . ."

"Robert Maxwell. Captain with the Twenty-sixth North Carolina. We woke up in a preacher's house. Federal surgeons had operated on both of us. Saved our lives. And this preacher, a very fine man, a widower, nursed us till we were well enough to travel."

"Not quite well enough," said Selden, "judging by Captain Maxwell's condition."

"I fear he's dying," said Barnhill. "But he's determined to make his way home." Barnhill took another swallow of bourbon and smacked his lips.

"I read the account of the Texas Brigade," said Selden. "Charging up that little hill. What did they call it?"

"Little Round Top." Barnhill looked into the distance.

"Remarkable. No wonder General Lee has such high regard for his Texans."

"Hood tried to persuade Longstreet to change his orders. To take the higher hill, in the Federals' rear, and turn their flank."

Selden sipped his drink with rapt attention.

"Old Pete refused, three times. I recall Hood's words. Suicide to attack that hill without taking the taller one first. And suicide it was."

"Well," said Selden, tipping the bottle to pour them both more whiskey, "I fear the chance to end the war with one decisive blow has been lost."

Barnhill nodded and took a sip of whiskey. "If only we'd taken that taller hill," he mused. "Our scouts reported it unoccupied. With a battery on that hill, we would have driven the Yankees on the flank and taken Cemetery Ridge."

"The fortunes of war," said Selden with a frown.

"Longstreet is a fine defensive general," said Barnhill. "But he's no Stonewall Jackson."

The doctors at the Confederate hospital concluded that Robert Maxwell's collapse at the depot was the result of exhaustion rather than infection and prescribed several days' rest with decent rations. They also judged neither Maxwell nor Barnhill fit for duty and issued them indefinite medical discharges. Preparing to board the train south to North Carolina, Barnhill warmly shook Selden's hand. "As soon as I'm well enough," he said, "I mean to make my way back to Richmond and rejoin my regiment."

"Haven't you heard?" said Selden. Barnhill shook his head. "Your division has been detached from Lee's army. Headed south to fight in Tennessee."

"Under Hood's command?" asked Barnhill. "I wasn't sure he survived Gettysburg."

"He lost an arm but is back in command."

"Well," said Barnhill, "I'll stay in touch, Edward, as you're in a position to know Lee's dispositions." Pausing at the locomotive's whistle, he reached for the handrail and climbed up the steps of the carriage, where Maxwell had already been borne on a litter. "Fare thee well, Edward," he said with a smile.

"Safe travels," said Selden with a wave. "Until we meet again."

Barnhill reflected on his blessings. Had it not been for the Bible in his shirt pocket, that minié ball at Fredericksburg would have taken his life. Unseen and unknown Federal troops had rescued him before he'd bled to death as dusk fell on Little Round Top. By the Lord's providence he'd been delivered into the hands of Reverend Bryan, without whose tender mercy he'd be languishing in a Union prison. And then Edward Selden had appeared on the platform at the Petersburg station. Barnhill believed profoundly in God and in his Savior, and though he prayed for God's protection and healing power over the sick and wounded, he doubted the ability of poor, ignorant mankind to call upon Almighty God to intervene in human affairs. The evidence was simply too overwhelming that a man, good or bad, would meet the fate ordained for him without regard for the desperate intercessions that he, or his friends, might fervently plead for. And yet, almost miraculously, he'd been spared, again and again. Barnhill bowed his head and thanked God. Looking up, he gazed out at the cultivated fields and pines of lowland Virginia, listening to the rhythmic *clack* of the rails, rocked by the gently swaying carriage. Robert slept peacefully on his cot. A fine plantation home, with sturdy columns and double chimneys, could be seen on a slight rise at the end of a row of live oaks. Old Virginia, Barnhill considered. The old country his father and mother had left for the Texas frontier.

Leaning his head against the window frame, Barnhill dozed, dreaming of home, of bird hunting on a fine October day with his favorite dog, a retriever named Buttermilk, and handing over his bag of quail to Hattie to fry up for supper. His eyes fluttered open at a change in the sound of the rails as the train passed over a high trestle bridge across the Nottoway River. Perhaps thirty miles to the east was Suffolk, the site of the brigade's winter encampment, forays into the Dismal Swamp, and skirmishing with Federal gunboats on the river. How many of those boys, warming themselves by the campfire on cold, clear nights, were now moldering in shallow graves in the Pennsylvania countryside? After a while Barnhill rose from his seat and walked to the front of the carriage where Robert Maxwell's cot was secured between two benches.

As Barnhill looked at him, Maxwell opened his eyes and raised himself on an elbow. "Where are we?" he asked sleepily.

"Somewhere near the state line, I reckon," replied Barnhill.

Maxwell looked out the window on the gently rolling fields and stands of tall pines. Rounding a wide curve in the tracks, the train crossed another bridge spanning a wide river. Gazing down at the water, Maxwell said, "It's the Roanoke. We're in Carolina now." He lowered himself on the pillow with a contented smile.

Within the hour the train came to a stop at the Rocky Mount Depot with a hiss of escaping steam. With Edward Selden's assistance, Barnhill had telegraphed ahead to the quartermaster of the local garrison, arranging a horse and buggy to take them the final leg of their long journey. As several Confederate privates helped Maxwell up on the buggy seat, he turned to Barnhill and said, "What day is it, Jamie?"

Barnhill glanced at the newspaper he'd bought in the depot, a day-old issue of the *Raleigh Standard*. "It's Thursday," he said, "the fourth of September." He grasped the frame of the buggy with his good arm and hauled himself up on the seat.

"September fourth," repeated Maxwell. "Almost two years since I left home."

"Much obliged, boys," said Barnhill to the privates, touching the brim of his hat. Before leaving Petersburg he'd donned his uniform coat, whose torn and bloodied left shoulder had been roughly patched, and traded his straw hat for a wide-brimmed slouch with a band of yellow twine. "He-ahh," he called to the horse with a yank on the reins.

After a final night at a roadside tavern, they arrived at the landing on the banks of the Chowan River at noon. Eyeing the steam-powered side-wheeler at the dock and the expanse of dark water, Barnhill turned to Maxwell and said, "Is this the river?"

Maxwell nodded. "Almost two miles wide where it empties into the sound."

Climbing down, Barnhill took the reins and led the horse and buggy down the rutted track to the ramshackle building that served as ticket office and residence for the ferryman. Hitching the mare, he purchased their tickets, lifted Maxwell down from the seat, and helped him to stand. Within the half hour, amid smoke swirling from the stack and a great rushing of the paddlewheel, the vessel moved away from the landing and turned into the wide river, with both men standing in the bow staring expectantly at the far shore. Before long Barnhill could make out the trees along the opposite bank and the wide curve of a harbor with stone fortifications, the facades of handsome brick and clapboard houses, and farther inland, a number of tall church steeples. "Edenton," commented Maxwell. As they approached the main wharf, Barnhill observed that the flag flapping on the tall pole was neither Union nor Confederate, but that of North Carolina. Throughout the short passage Maxwell remained quiet, studying the silent shore, immersed in his memories. With a clang of the bell atop the wheelhouse, the ferry shuddered alongside the moorings, which the deckhands secured with thick hawsers. Lifting their worn carpetbag and adjusting his hat, Barnhill took Maxwell by the arm and said, "Well, Robert, you're finally home." They crossed over the gangplank, and, as they slowly started down the pier, observed a tall man standing beside a fine coach, dressed in a black frock coat and tall silk hat. He stared for a moment at them and began walking, and then running, to greet them. Stretching out both arms he called out "Robert, Robert! Thank God."

CHAPTER SIX

DECADES LATER, after so many changes wrought by time and experience, Barnhill would often try to remember that particular time and place, an idyll in the midst of suffering and heartache, try to conjure up the sights, the smells, the sounds of that house and its environs, and most particularly its inhabitants. It was autumn, the wide lawn perfumed with fallen leaves, while others, red, orange, and brown, clung to the branches; the scent of woodsmoke in the air, the slap of the waves against the dock, and the distant peal of church bells. For a young man from the backwoods of East Texas, it was a magical place: Widewater, the graceful Maxwell home with its broad portico and fluted columns commanding a view of the mile-wide Chowan River, and Edenton, the nearby town, colonial capital of North Carolina, with its stately homes and churches and waterfront on Albemarle Sound.

The place was caught somewhere between war and peace, Union and Confederacy, slave and free. The majority sentiment had opposed secession until Lincoln called for an army of seventy-five thousand volunteers to subdue the South. In the winter of '62, Ambrose Burnside, before his elevation to command of the Army of the Potomac, led an expeditionary force to the coast of North Carolina. He landed a strong Federal brigade on Roanoke Island, located between the mainland and the Outer Banks, promptly defeated the Confederate garrison, and dispatched a raiding party across the sound, briefly occupying Edenton before retiring to his island sanctuary. No one in town, of course, considered the place under Federal control, and yet the experience vastly diminished the sense of belonging to, or being under the protection of, the Confederate States of America. Burnside, meanwhile, launched a naval flotilla to invade the Carolina mainland at New Bern, farther to the south, inflicting another defeat on the Confederate forces and occupying the important coastal city. To the dismay of wealthy planters like Josiah Maxwell, proprietor of Widewater, many in the coastal counties, especially in the aftermath of Gettysburg and Vicksburg, had turned against the war. Some young Carolinians went so far as to enlist in the Union army.

"Buffaloes," said Josiah Maxwell with a contemptuous frown. "That's what the traitors have taken to calling themselves." Tall and handsome, wearing a black frock coat over a scarlet silk vest, he strode before the fireplace with hands clasped behind his back.

"A strange choice of name," said Jamie Barnhill, seated in an easy chair with a cup and saucer on the table beside him. He looked comfortably around the elegantly appointed room, with its crystal chandelier, walls painted robin's-egg blue, and French ormolu clock on the mantelpiece.

"All the honorable men in the county," said Robert, reposing on the sofa under a knitted coverlet, "are up in Virginia fighting the Yankees."

The father looked admiringly at his son. "I well understand the independent streak of our people on the Outer Banks," he said, turning to Barnhill. "But for the boys of Chowan County . . ." He shook his head with a grimace.

"Don't dwell on it, Papa," said the young woman seated on a small, upholstered chair, Robert's sister Amelia, with her sewing in her lap. "It's bad for your digestion." Barnhill had learned in his first weeks with Robert at Reverend Bryan's home that his mother had died of typhus several years before the war, and that his younger sister, who closely resembled her mother, had become something of a surrogate caring for her widowed father.

"I wouldn't worry about the Federal forces on Roanoke Island," said Barnhill to Josiah Maxwell. "I should think your state militia can keep them at bay."

"I defer to your judgment," said Maxwell with a slight bow, "as you have faced Burnside." In the weeks since Barnhill's arrival at the plantation, Josiah Maxwell never tired of hearing stories about the great battles his son and his friend from Texas had fought in.

"Judging from his conduct at Fredericksburg," said Barnhill as the others keenly listened, "I would say Burnside was a reckless gambler..."

"And a fool," interjected Robert.

"Our regiment was not engaged at Fredericksburg," said Barnhill, "though we were perfectly situated to observe the Federal attack. A remarkable spectacle. Some fifty thousand men with nearly a mile of open ground to cover under all the guns Jackson could bring to bear." At the mention of the fallen Confederate hero, Josiah Maxwell reverently repeated the name with a nod. "Burnside ordered an attack on our entrenched positions, in broad daylight, with nothing to protect his men but a blue serge jacket and row of brass buttons."

"If you were not engaged," asked Amelia meekly, "how is it you were wounded?"

"I was ordered to seek out General Hill. Powell Hill, your great North Carolinian. His division was bearing the brunt of the attack. We—my cousin and I—got mixed up with another regiment, Maxcy Gregg's South Carolina boys, and found ourselves in the thick of the fighting..."

"How dreadful," said Amelia, putting her sewing aside.

"Spared by the Bible in your breast pocket," said Josiah. "A remarkable tale." He resumed his pacing by the windows.

"Father," said Amelia.

Maxwell halted.

"May I ask permission to take the phaeton into town? For sundries, and to see about mail."

"I'll go along," said Barnhill, springing up from his chair. "With your permission, that is."

"Naturally, Lieutenant," said Maxwell. "And now, I believe, dinner is served."

"You insist on driving?" said Barnhill as he examined the handsome two-seater carriage, painted bright green with red wheel spokes.

"I do," said Amelia. "Yellowjacket answers to my voice only. And besides, I know the way." Barnhill climbed up on the leather-upholstered seat beside her, and at her command, the tall bay started forward at a trot. Barnhill reached for the blanket folded at his feet and spread it over their laps. As they passed the brick gateposts and turned onto the road that ran beside the riverbank, Barnhill stole a look at Amelia, admiring her fair complexion, delicate nose and mouth, and the bounce in her light-brown curls as the wheels spun in the ruts.

"Ah," he said with a sigh. "A perfect October afternoon. Not a cloud in the sky."

Amelia briefly looked at him with a smile. "You're doing so much better," she said, holding the reins loosely in her lap since the horse knew the way into town. Barnhill nodded and stretched out his left arm. For weeks he'd gone without the sling and worked on rebuilding his strength. Barnhill gazed out on a broad cotton field, perhaps five hundred acres filled with white bolls as if blanketed in snow, and at the dozens of stooped black men and women with their burlap sacks toiling to harvest the last of the crop. Amelia turned the buggy at a crossroads, passing by a number of impressive houses, and after a trip of some thirty minutes turned again on Broad Street, which ran the length of the town. As Amelia waved or called out to acquaintances along the sidewalk, Barnhill silently studied the graceful two-story homes, some of them dating from the last century. Amelia reined in the horse at a storefront with the incongruous sign "United States Post Office" over the door. Barnhill climbed down and then walked around the phaeton to help her from the seat.

Holding his hand, she looked up into his eyes and said, "I have a letter to post, and I'll see if we have any mail."

"Fine," said Barnhill. "I'll take a look around town."

"Two blocks down is St. Paul's. It's worth a visit."

Barnhill watched as the door of the post office closed behind Amelia and then started down the sidewalk, crossed at the intersection of Broad and Church streets, and strolled into the quiet neighborhood adjoining the commercial district. Across from an ivy-covered brick home whose owner was burning a pile of leaves, he entered the churchyard through an iron gate, pausing to admire the massive magnolias and inspect the weathered headstones leaning at odd angles in the soft earth, with names and dates barely legible. He studied the handsome brick church with its arched windows and steeple atop a square Saxon base. Glancing at the cornerstone with the date 1774, he opened the heavy oak door and quietly entered. Daylight shone dimly through the old glass in the chancel, the wide plank floor creaked under his tread, and the musty air was fragrant with linseed oil. Barnhill sat on a worn pew and reached for the Book of Common Prayer in the rack. Raised a Presbyterian in a simple pioneer church, he was unfamiliar with the contents of the volume. Letting it fall open in his lap, he read:

> Eternal God, our heavenly Father, who alone makest men to be of one mind in a house, and stillest the outrage of a violent and unruly people . . . appease the seditious tumults which have been lately raised up among us. . . .

He closed the volume and returned it to the rack. Staring for a moment at the figures in the stained glass, he bowed his head with his hand at his brow, wondering if it was mere chance, or whether he had been meant to find the passage . . . *appease the seditious tumults raised up among us.* With a heavy sigh, he rose from the pew, feeling an ache in his injured shoulder that he suspected heralded a change in the weather.

The leaden sky gave no hint of change, though a chill in the air caused him to warm his hands in his coat pockets as he hurried back to the main thoroughfare and started up the sidewalk. He found Amelia gazing into a shop window, clutching a packet of letters. Eyeing his reflection in the glass, she turned with a smile and said, "Did you find St. Paul's?"

"Yes," said Barnhill. "It's beautiful, and so old."

"The first Episcopal church in the colony," said Amelia. "Founded in 1701."

"I see you have mail."

She nodded. "You never know when they'll deliver it, with the Yankee gunboats patrolling the sound. And there's one for you."

"For me?"

She sorted through the envelopes and extracted a bulky letter in his mother's blue stationery. "Postmarked in Texas," she said as she handed it to him.

Barnhill stared at the neat handwriting. "I'll save it till we're home," he said with a broad smile.

By the time the phaeton passed through the gateposts, a thin layer of clouds blotted out the sun and the freshening wind carried a sharp bite. Barnhill turned to Amelia and said, "Must be a norther on the way."

"A norther?" she repeated with a queer look. She steered the bay toward the barn behind the kitchen.

"That's what we call a cold snap in Texas."

"Well, then, Jamie Barnhill," she said with a toss of her curls as she reined in the horse, "I'd say we're in for a norther."

Amelia sat beside her father on the horsehair sofa facing the fireplace while Barnhill paced by the window, tapping the envelope on his palm. Robert, despite all his daydreams of hunting and fishing on the sound, had grown steadily weaker and this afternoon had been helped up the stairs to his old bedroom. Thomas, one of the house servants, entered the room with an armload of firewood, knelt to arrange it in the hearth, and struck a match to the kindling.

"Aren't you going to open your letter?" asked Amelia.

Barnhill nodded. "We get mail so seldom in the army," he said, "the men tend to savor it when a letter finally arrives." He watched the flames crackle in the logs and slit open the letter, removed its contents, and read by the light of the window:

October 3, 1863

My dear son,

> It was with great relief that I received your letter, though I knew from your previous correspondence from Gettysburg that the word you had perished in that terrible battle was, thanks be to God, mistaken. Your cousin Sam had written to his mother that he had seen you fall in an act of extraordinary heroism, leading your men.

Barnhill glanced at the fire, reflecting that, as he surmised, his poor mother had believed he was dead and grieved over him. Aware that Amelia and her father were watching, he continued silently reading:

> I am thankful beyond the power of words to express that you have been granted leave and are recuperating in the home of your friend Captain Maxwell. Please convey my deepest thanks to the family for their kindness. I pray morning and night for your full recovery and for your friend. How two badly wounded young men could have made their way from Pennsylvania to the coast of Carolina is more than I can comprehend.
>
> We are tolerably well here, Anna and I, though so many friends and neighbors are in mourning for lost sons and husbands. I am enclosing a letter Aunt Julia received from Sam, containing his

account of the recent great battle in Georgia. It seems they're sending the poor Texas boys from pillar to post, wherever the fighting's the hottest. Thank the Lord that again Sam was spared.

I must close now. Get well, dear son, and come home soon. Anna sends her love. Your devoted,

Mother

Barnhill briefly examined the letter enclosed with his mother's, written on cheap paper in his cousin's chicken-scratch, laid them aside, and turned to Amelia and her father.

"All is well at home?" inquired Mr. Maxwell.

"Tolerably well," replied Barnhill, "in my mother's words. It appears our division was sent to fight in this last great battle."

"But I understood," said Amelia, "that your division was in Virginia?"

"It was," said Barnhill, walking over to warm himself before the fire. "But as Robert and I were passing through Petersburg I learned from a friend that Hood's Division had been sent south to reinforce Bragg in Georgia." A wave of guilt passed over him as he reflected on his absence from his regiment.

"But this was a fine Southern victory," said Josiah Maxwell. "Was it not?"

Barnhill nodded. "According to the Richmond newspapers," he agreed. "The Battle of Chickamauga, they're calling it. But the account I read in *Harper's* . . ."

"Northern drivel," said Maxwell.

"I've found their accounts," said Barnhill, "to be quite accurate. In this instance, it would appear to be a slight victory for Bragg, gained at an enormous cost."

"And the Yankees have an inexhaustible supply of men," said Amelia quietly.

"Immigrants, mercenaries," muttered Maxwell.

"In any case," said Barnhill, "my mother enclosed a letter from my cousin, who serves in our regiment, with his personal account of the battle. I thought I would share it with Robert when he's feeling up to it."

At the early evening hour, following their customary time of prayer and scripture reading, the family gathered in the parlor before the fire, listening to the cold north wind as Barnhill read aloud in his sonorous voice the letter Sam Perkins had written his mother. "The Division boarded trains at Petersburg," Barnhill read, "boxcars and flatbeds fit for cattle, and for two days we journeyed south, with only water and hardtack to sustain us." Barnhill paused as an elderly servant entered the room with a salver and served each of the men a tumbler of whiskey and water. Barnhill took a swallow and continued:

> We departed on September 16 and reached Atlanta on the 18th. The men suffered terribly on the train and arrived in no condition to fight. We were served hot rations, however, and fitted out in new uniforms, and off we marched to join the Army of Tennessee.

Barnhill turned to Robert, who was listening raptly from his chair by the fire, and said, "Our train left Petersburg on the fourth of September, did it not? So the Texas boys passed through less than two weeks behind us." He turned back to Sam's letter:

> After a hard march we crossed a bridge over this crick, called Chickamauga, and bivouacked in the woods, our division and Kershaw's. Next day, the 19th, our beloved General Hood, whom we'd last seen in our charge on Little Round Top, arrived, not riding his roan, Jeff Davis, but a chestnut mare, which the men considered an ill omen. The country is rolling hills, red clay, and tall pines where the land hasn't been cleared for corn. By mid-day they rushed us into the line, the 4th Texas on our left and 3rd Arkansas on our right. At the command, "forward," Gen'l Hood was struck by a ball in the thigh, and fell from his horse into the arms of our men, who carried him from the field.
>
> We charged across an open pasture under a storm of shot and shell thicker than any the brigade had faced since the cornfield at Sharpsburg. The fire was so hot it set the sedge grass and fence rails ablaze. It was a terrible sight, dear mother, as so many comrades were struck, and yet we pushed the Federals—western men, who fought with great courage and tenacity. When it appeared the day might be lost, on came Kershaw's Georgians, whooping like wild Indians, and with the remnants of our three regiments, we drove the Yankees from the field.

"Splendid," interjected Josiah Maxwell.

"At nightfall," Barnhill continued,

> we managed to gather our wounded, and what was left of our regiment joined the march the following day toward the heights overlooking Chattanooga, where the Federals have retired. How I survived that hellish fight I cannot say, but after Gettysburg and this great battle there is little left of our once proud brigade, and I fear for the life of our great general. I must close, as we will soon be on the march again, and send my love . . .

Barnhill refolded the pages with an audible sigh. He looked up at the elder Maxwell, who was staring into the fire, and at Robert, whose blue eyes were soft and compassionate, and Amelia, whose cheeks were stained with tears. Taking another sip of his drink, Barnhill said, "If that's the price of victory, I fear we can't afford it."

Bright sunlight streamed into the library, situated beneath a gable on the second floor with a view across the lawn to the wide river. From his armchair, Barnhill gazed contentedly at the pale blue sky and naked branches of the hardwoods and at the leather-bound books neatly arranged on the shelves—a complete set of Pope, Gibbon's *Decline and Fall*, Dryden, and Shakespeare's major plays. And, he considered, Carlyle's *History of the French Revolution*, which he had been reading at Mrs. Webb's in Richmond. He thought back to that time, almost exactly a year earlier. Proud, gallant Edward Selden, the elegance and sophisticated banter of Mary Chesnut's table, General Hood wooing the beautiful Buck Preston. . . . A year had passed, and in the interval Hood had fallen twice from grievous wounds. What would become, he wondered, of that genteel way of life, of the patrician Southerners of Richmond and South Carolina? Conscious of another presence, he looked up to see Amelia in the doorway, wearing a simple woolen dress that, without underlying hoops and petticoats that were increasingly scarce, revealed her slender, well-proportioned figure.

"Sorry to disturb you," she said. "I didn't know . . ."

Rising from his chair, Barnhill said, "I wish you'd disturb me more often."

With a smile, she walked to the window and looked down on the lawn and river sparkling in the sunlight. "Tomorrow's Christmas Eve," she said. "You've been with us three months now, Jamie."

He walked over and looked in her eyes. "I don't want to leave," he said. "Though I know I should."

Lightly placing her hand on his arm, she said, "You mustn't. For Robert's sake."

"May I tell you something?" he said, putting his hand on hers.

"Of course."

"I . . . I've never felt this way before."

"What way?"

"About someone. The way I feel about you." He hesitated, searching for the right words. "You see, I've never really been in . . . love before." Amelia reddened slightly and gave his arm an encouraging squeeze. Gazing into her eyes, he said, "But everything about you, your gentleness and intelligence, not to mention your beauty, simply, well, swept me away."

On tiptoes, she lightly kissed him. They sat in armchairs facing the window, Barnhill with a handsome edition of Shakespeare's sonnets and Amelia with her well-worn Bible. After a while, closing the Bible, Amelia said, "As Christians, how can we justify owning slaves?"

"I've heard it done often, and convincingly, from the pulpit."

"But Jesus taught, in the Sermon on the Mount . . ."

"Yes, I know," said Barnhill. "And I agree with you. But at the very least the church teaches it's a sin to mistreat the slaves."

Christmas, the third of the war, had come and gone in a quiet, melancholy fashion, with Barnhill homesick for his mother and sister, Josiah Maxwell suffering from the loss of his wife, and Robert from a bad cold that drove him to his sickbed and further sapped his strength. Yet Amelia, when she wasn't waiting on her father or nursing her brother, was constantly at Barnhill's side, reading with him in the library or bundling up to take long walks along the riverbank, down to the sound shrouded in mist that concealed ducks and geese by the thousands, his hand circling her slender waist, her head leaning against his shoulder, pausing now and then to steal a kiss.

On New Year's Eve, Josiah Maxwell observed the traditional plantation celebration as it had been practiced in his father's and grandfather's day. The aroma of cornbread and baked ham with apples drifted from the kitchen and a cheerful fire burned brightly in the parlor while Amelia sat at the spinet piano. Somewhere in the distance the sound of singing could be heard, the rich harmonies and distinctive rhythms of Negro spirituals, as all of the slaves, save the cook and serving girl, had been given the traditional two-day holiday. Josiah Maxwell poured French champagne from one of the last bottles in his cellar and handed a crystal glass to Barnhill, standing beside him, his son, seated by the fire, and his daughter at the piano. Raising his glass, Maxwell proposed a toast:

"To the New Year. May it bring victory and an end to the war."

Barnhill raised his glass, thinking that such toasts were being drunk at countless firesides North and South. He turned to Amelia and said, "Will you play us a sentimental favorite?"

She reached for the sheet music on the piano, leafed through the pages, and said, "I'll play 'Aura Lea' if you'll sing it."

"Very well." Barnhill placed his glass on the mantel and sat beside her on the piano bench. She played the introductory chords and Barnhill sang:

> When the blackbird in the spring
> On the willow tree,
> Sat and rocked, I heard him sing,
> Singing Aura Lea. . . .

Her hands moving effortlessly over the keys, Amelia harmonized with him in the lilting chorus:

> Aura Lea, Aura Lea,
> Maid of golden hair,
> Sunshine came along with thee
> And swallows in the air.

As Barnhill savored the warm touch of her body and subtle fragrance of her perfume, she improvised a variant of the melody in a somber, minor key, and then, with a shy glance, resolved to the major seventh, and he sang:

> When the mistletoe was green
> Midst the winter's snows,
> Sunshine in thy face was seen
> Kissing lips of rose;

> Aura Lea, Aura Lea,
> Take my golden ring,
> Love and light return with thee
> And swallows in the spring.

As the closing notes died away, Barnhill looked up to see an elderly black woman, wearing a black dress with crisp white apron, standing in the arched entrance to the dining room, gazing lovingly at the girl she'd cared for since an infant, as did her father and brother, with identical expressions of loving approbation. For a moment, all of them were bound together by love, happiness, and family devotion . . . that was not to last.

CHAPTER SEVEN

WIDEWATER, BARNHILL REFLECTED FROM HIS VANTAGE POINT in a rocker on the broad portico, seemed not so much a plantation as a country house, an elegant estate in a park of some five acres with graceful trees and well-tended lawns and gardens, separated by a quarter mile from the cultivated cotton fields that supported it and the black field hands on whose labor it depended. So unlike his home in Texas, where the cotton fields lay just below the hilltop house, with a row of nearby cabins occupied by the blacks who intermingled freely with his family. At Widewater one might presume there were no slaves; merely the staff of black house servants—"darkies" as Josiah Maxwell referred to them with evident affection—the cook, the laundress, seamstress, and aging "houseboys" who lit the fires, hauled the water, and tended to Massa's every need.

On a bright, cold winter morning following weeks of dreary rain and ice, Barnhill sat at the breakfast table opposite Robert Maxwell, who looked haler and had a greater appetite for his eggs and country ham than at any time Barnhill could remember. "What do you say," said Barnhill as he put aside his cup of coffee, "if we venture down to the farm and have a look around? I'm curious to see how your methods compare to ours at home."

"Very well," said Maxwell, "though personally I haven't any interest in it. As you know, when I'm well, and the war's over, I intend to read the law."

"As do I," said Barnhill, tossing a piece of biscuit to the eager spaniel puppy at his knee. "Still, I might learn a thing or two from your overseer."

Maxwell responded with a brief, dark look and said, "Perhaps."

Bundled up in heavy wool coats, caps, and gloves, they made their way along a narrow path through tall oaks to the Maxwell cotton fields, eight hundred acres of rich, dark loam abutting the Chowan River. Pausing to rest, Robert sat on the hollow trunk of a fallen tree. "Our overseer, Mr. O'Grady," he said, "lives in that clearing just ahead. We'll pay him a visit and then take a stroll around." Overlooking a wide field of black, furrowed earth bearing the stubble of last summer's crop like an unshaved chin, a clapboard house, enclosed by a ramshackle fence, sat amid a squalor of broken glass, rotting vegetable vines, and rusting farm implements. Attached at the rear of the house was a pen enclosing two mules, a pigsty, and coops whose hens cackled in the morning sun. Barnhill trudged behind Maxwell to the front doorstep, noting the paint peeling from the boards and the grime on the windows. After giving the door a sharp rap, Maxwell stepped back, as if expecting trouble. His knock was answered by a threatening growl. A tall, beefy man, clutching a large yellow dog by the collar, flung open the door.

"Aha!" said the man, "if it ain't the young master hisself." He released the dog, which gave Robert a sniff and slunk off behind the house. Barnhill judged O'Grady to be in his early thirties, with thick forearms, a barrel chest, and ruddy Irish complexion.

"This is my friend, Mr. Barnhill," said Maxwell. "An officer in the Texas Brigade. Frank O'Grady." Barnhill reached out to shake hands.

"From Texas, eh," said O'Grady, stretching a gallus over the shoulder of his tobacco-stained shirt. "What brings you to these parts?"

"We were both wounded at Gettysburg," said Maxwell. O'Grady, an illiterate man, responded with an uncomprehending stare. "At any rate," Maxwell continued, "the lieutenant helped me to get home."

O'Grady walked out in the yard, impervious to the cold, turned to Robert and asked, "What can I do fer you gents today?"

"I'd like to show Mr. Barnhill around," said Maxwell. "How we do things here on the plantation. His family grows cotton."

"That a fact," said O'Grady.

"Yes," said Barnhill. "You plant the long-staple variety?"

"Nah," replied O'Grady with a shake of his large head. "Ordinary green-seed cotton."

"And your yield per acre?"

O'Grady scratched his chin and said, "Can't rightly say, but we'll make a crop of four hundred bales if I lean on 'em hard enough. How many do you make?"

"Six hundred," replied Barnhill. "In a good year."

"I'll be damned," said the overseer.

"We have a long season. Plant in March and don't pick till October."

"Well, you boys are welcome to have a look around," said O'Grady, idly kicking a half-buried bottle. "Taint much to see. The blacks as are well enough are workin' in the shop."

"Thank you," said Maxwell, touching a hand to his cap and turning to go.

"One more thing," said O'Grady. "Ye'd best keep away from them shacks."

"Why is that?" asked Maxwell.

"A lot of grippe goin' round," said O'Grady. "Had to bury a little gal yesterday."

Maxwell exchanged a brief look with Barnhill. "I see," he said.

"I can't abide that vile man," said Robert once they were out of earshot.

"Then why do you keep him?"

"My father believes that the . . . the slaves must be dealt with harshly. He has a great fear of an uprising, especially since Lincoln's proclamation and the Federal invasion of North Carolina." Barnhill walked along beside him, rubbing his arms for warmth. "He knows," said Maxwell, "he can depend on O'Grady to keep them in their place."

"I have no doubt of that," said Barnhill. "But how has he dodged conscription?"

"The so-called twenty-nigger law," said Maxwell with a shrug. Barnhill blinked uncomprehendingly. "One man," said Maxwell, "is exempt from conscription on every plantation with twenty or more slaves."

"Why?"

"So at least one white man is on hand to discipline the slaves and protect the womenfolk." As they rounded a corner on the path, an irregular row of shanties came into view amidst a copse of live oaks whose low-hanging boughs were draped with Spanish moss. A large, dilapidated shed stood to the right of the cabins with smoke pouring from a stovepipe.

"The shop," said Maxwell, pointing to the shed. "Let's pay the men a visit." As they drew near they could hear the clang of an anvil. Pausing at the partly open door, Barnhill peered inside the dimly lit structure, observing several black men working a bellows by a large fire at the far end while another—tall, muscular, and stripped to the waist—swung his heavy hammer to shape the glowing blade of a plow on the anvil. Other men were seated at a long workbench or slumped in the shadows on the dirt floor, discernible only by the whites of their eyes. Maxwell opened the door with a creak and stepped inside. Turning to look toward the shaft of bright sunlight, the men abruptly ceased their labors.

"Massa Robert," said one of the men at the bench, rising with a broad smile.

"Hello, Joe," said Maxwell, walking up to clap him on the shoulder. The others crowded around him as Barnhill watched from a distance.

"Home from the war," said a frail-looking man with white hair and beard. "They say you was shot."

"Yes," said Maxwell with a nod. "At the great battle of Gettysburg."

"Gettysburg," the men repeated among themselves. Barnhill drew closer, noting the virtual rags the slaves were wearing, many of them barefoot despite the bitter cold. "The Yankees came to town," said another man, "But then they went away again."

"Are you men all right?" asked Maxwell. "Are you getting enough to eat?"

The men merely nodded and shuffled their feet. The tall man who'd swung the hammer on the anvil stepped forward and said, "We needs a doctor, Massa. A lot of the chil'ren are mighty sick, and the mommas too." In the flickering light from the fire Barnhill could see that his broad shoulders and back were terribly disfigured with deep scars.

"They're dyin'," said another man from the shadows. "You got to help us."

"I'll see what I can do," Maxwell promised. "You men go back to work."

Stepping outside, Barnhill and Maxwell almost collided with a young slave with a light complexion who bore a striking resemblance to Robert and his father. "Sorry, sir," said the young man as he hurried inside the shed. Barnhill glanced at Robert, who turned away with a pained expression.

CHAPTER SEVEN

"We should go," said Robert. "I'm not feeling well."

"Massa Robert!"

Both men turned in the direction of one of the shanties where a young black woman, wearing a head scarf, gingham dress, and soiled apron, was standing in the doorway. "Massa Robert!" she repeated. "You got to help my little girl." In contrast to the neat, whitewashed slave quarters Barnhill was accustomed to, the shanty was a hovel, hewn of rough, weathered boards and mud bricks, with a low, sloping roof.

"You should wait here," Robert said to Barnhill. "While I take a look." He hurried to the cabin and followed the woman inside. Barnhill hesitated and then went after him. He stood at the threshold and peered in. By the light of a single candle Robert was kneeling on the dirt floor by a child's cot. Barnhill could hear her deep, hacking cough. He instinctively clasped his hand to his mouth, to ward off the stench of filth and protect himself from disease.

"Please," said the mother in a low, urgent voice. "Don't let my baby die."

Maxwell stood up, spoke briefly to the woman, and joined Barnhill outside the cabin. "The child's burning up," he said. "If we don't do something, they'll all be down with it. That damned fool overseer."

Robert and Barnhill stood before the fire in the parlor, warming themselves after the hour or more they'd spent in the cold. One of the house servants appeared in the doorway, coughed deferentially, and said, "Your father will be down shortly."

"Thank you," said Robert, dismissing him. Rubbing his hands together, he said, "It's frightful the way those poor creatures live. I can't say how long it's been since I've ventured down there."

Barnhill nodded, thinking out of sight, out of mind. He turned to Robert and said, "That one fellow, the big man with the hammer, why do you suppose he was whipped so badly?"

"He's a runaway," said Robert. "And every time they catch him, O'Grady . . . well, you saw for yourself."

"Why does he run?"

"They sold his mother and sister. Sent them a long way off, possibly Alabama, when Henry, I believe that's his name, was just a boy of fourteen or thereabouts." Robert's abhorrence of his father's treatment of his slaves was obvious. "A terrible thing."

"Yes," agreed Barnhill. "Just like in *Uncle Tom's Cabin.*"

"You've read it?" said Robert with a surprised expression.

Barnhill nodded. "It's no wonder that book got Northerners so riled up. But it doesn't have to be that way." Robert gave him an inquiring look. "The treatment of the slaves," said Barnhill.

"Good morning, gentlemen," said Josiah Maxwell as he strode briskly into the parlor, wearing his black frock and silk waistcoat. Looking at Robert, he said, "Thomas tells me there's something you're anxious to discuss."

"Yes, father. There's a fever sweeping the slave quarters. They're dying from it."

"What? I've heard nothing of the sort from Mr. O'Grady."

"Well, I'm not surprised," said Robert. "But I've spoken to the men myself and looked in on one of the children, running a high fever with a terrible cough."

"Haven't I instructed you to stay away from those shanties?" said the elder Maxwell angrily. "The very idea . . ."

"You must send for the doctor," said Robert calmly. He looked his father in the eye. "Before it's too late."

"Excuse me, sir," said Barnhill, "but the fault's mine. I asked Robert to show me around, to introduce me to the overseer."

"I see," said Maxwell.

"In fact," said Barnhill, "it was Mr. O'Grady who told us about the fever. He mentioned burying a child only yesterday."

"A child . . ."

"If I were in your position, sir," said Barnhill, "I would be concerned for the welfare of my field hands."

"Yes, of course," said Maxwell.

"I would be more than happy," continued Barnhill, "to ride into town and send for the doctor."

"That would be most kind," said Maxwell. "Robert, please tell the groom to saddle my best horse."

Astride a coal-black stallion, wearing his officer's coat, hat, and leather gauntlets, Barnhill couldn't rid his mind of images of the slaves, their miserable rags, the scars from their whippings, the pitiful child on the cot in the squalor of the shack. . . . And the young mulatto, he considered with disgust, obviously sired by Josiah Maxwell. Barnhill was convinced that most masters, like his own father, treated their slaves with far greater consideration, providing decent food, clothing, and shelter, with a paternalistic regard not only for their physical but their spiritual well-being. But there were far, far too many cruel masters like Josiah Maxwell . . . Lincoln and Seward were right; it had to end. Riding along the road by the river, Barnhill reined in his horse to watch as a flock of mallards noisily ascended from the mist-shrouded water. Yes, he conceded to himself, slavery had to end with this terrible war. He'd never before admitted the connection. The war, he'd insisted, was being fought for Southern independence. What was the remark General Longstreet supposedly had made? That the South should have declared an end to slavery and *then* seceded? Lincoln had been able to start a war to restore the Union, but Barnhill doubted he could win it without the high moral purpose of emancipation.

Arriving in Edenton, he dismounted at the general store on Broad Street, asked directions, and rode several blocks to turn on East King's Street where he located the doctor's residence, an ivy-covered brick house with a view of the waterfront and the slate water of Albemarle Sound. Shown inside, he explained the condition of the Widewater slaves to the physician, a slender, ascetic-looking man with wire-rimmed glasses and a wispy white goatee, who listened intently and agreed to come to the plantation as soon as his horse and buggy could be made ready. Returning to Widewater within the hour, Barnhill reported the result of his errand to Josiah Maxwell, who was attending to plantation business at the rolltop desk in his study, and ventured upstairs to the library, where he hoped to find Amelia.

She was sitting in her favorite chair, reading from a book in her lap by the pale light from the dormer window. "Is the doctor coming?" she asked.

"Yes," said Barnhill, lowering his tall frame into the chair beside her. "He should be here any minute."

"I wish you'd wear your uniform more often," she said with an affectionate smile. "You look so handsome."

Barnhill glanced down at the patched shoulder of his coat, and the sleeve stained with his blood. "It's a wonder I've still got it," he said. He thought about the dinner party at Mary Chesnut's, wearing the fine new uniform for the first time. "The Union doctors sent it along when I was taken to the reverend's house in Gettysburg. What's that you're reading?" he asked.

"The history of the French Revolution you're so fond of. I've found it difficult to understand. Could you help me with it?"

Barnhill complied, taking the identical chair facing her. Following his concise summary of Carlyle's account of the transformation of France from revolution to terror, she closed the thick volume in her lap and said, "I suppose that's the evil that came from destroying the old order. What did they call it?"

"The *ancien régime*."

She nodded. "Does it worry you, Jamie, what this war might do?"

"In what way?" Barnhill eased forward in his chair.

"Destroying *our* old order to save the Union. I'm sure the Jacobins, in the beginning, believed in the righteousness of their cause." Barnhill nodded encouragingly. "Just like the Republicans in the North," she continued. "But if they destroy our Southern way of life, to free the slaves, what will become of us, and who will look after the Negroes?" Barnhill gave her a brief, searching look. Blushing, she added, "Not that *our* Negroes have been well looked after."

Barnhill nodded and said, "Well, the sad truth is that the master, even the kind master, will lose all interest in caring for his slaves if they're no longer his property, and God knows what will become of the poor blacks. Lincoln's made this a war to end slavery, but with no idea what will take its place. And I fear we're losing it."

"It frightens me," said Amelia. "It frightens me terribly."

He looked up at the sound of hoofbeats on the drive below the window. Rising from his chair, he watched as the doctor climbed down from his buggy, clutching his black bag. "I should go down," he said, "and offer my assistance to your father."

The doctor, a man of Scots-Irish descent by the name of McDowell, stood before Josiah Maxwell, who was at his desk holding a match over the bowl of his clay pipe. Satisfied the tobacco was lit, he took a puff and said, "According to my son, some of the darkies have taken ill. The boy lacks the fortitude for these matters, however, and may be given to exaggeration."

"The child Robert looked in on," interjected Barnhill, "was indeed quite sick with a cough and high fever. And according to your overseer," he added, looking at Maxwell, "the grippe, as he termed it, is rampant among the slave quarters."

"Well, sir," said the doctor, "if you'd be so kind as to escort me, I shall have to examine them."

"I would be pleased, sir," offered Barnhill.

"No," said Maxwell, putting his pipe aside and rising from his chair. "I'll drive you in the buggy myself. At least as far as my overseer's cottage."

Barnhill stood with Amelia at the parlor window, waiting expectantly for her father's return with the doctor. The clock on the mantel struck four chimes. "I wonder," said Amelia, "why they're taking so long."

Gazing out on the drive, Barnhill rubbed his chin and said, "I suspect it's because the doctor found the slaves in a bad way. The men working in the shed pleaded with Robert to send for help, saying their women and children are dying."

"How terrible."

"Where is Robert?" asked Barnhill, turning to her and placing his hand on her arm.

"Upstairs in his room," she replied. "He wasn't feeling well."

They both turned at the sound of the approaching horse and buggy. Bringing the horse to a stop, Josiah Maxwell, with a stern expression, jumped down from the seat and started for the house, leaving the doctor to hitch his horse at the post.

"Well, Father?" said Amelia as Maxwell strode into the front hall and shrugged off his ulster.

Ignoring her, Maxwell said, "Mr. Barnhill."

"Yes, sir."

"If you would show Dr. McDowell to my study."

After thoroughly washing his hands in the kitchen, the doctor accompanied Barnhill to the study, where a plainly aggravated Josiah Maxwell was standing at his desk with his hands on the back of his chair. "Well, doctor," he said, "please repeat to young Barnhill your assessment."

"A contagion of influenza," said the doctor, turning to Barnhill, "has spread among the slaves. A virulent strain, judging from the high fever and catarrh. One child had a temperature of 104°. The children and elderly are especially vulnerable."

"In the experience of your plantation," Maxwell asked Barnhill, "have you dealt with such an outbreak?"

"In our part of the country," said Barnhill, "the danger is yellow-jack. We've seen entire plantations devastated, whites as well as blacks."

"The habitations of your slaves, Mr. Maxwell," said the doctor, "are deplorably unsanitary. You must act immediately, to avoid the disease infecting all of them, including the field hands."

"What do you suggest?" said Maxwell.

"You must separate those who have fallen ill from the others. The sick ones should be placed somewhere warm, under clean blankets, with ample water or tea. Clean water," he added with a frown.

"Perhaps at my overseer's," suggested Maxwell.

Barnhill and the doctor exchanged a knowing look. "I should think not," said the doctor. "I would recommend fashioning a hospital for them at your barn or stables, with cots on clean straw and a stove to keep them warm."

"A stove," muttered Maxwell.

"It's your choice, of course," said the doctor, snapping shut the clasp of his leather bag. "But if you leave them in their present condition, there's little doubt many will die, including the strongest of the men."

"Damn," said Maxwell quietly.

"I'll see to it, sir," said Barnhill.

"What? This is a job for Mr. O'Grady."

"I'd prefer to manage it," said Barnhill. "But I'll need help from the house servants."

"All right," said Maxwell. "You may take Thomas."

"All of them," said Barnhill.

Having unbolted the stove from the kitchen floor, Barnhill and the two men who worked in the house carried it outside and lifted it onto a flatbed wagon, which they hauled to the nearby barn. Henrietta, the cook, had swept the dirt floor, knocked down the cobwebs, and was spreading a layer of clean straw. "Can you saw a hole for the stovepipe?" Barnhill asked Thomas once they secured the stove in a corner. The man nodded.

"And bring plenty of blankets from the house," Barnhill instructed Henrietta. "And a demijohn of well water. I'll be back shortly with the first wagonload."

As the winter sun sank below the treetops, tingeing the horizon with a band of lilac, Barnhill hitched two horses to the wagon. As he reached for the reins, he observed Amelia walking down from the house in her heavy coat with a wool scarf over her head. Tying the reins on the railing, he met her halfway and said, "Is Robert coming?"

Biting her lip, she shook her head and said, "No."

"Well, I'm off for the first load. While there's still light."

"I'm coming with you."

"What? Amelia, you can't . . ."

"I'm coming," she insisted. "They know me and trust me."

Darkness was falling as they passed O'Grady's house. Barnhill could see him on the porch, clutching a bottle and a glass. Within minutes they reached the cluster of shanties among the live oaks. Barnhill had sent Fred, the other houseboy, ahead to instruct the mothers to prepare the sickest of the children and elderly to be moved. Two strong black men were waiting, holding a door from the shed to use as a litter. Working in the yellow light of a single lantern, Barnhill and Amelia went from shack to shack, supervising the selection of those most in need of nursing, loading eight children and six adults on the flatbed, shivering and groaning under blankets. Over the course of two hours, they completed three round trips in the darkness, eventually transporting nineteen children and twelve adults to the makeshift hospital, where they lay in tight rows on clean, sweet-smelling straw, under wool blankets in the warmth radiating from the glowing stove, with Henrietta dispensing water from a gourd and cups of hot, sweetened tea as Amelia passed from cot to cot, holding cold compresses to their burning brows. Throughout the long night, filled with the moans and hacking coughs of the sick, Henrietta and Amelia toiled away under Barnhill's compassionate eye, with no sign of the slaves' prideful master, nor his cruel overseer. When at last the cock crowed, Barnhill tenderly lifted Amelia, curled up on the straw, in his arms and carried her to the house.

There they found Josiah Maxwell, seated at his desk in a dressing gown, puffing on his clay pipe. "You look terrible," he said to Amelia as she paused in the doorway.

"I'm going upstairs to change," she replied.

"I'll never forgive you," said Maxwell to Barnhill once they were alone, "if something should happen to her."

"I'm sorry," said Barnhill with a downcast look. "I tried to stop her, but . . ." Returning Maxwell's cold stare, Barnhill turned away and started for the stairs, desperate to lie down for a few hours' sleep. In the upstairs hallway he found the door to Robert's bedroom ajar and heard soft voices. Looking in, he saw Amelia sitting on the bed with her hand on her brother's forehead.

"Oh, Jamie," she said with a stricken look. "He's burning up!"

CHAPTER EIGHT

AWAKENING IN A CHAIR WITH A BLANKET ON HIS LAP, Barnhill rubbed his eyes and looked around the dark room, a pale slant of light shining through a crack in the curtains drawn over the dormer windows. Was it morning or late afternoon? He listened to the rasp of Robert Maxwell's labored breathing. With a stifled yawn he rose from the chair, folded the blanket, and walked to the window. Parting the curtains, he looked out through the leafless branches at the dark waters of the river with the sun low in the winter sky.

"Jamie?"

Barnhill turned toward the recumbent figure in the four-poster bed. "Yes," he answered. "So you're awake, my friend." He drew back the curtains, filling the room with weak sunlight.

"Jamie, could you bring me something to drink?" Robert's voice was just above a whisper.

Barnhill poured a glass from the pitcher on the dresser and walked to the bedside. "It's water with a little lemon and sugar." He held the glass to Robert's cracked lips, studying his red-rimmed eyes and ashen complexion. Putting the glass aside, Barnhill lightly placed a hand on Robert's forehead, hot and dry to the touch.

"I'm cold," murmured Robert with a shiver. Barnhill reached for the blanket on the chair and spread it over the bedcovers. Robert moaned and then began to cough, a deep, congested hacking that left him gasping on his pillow.

To Barnhill's untrained eye, Robert's condition had clearly taken a turn for the worse on this, the second full day of the fever. Gently placing a hand on his friend's shoulder, he said, "Try to rest. I'm going down to get you a cup of hot tea."

Barnhill found Amelia alone in the parlor, sitting by the cold hearth with her head in her hands. At the sound of his footsteps she looked up and wearily asked, "How is he?"

Barnhill merely shook his head. He walked over and looked in her eyes. "He's worse," he said after a moment. "I'm afraid his constitution isn't strong enough to fight it after all he's been through."

"It has to get worse," said Amelia, "before it gets better. That's what the doctor said. Some of the slaves are better now who were in the worst way just a day ago."

Barnhill gave her a tender look, aware that she had tirelessly cared for dozens of sick slaves in the barn, almost without sleep, for the past forty-eight hours. With a glance at the dirty hem of her homespun dress, he said, "You should wash up and then take a nice, long nap."

Amelia shook her head. "No," she said with a sigh. "Not yet. I have to wait for the doctor."

"When is he coming?"

"Any time now."

"Good," said Barnhill. "We'll see if there's anything he can do for Robert. I'm going to take him some hot tea."

When Barnhill reached the landing at the top of the staircase, holding a lacquered tray with a teapot, cup, and saucer, he heard the creak of footsteps on the plank floor in the bedroom. Standing in the doorway, he watched as Josiah Maxwell, in his waistcoat and shirtsleeves, paced by the windows with his hands behind his back. He stopped and gave Barnhill a brief, inscrutable look. "Good afternoon," said Barnhill quietly. He'd scarcely seen the elder Maxwell since Robert had fallen ill. "I promised to bring him some tea."

Maxwell responded by walking over and taking the tray from Barnhill's hands. "No use," he said. "He's out of his head."

Barnhill hurried to the bedside. Though his eyes were shut, Robert tossed on the pillow, groaning, his cheeks flushed pink, shivering with chills. He's delirious, considered Barnhill, dimly recalling an incident from childhood when his sister was struck with a dangerously high fever his mother had battled with ice-cold compresses. Turning toward Robert's father, he said, "Do you have any ice?"

"Of course. In the cellar by the springhouse. But what for?"

"We've got to do something," replied Barnhill, "to bring down his fever."

Ten minutes later he returned with a pail in one hand and a stack of towels in the other. Josiah Maxwell was slumped in the chair in the corner, his face the same brooding mask. After quickly checking on Robert, who continued to toss and moan, Barnhill dipped a towel in the pail filled with water and a large chunk of river ice, wrung it out, and gently laid it across Robert's brow. Rolling up his shirtsleeves, Barnhill repeated the procedure every five or ten minutes, maintaining ice-cold compresses on the patient's face and forehead. After half an hour Robert seemed to grow calm, the feverish glow left his cheeks, and the shaking under the blankets abated. When Barnhill leaned down to change the compress, Robert opened his bleary eyes.

"What a strange dream," he said with a weak smile. Throwing back the covers, he added, "I'm burning up." The fine, blond hair at his temples was damp with perspiration and his palms were sweaty.

"Thank the Lord," said Barnhill under his breath. "His fever's broken."

Next morning, Dr. McDowell, wearing a long wool overcoat, stood before Josiah Maxwell's rolltop desk clutching his gloves and black leather bag. "All of your Negroes in the barn," he said, "should recover. And the outbreak appears to be contained, as I found no others in your slave quarters with symptoms."

"Very well," said Maxwell. He took a small key from a compartment of the desk, unlocked a metal case, and opened the lid. Removing a stack of bills, he began counting them.

"I would prefer gold, Mr. Maxwell," said the doctor.

"I'll settle your fee in the same Confederate banknotes," returned Maxwell, "that I'm paid for my cotton. And what about my boy?"

"The fever returned in the night," said McDowell, "and I fear pneumonia has set in."

"Surely there's something you can do . . ."

"There's no treatment for pneumonia, other than rest and fluids. It's simply a question of an individual's constitution."

"Robert is a strong man."

"I examined his abdomen, at the site of his wound. I suspect the internal injuries have not fully healed." Maxwell glared at the physician. "You should prepare yourself," said Dr. McDowell. "It may cost his life."

"No, no," said Maxwell. "Not my only son."

It was a vigil Barnhill would vividly remember for the rest of his life, the smell of camphor, the image of perfect solicitude on Amelia's face as she sat at her brother's bedside, the creak of the floorboards as Josiah Maxwell paced slowly before the curtained windows. Under such circumstances, Barnhill felt like an intruder, and occupied himself with small errands—refilling the water pitcher, bringing fresh towels, more ice water for the compresses. Robert sank deeper into the febrile miasma, sleeping without resting, wracked with nightmares, desperate for breath. Yet there were moments of lucidity: propped on his pillows, he gazed at Barnhill, standing at the foot of his bed, and thanked him for all he had done to care for him.

It was almost more than Barnhill could bear. He thought back to the bloodstained carpet in Reverend Bryan's house, Robert lying so still and pale that none of them thought he would live; his extraordinary courage and determination on the long journey south through the Shenandoah Valley; collapsing on the platform at the Petersburg station. And finally this, brought down by a simple act of kindness, caring for the sick child of a slave. Barnhill watched as Robert turned his face toward Amelia and whispered, "Read me a psalm . . . the twenty-third psalm."

Opening the Bible in her lap, Amelia read: "The Lord is my shepherd; I shall not want. He maketh me to lie down in green pastures: He leadeth me beside the still waters . . ."

Robert's features softened, and his eyes closed. The covers slowly rose and fell with each labored breath.

"He leadeth me in the paths of righteousness," Amelia continued, "for His name's sake. Yea, though I walk through the valley of the shadow of death, I shall fear no evil: for thou art with me; thy rod and thy staff they comfort me . . ."

In the yellow light of the oil lamp on the dresser, under the stern eye of his father, who had ceased pacing, a look of tranquility came over Robert, motionless with his arms folded over his chest. He drew a deep breath, slowly exhaled, and drew no more . . . no death rattle, no crying out . . . he died in peace listening to his beloved sister's voice. Closing the Bible, Amelia rose from her chair, leaned over her brother's still form and embraced him. "Oh, Father," she said with tears streaming down her cheeks, turning toward him, who was standing rigidly by the window. "Oh, Father, he's gone."

As if insensible to the words, or incapable of acceptance of the fact, Josiah Maxwell silently approached the bedside, glanced down at his dead son, and then slowly walked from the room. Barnhill went to Amelia's side, took her in his arms, and gently held her. After a moment a sound rose from the lawn below the windows, men and women singing together in rich harmony the old, old spiritual: "Swing low, sweet chariot, comin' for to carry me home . . ."

Barnhill's recollection of the weeks that followed was, in contrast, dim and hazy. He recalled an image of Josiah Maxwell standing in the cold rain at the graveside in his black coat and tall hat with the same impenetrable expression in his dark eyes, and the gut-wrenching fear that he would lose Amelia too, who had been struck with the influenza the very day of Robert's burial. But Amelia was strong, emerging from her sickbed on the second day, fully recovered on the fourth. Above all Barnhill remembered the slaves, the women weeping, the frequent sound of the spirituals . . .

A week after the burial, Barnhill found Amelia seated on the horsehair sofa in the parlor, her sewing in her lap and her eyes red from crying. He sat beside her, gently placed his hand on hers and said, "What can I do to help?"

Looking in his eyes, she said, "There's nothing anyone can do."

Barnhill nodded and said, "All we can do is trust in God."

"But I can't," said Amelia, her voice breaking. "I prayed so hard that Robert would be spared, and I just can't believe it was God's will that he should die."

Putting his arm around her, Barnhill said softly, "I know."

"Oh, Jamie," said Amelia, brushing back her tears, "I know we're taught to pray 'Thy will be done,' but I just can't. I fear I've lost my faith."

Lightly kissing her forehead, Barnhill said, "All we can do is try to keep going, and let the Lord take care of the rest."

Barnhill awoke one morning to discover the sudden arrival of bright color dotting the drab winter landscape, redbuds in bloom and the showy white and pink blossoms of the pear and cherry trees in the orchard. Shoots of new green grass appeared underfoot as he strolled down to the river with Amelia on his arm, aware that with the coming of spring his interlude at Widewater was nearing an end. Standing beneath their favorite oak, with its massive, gnarled trunk and wide-spreading boughs, Barnhill held Amelia in his arms, stared into her intelligent gray eyes, and leaned down to kiss her.

"Please don't leave," she murmured into his ear. "I couldn't bear it."

"I love you," he whispered. "I'll never love anyone else."

On tiptoes, she kissed him again. "Then why must you leave me?"

"We've been through it all before," he said, taking both her hands. She nodded and a tear appeared in the corner of her eye. "When the war's over," said Barnhill, "we'll go away someplace . . ."

"We'll take the ferry across the sound," said Amelia with a smile, "and walk for miles on the beach at Nags Head."

"We'll have a picnic with fried chicken and a bottle of champagne."

"Promise me?" said Amelia. "Or is it just a daydream?"

"I promise. I'll come back for you." With her arms around him she pressed her face to his chest. "I want to marry you," said Barnhill, running his hand through her hair.

"Oh, Jamie," she murmured, holding him tighter.

Gently holding her shoulders, he looked in her eyes and said, "Will you marry me?"

Fighting tears, she nodded and said, "Yes. Yes, I will. With father's permission."

"Oh, Amelia," said Barnhill, holding her tight. "I'll speak with him just as soon as I've decided on my plans."

For the first time since Robert's death the family resumed its customary practice of scripture reading and prayers in the parlor before retiring to the dining room for supper. As Amelia read from the Psalms and John's gospel, Josiah Maxwell seemed distracted, his mind elsewhere, and his participation in the prayers was mechanical and unfeeling. Afterward, he took his customary place at the head of the dinner table, where a place had been set with a vacant chair for the departed Robert. But Josiah Maxwell added little to the conversation, which turned from the weather, the likelihood of another frost before planting, to the resumption, with the coming of spring, of the Yankees' offensive threatening Atlanta. Finishing his plate of ham and corn pudding, Barnhill put his silverware aside and said, "I'll be leaving shortly, sir, to rejoin my regiment." Apart from slightly raised eyebrows, Maxwell made no response. "To be honest," Barnhill continued, "I'm not sure where to find them."

"I pleaded with Jamie to stay," said Amelia, "but he wouldn't hear of it."

"He must do his duty," said Maxwell coldly.

"I'm deeply indebted to you for all your hospitality," said Barnhill.

"And I'm thankful to you for your kindness to . . . my son," replied Maxwell, unable to utter Robert's name. The room fell silent as Henrietta arrived to clear the table.

As Maxwell pushed back, Barnhill spoke up: "There's a matter I'd like to discuss with you, sir. In private."

Eyeing him curiously, Maxwell said, "All right. We'll talk in my study."

Josiah Maxwell reached for his tobacco pouch and carefully filled his clay pipe as Barnhill stood nervously before his rolltop desk. Striking a match and cupping it over the bowl, Maxwell expelled a cloud of aromatic smoke and said, "Have a seat, son. What's on your mind?"

Barnhill lowered his tall frame in the chair facing Maxwell and said, "I've come to ask for Amelia's hand."

"What?"

"I love her very much, sir."

Maxwell shook his head and muttered, "She's all I have." Looking Barnhill in the eye he said, "I understood you're returning to your regiment."

"Yes, sir, but we . . . we've decided to marry . . . that is, before I leave. With your permission."

Maxwell drew on his pipe and stared into the distance. "What will you do," he asked after a moment, "when the war's over?"

"I intend to go home, of course."

Maxwell frowned. "To Texas. Your father's deceased?" Barnhill nodded. "And you have no brothers?"

"No, sir. A sister."

"Then the plantation will be yours, I assume? A rather large plantation, as I recall?"

"Well, sir," said Barnhill, shifting in his chair, "it's not my intention to manage the farm. I intend to study law . . ."

"What will become of your property?"

"My mother is looking after the farm . . ."

"Your mother." Maxwell put aside his pipe. "You would take my only child to the backwoods of Texas, and eke out a living as a country lawyer. Sir, I cannot consent."

Barnhill rose from his chair and gazed down on Maxwell, who seemed to have aged in the weeks since Robert's death. "I beg you to reconsider," he said evenly. "Texas is a rich country, and my father, one of the pioneers, had large land holdings, rich river bottom, one of the wealthiest men in the county. I will provide a comfortable life for your daughter, Mr. Maxwell. Amelia and I are very much in love."

Maxwell sat with his chin in his hand. "First Robert," he said, "and now this. There's a war to be fought, Lieutenant. An enemy to be whipped. An enemy I hold responsible for my son's death. Do your duty, and then we can discuss Amelia."

As much as she resented her father's refusal to give his consent, Amelia, accustomed to caring for him in the years since her mother's death, would not dare go against his wishes. And so she and Barnhill decided to view her father's position in a more optimistic light than perhaps was prudent, as a *conditional* acquiescence in their marriage, when Barnhill returned from the war, assuming he could demonstrate that he could provide for her in the style to which she was accustomed. Barnhill's departure was delayed by his complete lack of information concerning the Texas Brigade, which had been detached from Lee's army the previous September to fight under Bragg in Georgia and Tennessee. The infrequent letters he received from his mother made no mention of the movements of the Texans after the Battle of Chickamauga, although she did disclose, in an offhand way he supposed was intended to spare his feelings, that Kate, as he surmised, had indeed fallen for another young man, new to the county, to whom she was now betrothed. And so Barnhill had written to his friend Edward Selden in Richmond, inquiring about the whereabouts of Hood's Division.

CHAPTER EIGHT

After weeks, Barnhill's regular trips into town to the post office were rewarded with a letter on the official stationery of the Army of Northern Virginia. "Come to the capital," Selden wrote, "and join me on General Lee's staff. We're having a jovial time, notwithstanding the depressing news of the war. Or, if you prefer, come and await the return of your fellow Texians, who have been ordered back to Virginia."

Barnhill leaned back in his chair in the upstairs library, tapping the letter in his palm as he gazed affectionately at Amelia.

"What did he write?" she asked.

"My old regiment's returning to Virginia." He considered mentioning Selden's offer to join Lee's staff but decided against it, duty-bound to return to his men. "I should pack my things and leave in the morning."

"Oh, Jamie," she said with a forlorn look. "Promise you'll write me every day."

He leaned over and took her hand. "There's one thing I need to do before leaving. I'm going into town."

"Why?"

"To buy your ring. Your engagement ring."

Having somehow managed to hang on to his wad of Confederate banknotes and the remaining gold dollars Robert had entrusted to him, Barnhill returned to the shop on Broad Street he'd often passed on his trips to the post office, with its display of ladies' hats, shoes, and coats in the window. Inquiring at the counter inside, the shopkeeper unlocked a cabinet and produced a chinoiserie jewelry box. "Folks bring me odds and ends," he said, "to sell on consignment. Grandma's brooch, that sort of thing. What is it you're looking for?"

"A ring," said Barnhill. "A gold ring with a gemstone."

Removing a velvet cover, the shopkeeper held up a slender gold band for Barnhill's inspection. "The stone's garnet, not ruby," he said, "but who can tell the difference?"

With the small box secure in his waistcoat pocket, Barnhill rode out of town, admiring the delicate new foliage on the oaks and chestnuts and the profusion of tulips and daffodils in the neatly tended beds surrounding the handsome two-story residences. He briefly contemplated what it would be like to return to Edenton after the war, to settle there with Amelia. Reaching the road along the riverbank, the mare broke into a canter, as eager to return to the barn as Barnhill was loath to leave the idyllic town on the shore of Albemarle. A quarter mile from the Widewater gate, passing by the stand of tall pines that separated the tilled plantation fields from the river, Barnhill was arrested by the piercing sound of a human scream. Reining in the mare, he heard it again: a man's agonized cry, followed by the sound of women wailing. Through a break in the trees he could make out the roofline of the overseer O'Grady's cottage. His heart pounding, he turned the horse onto a narrow path through the woods as the screams and wails grew louder. He swung out of the saddle at the verge of a clearing and tied the reins to a pine seedling. Beyond the overseer's ramshackle house, a large group of black men and women were clustered in the direction of the slave quarters. Mingling with the screams and wailing, Barnhill could now distinctly hear the loud slap of a whip. In a moment he could see the object of the spectacle: a tall, muscular black man, stripped to the waist, with his legs splayed and wrists bound to a wooden frame. Bright red blood streamed down his back, staining his pants and pooling on the ground.

Frank O'Grady, likewise stripped to the waist, stood with his back to the slaves, his broad shoulders mottled pink with exertion, clutching the handle of a long leather whip. As Barnhill watched with disgust, O'Grady raised his powerful right arm, hesitated, and delivered another lash with all his might. As the victim howled in agony, arching his deeply gashed back, the women swayed and moaned, "Ohh Jesus!"

Barnhill suddenly stood in their midst. Oblivious, sweat streaming from his neck and face, the overseer raised the whip to deliver another blow. "Stop," said Barnhill.

O'Grady spun around, panting and staring at Barnhill with a look of surprise and malice. "You," he said. The thick hair on his barrel chest was matted with dirt and sweat. "The boy from Texas." He spat and turned back to the bleeding slave.

"I said stop," said Barnhill, taking a step closer. "You're liable to kill that man."

"Serve him right," growled O'Grady. "Runaway nigger."

The crowd parted as Barnhill walked up to the overseer. "Put down the whip," said Barnhill. His face contorted with fury, O'Grady turned, dropped the whip, and took a powerful swing at Barnhill, who, quicker by far, evaded the blow and delivered a sharp uppercut to O'Grady's midsection.

"Ohh," he groaned, the wind knocked out of him. His blood up now, Barnhill stepped in and threw a rapid series of punches, drawing blood from O'Grady's nose and eyebrow. In a matter of seconds, the overseer was down on his hands and knees, spitting blood and a tooth into the dirt.

"Take him down," Barnhill instructed the astonished slaves, gesturing to the man on the rack. At the sound of hoofbeats, he looked over his shoulder as Josiah Maxwell rode up on his black stallion.

"What's this!" demanded Maxwell.

Picking himself up, with puffy eyes and blood streaming from his nose, O'Grady shook his finger at Barnhill and said, "He tried to stop me, sir, from deliverin' the punishment you ordered."

"He did what!" said Maxwell angrily, staring down at Barnhill.

"It was wrong, sir," said Barnhill. "He could have killed that man . . ."

"And then," continued O'Grady in a loud voice, "he come after me. He snuck up on me and hit me . . ."

"A damned lie," said Barnhill. "I asked him to stop. You can see for yourself the condition of that poor man. Your overseer took a swing at me and I defended myself."

"Fighting with my overseer!" said Maxwell with barely controlled fury. "Interfering in the discipline of my slaves! I'll not tolerate it!"

Briefly making eye contact with Maxwell, Barnhill said, "You'll excuse me, sir." With a glance at O'Grady, he walked quickly from the clearing.

By the time Barnhill unsaddled the mare, Josiah Maxwell had returned to the house and was waiting for him in the front hall. As soon as Barnhill entered and removed his hat, Maxwell said sharply, "I'll see you in my study."

"What is it, Father?" said Amelia, rising from her chair in the parlor.

"Nothing that concerns you." Maxwell followed Barnhill into the study, closing the door firmly behind them. Barnhill could feel a flush on his cheeks and perspiration beading his forehead as Maxwell walked over to the tall window, partially shrouded with heavy drapes, and stood with his back to him. After a moment he turned, staring at Barnhill with ill-concealed hostility.

"Sir," began Barnhill, "if I might explain . . ."

"There's nothing to explain. You've attacked and beaten my overseer before the very eyes of my slaves. You've undermined my authority, you've utterly humiliated me."

"What he did was wrong, sir."

"Wrong? Wrong to discipline my slaves! How dare you!"

Amelia stood in the hallway, wringing her hands as she listened to the terrible wrath in her father's indistinct voice through the heavy oak door.

"It's wrong to beat a man to death," countered Barnhill with equal vehemence, "for no crime other than the desire to escape his bondage. It's still murder, even if he's a slave."

"Murder," repeated Maxwell with contempt. "It's clear to me, young man, that you have no understanding of our way of life. It requires harsh measures, very harsh, to keep these creatures in their place."

Barnhill shook his head. "Maybe you're right, Mr. Maxwell. Maybe I don't understand."

Maxwell took a step closer to him. "I'd advise you to leave, Lieutenant. Without delay."

"Yes, sir." Barnhill turned to go.

"And I forbid you to marry Amelia."

Barnhill turned and stared into the older man's eyes.

"Or ever again to return to this house."

With the battered old valise at his feet, wearing his Confederate uniform and campaign hat, Barnhill stood at the gatepost, gazing at Amelia in a lilac cotton dress with full hoop skirt, and at the handsome white house behind her on the knoll overlooking the river. He pressed the small box into her hands and leaned down to kiss her. "I love you," he said. "I always will."

Fighting back tears, Amelia said, "I love you, Jamie. I'll be praying for you every day."

With a final kiss and embrace, he said simply, "Goodbye," and started down the road into town.

CHAPTER NINE

AFTER AN ABSENCE OF OVER NINE MONTHS from the Southern army, the inviting aromas of coffee and frying bacon in the morning, woodsmoke and pipe tobacco around the campfire, and the sound of banjo and fiddle were pleasingly familiar to Jamie Barnhill. But the faces of the men, with few exceptions, were unfamiliar. Most of his comrades from the old Fifth Texas were gone, either killed or disabled, or had deserted to return to their farms after three years of war. The few who remained, including his cousin Sam Perkins and Major Harry Sellers, rejoiced at Barnhill's unexpected reappearance and elected him captain, second in command of the regiment. Among the departed was General Hood, in Richmond courting the beautiful Buck Preston while he recovered from the loss of a leg at Chickamauga.

The brigade was now commanded by General John Gregg, a handsome Texan with no previous experience in the Army of Northern Virginia. It was early May, almost a year to the day after Stonewall Jackson's great flanking maneuver that routed the Union army at Chancellorsville. Though the brigade and the rest of Longstreet's Corps had played no part in that great victory, they now marched within a few miles of the battlefield, littered with the bleached skulls and bones of men buried, if at all, in shallow graves, to confront the threat of the massive Federal army. Now under the command of General U. S. Grant, the Federals had crossed the Rapidan into the almost impenetrable expanse of Virginia woodland, bogs, and sloughs known as the Wilderness. The Texas Brigade, after a night bivouacked on the cold ground, rose at 3:00 a.m. on the morning of May 6 and, without coffee or a hot meal, resumed its march toward A. P. Hill's Corps, eight miles distant.

Barnhill was at the head of the column, two men abreast, rifles at their shoulders with fixed bayonets, listening to the *chirr* of the crickets, the call of the mourning doves, and the occasional hoot of an owl, as they tramped blindly on a narrow defile through the tangle of creepers, briars, and witch hazel that snagged their shirts and tripped boots and bare feet. At the sound of musket fire and the far-off boom of cannons, Barnhill halted the column to listen. "I'll be danged," said the lanky corporal standing beside him. "You'd figure they'd wait till sunup to start shootin'."

Brushing back a low-hanging branch, Barnhill started the men forward. "Not much to aim at in the dark," he said. "The Yanks must be itching for a fight." The sound of firing intensified at the first hint of dawn.

"I heard tell," said the corporal, "there's a hundred thousand men in the Federal army."

"More like a hundred and twenty-five thousand," said Barnhill, "led by our old friend Edward Meade. Which gives the Yankees a two-to-one advantage."

"About the odds," said the corporal with a grin that revealed a row of white teeth in the darkness, "we're accustomed to."

The column slowed, came to a stop, and began moving again beneath the canopy of new green foliage that appeared with the first light. Barnhill looked over his shoulder at the sound of an approaching rider. General Gregg reined in his chestnut mare and studied a map he unfolded from his pocket. "Our orders," he said, "are to cross the Orange Plank Road and report to General Lee at the Widow Tapp Farm. The brigade is in the van of the division."

"Yes, sir," said Barnhill, touching a hand to the brim of his hat. Both men looked up at the thunderous report of cannons less than a mile ahead, and a rolling volley of rifle fire that filled the air with the acrid smell of black powder. As Gregg rode to the rear, Barnhill spoke briefly to the corporal and picked up the pace of the march. He was conscious of the racing of his heart, the knot in his belly, and other manifestations of intense fear that preceded battle; but something else as well: a longing for Amelia so deep that, despite his doubts about the power of prayer, he implored God to grant him deliverance that he might see her again. As the column approached the Plank Road, one of the few means of passage through miles of impenetrable woodland, the almost continuous volleys of musketry and boom of cannons blended with other sounds: hoarse shouts, curses, and hoofbeats. Arriving at the roadside, they encountered pandemonium on a scale hitherto unseen in Lee's army: riderless horses galloping away from the sound of fighting, dozens of wagons, some overturned, others clattering down the corduroy under the lash of frenzied muleteers, and hundreds of men in butternut streaming down the road in wide-eyed terror; Heth's and Wilcox's divisions in full, panicked retreat.

"Runnin'," said the corporal at Barnhill's elbow with disgust. "What a sorry sight."

General Gregg, astride his tall horse, calmly appeared in the midst of the chaos. "On the double quick!" he commanded with upraised saber. "March!"

Wheeling to the right, Barnhill's men shifted to a shuffling trot. At the sight of such coolness and discipline, many of the retreating soldiers paused and then joined the Texans trotting down the Orange Plank Road toward the advancing Federals. After several hundred yards, the regiment reached a clearing with a nearby farmhouse and a battery of Confederate artillery firing rapidly at the Federal troops concealed in the tree line on the far side of the clearing. Hill's Corps, Barnhill quickly surmised, had been routed by an overwhelming Federal force. The fresh troops of Longstreet's Corps, with the Texas Brigade in the lead, were all that stood in the way of Grant's powerful army breaching the Confederate center and opening the way to Richmond, a mere fifty miles to the southeast. As the column halted, Barnhill wondered if they might actually see General Lee, whom he'd hoped to catch a glimpse of at Gettysburg before the attack on Little Round Top. At the thought of that terrible day he was wracked by a spasm of fear that left him queasy. He slowly exhaled and, with trembling fingers, fastened the row of brass buttons on the front of his patched and bloodstained jacket. Barnhill gripped the handle of the .45 in its holster and tapped the envelope in his breast pocket—the letter his cousin Sam had entrusted to him in exchange for a letter he had penned to Amelia to be sent in the event of his death. As smoke from the cannons swirled before the rising sun, he observed an officer with a full white beard riding toward them on a dappled gray—Robert E. Lee on Traveller.

Cantering up to General Gregg, Lee inquired, "Sir, what brigade is this?"

"The Texas Brigade," replied Gregg with a salute.

"I am glad to see it," said Lee, surveying the men crowding eagerly around the two horsemen. "When you go in there," said Lee, pointing toward the tree line, "give those men cold steel. They will stand and fire all day, and never move unless you charge them."

"That is my experience," answered Gregg.

An aide from Longstreet galloped up and announced: "Advance your command, General Gregg."

"Attention, Texas Brigade!" called out Gregg in a strong voice. "The eyes of General Lee are upon you!"

Lee lifted his hat and raised himself up in his stirrups. "Hurrah for Texas!" he shouted. "Texans always move them!"

The men began to cheer, and as Lee's words were passed down the line, the cheering turned to a chorus that drowned the deafening cannon fire. "I would charge hell itself for that old man," declared a tattered, barefoot private standing beside Barnhill. As the columns formed, Lee rode to the front with the evident intention of leading the attack. "Go back!" cried the men. "Lee to the rear!" Several of them lunged for Traveller's reins and forced the general to retire.

"Texas Brigade!" commanded Gregg, tall in the saddle. "Forward, march!"

It would prove to be the brigade's last great action in the war, and perhaps its finest hour. Like its famous stand in the cornfield at Sharpsburg, the Texans' reckless charge in the Wilderness, facing an entrenched enemy far superior in numbers, proved decisive in turning back a Federal advance that threatened to engulf the entire Confederate army. Spurred by the effusive praise of their beloved commander, the three Texas regiments, joined by the Third Arkansas, moved forward, advancing perpendicularly across the half-mile-wide clearing toward the trees; marching at the double quick as the first volley of Union rifles and artillery at point-blank range decimated their lines, kneeling to fire, and then charging with a chorus of Indian whoops and Rebel yells into the thicket of briars and brambles, driving the defenders from their pine-log breastworks with bayonets and rifle butts. Pursuing the fleeing Federals through the dense woods, the Texans found themselves cut off, unsupported on their left or right, subjected to enfilading fire that further tore their ranks. When

CHAPTER NINE

the charge subsided, after driving the men of Hancock's Corps from successive lines of battle, General Gregg ordered his men to retire, no dash to the rear, but an orderly rearguard march, recovering their dead and wounded who lay bleeding by the hundreds amid the shredded leaves and branches on the forest floor.

Barnhill played little part in the splendid charge. Surviving the first three hundred yards unscathed, he caught an ankle in his leap over a Union parapet, twisting it so badly that, unable to keep up with his men as they dashed after the fleeing enemy, he lay among the dying defenders, gasping in pain until helped by a stretcher bearer to the rear. The attack saved the day for General Lee, further confirming his high opinion of the Texas Brigade, but represented no victory for the Southern army—rather the avoidance of a decisive defeat at the hands of a new Union commander relentless in his determination to press the enemy, no matter the cost in Northern lives.

From the Wilderness, Lee maneuvered his pitifully clothed and fed troops to the southeast toward Spotsylvania Court House, facing the largest, and certainly the best equipped and provisioned, army in modern history. There Grant delivered another hammer blow, sending Union forces by the tens of thousands in frontal attacks on the Confederate breastworks and abatis of the Bloody Angle. Repulsing the far more numerous Federals, Lee sidestepped again to the south and east, taking up positions at Cold Harbor, a mere ten miles from Richmond, where Grant launched another series of fruitless frontal assaults. By early June, Union losses were appalling: fifty thousand dead or wounded men over the course of a five-week campaign.

Seated on a stump by the crackling campfire, Barnhill poured an inch of bourbon into a tin cup, stirred in water from his canteen, and handed the drink to Sam Perkins, whose left arm was in a sling. After taking a sip, Sam said, "The way this new Union general fights, I reckon we kill two Yankees for every one of ours."

"Grant doesn't seem to care," said Barnhill, "how many men he loses. He's determined to wear us down."

"I'll bet a lot of Northern folks," said Sam, leaning closer to the fire, "think Grant's a butcher and are sick to death of the war."

Barnhill nodded in agreement. "Our only hope," he said, "is to hold him off till November."

"Why November?" asked a man in the shadows, puffing on a corncob pipe.

"The election," said Barnhill. "If Lee can keep Grant at bay, and Hood can hang on to Atlanta, Lincoln might just lose to one of those Copperheads."

"Like McClellan," said Sam, staring into the fire as darkness enfolded the encampment. "But I'm not sure Hood can hang on to Atlanta." Despite the loss of an arm at Gettysburg and a leg at Chickamauga, John Bell Hood had recently replaced Joe Johnston as commander of the Army of Tennessee.

"If Atlanta falls," said Barnhill, "it's just the news Lincoln's hoping for."

"You're sayin' the war's lost?" said the man in the shadows in a truculent tone.

"Our only chance for peace," countered Barnhill, "is if Lincoln loses the election."

"So if the Democrats beat Lincoln," considered the other man, "they'll make peace with Jeff Davis."

"Yep."

"You reckon they'll let us keep the slaves?"

"If we go back to the Union, they will," said Barnhill. "Just think about it. After all those men lost, all the destruction, and we'd end up right back where we started."

"Sometimes I think you're too smart for your own good," said Sam. He tossed back the last of his drink. "All our men who died, or lost an arm or leg, weren't fighting for some *slaveowner's* rights."

Barnhill stared into the glowing embers. An image of Widewater and the overseer whipping the runaway slave came to mind. If Jeff Davis had any sense, he reasoned, he'd announce that the South was abolishing slavery *before* the November election. What would Old Abe have to say about *that*? "Don't be a fool, Sam," said Barnhill with surprising bitterness. "Defending slavery is what this damned war is all about."

"I don't care a fig about slavery," said Sam. "Ought to send the blacks back where they came from. *I'm* fightin' for the Confederacy." In the ensuing silence the pale orange disk of the full moon began its slow ascent through the pine boughs. "What'll you do, Jamie," asked Sam, "when the war's over? Go back to North Carolina?"

CHAPTER NINE   105

Barnhill picked up the bottle and poured himself more bourbon. "Yes," he said after taking a sip. He'd written Josiah Maxwell a letter of apology and explanation months ago and never received a reply. "I'm going to marry Amelia, Sam. But first I'll head home to see about Mother." Barnhill, of course, had written Amelia, not daily as she had asked him, but at least a brief note each week or ten days. He'd received nothing in return, nor was there any way of knowing whether his letters reached their destination. Taking a final swallow, he stood, stretched his arms over his head, and said, "Good night, Sam. I'm up at three to relieve the pickets."

After weeks of skirmishing on the north bank of the James River, blocking the Federals' approach to Richmond from the east, the Texas Brigade was shifted south to the Confederate fortifications ringing Petersburg, living a mole-like existence in a labyrinth of caves and trenches, in constant terror of being buried alive by massive Federal siege mortars and mines. In the first week of September the Richmond papers reported the fall of Atlanta, a stunning blow to Southern morale that strengthened Barnhill's belief in the inevitability of Lincoln's reelection. As the noose tightened around Richmond, he was convinced that it was only a matter of time before Lee would abandon Petersburg and march the pitiful remnant of his once-proud army west to link up with the Confederate forces in the valley for a final stand against a far more powerful adversary.

In the desultory fighting of that fall of 1864, Barnhill occupied his time with reading—his tattered volume of Carlyle, another miniature Bible that had taken the place of the one that saved his life, and the Richmond newspapers. And writing letters to Amelia and his mother, all unanswered. He considered the war lost, and though he prayed constantly to be spared from the death that seemed right around the next bend of the trench, he shared his men's conviction that they should fight to the finish, that surrender would dishonor all they had fought for so long and at such a terrible price, that their honor was all they would take with them when, in the end, they returned to their faraway homes.

Decades later, one incident remained indelibly imprinted on Barnhill's recollection. Awakened at 3:00 a.m. on a frosty October morning, hastily assembled without lighting the cookstoves, with instructions to fill their cartridge boxes and fix bayonets, the depleted ranks of the Fifth Texas regiment took up positions, passing along the order: with the other brigades of Field's Division, a reconnaissance in force of the Federal entrenchments across the Darbytown Road. Concealed by a cloudy, moonless sky, the men moved out of their trenches. Listening to the jangling of gear and the soft tread of boots on dusty ground, Barnhill apprehended an officer on horseback, whose identity was excitedly whispered from man to man: "Marse Robert! General Lee!"

Barnhill stared at the dim figure on the dappled gray, calm, dignified, assured in command. Leaning down from the saddle, he asked a nearby aide, "Are the commands ready to advance?"

"None but the Texas Brigade, sir."

"The Texas Brigade is always ready," commented Lee. Though spoken softly, every man could distinctly hear his words in the still, cold air of early morning. The order was given, and, with the first rays of sunlight bathing the bomb-pocked roadway separating the two armies, the men surged forward, crashing into dense woods until the attacking lines broke on the Federal breastworks like waves on a rocky shore. His jacket torn and face bleeding from the sharpened stakes, Barnhill struggled back, supporting a badly wounded man on his weakened shoulder and collapsing into the safety of the trench with a loud groan and unuttered prayer of gratitude. Among the many Texans who perished in that fruitless charge was John Gregg, the last general officer to command the brigade.

By November, Lee's army of forty thousand men tenuously held a line that stretched for forty miles from Hatcher's Run south of Petersburg north to the Chickahominy, subsisting on a daily ration of a quarter pound of bacon and a pound of cornmeal per man. With supplies piling up on railroad sidings in Georgia and the Carolinas, the meager ration was reduced by half, barely enough to keep the men alive. From their entrenchments they gazed out on the comfortably tented winter quarters of the vast Federal army, 125,000 strong, fully provisioned by the quartermaster with beef, pork, potatoes, and flour, and by the sutlers' trains with ample liquor, wine, and tobacco. In November Grant openly declared his strategy: after the disastrous campaign of the summer he would avoid maneuver with the wily Confederates and break the back of the Rebels in a war of attrition.

Swept by December's bitter cold, the Confederates desperately sought shelter. Lacking nails and timber, and with few axes, saws, or hammers, they fashioned crude hovels in the Virginia clay, roofed with tents or blankets, absorbing the heat from mud chimneys and passing the hours in endless games of cards, checkers, cribbage, and chess. With his back to the wall, Barnhill turned the page of a week-old copy of the *Richmond Enquirer*, reading with disgust a long account of the depredations of Sherman's army in its infamous March to the Sea: beautiful homes put to the torch, crops and livestock wantonly destroyed, hundreds of miles of railroad tracks twisted into useless heaps. Barnhill felt the old anger and indignation rising in his chest at the thought of Sherman punishing innocent civilians for the audacity of declaring their independence. Hearing an unfamiliar voice, he put the newspaper aside.

"Barnhill," repeated a man outside the shelter. "Lieutenant Barnhill?"

On hands and knees, Barnhill pulled open the flap. "I'm Barnhill," he said. He eyed the man curiously, a soldier he'd never seen before, bundled up in a heavy coat with muddy cavalry boots that reached his knees.

"I've got something for you," said the man, removing an oilskin-wrapped envelope from a leather pouch and handing it over.

His heart pounding, Barnhill rose and studied the address: "Lt. James Barnhill, 5th Texas, Hood's Div., Army Nrth. Va." Printed in Amelia's neat hand. "Much obliged," he said, giving the courier a quick handshake.

With a quick glance at the leaden skies, Barnhill ducked inside his shelter, added a few sticks of kindling to the crude hearth, and sat against the earthen wall. With a deep breath he carefully unwrapped and slit open the envelope. At the top right corner Amelia had written: "November 18, 1864, Widewater Plantation, Chowan County, N. Carolina." With a trembling hand, in the flickering light of the fire, Barnhill read:

My dear Jamie,

After so many months without a letter, and the news of the terrible battles in Virginia, I confess that I despaired I had lost you forever. And so it was with utter amazement that I received your tender letter, written in September, that somehow found its way here. For many months we have been unable to send or receive mail, since the Yankees captured the railroad north of Rocky Mount and constantly patrol the Sound with their gunboats. My dear boy, I'm so thankful to God you're alive and well, and I love you with all my heart.

You would scarcely believe the change that has come over this place. We have little to eat, paper money has no value, and coffee and sugar are worth their weight in gold. Many have turned against the war, voting for Holden for governor on his pledge to return North Carolina to the Union. So many families have lost sons that grief and sadness are ever present. Worst of all, Father is filled with gall and hate: hate for Lincoln and Seward and the others, and bitterness for Robert's death, which he blames on the Yankees and, without reason, on the poor coloreds. He almost never goes out, but sits for hours brooding in his study, leaving the overseer to run the plantation with terrible cruelty. I want to escape from this place, Jamie, to run away with you to some sunlit, happy shore, far away. How I dream of it!

But in my heart I know it cannot be. Father has not softened in his angry opposition to our marriage. He insists that I take care of him, declares that he cannot live without my attentions, and forbids even the mention of your name. In some perverse way he associates you with Robert's death, and, I am sorry to confess, blames you for it.

Barnhill looked up from the page, staring at the blanket draped over the "door" of the dugout as he thought back to the deathbed scene in Robert's bedroom, Amelia holding his hand and reading to him from the Bible while Josiah Maxwell stood grimly at the window. He turned back to her letter:

Our world is crashing down around us, and I am so frightened. I would beg you to come for me, if I could, but I must beg you to stay away. Please keep safe, as the war must end soon. If you receive this letter, do your best to acknowledge it. I have used what little money I had to send it with a courier.

I love you dear Jamie and always will. Come what may, I will keep your ring. May God bless you and keep you,

Your dearest,
Amelia

Carefully folding the pages and fitting them in the envelope, Barnhill suppressed a sob at the thought of Amelia trapped in that place, and the bitter realization that marriage was out of the question and that he might never see her again. Cold wind gusted down the mud chimney, filling the dugout with smoke that stung his tear-filled eyes. He drew back the blanket, preferring the cold to the smoke, and watched as it began to sleet, pebbles clattering noisily in the trench. The storm muffled the boom of a Union mortar, raining death on unsuspecting souls sheltering like vermin in the miserable caves and trenches. After a while he drew back the blanket and tended to the fire, vowing that he would survive and somehow, some day, see Amelia again.

By January their plight was truly desperate, thousands of emaciated men just surviving in the bitter cold, risking death from sharpshooters each time they ventured out to refill canteens from the single source of drinking water, their ranks thinned by a constant stream of deserters. At last, with the first signs of spring in early April, they received orders to abandon their wretched fortifications, cross the river under the cover of darkness, and make a final, desperate march to the west towards Lynchburg, hoping to link up with the Confederate force under Jubal Early for a final stand against Grant's enormous, well-fed and rested Army of the Potomac.

It was not the same army that had so deftly evaded Grant's advances in the summer. Shrunk by desertion, crippled by disease and near starvation, the regiments marched to the west, fording rivers and streams, with Grant's powerful infantry and cavalry in hot pursuit. Amid the beauty of early spring in the Piedmont, rolling hills carpeted with wildflowers, the Texans camped for the night, two miles from the county courthouse at Appomattox. Fearing an attack that never came, they received word of the Confederate surrender as they were finishing their cornbread and ersatz coffee around the remains of their campfires. A single horseman rode into their midst, wearing a plumed cavalry hat with a saber at his side, dismounted, and saluted to Major Sellers, who called his men to attention.

"Sir," said the horseman, removing a folded paper from his breast pocket. "I have instructions to read aloud an order from General Lee."

In silence broken only by the caroling of the songbirds, the major nodded and said, "Please proceed."

Waiting for the men to assemble around him, the officer cleared his throat and then read in a strong voice:

General Order No. 9

After four years of arduous service marked by unsurpassed courage and fortitude, the Army of Northern Virginia has been compelled to yield to overwhelming numbers and resources. I need not tell the brave survivors of so many hard fought battles who have remained steadfast to the last that I have consented to this result from no distrust of them. But feeling that valor and devotion could accomplish nothing that could compensate for the loss that must have attended the continuance of the contest, I determined to avoid the useless sacrifice of those whose past services have endeared them to their countrymen.

By the terms of this agreement, officers and men can return to their homes. You will take with you the satisfaction that proceeds from a consciousness of duty faithfully performed, and I earnestly pray that a merciful God will extend to you His blessings and protection.

With an unceasing admiration of your constancy and devotion to your Country, and a grateful remembrance of your kind and generous consideration for myself, I bid you all an affectionate farewell.

R. E. Lee, Gen.

The men stood in silence as the officer folded the order in his pocket, mounted his horse, and cantered away. After a delay of some hours, the regiment formed columns and marched, rifles at their shoulders and bayonets fixed, with the rest of the division, some 450 survivors of the original four thousand who left Texas at the outbreak of the war, to the redbrick courthouse with the Stars and Stripes waving over the entrance. Passing between two long rows of bluecoats, the column halted before a tall Union officer with a drooping mustache, holding a saber at his shoulder. Listening to the snap of the flag in the cool April breeze, Barnhill turned to Major Sellers, standing beside him, and quietly asked, "Who is that Yankee general?"

"Joshua Chamberlain," Sellers replied, "if I'm not mistaken. Who commanded the Maine regiment at the summit of Little Round Top."

The order was given and the men filed slowly past the dignified Union general, quietly placing their rifles in neat stacks. With a lump in his throat as he turned to walk away, Barnhill noticed a familiar figure mounted on a fine black stallion at the verge of the courthouse square. Walking quickly up to him, Barnhill said, "Hello, Ed."

Leaning down from the saddle, Edward Selden gave Barnhill a firm handshake and said, "Well, Jamie, what will you do?"

"Make my way back to Texas."

"And then?"

"Not sure."

"You always said you intended to be a lawyer."

Barnhill nodded.

"Well, then," said Selden with a smile, "go home and see to your mother. And then come back to Virginia and we'll study the law together. At Charlottesville."

"Goodbye, Edward," said Barnhill. "There's a lot I need to sort out. But I'll think about it."

PART TWO
RECONSTRUCTION

CHAPTER TEN

"THE FIRST CLASS TO GRADUATE AFTER THE WAR," said Edward Selden, "and you're not even staying for the celebration."

Jamie Barnhill stood by the window gazing out on the emerald quadrangle and the symmetrical rows of redbrick buildings facing the Rotunda, resplendent in the bright June sunshine. Turning to Selden, he said, "When I walk across that platform, and Dean Brown hands me that sheepskin . . ."

"You're assumin' facts not in evidence . . ."

Barnhill smiled. "I intend to bid a fond farewell," he continued, "to the Old Dominion and catch the first train south. You can take my place in all the revelry."

Leaning on his silver-handled cane, Selden limped to the coatrack in the corner, lifted up a long black gown, and walked over to drape it on Barnhill's shoulders. "There," he said, giving Barnhill an appraising look. "Fitting, I should say, for a man who finished near the top of his class. A St. Anthony man, no less." Barnhill stretched his arms into the sleeves of the gown and studied his reflection in the hallway mirror. "Who would have imagined it," said Selden, "in that bleak September of '65?"

Barnhill thought back to the day he arrived at the Charlottesville station, lugging a heavy valise bulging with clothes and books and hiring a buggy for the short trip to the campus, whose stately architecture and manicured grounds had taken his breath away. He could scarcely believe that in a few hours he would be finished, returning home to Texas with his law degree. Wearing the black gown, Barnhill had something of the aspect of a judge, aided by the neatly trimmed mustache and beard he'd worn during his three years at the university. At age twenty-nine, he looked older, prematurely graying at his temples and with a gravity of demeanor attributable to the hardships he'd endured in the army and the travail that followed him after the surrender. "We've traveled a fair distance, Edward," he said as he shrugged off the gown and laid it over the back of a chair, "since that dark day at Appomattox."

"We have indeed," said Selden. "I only wish you'd reconsider. Spend a few weeks with me in Richmond. You could meet Eppa Hunton and some of the others...."

"My mind's made up," said Barnhill with an upraised hand. "As much as I love Virginia, I'm needed at home." The situation in Texas, he considered, was growing worse, judging from recent letters from his mother and cousin Sam; with utterly corrupt opportunists, widespread poverty, and an embittered populace that frequently resorted to vigilante violence. Barnhill thought back to the long, arduous journey home after the surrender; marching with the remnant of his regiment to Lynchburg, boarding a freight train south to Montgomery whence they were forced to walk, many on bare feet, all the way to Mobile; loitering on the wharves under the broiling sun until at last they crowded on a paddle wheeler for the trip across the Gulf to Galveston. From that point his recollection dimmed, until the moment he at last opened the latch on the picket gate and walked slowly up the path to his home at the top of the hill.

Barnhill slumped on the sofa in the small apartment he shared with Edward Selden and thought back to his homecoming in June of '65. Apart from paint peeling from some of the boards, he'd found the house just as he remembered it: the broad, galleried porches above and below, the fanlight over the door, and the brick chimney at one end of the handsome building. Home—which, unlike the pretentious plantations of Virginia and the Carolinas, bore no name but "the Mountain Farm," an exaggeration of the promontory his father had chosen on which to build it—had largely been untouched by the war. Virtually all of the former slaves remained, living in their old quarters and farming the land for their own sustenance while the house servants continued to support their mistress in return for her kindness and generosity. Barnhill's father had wisely sold a parcel of rich bottomland for a good price, paid in gold, a year before the war, providing an endowment for his wife to maintain the house and to feed and clothe the family and servants for the duration. But Barnhill had found the surrounding country vastly changed from the prosperous cotton district he'd left behind in the summer of '61: families embittered by the loss of sons or fathers; slaves converted to freedmen without any social, legal, or spiritual guidance for their transformation; fields untilled, crops unpicked, bankruptcy widespread as a consequence of debt and devalued paper money; and the oppressive, shameful sense of defeat as hard to rid as a sour taste in your mouth. People walked the streets in the nearby town of San Augustine with eyes downcast, the shelves of the dry goods and grocery stores were largely empty, and the sheriff and other local officials were forced at the point of a bayonet to surrender their offices to hated carpetbag Northerners bent on teaching the Rebels a lesson—and lining their pockets in the process. But the returning soldiers, especially those like Barnhill who'd fought in Virginia or Tennessee, were immensely relieved that the country had been spared the true ravages of the war; that their homes, barns, fences, and livestock were intact; that there were telegraph wires and bridges spanning the streams and rivers.

At first Barnhill had clung to the hope of returning to North Carolina to marry Amelia that had sustained him through the final, terrible months of the war. And then, as the depth of the economic collapse and privation sunk in, he had been bitterly forced to concede that he could never keep the promise he'd made to Josiah Maxwell in an effort to gain his consent—to provide Amelia the same degree of comfort and prosperity to which she was accustomed at Widewater. With so many of his boyhood friends killed or maimed in the war, and so many of his father's generation ruined, he was convinced that East Texas desperately needed a new generation of leaders, educated men with a new vision. And then, as he weighed Edward Selden's proposal to join him in the study of law at the University of Virginia, Barnhill received a final letter from Amelia, informing him that, under "the terrible economic circumstances," she had assumed full responsibility for caring for her father and the plantation. "All I feared, dearest Jamie," she wrote, "has come to pass. Our former life is no more." With an expression of heartfelt thanks for all that Barnhill had done, she closed with the "fervent hope" that some day she would see him again.

CHAPTER TEN

Barnhill sat in cap and gown on the first row, admiring the classical lines of Jefferson's rotunda and the colorful display of regalia of the robed faculty seated on the stage set before the dais and graduating seniors. Following the remarks of the aged university president, Dean Brown, erect and distinguished with his long gray beard and the blue and white silks of Yale on his hood, took his place at the podium. Clearing his throat, in a strong voice that reached the last row of chairs, he said, "And now, the Class of 1868."

As there were fewer than one hundred graduates, it did not take him long to reach Barnhill's name. "James Madison Barnhill," intoned the dean, "bachelor of law, *magna cum laude*." Barnhill rose from his chair, walked up the steps amid a smattering of applause and reached out to accept the scrolled-up parchment. "Congratulations, Mr. Barnhill," said the dean. "You have distinguished yourself." His heart pounding, Barnhill mumbled his thanks and returned to his seat with an overwhelming feeling of sadness that no one in his family, his father especially, was present to witness the momentous occasion.

Barnhill did not entirely boycott the afternoon and evening celebrations for the graduates, attending a reception on the quadrangle where he enjoyed several glasses of champagne punch and visited with Edward Selden's gracious mother and father. His heart rose with the rumor that Robert E. Lee, who had recently assumed the presidency of Washington College in nearby Lexington, would attend. But to the disappointment of all, the beloved general sent his regrets.

Afterward, Barnhill returned to his rooms, where his few belongings were already packed. By the light of an oil lamp, he placed several sheets of stationery on his scarred oak desk. For a moment he closed his eyes, remembering the words of the brief note from Amelia forwarded to him by his mother in the spring of '67, then dipped the nib of his pen in the well and thoughtfully wrote:

> June 5, 1868
> Charlottesville, Va.

Mrs. Albert Bondurant
Widewater Plantation
Chowan County, N. Car.

Dear Amelia,

    I wish you could have seen me today, on the occasion of my graduation from the University of Virginia with a degree in law. I finished near the top of my class, though it was a small one, and it would have made me so proud if you had been there to see it. If he could have known that I would manage this accomplishment, I wonder if your father might have viewed me in a different light.

    In the morning I will board the train to Atlanta, whereupon I will take another to Birmingham and, eventually, to Texas. When I return home I will be one of the few men with a university education, and it is my intention to enter into practice with one of the ablest lawyers in the area.

    Though I often think what might have been, I try to look to the future and not dwell on the terrible losses we have all suffered. I think often of Robert and hold him up as an example of what a true gentleman should be. I will not say that I miss you, but rather think of you often in the hope that you are happy and content and that you receive your share of God's blessings. I doubt I will ever have occasion to pass your way, but if I should I certainly will call on you and your husband. With all best wishes,

    Yours sincerely,
    Jamie

Barnhill blew on the sheets to dry the ink and then leaned back to reread the letter in the yellow lamplight. With a sigh, he withdrew a cheroot from his pocket, reached for a box of matches, and struck one on the sole of his boot. Lighting the cigar, he took a puff and then held the flame to the edge of the letter and tossed the burning pages on the cold grate of the fireplace.

    At the brow of a long, gentle hill, Barnhill tugged on the reins, halting the mare, which gave an impatient stamp of her forelegs. He'd purchased the buggy and horse, a plodding swayback, in New Orleans for the final leg of the journey. He surveyed the familiar vista: a wide swath of cultivated soil planted with early cotton to the left of the rutted track and, to the right, an expanse of virgin longleaf pine that reached to the horizon. Faith, he considered: the substance of things hoped for, the evidence of things not seen. He had faith in his future, and in the future of his homeland and people. Taking a kerchief from his back pocket, he wiped the sweat from his face and slapped the reins, starting the horse down the slope with a swish of her long tail, the wheels of the buggy creaking on their springs. As they drew near the cotton field Barnhill studied the dilapidated fence rails and weeds growing in the furrows, which veered unevenly across the sloping ground. With the approach of high noon, the summer sun beat down on his wide-brimmed hat and suntanned forearms, lathering the haunches of the mare. At a bend in the road, Barnhill decided to take a shortcut through the forest, cool, shady, and completely free of undergrowth beneath the canopy of towering pines, four feet or more in diameter at their base. As the buggy passed through the cathedral-like forest, he listened to the wind singing in the boughs high overhead and inhaled the sweet bouquet of the sap and needles. He thought pleasantly of arriving at last at his hilltop home with its graceful parlor and snug library and the imminent reunion with his mother and sister from whom he'd been separated for the better part of seven years. After a quarter mile, he reached the banks of a muddy tributary of the Sabine, where the pine forest turned to sweet gum, live oak, and chinquapin. As the buggy approached the hardwoods, Barnhill detected motion in the dense underbrush, a blur of black fur and crash of branches. Bear, he thought with quickened pulse. The woods were thick with them, and plentiful deer and wild turkey.

Emerging from the shade of the forest, he turned back on the rutted road and urged the mare on to a trot, bouncing him on the wooden seat, until she abruptly halted with a nervous whinny and shake of her head. What is it, girl? wondered Barnhill, staring ahead at the gnarled trunk of a massive live oak. And then he saw it: bare black feet protruding from ragged pant legs, dangling from a thick bough overhanging the roadway.

"Steady," said Barnhill as he jumped down and looped the reins on the footrail. He walked cautiously up to the tree and studied the limp body of a young black man hanging by a rope as straight as a plumb line. With a brief glance at the look of terror frozen in the dead boy's eyes, he turned away and spat on the red clay at the roadside. There was nothing around the site to suggest the motivation for the lynching, though Barnhill suspected he knew the pretext. Hurrying back to the buggy, where the mare was contentedly munching shoots of grass, he leapt up on the seat and started her into a canter with a slap of reins on her rump and a shout. He ignored the sorry condition of the fences and barns along the final mile into town, his disgust contending with seething anger that blotted out any pleasant thoughts of his imminent homecoming.

San Augustine was just as he remembered it, a humble collection of buildings surrounding a courthouse square choked with weeds. He drove straight to the livery, hitching the horse at the railing without bothering to go inside. Passing by the McPherson general store, he hurried to the sheriff's office on the north side of the square. An unfamiliar figure was seated inside, in shirtsleeves with a tin star pinned to his suspenders and scuffed boots up on the cluttered desk, looking at an illustrated magazine.

"Afternoon," said Barnhill, noting the man's rough attire and the worn-out soles of his boots.

The man eyed him curiously over the top of his magazine. "Who're you?" he asked. "New to these parts?"

"Me?" said Barnhill with a smile. "The name's Barnhill. Been here all my life, though I've been away, with the war and . . ."

"Oh, another Johnny Reb," said the man, lifting his boots from the desk. "Well, goddam."

Barnhill's smile vanished. "Is the sheriff in?"

"Nope," replied the deputy, rubbing his unshaved chin. "What seems to be the problem?"

Barnhill considered excusing himself, instinctively distrusting the stranger. "The problem," he said after a moment, "is a dead man, or rather, boy. A colored boy." The deputy's eyes narrowed. "Hanging by a noose from a live oak about a mile outside of town on the Carthage road."

"Who done it?" said the deputy, rising from the desk. "These goddam people."

"I have no idea," said Barnhill. "I happened by the body on my way into town."

"For your sake, mister," said the deputy, "I hope you're tellin' the truth. Sheriff Dinwoody means to make an example out of the first one of them crackers he catches."

"If I had anything to do with it," said Barnhill, "you reckon I'd have come to the sheriff to turn myself in?"

"Reckon not," said the deputy, hitching up his dirty trousers and reaching for his holster and revolver hanging from a peg. "I'd best go take a look."

CHAPTER TEN

"Good day, sir," said Barnhill, turning to the door and letting himself out. Standing on the sidewalk, squinting into the bright sun, he weighed the curious fact of an outsider in the position of deputy sheriff—and of sheriff, whoever this man Dinwoody might be. He watched as an elegant four-in-hand carriage rounded the corner onto the square, drawn by a matched team of white horses, with a black driver on the seat wearing a frock coat and top hat and brandishing a long whip. Halting before the courthouse above whose cupola, Barnhill noticed for the first time, the Stars and Stripes were flying, the absurdly attired driver climbed down and held open the door for the carriage's occupant, another unfamiliar face, a short, portly figure also dressed in a black frock coat and yet another stovepipe hat. Emulating Abe Lincoln, perhaps, thought Barnhill with an inward smile as the black man bowed obsequiously to his passenger, who straightened his coat with a self-important air and strode up the steps to the courthouse.

Barnhill strolled along the sidewalk toward the other side of the square. Crossing the dusty street, he was relieved to see his old Sunday-school teacher walking toward him, clad in a faded cotton dress whose hem, he observed, was uncharacteristically ragged, her elderly face obscured by a sunbonnet. "Mrs. Walker," he said, meeting her midway across the street.

Looking up with a surprised expression, she studied him for a moment and then exclaimed, "Praise the Lord! It's Jamie Barnhill." Taking her by the arm, he escorted her up to the sidewalk just as another old acquaintance, Ezekiel Henderson, emerged from the hardware store. "Mr. Henderson," called out Mrs. Walker. "Come and see who's home."

Striding quickly up to them, Henderson said, "Why, it's young Barnhill," warmly clasping his hand. Barnhill scarcely recognized the man, the owner of a neighboring farm, whose hair had gone completely white since he'd last seen him in the summer of '61. He recalled that he'd lost two of his three sons in the war, one at Sharpsburg and the other to illness in Arkansas. Reluctantly releasing Barnhill's hand, Henderson said, "Your mother will be mighty proud, son. A college man."

"Thank you, sir."

"One of these days, Jamie, when you have a minute, maybe you could stop by . . ." Henderson paused and cleared his throat. "Tell me about Billy."

"Yes, sir," said Barnhill with a nod.

"You see, nobody else . . ."

"I understand." Anxious to be on his way, Barnhill said goodbye and started down the sidewalk toward the livery stable. He halted at the sound of approaching horses and watched as a large man on a black horse, wearing a slouch hat and a silver star on his lapel, galloped into the square in a cloud of brick-red dust, accompanied by two Federal cavalry troopers armed with carbines and sabers.

"Damned Yankees," muttered a man on the sidewalk leaning against a storefront. With a missing leg and wearing a faded Confederate jacket, he lifted a tin cup toward Barnhill. Briefly studying the man's unkempt hair and stubble of beard, he dimly recognized him, a local farmer several years his senior, from before the war. Barnhill made eye contact, fished in his pocket for a fifty-cent piece, and dropped it in the cup. "Much obliged, sir," said the man vacantly as Barnhill stepped down from the sidewalk and hurried across the street. He glanced at McPherson's general store in the next block, with its half-curtained windows, debating whether to stop and inquire about Kate before heading out of town. He continued in the direction of the livery and then felt a gentle tug from an unseen hand, drawing him back in the hope of seeing the girl, now married, that so many years ago he'd fancied he was in love with. Walking back down the block, he opened the door, slipped off his hat and looked around the familiar shop, with shelves that reached to the patterned tin ceiling and a long counter at the back. The store was empty, as were many of the shelves. The wide cypress boards creaked under his tread as he examined a few bolts of gingham and muslin, neat spools of sewing thread, stacks of pottery, and boxes of candles and canning jars. He ran a finger along an empty shelf, leaving a trail in the thick dust. Approaching the worn counter, he inspected a complete set of English china—dinner and dessert plates, soup bowls, cups and saucers—someone was hoping to sell on consignment, and an array of cast-iron skillets next to a Dutch oven. He put his hat on the counter, where a thick ledger lay open beside a stack of receipts, wondering if the shop was closed and the clerk had simply neglected to lock up. Resisting the temptation to leave, he reached for the small silver bell and gave it a tap.

"Coming," said someone from the stockroom in back. A woman's voice: "Hold your horses." In a moment a slender young woman wearing a long black dress appeared in the doorframe. She suddenly froze, staring at Barnhill like an apparition and raising a hand to her mouth as if to suppress a cry.

"Kate," said Barnhill with a wide smile. "I was hoping to find you here."

"Jamie . . . Oh, my goodness." She folded her hands at her chest. "You liked to take my breath away." Barnhill studied her for a moment, the same auburn hair parted in the middle and tied with a ribbon at the back, but her flesh pale and worn and so thin her dress hung loosely on her frame. "Well," she said, regaining her composure, "this is quite a surprise."

"Seven years, Kate. A long time." She looked down at her hands with a pained expression. "Your father's well?" he asked.

She nodded, avoiding his eyes, and softly said, "I suppose so. Considering."

"And your husband?"

She met his gaze with an anguished expression and suddenly burst into tears.

"What is it, Kate?" He reached across the counter to take her hand.

"Dead," she said as tears streamed down her pale cheeks. "Murdered."

"My God," said Barnhill, noticing that she was dressed in mourning. "When did this happen?"

"A month ago," she said, brushing back her tears. "There was a fight. Calvin—my husband—called down this Yankee officer for . . . for insulting me. He drew his pistol and shot my husband dead!"

"I'm so sorry," said Barnhill. "What have they done with this man?"

"Scot free," she said with a sigh. "Claimed it was self defense. And Calvin didn't even own a gun."

Barnhill considered the deputy at the jail, with his sneering comments about "crackers" and "Johnny Reb" and the sheriff riding on to the square with his escort of cavalry troopers. "Why don't you sit down," he suggested, "and let me get you something."

"There's a pitcher of lemonade in the back," said Kate, settling on the stool behind the counter. "Why don't you close up the store."

Barnhill turned the bolt in the front door, put the "closed" sign in the window, and went to the stockroom to pour Kate a glass from the pitcher on the shelf.

After taking a swallow, she ran the back of her hand over her forehead and said, "I'm sorry, Jamie."

Barnhill sat on the counter and gave her an affectionate smile. "Sorry for what?"

"For not writing. Especially after we heard you'd been . . ."

"What? Killed? You don't write a dead man."

"No," she said softly. "I grieved for you, Jamie. And that's when I met Calvin, before we learned you'd been spared."

"I see," said Barnhill, suspecting she was being less than truthful. "But you shouldn't be sorry."

She brightened a little and said, "So now you're a lawyer." Barnhill nodded. "A law degree won't do much good around here," she added.

"Why's that?"

"The only law is the Union cavalry. And the carpetbaggers have taken over the courthouse . . ."

"I met the deputy sheriff," said Barnhill.

"That awful man," said Kate with a grimace. "You won't find any justice around here. You'd have been better off staying away. Where were you, in Virginia?"

"Yes, in Virginia. Well, I aim to see if these men will enforce the laws on the books. And I came home to look after my mother." He slipped off the counter. She nodded glumly and took another swallow of lemonade. "I have to go, Kate," he said. "It's good to see you. And I'm sorry about your husband."

"Thanks." She rose from the stool. "Thanks for dropping by, Jamie. I hope to see you again."

CHAPTER ELEVEN

THE BUGGY TRAVELED SLOWLY DOWN THE RUTTED ROAD in the stifling mid-afternoon heat, trailing a cloud of orange-brown dust. Jamie eyed the thunderclouds building beyond the line of hills to the north. He flicked the reins and called to the chestnut mare. After a moment's hesitation and toss of her mane, she started into a trot. How many times had he visualized this homecoming, lying awake on the straw mattress in his small bedroom at the Charlottesville boarding house, listening to the wind through the open window? The mare's ears pricked up as a lightning bolt arced across the charcoal sky, followed after a few seconds by an angry rumble of thunder. "C'mon, girl," said Barnhill reassuringly, "just another mile, after we've come so far." Now every aspect of the roadside was familiar: the board fence at the boundary of the Lucas farm, the sturdy bridge over the muddy creek, and the tall trees bordering the arrow-straight stretch of road to the top of the hill and the turn into Mountain Farm.

There was the mailbox, with "BARNHILL" stenciled on the side, and the split-rail fence enclosing the north pasture, cleared of trees and pale green with the coastal grasses planted by his father. Barnhill turned the rented rig through the gate onto the neat track, his heart beating faster with anticipation. The sky was bright blue above the billowing cumulus, the breeze fresh and cool from the nearby thunderstorm. As he passed through the pecan orchard and breasted a gentle rise, the house came into view at last on the hilltop, just as he'd left it, the wide galleries above and below, the redbrick chimney on the left, surrounded by pines. With a slap of the reins he urged the weary horse back to a trot, bringing the buggy to a stop beside the picket fence that enclosed the yard. After tying the reins to the iron loop of the hitching post, Barnhill retrieved his bag from behind the seat, unlatched the gate, and walked quickly up to the front door. He paused to glance at the pair of rocking chairs on the wide porch, for a moment imagining his father in his favorite spot, contentedly gazing out on the panoramic view. Placing his bag at his feet, Barnhill lifted his hand to knock and then decided to surprise them. He tried the knob and, finding the door unlocked, quietly let himself in.

He hesitated for a moment, inhaling the familiar musty air and looking around the front hall and arched entrance to the parlor, unchanged since he'd last seen them. The *ticktock* of the grandfather clock was the only sound. He considered calling out, but then walked slowly into the parlor, observing his mother's sewing on the table beside her favorite chair, the cypress floors neatly swept, furniture dusted and smelling faintly of lemon oil. A gentle breeze furled the curtains at the tall windows. He moved from the parlor to the dining room with its dull green paneling and the heavy mahogany buffet where the good china and silver were kept, and paused again to listen. No sound came from the kitchen, nor from the stairs . . . Not even Hattie humming to herself; she was always humming . . . Barnhill opened the door and walked down the hall to the pantry at the back of the house, whose shelves were crammed with canned fruit, preserves, and pickles, with a broom, mop, and pail in the corner, and just beside the door to the outside, two pairs of ladies' shoes. He put his hands on his hips and shook his head. His mother's shoes? And then he detected the sound of men talking, deep voices in animated conversation. He flung open the door, observing two black men wearing faded bib overalls and straw hats walking up the path to the house. They halted at the sight of the tall man on the steps, studying him as they rested on their hoes. Beyond the path Barnhill gazed out on the neatly furrowed cotton fields that stretched all the way to the tree line in the distance and, to the left of the path, a large garden, enclosed by a board fence, filled with ripening corn, beans, peas, tomatoes, and squash. He strode down the back steps toward the two black men.

Eyeing him curiously, the older of the two said, "Mista James? That you?"

Barnhill broke into a grin and said, "Why, it's Parker." He reached out and shook the man's outstretched hand. "I scarcely recognized you after all these years."

"Home at last," said Parker. "Yore momma's gonna be mighty pleased."

"Where is she?" asked Barnhill. "There wasn't a soul in the house, not even Elijah or Hattie."

A sad look clouded the black man's face. "Elijah's gone to his reward. Buried him last month."

"Good old Elijah," said Barnhill with a shake of his head.

"And Hattie's hardly fit to get around," said Parker. "She's takin' it easy . . ."

"And my mother?"

"Oh, she's right there in the garden," said Parker, hooking a thumb over his shoulder. "Pullin' weeds, I spec."

Barnhill walked quickly to the garden gate and peered through the chest-high corn. At the far end, two figures were on their hands and knees, toiling in the reddish-orange clay, their heads obscured by rows of staked beans. As he drew nearer, he could see that they were women, one wearing a sunbonnet and the other with a red kerchief tied over her hair. Barnhill smiled when he saw their bare feet curled up under them. "Afternoon," he said.

His mother looked up over her shoulder, holding a trowel in one hand and raising the other to shield her eyes from the afternoon sun. "Who's there?" she said.

Before he could answer, Barnhill's sister Anna sprang up and held out her dirty hands. "Why, it's Jamie!" she exclaimed.

"Jamie?" repeated his mother.

Barnhill reached down and, taking her by the arms, lifted her up and embraced her. "Hello, Mother," he said gently, surprised by how thin and feathery light she was.

"Oh, dear," she said with a stifled sob, "just look at me."

Letting her go, he took a step back and gave both mother and sister an appraising look. "You look more like a cotton picker," he said with a smile, "than the mistress of the house."

"You don't know the half of it," said Anna with a laugh. Barnhill could now see she was wearing a baggy pair of men's trousers, cinched at her slender waist with a belt. "But Ma and I are right good gardeners, and it keeps food on the table."

"And cow milkers and hog callers," added Mary Barnhill with a shake of her head. "Oh, Jamie. Thank the Lord you're home."

Standing by the bookcase in his father's library, Barnhill lightly ran a finger over the spines of the fine leather volumes, remembering the hours he'd happily spent there before the war, traveling the world through the medium of books. . . . He listened to the cicadas in the trees outside, a shrill chorus that rose and fell, strange, but comfortingly familiar. He was, he realized, enormously happy to be home. Recalling that his father had stocked the good whiskey in a cabinet below the bookshelf, he bent down and opened it, removing a bottle of Kentucky bourbon. The servant, a quiet man named Watson who'd taken Elijah's place, had left a tray on the table with a water pitcher and several glasses. Pouring an inch of bourbon and adding water, Barnhill walked to the window and gazed out at the undulating hills, clad in pine forest and folded in the purple and rose of dusk. Hearing footsteps, he turned as his mother entered the room, fresh from her bath with her dark hair, streaked with gray, put up, and wearing a blue cotton dress trimmed with grosgrain and a pendant at her neck. Barnhill walked over and lightly kissed her cheek, fragrant with talcum powder that took him back to his childhood.

"You're drinking," she said in a mildly disapproving tone.

"I'm a grown man," said Barnhill. "Well beyond my years. Good bourbon is something I learned to appreciate in Virginia."

"I wonder," she said, "why you didn't choose to stay there. With your degree from the university and your friends in Richmond."

"You mean," said Barnhill, "considering the sad shape things are in here?" She nodded. After taking a sip of his drink, he said, "As much as I like Virginia, I was ready to leave. You have no idea how glad I am to be home."

Sitting on the arm of a wing chair, she smiled wistfully and said, "You did it for me. And for Anna. I know that, and I thank you, Jamie."

"I always intended to come back," he said. "But you seem to have managed very well. It almost seems like the old days. . . ."

"Thanks to your father, bless his soul. He left enough to get through the war, and the Negroes have been content to farm their plots and help with the house and chores. But if they venture outside the front gate . . ."

"I know," said Barnhill, taking another sip. "I saw enough passing through town."

"It's terrible, Jamie. These Northern men have taken over everything. And why? To help the poor blacks?" She shook her head and walked over to the window to look out on the gathering darkness. Barnhill struck a match and lit the wick of the oil lamp on the rolltop desk. Turning toward him, she said, "They're in it for the money. And to punish us, as if the war wasn't punishment enough." She brushed back a tear.

"You could argue that the war," said Barnhill, "was our own fault. But how do they do it? I'm not sure I understand."

"Why, they get themselves elected. They line up all the blacks and tell them who to vote for, as none of our people can cast a ballot. And ever since that Yankee general . . ."

"Sheridan?"

"Yes, Sheridan, removed the governor, why the army's taken over and put the men they want in charge. Every one of them a carpetbagger. Take this man Newton, for instance. A store clerk from Rhode Island who came down here and got himself elected county judge."

"Why do the people stand for it?" Barnhill sat in the swivel chair at the desk.

"Some of them have thrown in with the Republicans, looking for plums. And then there's the Yankee cavalry in case anyone makes trouble."

"And all this folderol about protecting the blacks' rights," said Barnhill with a frown.

"Oh, they have the suffrage, all right. And a few of them are rewarded with jobs in the courthouse, that sort of thing. Making an example. But as for the rest, unless they stay on the farm and work for their old masters they're liable to be . . ."

Barnhill studied his mother's pained expression. "Yes," he said after a moment. "I came across a black boy hanging from a live oak on my way into town."

"Lynching. The work of drunken white trash," said Mary Barnhill with surprising fervor. "Protecting the Southern woman's honor. Good Lord, where will it end."

"I paid a call on Kate," said Barnhill. "On my way out of town."

"That poor girl."

A servant appeared, a young black woman wearing a starched white dress and apron. "Supper's 'bout ready, Missus," she announced.

"We'll be in directly," said Mrs. Barnhill. Turning to Jamie, she said, "Kate's husband was a fool. A hothead who didn't do a thing in the war. He challenged a Yankee officer. Claimed he insulted her . . ."

"Who shot him dead," said Barnhill. "According to Kate, the man got off Scot free with cold-blooded murder."

Mary Barnhill nodded. "The sheriff didn't even bother to bring him in. So now they'll be gunning for him on some dark night. Vigilantes."

Barnhill sat to his mother's left at the rectangular dining-room table, illuminated by a fine old silver candelabra; his father's place at the head of the table was still vacant. Anna took her seat opposite her brother, and after the servant had passed a tray of pork chops with bowls of black-eyed peas and okra, Mrs. Barnhill folded her hands on her napkin and asked her son to return thanks. Giving her a fond look in the flickering candlelight, he reflected for a moment, and then bowed his head and prayed: "Heavenly Father, bless this food to our nourishment and us to thy service. Grant us the strength to remember in these trying times all the blessings that have been bestowed on us. In Jesus's name, Amen."

"Amen," murmured Mary and Anna in unison. As they helped themselves to the side dishes and passed the bowls, the servant returned with a plate of hot biscuits. When she was out of earshot, Mary Barnhill, spreading a pat of butter, remarked, "That girl just can't seem to learn."

"Not like Hattie's," agreed Barnhill, taking a bite of biscuit. "Something about the way she spanks the dough."

"Hattie," said Mary, "would probably rise from her deathbed if it meant a chance to fix supper for her dear boy."

"Well, by all means," said Barnhill as he sliced a thick pork chop, "let's give her the opportunity."

Anna, hitherto silent, said, "You don't seem to realize it, but if it weren't for Mama and me, workin' like . . . well, like field hands, you wouldn't have that glass of milk, or that butter, and certainly not those peas and okra."

"I obviously don't appreciate," said Barnhill equably, "how much things have changed, or how hard you've had to work." He paused to sample the okra. "I'm curious about the division of labor."

"Well," began Anna, "we do all the . . ."

"The blacks," interrupted Mrs. Barnhill, "at least the ones who live here, are free to farm their own land. They make a small cotton crop and raise their own food. Not sharecrop, mind you. I provide credit for their furnish. They repay me with interest, and what's left over belongs to them."

"It's just not right," muttered Anna.

"Going on eight years now," continued Mary mildly. "We have Alma to do the laundry, and Watson and Maggie, now that Elijah passed and Hattie's laid up."

"And you have money in the bank?" asked Barnhill. "For a rainy day?"

Mary looked at her son and then made eye contact with Anna, whose suntanned face was a blank mask. "A little," said Mary. "The money from the River Farm tided us through the war and helped us to keep things going. . . ."

"She won't say it," blurted out Anna, "but Mama spent that money to buy medicine for the blacks, and pay their doctor bills, and loan enough to the widow Lucas to have her son sent home and buried, and, oh, for anytime a neighbor was in trouble."

"Anna," said her mother with a trace of asperity.

"And now it's gone, or almost," Anna finished.

"We have land," said Mary Barnhill. "In fact, I intend to . . ."

"Papa left the good land to the slaves," interrupted Anna. "All we have left is the north pasture and the pine barrens."

"Not all at once," said Barnhill, raising a placating hand. "Let mother finish. Are you thinking about selling more land?"

"Yes," she admitted in a self-reproachful tone. "Land is fine, but we need the cash."

"I'm starting work," said Barnhill. "It's why I spent three years getting my degree . . ."

"While we were struggling," said Anna under her breath.

Barnhill stared at her, surprised by the depth of her resentment of his long absence to pursue something of such dubious value as a college education. "I'm sorry," he said, looking at her. "I'm sure it was very hard. But from what I've seen, this place could use a little honest justice . . ."

"You try taking on these Northerners," said Anna, "and you'll be up against the Yankee cavalry."

"I've dealt with my share of Yankee cavalry," countered Barnhill. "Judge Withers has invited me to join his law office. I'm starting in the morning."

"I'm proud of you, Jamie," said Mary. "It's your future. And it's just a matter of time before these *people* leave us alone to manage our own affairs."

"Thank you," said Barnhill. "But I'm curious. Who's been talking to you about buying property?"

"That man Newton," said Mary, staring into her lap. This elicited a gasp from Anna.

"Leave it be for now, Mother," said Barnhill. "Let me get the lay of the land."

Barnhill swung down from the saddle and tied his horse at the railing. Giving the colt a reassuring pat, he unfolded his coat—a black frock—from the saddlebag and shrugged it on. The law office was in a storefront of the two-story Wagner building facing the courthouse. As Barnhill stepped up on the sidewalk, he noticed the same fancy black carriage he'd seen on his last trip to town, with the driver on the seat in his stovepipe hat.

Glancing at the words stenciled in gold leaf on the glass—*Jno. H. Withers, Attorney at Law*—Barnhill reached for the knob and let himself in. A pale young man, perhaps twenty, sat behind an ink-stained desk cluttered with stacks of papers. With armbands over his shirtsleeves, he peered up at his visitor over the top of his spectacles.

"Mornin'," said Barnhill, slipping off his wide-brimmed hat. "Is the judge in?"

"And you would be . . ." the young man asked diffidently.

"James Barnhill. He's expecting me."

"Oh, Captain Barnhill." The clerk struggled to his feet. Barnhill looked around the small outer office, with a facsimile map of the Republic of Texas on one wall and a floor-to-ceiling bookcase filled with the state's statute books bound in black buckram. "I'll let the judge know you're here," said the clerk with a slight bow before exiting through a

CHAPTER ELEVEN

frosted glass door. After a moment the young man reappeared and held the door open for Barnhill. The judge's spacious office was at the end of a hallway lined with glass-encased bookshelves. Barnhill paused at the threshold, inhaling the pungent aroma of good cigars. Judge John H. Withers, in shirtsleeves with a brocaded waistcoat, was seated at a leather-tooled library table before a bronze inkstand. Short and compact, with china blue eyes and flowing white hair, he rose from his chair and reached out to give Barnhill a firm handshake.

"Mornin', Judge," said Barnhill with a smile.

"I've been expecting you, Jamie," said Withers. He studied the tall young man with the neatly trimmed beard and mustache. "I remember the skinny kid with a cane pole over his shoulder and not a care in the world. And here you are, a captain in Hood's famous brigade and graduate of Jefferson's university."

"I'm just glad to be home," said Barnhill. "And anxious to get to work."

"It's a pity," said Withers, slumping in his chair, "that your father didn't live to see the day. Have a seat." He motioned to an armchair. "Harrison," he called to the clerk, who was waiting outside the office. "Bring us two cups of coffee. You take it black?"

"Yes, sir." Barnhill sat in an armchair facing the desk.

Withers walked to the window and lifted the sash. "Another hot one," he commented. Turning back to Barnhill, he said, "So you're eager to start work?" The clerk returned and carefully placed two steaming cups on the desk.

"Yes, sir," said Barnhill, reaching for his cup. "I am."

Returning to his chair, the judge said, "There's not much work to go around, I'm sorry to say. You'll have the office across the hall, do my briefing, and assist when I have a case. Before long you'll be admitted to the bar."

"I have a lot to learn," said Barnhill, taking a sip of strong black coffee.

"Let me be plain," said the judge, resting his elbows on his desk. "These Northern men control the courthouse, from the trial judge to the bailiff. They'll seat poor, ignorant blacks on a jury. And the laws coming out of the legislature . . ." Withers shook his head. "God help us."

"And so how," said Barnhill, "does a lawyer make a living?"

Withers took a sip of coffee and then leaned back in his chair. "The people of this community," he said, "still need their wills drawn, which need to be construed and probated when they die. They occasionally require a deed or contract written, or help in settling a dispute with a neighbor. But more often than not, the fee consists of a bushel of corn, a parcel of land, or a share in the cotton crop."

"I see," said Barnhill, thinking back to Josiah Maxwell's prophetic warning about eking out a living as a backwoods lawyer.

"Of course," said Withers, "our people need skilled and honest attorneys. Not the charlatans masqueradin' as lawyers all over the county. You've got the brains and the education, Jamie. The people look up to you, an honest-to-goodness hero from the war. And I'm getting along in years. Sit second chair with me for a while, and you can take over my practice."

"I'm mighty grateful, Judge." Barnhill sipped his coffee and said, "What can you tell me about this man Newton?"

The older man's eyes narrowed. "Archibald Newton," he said sourly, "is the worst sort of carpetbagger. Came down from New England and managed to get himself elected county judge. If it weren't for the sheriff and that bunch of Yankee cavalry, by now the people would've ridden him out of town on a rail." He shook his head. "He's like the Sheriff of Nottingham, exacting tribute from everyone in town."

Barnhill smiled. "Maybe," he suggested, "the town could use a Robin Hood."

Withers returned the smile and said, "Maybe. But steer clear of Newton," he cautioned.

"He's been out to see mother," said Barnhill. "About buying some of our land."

"Oh, really? On the north side of the highway?"

"I'm not sure." Barnhill gave Withers a curious look.

"The carpetbaggers are working on passing a bill in the legislature," said the judge, "to extend the Union Pacific line from Dallas to Galveston."

"The Southern Branch of the Union Pacific," explained Judge Withers. "Out of Topeka, Kansas, but controlled by New York bankers."

"I see."

"Naturally," Withers continued, "Newton is in on it, and undoubtedly knows where the right-of-way is going. And so he's buying land. Cheap."

"Well, we're not selling," said Barnhill.

"Beg pardon, Judge . . ."

Barnhill looked over his shoulder at the clerk standing in the doorway.

"The widow Blount is here to see you," said Harrison.

"Very well," said Withers, rising from his chair. "You'll find this interesting, Jamie," he added with a smile. "Her neighbor's bull busted down a fence and scattered her livestock all over creation."

"Who's the neighbor?" asked Barnhill.

"Oh, a sharecropper. But the land . . . and the bull . . ." —Withers reached for his coat on the rack—"belong to one Archibald Newton."

CHAPTER TWELVE

STANDING BY THE WINDOW, Barnhill pushed aside the curtain and gazed out at the flag waving over the cupola of the county courthouse. After a week riding back and forth to the farm, he'd taken a room at the town's only boardinghouse, a two-story clapboard structure managed by the widow Goldfarb, whose husband, a Jewish cotton broker, had died at the Battle of Shiloh. Lifting the sash, he savored the fresh, cool breeze after months of torpid heat and humidity and imagined a different flag rising over the courthouse, a single white star on a blue field, which brought to mind the words and melody of the lively Confederate anthem.

Looking around the small, spare room, with its stained and peeling wallpaper, he slumped on the bed and dimly recollected the long-ago winter in Richmond recuperating at Mrs. Webb's, when the "Bonny Blue" Confederate flag flew proudly throughout the capital, and the expectation hung in the frigid air that, with the coming of spring, Lee's army would overwhelm its Federal adversary and force an end to the war. As was almost always the case, these ruminations ended with bitter thoughts of Amelia and the interlude at Widewater before Robert Maxwell's tragic death. With a rueful shake of his head, Barnhill bent over the washstand for his usual ablutions, dressed in a clean white shirt, and donned his frock coat for the short walk to the law office. Bounding down the stairs, he paused in the dining room to pour a glass of milk and take a slice of cornbread from the plate on the sideboard, bid the black cook good day, and hurried out into the bright sunshine.

Barnhill had known virtually all of the inhabitants of the small town since he was a boy. Of course, some of the most familiar faces were gone, perished in the war, and other faces, the new arrivals from the North, were utterly foreign. What mattered was that he belonged to the kindred people of his community. As he passed by the Reynolds house, one of several constructed of dark-red brick from the kiln at Nacogdoches, the matron of the house paused from her sweeping on the front porch to call out, "Mornin', Captain Barnhill. Fine day." He smiled and waved, reflecting that it was commonplace to address him thus, out of respect that verged on adulation for the few survivors of the storied Texas Brigade, especially an officer who, at war's end, was second in command of one of its regiments. As soon as word circulated that he'd hung out his shingle with Judge Withers, the townspeople had flocked to his office to pay their respects and welcome home the returning hero. Naturally gratified, he soon realized that none had any need for the services of a young lawyer.

Arriving at the town square, Barnhill stopped to gaze again at the national banner atop the flagpole, a deliberate insult to the people who had flown the Lone Star flag of Texas at the courthouse throughout the war. As usual, despite the invigorating change in the weather, there were few people about: several men unloading lumber from a mule-drawn wagon at the Tucker hardware, a woman with a little girl at her side entering McPherson's general store. Barnhill mounted the steps to the sidewalk, passed the crippled Confederate veteran with his missing leg and outstretched cup, and arrived at the office just as the clock at the courthouse struck nine. The clerk glanced up over his spectacles, put aside the document he was copying, and said, "Good morning, sir. May I be of service . . ."

"If there's coffee on the stove," said Barnhill, slipping off his hat, "I'll have a cup." He resented the young man's unctuous servility, which reminded him uncomfortably of Uriah Heep's attitude toward Copperfield. Aware that the judge seldom arrived before ten, Barnhill reached into his pocket for a key and unlocked the door to his office. Striking a match from the box on a table, he lit the lamp, adjusted the wick, and surveyed the small, windowless room with a satisfied expression. The sturdy oak desk with lion's clawed feet came from the office his father had maintained in town; behind the desk a pine bookcase held his law books and, on an otherwise empty shelf, a glass jar with the minié ball extracted from his chest following the Battle of Fredericksburg. His parchment diploma from the University of Virginia was framed on the wall behind the desk next to an engraving of Robert E. Lee on Traveller. Lastly, the frayed and torn battle standard of the Fifth Texas, presented by his men following the surrender at Appomattox, hung on a stand in the corner.

Draping his coat on the back of a chair, Barnhill sat in his creaking swivel chair and removed a ruled tablet and sharpened pencil from the desk. Lost in concentration, he looked up to observe Harrison in the doorway, who bowed humbly and wordlessly handed Barnhill a cup of strong black coffee.

"Anything else, sir?"

"No." The clerk softly closed the door. Barnhill stared at the blank page, blew on the surface of the hot coffee and took a sip, thinking back to the cold mornings when boiled peanut grounds had sufficed for a cup of ersatz coffee. Putting his cup aside, he held the sharpened pencil over the page and wrote . . . nothing. After another sip, he snapped the pencil between his fingers and flung the pieces on the floor. He had no clients, nor was he likely to attract any in the impoverished backwater of San Augustine County. His father had bequeathed the family's only decent farmland, he bitterly reflected, to his slaves, perhaps out of deep-seated guilt for their enslavement, and now his mother and sister were reduced to working in the garden, milking the cows, while he . . . He looked up at a soft tap on the door. "Come in," said Barnhill.

Judge John H. Withers, wearing a dark green waistcoat under his black frock, opened the door and stood at the jamb. With a quick glance at the broken bits of pencil on the floor, he said, "Hard at it?"

Feeling a flush of embarrassment, Barnhill said, "Mornin', Judge. I, ah . . ."

The judge pulled back a chair and sat down. "It's high time we put you to work," he said, crossing one black boot over his knee. "See what they taught you at the university."

"Yes, sir." Barnhill leaned forward with elbows on the desk.

"I mean to test the limits of this rigged judiciary," said Withers. "Are you familiar with an action for replevin?"

"Why, yes. One of the common law writs. To recover property wrongfully taken."

Withers nodded. "One of *our* clients," he explained, "has been swindled out of a parcel of land with a valuable gravel pit. Right valuable, considering the plans to lay a road-bed for the new railway."

"Who are the parties?"

"The widow Goldfarb—your landlady—was induced by a fellow named Thornberry, a crony of our county judge, to relinquish the property on the basis of a forged instrument, purporting to be a mortgage executed by her husband. Rather than sue for damages . . ."

"An action for replevin," said Barnhill. "Put the judge to the test, rather than look to a jury for damages . . ."

"That's the idea, my boy," said the judge with a smile. "Now, I'd like you to brief the law. See if you can find a Texas case."

Barnhill rose from his desk and pulled a thick volume from the shelf. "I'll see what I can learn from Blackstone," he said, opening the famous *Commentaries* on his desk. "And then have a look in the library at the courthouse."

After an hour reviewing the elements of the venerable common law tort, Barnhill returned the thick volume to its place on the shelf and, with a satisfied smile, tore three pages of notes from his tablet. Placing paper and pencil in a leather case, he grabbed his hat and coat and headed out without a word to the servile scrivener at his cluttered desk. With a deep, invigorating breath of cool autumn air, he began to step down from the sidewalk when he heard the loud clatter of wheel rims and hoofbeats and watched as the sheriff drove a wagon into the square with his usual escort of cavalry troopers. As they sped past, Barnhill could see that a man, bound hand and foot with ropes, was lying in the back.

Bringing the wagon to a halt with a shout and a cloud of dust, the sheriff leapt down from the seat and tied the reins at the railing. After a moment the deputy appeared, stretching galluses over the shoulders of his dirty shirt, and in a voice loud enough that Barnhill could easily hear him, said, "Well, well! Where'd you catch 'im?" Barnhill started walking slowly toward the jail, as did a number of others who emerged from stores and offices.

"Whar do you reckon?" said Sheriff Dinwoody. "Down on Sweet Gum Holler."

Sweet Gum Hollow, considered Barnhill, a collection of pitiful shacks that was chiefly known as the site of a notorious brothel whose madam was a large woman by the name of Aunt Betsy. The crowd of onlookers slowly converged in a semicircle around the wagon. Heeding the sheriff's instructions, the troopers dismounted, lowered the tailgate, and flung the bound man on the ground like a sack of flour. Barnhill clenched his fists with a sharp intake of breath, deeply repelled by an act of such senseless violence. He turned to the man standing beside him, owner of the hardware store, and asked, "What's this all about?"

With a look that suggested caution, the man quietly said, "Haven't you heard? They got him last night. The vigilante who shot that Yankee."

"Take him in," ordered the sheriff. The troopers hauled the prisoner to his feet, facing the crowd. With his bleeding and swollen face, Barnhill didn't recognize him. Then the man beside him uttered a name and Barnhill realized the prisoner was Jethro Banks, a dirt-poor farmer with a reputation for brawling who was rumored to have a connection to Aunt Betsy's house of ill repute. Briefly scanning the faces in the crowd, Banks made eye contact with Barnhill and called out, "Hey! Lawyer!"

Barnhill took a step forward.

"Yer a lawyer, ain't you?"

Barnhill, feeling the eyes of the crowd, merely nodded.

"Take him in, goddammit," said the sheriff. "You people get along!" he shouted to the onlookers as the troopers dragged the prisoner up the steps toward the jail. "Get on back to your business!" The people turned and slowly began to drift away. "By God," the sheriff called to them. "That man will hang."

His stomach churning and his neck flushed with anger, Barnhill was in no mood to sift through cases in the law library for an obscure ruling on property rights. Something impelled him to see Kate. When he reached the general store, he peered through the half-curtained windows and then tried the door, finding it unlocked. As on his previous visit, the shop was empty. Walking slowly toward the back, he noticed an old man sitting on a stool, barely visible in the dim light, hunched over a ledger book. When Barnhill cleared his throat, the old man looked up, staring curiously at Barnhill through the thick lenses of his spectacles. "Mornin'," said Barnhill, slipping off his hat. It suddenly dawned on him that the man was Kate's father, though he bore almost no resemblance to the man he'd last seen when he departed for the war. "Mr. McPherson?" said Barnhill, noticing his thinning and almost completely white hair, the bags under his bloodshot eyes, and stubble of whiskers on his chin and jowls.

"Yessir," said Donald McPherson. He blinked uncomprehendingly.

"It's me, Jamie Barnhill. I dropped by to see Kate."

"Oh," said McPherson, who seemed much older than his fifty years. "Barnhill. Been a long time." He scratched his chin.

"I'm awfully sorry about Ted," said Barnhill. Kate's only brother had been one of Barnhill's closest friends since boyhood.

The old man shook his head. "Measles," he said after a moment.

Unsure what to say, Barnhill pressed his lips together and nodded.

"Measles," Mr. McPherson repeated. "You got shot, didn't you?"

"Yes, sir."

"Where?"

"In the chest," replied Barnhill. "And the shoulder."

"And here you are," said McPherson. "And Theo dead."

"I'm very sorry, sir. Is Kate in?"

"Kate? Oh, sure. She's in the back." Turning toward the half door to the stockroom, he called out, "Kate! Jimmy Barnhill's here to see you!"

Barnhill smiled, the first time he'd been called by that nickname since he was twelve. "Oh, dear me," he heard Kate say from the back. In a moment she appeared, rubbing her hands with a washrag.

"Hello, Jamie," she said with a nervous smile. "I look a fright."

He gazed at her—the same auburn hair, parted in the middle and tied back; the same pretty face, but thinner and careworn, with crows' feet at the corners of her eyes. "I thought I'd drop by for a visit." They both glanced at Kate's father, who sat immobile on his stool.

"I'd love a breath of air," she said. "Perhaps we could . . ."

"Mind if I take your pretty girl on a stroll?" Barnhill asked.

"What? Mind? Why, no."

Putting aside her rag and moving from behind the counter, Kate gave Barnhill a hopeful look and walked with him to the door and out on the sidewalk. "It's a pretty day," she said, looking up at the cloudless sky and feeling the cool breeze on her face.

"There's something about the first norther of the season," he said, starting slowly down the sidewalk. They paused to speak to Mrs. Hodges, leaving the greengrocer's with a basket of sweet potatoes on her arm, and walked on to the corner. "I wonder if there's someplace," said Barnhill, "where we could sit and visit?"

"Well," said Kate, "there's the Methodist church. The bench out back."

There was no one at the tiny whitewashed church, and they sat on the wooden bench looking out on grass that sloped down to the muddy creek that meandered through the town. "Jamie," said Kate. "I'm awful glad you dropped by."

Barnhill, resting his elbows on his knees listening to the songbirds in the tall oaks, turned to give her a smile.

"Do you still care for me?" she asked coyly.

He thought back to his youthful professions of love in the months and weeks leading up to his regiment's departure in the summer of '61. It seemed much longer ago than seven years. "Of course," he replied. He noticed that she was no longer wearing her widow's weeds. "I hardly recognized your father," he said after an awkward moment of silence.

Kate looked down in her lap with a frown. "He's turned into an old man," she said quietly. Giving Barnhill a sidelong glance, she added, "Taken to hard drink. Drinkin' himself to death."

Barnhill felt a pang of deep sadness, thinking about Kate's brother Ted and so many others who never came home, and her father, who had fiercely opposed secession, utterly broken by the war. "I'm sorry," he muttered. Sitting up straight, he said, "Did you hear all the commotion a while ago?"

"Commotion?" She shook her head.

"Down at the jail. They arrested Jethro Banks."

"That comes as no surprise," said Kate, "with all his fightin' and goodness knows what else."

"They mean to hang him."

"Hang him? What for?"

"Killing the man . . . the Federal officer . . . who shot your husband."

She gave him a blank stare.

"Did you know about this?"

"About what?" There was an angry, defensive edge in her voice.

"Well, about the killing."

"It's the first I heard of it. But I'm not surprised. Everybody knows they were gunnin' for him."

"They?" said Barnhill. "You mean Banks?"

"Listen, Jamie," said Kate earnestly, leaning toward him. "I don't know anything about Jethro Banks being mixed up in this. There's a group of men callin' themselves the clan, or something like that, who aim to get even with the Yankees and swore they were gonna get the man who shot Calvin."

Barnhill nodded.

"And," Kate added, "I'm glad they did."

Barnhill stared at the courthouse in the distance. "These men," he said, turning back to her, "this so-called clan, are they the nightriders I've been hearing about?"

"I suppose so," said Kate. "Wearing hoods over their heads. There's certain places it's not safe for the Yankees after dark."

"Like Sweet Gum Hollow," said Barnhill grimly. "Listen, Kate, I'd better go. But you answered my question."

"Will I see you again?"

"In church on Sunday?" he suggested, rising from the bench. "Could you come for dinner? Hattie's frying chicken."

Kate smiled. "I'd be delighted."

Barnhill stood at the railing outside the sheriff's office, glanced at the watch he pulled from his fob pocket, and started up the steps. Letting himself in, he studied the deputy, asleep with his hands folded over his belly and his boots up on the desk. "Pardon me," said Barnhill.

"Huh?" said the startled deputy, rubbing his eyes and dragging his boots from the desk.

"Sheriff in?"

"Who're you?"

"We've met. The name's Barnhill."

"Don't recollect it. Sheriff's busy."

"I'm here to see the prisoner," said Barnhill. "I can wait."

"The prisoner? Oh, you mean . . ."

"Barnhill," said Sheriff Dinwoody, standing in the doorway, a tall, heavyset man with a drooping black mustache. "Don't believe we've met."

"No," said Barnhill. "Maybe we could talk in your office."

Dinwoody studied Barnhill for a moment and then said, "All right." He turned and walked to the office in the back. Sitting at his desk, he said, "So you're here to see the prisoner."

"That's right." Barnhill sat in a hard-back chair. "My client."

Dinwoody smiled. "Your client," he repeated with a stroke of his mustache.

"Mr. Banks. Has he been charged?"

Dinwoody opened a pigeonhole drawer and pulled out a plug of tobacco. He broke off a piece and carefully placed it between his cheek and gum. He glared at Barnhill and said, "Listen here. Ain't nobody seein' that whore's dog Banks."

"Speaking of whores," said Barnhill mildly, "I gather the *deceased* had been down at Aunt Betsy's when this incident occurred?" Dinwoody stared malevolently, working the chaw of tobacco like a cow its cud. Barnhill rose from his chair. "The deceased," he said evenly, "is the same man, if I'm not mistaken, who shot and killed Calvin Jones. In cold blood."

"I oughtta throw yer sorry . . ."

"Where are you from, Sheriff?" asked Barnhill.

"Kansas." He aimed a brown stream at the spittoon.

"I see."

"That's right," said the Sheriff. "Fought with Doc Jennison and the Jayhawkers."

Barnhill nodded, aware of the Union commander's notorious depredations against the civilian population during the war.

"And, by God," said Dinwoody, "if you people think you can . . ."

"Sheriff," interrupted Barnhill. "The war's over. If you act like you're above the law there'll be no end to these killings. Now, I'd like to talk to my client."

"Fine," said Dinwoody with a smile. "You go right ahead. But the man will hang."

Following a brief interview in the squalid cell, Barnhill reflected that he couldn't have made a poorer choice for a client, a man as foul in his appearance as his speech, reeking of liquor, the sort who wouldn't have lasted a fortnight in the army. Of course, every word spoken by both men had been overheard by the deputy, presumably Dinwoody's intention in granting the interview. But Jethro Banks was wily enough to avoid any incriminating comments, instead insisting that he knew nothing of the fate of the murdered cavalry officer and that there were any number of men who could vouch for the fact that he was engaged in a perfectly innocent poker game at the time of the midnight attack. Of more interest to Barnhill was Banks's sneering remark that the "sorry Yankees" were frequent visitors to Aunt Betsy's "establishment." After advising the accused that he could make no commitment to represent him, Barnhill quickly departed without a word to the deputy, anxious for a breath of fresh air and a quiet moment to reflect.

CHAPTER THIRTEEN

BARNHILL LOOKED UP AT THE SOUND OF A TAP ON THE DOOR. "What is it?" he said with some annoyance.

Harrison, the clerk, opened the door a crack and peered inside. "Pardon me, sir," he said with a deferential bow. "You have a visitor. A Mr. Perkins."

"Well," said Barnhill, rising from his chair, "show him back. And let me know as soon as the judge arrives."

"Of course," replied Harrison with another bow.

"Jamie," said Sam Perkins, pushing his way past the clerk and taking Barnhill's outstretched hand.

"Hello, Sam." Apart from a late-summer family gathering, Barnhill had not seen his cousin, who was managing his father's cotton farm in nearby Nacogdoches County, since his return from Virginia.

Perkins walked around behind the desk, pausing to inspect the diploma on the wall, the first he'd ever seen. He reached for the jar on the shelf and rattled the minié ball inside. "You were damned lucky," he said as he placed the jar back on the shelf.

"You were the lucky one," said Barnhill with a smile. "Lucky Sam."

"I reckon. Ever see any of the men?"

Barnhill shook his head. "No," he said, "though Will Barrett lives just outside of town."

"Micah Jenkins settled in Nacogdoches," said Sam. "Saw him the other day, and he asked about you."

Barnhill slumped in his chair and stretched his hands behind his head. "Those were fine men," he said. "Especially the ones who lasted till the end."

Perkins sat in a straight-backed chair facing the desk. "They would've kept on fighting," he said, "if it hadn't been for General Lee's order." He looked past Barnhill at the engraving of the beloved general. "So how do you tolerate it," he asked, "cooped up in a little office like this?"

Barnhill smiled. "I was never cut out to be a farmer," he said. "I prefer the company of my law books. I just wish there was more business. How are Aunt Julia and your father?"

"Fair to middlin', I suppose. Scrapin' by. But we should make a decent crop. And," Perkins said with a grin, "I'm gettin' hitched."

"Married?"

"Yep. To little old Martha Johnson. Her daddy has the cotton gin . . ."

"She's just a child."

"Nineteen."

"Sorry to interrupt, sir." Harrison stood awkwardly in the doorway. "Judge Withers is in his office."

"I'll be right there," said Barnhill, rising from his chair. "Well, congratulations, cousin," he said, reaching across the desk to shake hands. "You'll have to bring her for supper. Let Mother and Anna inspect the merchandise."

Once Barnhill had seen Sam to the sidewalk, he returned to his desk for a neat sheaf of papers, donned his coat, and strode to the corner office, where he found the compact Judge Withers at his broad desk, puffing on a cigar as he perused a day-old newspaper.

"That your cousin?" asked the judge, peering over the top of his paper.

"Yes, sir," said Barnhill, settling in an armchair.

"Fought in your regiment?"

"Yes, sir. Every engagement from Seven Pines to Petersburg, even Chickamauga, where I was absent. Lucky Sam, they called him. Never had more than a scratch."

Putting the paper aside, Judge Withers drew on his cigar and expelled a bluish cloud. "You have that brief?" Barnhill leaned forward and handed him the sheaf of papers, fifteen pages in his neat cursive script. As the judge slowly turned the pages, Barnhill sat quietly, one long leg draped over his knee, gazing absently out the window through which a cool breeze rustled the newspaper on the desk.

"Hmm," said Withers, thoughtfully rubbing his chin. "Almost a white-horse case." He turned to the final page and, when he had finished and carefully arranged the pages in a neat stack, said, "A fine piece of work, Jamie. Too bad there's not a Texas precedent, but that's to be expected. But that Ohio case, almost on all fours."

"It was a lucky find," said a plainly pleased Barnhill. "The court held the gravel from the pit constituted a chattel . . ."

"Subject to replevin," said the judge with a nod. "I'd like to have the petition ready to file this afternoon. And then we'll serve the writ on Mr. Thornberry."

"The widow Goldfarb will be pleased as punch," said Barnhill.

"She's crediting your rent?"

"Yes, sir. As part of your fee."

"Very well."

"Judge . . ." Withers looked Barnhill in the eye. "I was wondering when you were planning to propose my admission to the bar?"

"Soon enough. Is there some reason . . ."

Barnhill nodded. "I've decided to take on a case, an indigent case."

"What manner of case?" Withers leaned back in his chair and drew on the cigar.

"A man charged with murder. I intend to file a writ of habeas corpus."

"Who is this man?"

Barnhill hesitated and then said, "Jethro Banks."

Withers abruptly rose from his desk and began to pace. "Jethro Banks," he repeated, almost to himself. "Charged with killing that Union officer."

"Yes, sir."

Withers halted and stared at Barnhill with his penetrating blue eyes. "Why in the name of God would you agree to represent that scoundrel?"

"Look, Judge, he's a shiftless troublemaker. But it's the principle of the thing. That lawman doesn't have a scrap of evidence to implicate Banks. They might as well lynch him."

Withers stubbed out the cigar in a bronze ashtray and rested his palms on his desk. "Listen to me, son," he said. "Banks is one of these so-called Klansmen. The Ku Klux Klan, as they've taken to calling themselves. And there's no doubt in my mind they're the bunch who ambushed that officer."

"Well, then," said Barnhill, "the district attorney ought to be able to prove it. In a fair trial."

"A fair trial," said Withers with a shake of his silvery locks. "When you decide to take on that corrupt courthouse, you should choose an innocent man to defend, wrongly accused, and not some vigilante everyone in town knows is guilty."

"But, sir," said Barnhill, leaning forward in his chair, "don't you think it's just as important, or maybe more important, to give the man a fair trial, even if he's guilty? Otherwise, these men will just keep on . . ."

"That may be," said Withers, lowering himself in his chair. "But the Federals are determined to put these people out of business, and I don't blame 'em. They'll hang Jethro Banks to make a point. I'd strongly advise you to stay out of it. Pick a different fight, son."

"Yes, sir," said Barnhill, staring at his bootlaces.

"Now, let's get to work drafting our petition."

Barnhill sat with his back to the windows that opened to a pasture, facing the tenors on the opposite side of the music room that adjoined the small, whitewashed church. On his left sat two rows of sopranos, women ranging from their teens to their seventies, with the altos seated on his right. A choir of perhaps forty men and women, gathered on Sunday morning from the town and surrounding farms at the Laurel Grove Presbyterian Church. At the center of the room, with her worn volume of *The Sacred Harp*, 1860 edition, open on a music stand, stood Miss Ellen Graves, thin and erect with her graying hair in a bun, wearing a long black skirt and white blouse buttoned at the neck. "All right, then," she said with a smile, raising her hand as the singers rose from their chairs. The pianist in the corner played a simple chord, and on Miss Ellen's downbeat the choir, in rich, four-part harmony, sang:

> Just as I am without one plea
> But that Thy blood was shed for me,
> And that Thou biddest me come to Thee,
> O Lamb of God, I come, I come!

Following the "Amen," Miss Graves smiled and said, "Captain Barnhill? Would you care to lead us?"

Barnhill made his way around the others in the bass section and joined Miss Graves at the center of the room. Turning the pages of the venerable songbook to a personal favorite, he glanced at the music with its distinctive shaped notes. "Let's sing 'Jerusalem,'" he said. "Number 70." Waiting for the others to find their place, Miss Graves motioned to the pianist for the chord, raised her hand, and Barnhill, accompanied by the a cappella choir, sang:

> Jesus, my all, to heaven is gone,
> He whom I fix my hopes upon,
> The way the holy prophets went,
> The road that leads from banishment . . .

As he sang the closing bars of the final stanza, he noticed that Kate had slipped into the room and was standing by the door, watching him with a shy smile.

Miss Graves consulted a thin watch she slipped from her pocket and announced, "That's all we have time for this morning. Please leave your songbooks on the shelf on your way out." Amid the scraping of chairs and friendly banter, she turned to Barnhill and said, "May I have a private word with you, Captain?"

"Of course," he replied. "If you'll excuse me a moment." He walked over to Kate and asked her to wait for him in the narthex of the small chapel. Returning to Miss Graves, he said, "What is it, ma'am?"

"I'd appreciate your advice," she said in her no-nonsense manner. "You recall that I taught Bible classes on the plantations before the war. For the slave children."

Barnhill nodded and said, "As did my mother."

"I would like to offer such a class here, at the church," said Miss Graves.

"For the black children?"

"Yes."

"Well, ma'am," said Barnhill, "I'm not the best person to ask for advice. I'd think Reverend Blackmon . . ."

"He opposes it," she said flatly. "As do the elders. Let them go to Sunday school at their own churches, and so forth." Barnhill began to speak, but she cut him off. "The problem, Captain, is that the blacks are intimidated from even *attending* church. Most of them worshiped on the plantation, apart from that tiny black Baptist church outside town."

"I see," said Barnhill. "But why ask my opinion?"

"Because you're respected. They look up to you. And the poor children need help."

Barnhill considered. In the highly combustible atmosphere pervading the county, the idea of bringing black children to a white church might provoke violence. But coming from someone with the reputation and rectitude of Miss Ellen Graves, it might send a sorely needed gesture of reconciliation to both races. "All right," he said. "I'll speak to some of the elders about it."

"Thank you," she said with a smile. "And I so enjoy your singing. Your voice is truly a sacred harp. "

At the conclusion of the worship service in the sanctuary, in which the Reverend Blackmon, a thin, elderly man with long silver hair, had chosen for his text a passage from Jeremiah and likened the plight of the South to the tribulations of the Israelites in captivity in Babylon, Barnhill stood on the sunlit lawn outside the whitewashed building with Kate at his side, who lightly placed her hand on his arm, eliciting a disapproving look from his sister Anna. "Are we ready?" he said to his mother.

"I'm starved," said Anna. "I thought that sermon would never end."

After a journey of half an hour on dusty roads, Barnhill brought the two-seater surrey to a stop by the picket fence in front of the family homestead and helped the three women to climb down. "Wash up," said Mrs. Barnhill, "and dinner will be on the table directly."

Barnhill sat next to Kate, opposite his sister, with his mother on his right, inhaling the inviting aromas wafting from the kitchen, where Hattie, stooped with old age, could be heard softly singing to herself. After a moment the servant girl, wearing a starched white apron over her gingham frock, appeared in the doorway and announced that dinner was served. At his mother's request, Barnhill offered a blessing, giving thanks for the bounty of the table and their many blessings, not least, he considered, his budding romance with Kate.

"Amen," repeated Mary Barnhill. "Maggie," she said with a nod.

As the serving girl passed a platter of fried chicken, accompanied by sweet potatoes, creamed corn, and lastly, Hattie's flaky silver-dollar biscuits, Barnhill surveyed the dining room with its dull green paneling, gleaming mahogany, and old silver from Virginia, with a feeling of deep contentment. As he savored the chicken with cream gravy—drumsticks were his favorite—and biscuits, the women occupied themselves with small talk: who was getting engaged or expecting a baby, the peculiar hat Mrs. Davis had worn to church. "Well, Jamie," said Mary Barnhill during a pause, "how was the box singing this morning?"

"Right good," he replied as he reached to pour another glass of milk from the blue glass pitcher. "Apart from the sopranos screechin' on the high notes."

"I slipped in to listen," said Kate. "Miss Ellen had Jamie down to lead the choir."

"I'm not surprised," said Mary. "He has a beautiful voice. Like his father's." Anna responded with a sour expression.

"Sis," said Barnhill with a smile. "Would you pass the butter?" As he spread a pat on another biscuit, he said, "Speaking of Miss Ellen. She's planning to teach the black children Sunday school."

"Oh, really?" said Mary. "Whereabouts?"

"At the church," replied Barnhill.

"The church?" said Mary and Anna in unison as Kate laughed out loud.

"I don't see what's funny about that," said Barnhill. "Miss Ellen's determined to do something for them."

"They can go to their own church," said Anna.

Barnhill noticed the serving girl Maggie standing just beyond the entrance to the kitchen. "That's just the point," he said. "They *can't* go to their own church. Not with these damned Klansmen . . ."

"Jamie," said Mary sharply. "Mind your tongue."

"Miss Ellen asked for my help," he continued. "I intend to speak to the elders about it. I don't see why we couldn't bring the children to the church on Sunday afternoon." He looked Mary in the eye. "Perhaps, mother," he concluded, "you might want to help teach them."

Folding her napkin on the table, she met her son's gaze and said, "Perhaps."

Barnhill rose in the dark with a shiver, remembering the loud thunderclaps in the night and rain that lashed his boardinghouse window.

CHAPTER THIRTEEN

Striking a match, he lit the wick of the lamp on the dresser, splashed water on his face from the basin, and lathered his face with shaving soap. After several months at the law office he'd decided to shave the beard he'd grown at the university, leaving a neatly trimmed mustache and sideburns. Putting the razor aside, he toweled his face and reached for his shirt on the chair back. Stretching his arm into the sleeve, he winced at a sharp stab of pain in his shoulder. The old wound never failed to warn him of a change in the weather.

The skies outside were leaden, and a cold north wind swept the fallen leaves from the lawns and muddy streets. By the time he reached the office his hands were stinging from the cold. Stripping off his coat and hanging his hat on the stand in the corner, he inhaled the inviting aroma of brewing coffee. The judge kept a small woodburning stove in the storeroom in back, whose shelves were filled with case files and supplies. The clerk Harrison was bending over the stove, adding a few sticks of firewood to the potbelly. Drawing near, Barnhill felt the radiant heat and observed the coffee percolating in the spatterware pot. "Cold day," he said.

Startled, Harrison awkwardly stood up, nearly dropping the piece of wood cradled in his arm. "Uh, yes," he said. "Yes, sir, it sure is."

Barnhill studied the young man, with his perpetually cowed expression and tendency to bow when spoken to. A stint in the army, with its rigors, discipline, and comradeship would have done him a world of good. Reaching for a cup on the shelf above the stove, Barnhill tested the handle of the pot and then poured a cup, which he handed to Harrison.

"Why, thank you, sir," he said with another small bow.

"You don't need to call me sir, Harrison. Mr. Barnhill would be fine."

"Yes, sir."

Barnhill reached for another cup and helped himself to coffee, inhaling the aromatic vapors before taking a sip. "Good coffee," he said, "with a touch of chicory."

"Yes, ah, Mr. Barnhill. The judge orders it from New Orleans."

Barnhill nodded. After taking another sip, he said, "What are your plans, Harrison?"

"Plans? I'm not sure I . . ."

"For the future," said Barnhill. He put down his cup and warmed his hands at the stove. "What do you aim to do with yourself?"

"I don't rightly know."

"You should read the law," said Barnhill. "Study under the judge, and me, of course."

"Really?"

"Why not? I'll lend you Blackstone's *Commentaries* to get started. You can read it in your spare time."

"Why, thank you, sir," said Harrison. "I'd be much obliged."

Taking his cup, Barnhill gave Harrison a reassuring smile and went to his desk. After working for a half hour revising a trust indenture for an elderly farmer, he looked up to see Judge Withers standing in the doorway with a grim expression. "Mornin', Jamie," he said. "Let's visit in my office."

Though the windows were firmly shut, a cold draft seeped under the sill and rain beaded the panes. The expression in the judge's clear blue eyes was as frosty, Barnhill noticed, as the late November day. In the distance he could hear what sounded like hammer blows.

"Hear that?" asked Withers. Barnhill merely nodded. "They're building the gallows," said the judge.

"Oh," said Barnhill.

"I dropped by the courthouse on my way in. The clerk advised me the trial's set for ten o'clock this mornin'." Resting his arms on his knees, Barnhill stared dejectedly at the floorboards. "You've spoken with Jethro Banks?" asked Withers.

Looking up, Barnhill nodded and said, "I saw him yesterday."

"And . . ."

"I advised him I was not in a position to take the case."

"Good."

Barnhill exhaled audibly. "I hated to do it," he said. "He's a condemned man, without a lawyer . . ."

The judge withdrew a silver railroad watch from his waistcoat pocket and snapped open the cover. "Right about now," he said, "they're marching him into the courtroom. They'll pick a jury, and within the half hour he'll be tried for murder, convicted, and sentenced to death. As simple as that."

Barnhill met the judge's steady gaze. "I'm sorry," he said, "but I still don't feel right about it. Someone's got to take these men on."

Withers picked up a silver letter opener and tapped it on his palm.

"It's one thing," he said, "to take on the sheriff and the district attorney. A hopeless cause, just to make a point. And quite another," he cautioned, "to take on this pack of vicious dogs out to kill Yankees. Men like Mr. Jethro Banks."

Cold rain was falling in sheets as Barnhill stepped from the sidewalk onto the muddy street, obscuring his view of the hewn-pine gallows on the courthouse lawn where a large crowd was assembling, heedless of the miserable weather. When he reached McPherson's store he shook the rain from his hat and unbuttoned his ulster before letting himself in. The aisle was blocked by a heavyset man wearing a bright green jacket over his silk waistcoat and a brown derby perched on his large, round head, bending down to inspect a collection of china dishes. Noticing Barnhill, he stood up and clasped his hands over his ample belly. "Mornin'," he said with a broad smile. "Nice merchandise."

With a glance at the gold rings on both of the man's hands, Barnhill nodded and said, "Mornin'. Pardon me." He made his way past the man to the back of the store, where a petite young woman wearing a dark blue dress with matching hat and a red knitted shawl stood at the counter. As Barnhill walked up, she dropped a silver dollar on the floor, which he quickly knelt and recovered. Looking up, he instantly recognized Sally Porter, with the same pretty face and blond curls he'd known since they were in Sunday school together as children.

"Why, Jamie," she said, taking the coin and briefly holding his hand. "Lord have mercy."

"Hello, Sally," said Barnhill with a smile, noticing the soft kid gloves that reached her elbows. "I haven't seen you around town."

"I've just moved back. To be with Alex's parents."

Sally's husband Alex Porter, another of Barnhill's boyhood companions, had been killed in '64 in the fighting along the Red River. His family owned a cotton plantation, one of the largest in the area. "I'm glad to hear of it," he said.

"Hello, you two," said Kate, wearing a black muslin dress, standing in the doorway to the stockroom.

"Why, Kate," said Sally with mock reproach. "You didn't tell me Jamie was back in town." Giving Kate a knowing look, she took her purchases from the counter and bid them both a cheerful adieu. After a moment

Mr. McPherson emerged from the stockroom, peered at Barnhill with bloodshot eyes and, leaning a hand against the counter to steady himself, slowly moved to his stool.

"Good morning, sir," said Barnhill.

"Mornin'," said McPherson. He rubbed the white stubble on his chin and then lifted a glass of amber liquid from the shelf below the counter and took a large swig. The customer appeared and lowered a blue-willow-pattern soup tureen onto the counter. McPherson stared at him vacantly.

"How much?" inquired the customer.

"It should be marked," said Kate. "Three dollars fifty cents."

Reaching a hand into his pocket, the man produced a handful of silver dollars and counted out four. "Keep the change, missy," he said with a smile and wink.

"Much obliged," she replied as she scooped up the coins. After the customer started for the door, Kate whispered, "I don't know where these people get the money, but thank the Lord they're spending it."

"Working for our county judge, I reckon," said Barnhill. Looking at Kate with a serious expression, he said, "You're sure you want to do this?" Her lips pressed firmly together, she nodded. "You'll need a warm coat," he added. "And a hat."

"I have an umbrella," she said. "Father—we're going out. I'll be back after awhile. I'll lock up." Kate's father merely nodded and took another sip of his drink. Returning from the back wearing a long black coat buttoned up to her chin and a black silk scarf over her hair, Kate put her arm through Barnhill's and walked with him to the front. After locking the door, she handed him the umbrella, which he opened and held over their heads. "Ready?" he said.

Despite the thick curtain of rain, Barnhill could see that an entire troop of mounted cavalry lined the north end of the square, facing the gallows and the large crowd, perhaps the entire town, gathered on the lawn. For a moment he stopped and stared at the Federal troopers in their dark blue jackets and pale blue trousers with the yellow stripe, just as he remembered them mustered outside the redbrick courthouse at Appomattox. As he and Kate drew near, the crowd slowly parted, allowing the widow of Calvin Jones, escorted by a tall, handsome captain, to pass. The hand of the courthouse clock moved to one minute before noon as they took their place on the first row, within yards of the platform. The noose suspended from the gallows swung eerily in the gusting wind.

Precisely at twelve o'clock the sheriff, wearing a wide-brimmed black hat and long coat, emerged from the jail, briefly surveyed the large assemblage, and walked up the steps to the platform. He was followed by a delegation consisting of Archibald Newton and his underlings, and lastly the prisoner, hatless with his hands bound behind his back and legs in irons, slowly led by the deputy. The crowd remained silent amid the wind shaking the trees, as the line of grim-faced men ascended the platform. Within minutes the condemned man stood beneath the gallows, facing the crowd with a blank expression, the noose cinched tightly around his neck. As the sheriff stepped forward, clutching a sheet of rain-soaked paper, the deputy hurriedly fastened a hood over the prisoner's head. Raising his voice, the sheriff announced, "On the order of the District Court of San Augustine County, Jethro Banks, convicted of murder, shall hang by the neck until dead."

Barnhill turned to Kate, whose tears mingled with the raindrops on her cheeks, and gently squeezed her hand.

With a loud crash, the trapdoor opened, and the hooded figure dropped, twisting slowly in the wind before the hushed, angry crowd.

CHAPTER FOURTEEN

ENCLOSED BY A RUSTING WROUGHT-IRON FENCE, the new cemetery had been laid out on a low hill, cleared of pines, a mile out of town on the Carthage road, after the small churchyards had begun to fill up during the war and the townspeople had grown weary of daily reminders of the deaths of so many sons and husbands. Barnhill pushed open the gate and studied the modest row of grave markers amid the weeds, fallen leaves, and pine straw. Taking Kate by the arm, he walked slowly with her to the simple headstone where her father had been laid to rest. He stared at the inscription etched on the smooth gray granite—Donald R. McPherson, born March 11, 1816, died January 20, 1872—and shivered in the whipping wind, raw with moisture.

With a glance up at the pewter sky, Kate snuggled against Barnhill's wool coat and said, "Looks like it might snow."

"Wouldn't be surprised," he said, placing an arm around her shoulder. "We should get you out of the wind. Don't want you to catch cold."

Kate nodded. "Bye, Papa," she said, wiping away a tear before tossing a branch of viburnum on the mounded earth. After a moment, they turned and walked away, closing the gate with a parting look back at the fresh grave. Barnhill helped her up onto the seat of the buggy, climbed in beside her, and spread the thick blanket over their laps. With a slap of the reins he started the mare down the muddy track. Rain was falling by the time they turned on the highway; it soon turned to sleet clattering on the canvas top, and then, as they entered the driveway at the back of their two-story clapboard house, to wet snow, fat flakes that clung to the horse's black mane. Barnhill lifted Kate down and hurried her inside as he unhitched the mare and led her to the barn.

Barnhill had moved into the McPherson household following his marriage to Kate in the summer of '70. For a year and a half they'd shared the house with Kate's father, who often was too ill from his bouts of drinking to go to the store, either remaining in his upstairs bedroom or slouched in a chair in the parlor with a bottle and glass nearby. Now, at last, the house was beginning to feel like home, with Barnhill's growing collection of books on the shelves and favorite lithographs displayed on the walls of the parlor, which Kate had brightened with new wallpaper and fresh paint. Entering with an armload of wood, he knelt by the fireplace, arranged the logs, and struck a match to the fatwood kindling. He stood up, dusted his hands on his serge trousers, and smiled at Kate, who was sitting in her favorite armchair with her knitting in her lap. "Are you all right?" he asked. "Bring you anything? A glass of milk?"

"No, thank you. Not now anyways. I'm just feeling a little blue."

"Well, I don't blame you. Your first trip out there since . . . the funeral."

"Sometimes, Jamie," she said, putting her knitting aside, "I try to remember Papa back when Mama and Theo were alive, before the war. But I can't. I just remember that poor sick old man."

Barnhill walked over and gently put a hand on her shoulder. "I understand," he said. "But the day will come when you forget all that and remember the good times." With a glance at the cheerful fire blazing in the hearth, he said, "Why don't I fix us a pot of tea?"

He stared contentedly at the thickly falling snow swagging the pine boughs outside the window and listened to the clicking of the knitting needles and crackling of the logs as he sipped his cup of hot sugared tea. It was Sunday, and a melody refused to leave his head, one of the fine old hymns from the *Sacred Harp* songbook. He smiled inwardly as he thought of Miss Ellen leading the choir; she was his ideal of a true Christian woman dedicated to serving the Lord and caring for the least fortunate. Despite the opposition of the church elders and the occasional dark threats muttered by some of the low, violent men around town, she had calmly persevered in her determination to establish a Sunday school for the black children, which now, after almost two years, was an accepted feature of the small farming community. Barnhill silently recited Jesus's words to his disciples: "When I was hungry, you gave me meat; I was thirsty, and you gave me drink; I was a stranger, and you took me in; naked, and you clothed me; I was sick, and you visited me; I was in prison, and you came unto me . . . whatever you have done for the least of these, you have done it unto me . . ." Briefly closing his eyes, he thought of the Reverend Bryan and sweet little Dora. Of Robert Maxwell lying motionless on his pallet in the parlor.

Barnhill opened his eyes and looked at Kate seated by the fire with her ball of yarn, at peace now that the ordeal of caring for her poor father had ended, happily married, and . . . expecting their first child.

Though Sunday's snowfall, a good five inches, had largely melted, white patches remained in the crooks of the oak trees on the courthouse lawn and frosted the tops of the buggies parked on the square. Wearing a long black coat and leather gloves, his breath clouding before his face, Barnhill stood on the sidewalk outside the new gold-leaf sign on the window that read "Withers and Barnhill, Attorneys-At-Law." After a moment the clerk Harrison emerged, carrying a leather briefcase bulging with documents. "Ready?" said Barnhill.

"Yes, sir," replied Harrison with a nod.

Barnhill crossed the street, strode up the flagstone walk, and entered the two-story limestone courthouse, pausing to look at the Lone Star flag atop the cupola just as the clock over the tall doors struck the hour. He was a familiar and highly respected figure, eliciting courteous smiles from the men, black and white, employed in the tax assessor's and registrar's offices on the first floor, and a warm handshake from a fellow attorney he passed in the hallway. He was gaining a reputation as a gifted trial lawyer, beginning with his victory in the action for replevin and spreading rapidly with the verdict he obtained against Archibald Newton, the powerful county judge, for the damages caused to the widow Blount's fences and livestock by Newton's escaped bull. Barnhill had a natural way with the black jurors, most of whom knew him by name and held him in high esteem, and the fact that a jury of illiterate Negroes would return a verdict against the notorious carpetbagger had dumbfounded the townspeople. Thus Barnhill, early in his legal career, had exhibited both a scholarly knowledge of the law and a persuasive touch with a common jury.

CHAPTER FOURTEEN   161

Ascending the wide staircase with Harrison hauling the heavy briefcase and struggling to keep up, Barnhill felt a momentary rush, nervous anticipation mixed with excitement that reminded him of his feelings at the approach of battle. The previous day had been consumed selecting a jury, the tedious *voir dire* examination of the prospective jurors, predominantly black, selected from the voting rolls. Midway down the hall, he opened the frosted-glass door and surveyed the high-ceilinged courtroom: two heavy oak tables arranged before the elevated bench, the empty jury box on the left beneath a framed portrait of President Ulysses Grant, and the flag of Texas on the right of the witness stand. He strode down the aisle between the pew-like rows of seats, opened the gate, and walked to the table on the right—the plaintiff's table. Resting his palms on the smooth surface, he considered that today, at last, he would try the case he'd been carefully preparing for the better part of a year. As Harrison unpacked the contents of the briefcase—the petition, brief of the Texas citations, and various exhibits to be introduced as evidence—Barnhill removed the slender gold watch on a chain from his fob pocket and checked the time: 9:25 a.m.

"Oyez, oyez," called the bailiff, a rotund, balding man rumored to be a cousin of Archibald Newton from New England. "All rise!"

Barnhill stood, pushing back his chair with a scrape on the hardwood floor. Hooking his thumbs in his waistcoat, he watched as the judge entered from his chambers, ascended the bench, and sat in his tall, leather-upholstered chair. Herman Fischer, a short, bilious Pennsylvania Dutchman with thick ginger sideburns, had recently been elected district judge when the incumbent was appointed by the Republican governor to the state supreme court.

"Be seated," instructed the bailiff. Barnhill returned to his chair amid the low, murmured comments of the townspeople who packed the courtroom. He turned and smiled reassuringly at his client, Edwina Lucas, owner of the five-hundred-acre cotton plantation that adjoined Mountain Farm. Prim and erect, with steel-gray hair, she was seated on the first row flanked by her two sons, whose older brother, a friend of Barnhill since boyhood, had died in the Battle of the Wilderness. Barnhill briefly exchanged looks with the judge as the bailiff exited through a side door and returned after a moment with the twelve men of the jury. With the exception of a balding man dressed in a rough wool coat and trousers, all of the jurors, black and white, were wearing bib overalls, homespun shirts, and sturdy laced-up boots. Once they were seated in the box, looking uncomfortably around the crowded courtroom, Barnhill attempted to make eye contact with each of them; the first, subtle attempt to establish a connection, as if to say, "I trust you. Trust me."

With a rap of the gavel, Judge Fischer announced the style of the case, *Lucas v. Johnston,* and the assigned docket number. With a nod toward Barnhill, he said, "Mr. Barnhill, your opening statement."

Barnhill glanced at his opposing counsel, a team of three lawyers from Nacogdoches, the leading town of East Texas, and the defendant, a heavyset man in his midfifties wearing an expensive checked suit with a pearl stickpin through the satin tie knotted in his stiff, upturned collar, and black boots shined to a high gloss. Holding a single sheet of paper with his notes, Barnhill rose, smiled to the jurors, and began.

The case arose out of Barnhill's suspicion, based on information gleaned from Judge Withers, that powerful Northern railroad interests were manipulating the Reconstruction legislature to open a new line south from the Indian Territory, through Dallas, and on to Houston and the important port city of Galveston. Local speculators like Archibald Newton had tried, with limited success, to buy land cheap along the right-of-way from local farmers in dire need of cash. But others were more successful: strangers to the county, more polished, purporting to be mere businessmen, with ample financial resources; men such as Hiram Johnston, the defendant seated on the first row directly behind his attorneys.

As his first witness, Barnhill called his client, Mrs. Lucas, who, heeding Barnhill's instructions, looked the jurors squarely in the eyes and calmly testified that after receiving a letter from Mr. Johnston she agreed to meet with him at her home, where he identified himself as a businessman interested in purchasing land for investment. Barnhill introduced Johnston's letter into evidence as well as a contract for the purchase of 750 acres from Mrs. Lucas at the price of $1,875, or $2.50 per acre.

"And did you agree to the contract?" inquired Barnhill.

"Yes," answered the witness in a voice so soft the jurors leaned forward in their chairs to make it out.

"And how was the price to be paid?"

"Objection," said the portly, balding defense counsel, rising from his seat. "The document speaks for itself."

"I'm asking the plaintiff to explain her understanding of the terms," said Barnhill, "not to interpret the contract."

Looking down at the witness over the top of his spectacles, the judge said, "You may answer."

"Well," said Mrs. Lucas, "a little bit down. Two hundred as I recall. And then paid out over time."

"What period of time?" asked Barnhill.

"Your honor," said the defense lawyer testily, "we will stipulate that the contract provided for $200 down and the balance in equal annual installments over ten years."

"Very well," said Barnhill, grasping the lapels of his black frock. "A contract for deed, paid out over ten years, without interest. Did you discuss this with your boys, ma'am?"

"No, sir." She lowered her eyes.

"And you agreed?" The witness nodded. "And signed a deed?"

Looking up, she said, "Yes, sir."

Approaching the bench, Barnhill handed the judge a document, several pages in length, with a blue stamp on the lower right hand corner. "A certified copy of the deed, your honor," he said, "from the Registrar. Plaintiff's Exhibit 3."

"No objection," said the defense.

"Mrs. Lucas," said Barnhill mildly. "Would you tell the gentlemen of the jury what has happened to the land you sold to Mr. Johnston?"

Looking from Barnhill to the jurors and back again, she replied, "I don't rightly know."

"That's fine," said Barnhill. "No more questions. Pass the witness."

Rising from his place at the counsel table, the defense lawyer approached the witness and smiled indulgently. "Now, Mrs. Lucas," he began. "Your husband is deceased?"

"Yes, sir."

"He was a secessionist, was he not?"

"Objection, your honor," said Barnhill, quickly rising. "What possible relevance . . ."

"Overruled," said the judge harshly. "Answer the question."

Mrs. Lucas nodded and softly said, "Yes. Mr. Lucas supported secession."

"And," said the portly lawyer as he paced before the witness stand, "your boy fought in the Confederate army?"

Barnhill started to rise and lodge an objection but returned to his seat.

"Yes," replied Mrs. Lucas in a stronger voice. Turning toward the jury, she added, "And he died of wounds at the Wilderness in Virginia."

"And your other boys," said the lawyer, gesturing toward them. "Have they signed the oath?"

Barnhill shot up and said, "Your honor, what can this possibly have to do with the case? These boys were too young to vote at the end of the war. They . . ."

"No more questions," said the defense lawyer smugly. "Pass the witness."

Though the clerk Harrison's tendency to grovel was an annoyance to Barnhill, he had proven to be surprisingly adept at gathering information, perhaps because he was so unassuming. Acting on a hunch, Barnhill had dispatched him to Tyler, where the railroad interests were believed to have opened an office, to see what he could learn about Hiram Johnston, who had succeeded in purchasing a sizable swath of land to the west of San Augustine. Harrison had ingratiated himself with another young man employed at the Farmer's Bank & Trust, who confided in him that the Missouri, Kansas, and Texas Railway, or the "Katy," as the southern branch of the Union Pacific was now known, maintained large balances with the bank. At length, he had reluctantly provided Harrison with even more valuable intelligence regarding the railroad and Mr. Johnston.

Barnhill rearranged the papers on the counsel table and studied the jurors as they returned to their seats following an afternoon recess. The four white members of the panel remained aloof from their black counterparts, who seemed largely indifferent to the confusing dispute among white folks over the sale of a parcel of land. Barnhill gave the jurors a small, inscrutable smile, as if to indicate he was about to share a secret with them. The judge returned to the bench and said, "Mr. Barnhill. Your next witness."

With a glance at the well-dressed man seated to his left, Barnhill said, "Hiram Johnston."

After the witness was sworn, Barnhill looked him in the eye and said, "Now, Mr. Johnston, would you tell the court where you reside?"

"Tyler, Texas." Johnston seemed relaxed and confident, with arms folded across his broad chest.

"Are you a native of the state?" asked Barnhill.

"No, sir." Smiling briefly at the black jurors, he added, "I came to Texas from Ohio, after the war."

"What attracted you to Texas?" asked Barnhill.

"I am a businessman, sir," replied Johnston. "I believe there is great opportunity here."

"I see," said Barnhill, "though you might get an argument on that subject from some of *our* people." He briefly made eye contact with the white farmers on the jury, who appeared to be following the colloquy with great interest. "And that is your occupation?" asked Barnhill. "Businessman?"

The witness nodded. "I am an investor. In land."

"A speculator?"

The defense counsel rose and uttered, "Objection."

"I withdraw the question," said Barnhill. "Now, Mr. Johnston, in addition to the land you purchased from Mrs. Lucas, how much other land have you bought in this part of the state?"

"Oh, I don't rightly know," said Johnston. "Maybe four or five thousand acres."

Even the judge raised his eyebrows at this revelation as the white jurors exchanged looks of astonishment. "And your intention," asked Barnhill, "in buying all this land?"

"As I said," replied the witness with a bored expression. "For investment."

"And what has become of this land? Have you sold any of it?" Johnston responded with a shrug. Barnhill looked to the judge and said, "May I approach the witness?" Handing Johnston a document, he said, "Would you tell the court what this is?"

The witness scratched his chin, hesitated, and said, "A deed."

"A deed for the same 750 acres you purchased from Mrs. Lucas, is it not?"

"Your honor, I object," said the defense counsel. "I fail to see why we're goin' down this rabbit trail . . ."

"Overruled," said the judge.

"So what if it is?" said Johnston.

"Would you tell the gentlemen of the jury the name of the buyer of the property, and the price you were paid?"

The witness pursed his lips, looked to his lawyer, and then said, "The Missouri, Kansas, and Texas Railway. At a price of four dollars an acre."

"Three thousand dollars," said Barnhill. "In cash, correct?" The witness nodded. "A tidy profit," said Barnhill, "for a parcel of timberland you bought from Mrs. Lucas for $200 down."

"A man's entitled to a fair profit," countered Johnston. "Besides," he volunteered, "it was eminent domain."

"Thank you, sir," said Barnhill, "for that bit of information. You see,"—he turned to the jury—"the legislature in Austin has passed a bill giving this railroad—the 'Katy' I believe they call it—the right to build a line through East Texas. And the power to buy land for the right-of-way, what's known as 'eminent domain.' And pay for it with public funds."

The chief defense lawyer slumped back in his chair, scowling.

"Now, Mr. Johnston," said Barnhill. "I wonder if you could identify this document."

The witness accepted a single typewritten sheet and examined it. "I never seen this before," he said after a moment.

Retrieving the paper, Barnhill said, "Your honor, this is a certified copy of a resolution passed by the Board of Directors of the Missouri, Kansas, and Texas Railway Company on November 11, 1869. Obtained from the files of the Farmers Bank & Trust of Tyler, Texas. The vice president of the bank is here in the courtroom, prepared to testify to its authenticity." He walked slowly to the defense table and handed it to the scowling lawyer. "Move to admit the bank resolution," said Barnhill. "Plaintiff's number four."

After allowing the judge briefly to inspect the document, Barnhill faced the jurors and said, "When a corporation, such as this railroad corporation, opens a bank account, the bank requires a so-called resolution indicating which of its officers have authority to sign on the account." He paused, noting that most of the jurors indicated their comprehension with a nod. "And in this particular resolution," said Barnhill, "one of the officers of the Katy Railroad authorized to sign on the account was an assistant vice president by the name of . . . Hiram Johnston." Barnhill held up the document before the jurors. "This," he said, tapping on the paper, "is his signature." Turning to the witness, he said, "You, sir, are the officer of the railroad named in this resolution, are you not?"

An audible murmur passed through the courtroom. "You see," said Barnhill, facing the jurors, "the railroad, acting through its officer, Mr. Johnston, induced my client, Mrs. Lucas, to sell them her land for far less than it was worth, by concealing the fact that the buyer, supposedly Mr. Johnston but in truth the railroad, was their employee." At this a number of jurors nodded in vigorous agreement. "And for his effort, Mr. Johnston pocketed a large windfall, paid for by the taxpayers of Texas." Approaching the bench, Barnhill said, "Your honor, I move for a directed verdict. For the amount of the ill-gotten profit on my client's land, with interest. For fraud and deceit. And, I might add, for flagrant illegality on the part, not only of the defendant, but of his employer, the Katy Railroad."

After a feeble effort to object, the other lawyer remained in his chair, stunned and immobile, as the judge hurried from the courtroom filled with the boisterous cries of the spectators. Barnhill warmly thanked Harrison and slowly made his way down the center aisle. Waiting for him by the door was a tall man, unfamiliar to Barnhill, with side-whiskers and a neatly trimmed mustache, clad in an immaculate black wool frock and crimson waistcoat. "My congratulations, sir," he said as Barnhill walked up, "on an impressive victory." He reached out to shake Barnhill's hand.

"Why, thank you," said Barnhill.

"My name's Parker," said the other. "Addison Parker. My card." He produced an engraved card from his breast pocket and handed it to Barnhill. "I'd appreciate it if you'd drop by my office when you have a spare moment."

CHAPTER FIFTEEN

BARNHILL STOOD AT THE DOOR, RAISED HIS FIST TO KNOCK, then thought better of it. The two-story house was freshly painted white, with dark green shutters and trim. He straightened his coat, turned the bronze door handle, and let himself in. In the dim light he observed an old man, with long snow-white hair, seated at a writing desk; possibly hard of hearing, he took no notice of the visitor. The small anteroom was elegantly appointed in dark walnut, with a thick Persian carpet and furniture upholstered in green leather. Slipping off his hat, Barnhill cleared his throat and said, "Good morning."

The old man put aside his quill and gave Barnhill a curious look. "May I help you?" he asked after a moment.

"I'm here to see Mr. Parker," said Barnhill. "He asked me to drop by."

"I see. Your name?"

"James Barnhill."

Rising from the desk, the old man, presumably Parker's secretary, said, "Have a seat, Mr. Barnhill. I'll let him know you're here."

Sinking into a plush armchair, Barnhill crossed one boot over his knee and inhaled the aroma of abraded leather. He glanced at the painting over the fireplace, a portrait of a distinguished-looking gentleman who bore a vague resemblance to the man who'd introduced himself at the courthouse. Barnhill knew little about Addison Parker, apart from the fact that he was new to the county, had established an office in the house on Houston Street, and was rumored to have made a large fortune during the war. The secretary reappeared, held open the heavy mahogany door to the hall, and said, "Mr. Parker will see you now."

Barnhill ascended a wide staircase to the second floor, where he found the door open to Addison Parker's office, a spacious room overlooking the street with another Persian carpet over the wide floorboards and bookcases filled with leather-bound volumes. Parker, who was wearing an expensively tailored coat with a stiff collar and black silk tie, was seated at an elaborately carved mahogany desk. As Barnhill entered he rose from his chair and extended a hand. "Good morning, sir," he said. "Have a seat." Barnhill sat in one of the chairs facing the desk and briefly studied Parker, whom he judged to be in his midfifties, heavyset with thick, dark hair streaked with gray and a neatly trimmed mustache and goatee.

"I appreciate your coming by," began Parker. "I was very impressed by your handling of the Lucas case. The cupidity of these railroad scoundrels is remarkable. You'd have thought that man Johnston would've had sense enough to use a straw man."

"Well," said Barnhill, "our people are generally honest and trusting, but easily duped, I'm afraid."

Parker spread his palms on the desk and gave Barnhill an appraising look. "You served as an officer in Hood's Brigade?" he said after a moment.

"That's right," replied Barnhill, noticing Parker's immaculately trimmed and polished nails.

"Twice wounded," said Parker, "and greatly admired by the men, as I understand it." Barnhill met his steady gaze. "And," concluded Parker, "an honors graduate of the University of Virginia."

"Well, sir," said Barnhill, "you appear to know quite a bit about me."

"I'm careful, especially when it comes to choosing men in whom I intend to place great confidence."

"I see," said Barnhill. "Perhaps you could tell me . . . about yourself?"

"Fair enough," said Parker. He opened a burl elm box and removed a cigar. "Smoke?" he said. Barnhill shook his head. After biting off the tip, Parker struck a match and lit his cigar. Expelling a cloud of bluish smoke, he said, "I came to Texas in '54. From Ohio. Settled in Austin and went into banking. Like Governor Houston, I was strongly opposed to secession."

"Many men were," said Barnhill.

"First and foremost," continued Parker, "I'm a businessman, not a moralist. The South desperately needed arms, and Mexico was the logical source. I provided the capital and arranged the shipment of large quantities of rifles, cartridges, and powder across the Rio Grande." Parker drew on his cigar and expelled another puff of smoke.

"No offense, sir," said Barnhill, "but I'm surprised the Federals didn't have you arrested."

"I was discreet in my dealings," said Parker, "and never ceased to voice my opposition to Southern independence."

Barnhill was offended by the older man's war profiteering and dismissive attitude toward the Confederate cause. He considered raising an objection, but instead said, "What brought you to East Texas?"

"The longleaf pine," replied Parker. "The greatest stands of timber in North America, in my estimation."

"Folks around here," said Barnhill, "regard the pine forest as something that's only good for bear and deer hunting. Too much trouble to clear, with soil that's no good for growing cotton."

"Cotton," said Parker with a frown. "King Cotton. What brought all these poor blacks to the Gulf States and caused the war."

"Sir, I must object," said Barnhill. "The war . . ."

"You'd have thought the planters," continued Parker, "would have turned to something else when their glorious cause was finally crushed, but, no. The Negroes, in theory, may be free, but they're right back to picking their masters' cotton."

Barnhill found himself disliking and agreeing with Parker at the same time. Rubbing his chin, he said, "You strike me as an educated man."

"Harvard College," said Parker proudly. Barnhill noticed the Phi Beta Kappa key that hung from a chain on his waistcoat. "You and I may be the only college men in the county, Barnhill."

"So what do you aim to do with the pine forest?" asked Barnhill.

"As you well know," said Parker, "the Northern railroad interests are building new lines—financed with state bonds and watered stock—that ultimately will open commerce from the port at Galveston as far north as St. Louis and Chicago. There are vast quantities of virgin timber in East Texas. I intend to purchase as much land as possible and mill lumber on a large scale."

"Very ambitious," said Barnhill, "particularly in times like these. But what is it you wanted to discuss with me?"

"I hardly need to tell you that these railroad men are utterly corrupt. I will not resort to bribery or graft. I have the resources to fight them, if necessary, and I think you're the lawyer to take them on."

"Well, sir," said Barnhill. "Though I thoroughly disagree with your views on the war—Lincoln should've let the South go in peace, and frankly the blacks would be far better off—I share your opinion of the cotton economy. I'd be pleased to have you as a client."

"Excellent," said Parker with a smile. "I'd suggest a retainer of $200 a month for the first year. You can charge your services against it and bill for any overages."

"Most generous," said Barnhill.

"Very well," said Parker. "Draw up a contract and we'll sign it in the morning."

Barnhill rose, clasped Parker's hand, and said, "Thank you, sir."

Arriving home at the unusually early hour of four, Barnhill bounded up the steps to the porch and hurried inside. "Kate!" he called out, glancing around the empty parlor. "Kate! I've got good news!" He paused at the foot of the stairs, thinking he heard low voices from an upper room. Taking the stairs two at a time, he strode to their bedroom, halting in the doorway. Kate was lying in bed propped up on pillows, her face pale and auburn hair dark with perspiration. Dinah, the young black servant, was seated at her bedside with a worried expression.

"Ohh," said Kate, wincing in pain.

"What is it, sweetheart?" said Barnhill, hurrying to her.

"Why, it's the baby," said Dinah. "The baby's comin'!"

"The baby?" said Barnhill. "Dinah," he commanded, "run along and send for Doc Smithers. And then put some water on to boil."

"Yes, sir."

"Oh, Kate," said Barnhill, bending down and gently touching her cheek. Squeezing his hand, she gave him a wild look and then gasped with the next contraction. Within ten minutes the doctor arrived, accompanied by his black midwife, who banished Barnhill to the parlor, firmly closing the door behind him.

It proved to be a long and difficult labor, reaching into the small hours of the morning. When the clock over the mantel chimed four times, Barnhill looked up from his chair, wearing the same rumpled clothes he'd dressed in that morning, unable to rid his mouth of the sour aftertaste of cigars and black coffee. Dear God, he prayed, squeezing his eyes shut. Please, dear God, spare my wife and bring my child safe into this world. He opened his eyes and slowly exhaled. It was just like he'd prayed all through the war, not really believing that Almighty God could be swayed by a poor man's plea, but pleading nevertheless with enormous conviction. And then he was startled by the sound, unmistakable, the piercing cry of a newborn. Racing up the stairs, he threw open the door to the bedroom. Kate cradled the child in her arms, her face drawn yet radiant. The doctor, with sleeves rolled up and hands covered in blood, stood at the bedside with a satisfied if exhausted expression. Barnhill slowly walked forward and looked from the tiny face of the child to Kate, who managed a weak smile.

"Jamie," she whispered. "We've got a son."

The upstairs sewing room had been transformed into a nursery, with the old cradle Barnhill had brought from the attic at Mountain Farm, a rocking chair, and a cot for a black woman named Annie he'd engaged to help with the baby and, if need be, double as a wet nurse. Barnhill had supposed that Kate would prefer to nurse the child, but in the first weeks she seemed exhausted, preferring to allow the child to suckle at the ample breast of the nurse than to rise from her bed in the middle of the night. Barnhill, however, was unconcerned by Kate's evident lack of interest in the baby, so awed was he by the transformation of their lives, taking every opportunity to hold the baby in his arms as he gently rocked in the chair, softly singing the lullabies he remembered from his own mother, gazing into the child's dark, inscrutable eyes. His son. James Madison Barnhill Jr.

Rising at first light on a late May morning, Barnhill ground the coffee and struck a match to the kindling in the kitchen stove. He sat down at the small enameled table, inhaling the faint lemony bouquet of the magnolias through the open window and listening to the carol of the songbirds. As daylight and the aroma of brewing coffee filled the room, he was conscious of a feeling of deep contentment, with his wife and baby safely asleep upstairs, a steady income from his law practice filling his bank account, and a growing reputation among the upstanding men of the community. When the percolating coffee subsided, he poured a cup and turned to see Kate standing in the doorway, clutching her dressing gown to her breast, her long, uncombed auburn hair lying on her shoulders. "Good mornin'," he said with a smile. "I didn't hear you come down."

"I tippy-toed," she said quietly, moving into the kitchen and sitting at the table. "Didn't want to wake up the baby."

Barnhill rose, poured her a cup of coffee, and placed it on the table. "Why not?" he said. "Annie can look after him."

"We can't keep that gal forever, Jamie. And I scarcely know what to do."

"But Kate." Barnhill sat down beside her. "You can learn. Just get Annie to show you."

"I don't know," said Kate, closing her eyes and massaging her brow. "I'm just so tired."

"You'll get your strength back," he said, patting her hand. "And you'll do fine with the baby."

Three months passed, long months of summer torpor, and a return to the quotidian rhythms of life before the war, of sweltering days, with blacks and poor whites toiling in the cotton fields, and evenings on porches, refreshed by cooling breezes, listening to the shrill chorus of the cicadas and the plaintive calls of the mourning doves. Only a vestige remained of the detested Yankee occupation, with the retirement of the Federal cavalry following their ruthless suppression of the so-called Klansmen, and even the departure of the hated Sheriff Dinwoody and his deputy, though Mr. Newton, a master of patronage, had clung to his powerful position as county judge. Sunday mornings found Barnhill and Kate in the family pew at the Presbyterian Church, followed by a fried chicken dinner with his mother and sister at Mountain Farm. The wet nurse was long since gone, replaced by young Dinah, who'd been raised the eldest of nine children and consequently had ample experience both with housework and caring for babies. Barnhill, laboring under the misapprehension that Kate was as satisfied as he with their good fortune, worked tirelessly to advance the interests of his wealthy client, examining title to the tens of thousands of acres of pine forests Addison Parker was amassing and frequently sparring in court with the railroad's lawyers. Hard work, for Judge Withers had now retired—and the satisfaction of an income sufficient to support his mother and sister and surprise Kate with a new set of English bone china—had convinced Barnhill that their marriage was thriving, despite Kate's perplexing lack of interest in domestic life. She was, Barnhill reasoned, still grieving for her father, and lonely, with few other young women to befriend in the small town.

Barnhill was troubled by a vague premonition—reminiscent of the sensation of imminent danger he'd experienced during the war—as he unlatched the picket gate. At the end of another long, oppressively hot day, the still air had the heavy, charged feeling that often preceded a sudden, violent thunderstorm. As he mounted the steps to the front porch he observed that the door was slightly ajar, triggering another pang of unease. "Kate," he called as he stepped inside. He paused to listen but heard only the sound of the baby crying from somewhere in the back of the house. "Kate?" he called again, stepping over a small pile of infant clothing and toys strewn over the parlor floor. He found his six-month-old child alone in the crib in the small room adjoining the kitchen, his chubby face red from crying. Reaching down to lift him, Barnhill turned his face away from the stench of the child's dirty diaper. "Poor baby," he murmured, trying to quiet him. "Where's your mama?"

"I'll take him," said Kate, suddenly appearing in the doorway. Her voice had a hard, defensive edge.

Holding the child, Barnhill briefly studied her: pale and disheveled, barefoot, her hair uncombed, and wearing her father's frayed robe. "Are you all right?" he asked. "And where's Dinah? The house is a mess."

"I gave her the afternoon off," said Kate wearily as she walked over and reached for the baby.

Reluctantly surrendering the child, whose crying intensified, Barnhill said, "He needs a change, and probably a . . ."

"Don't tell me," said Kate with asperity, "how to tend to the baby. What do you suppose I do all day?" She turned her back on Barnhill and hurried from the room.

Listening to her footsteps on the stairs, Barnhill sighed and walked absently back to the parlor, where he stooped down to pick up the clothes, baby blanket, and toys. Before the arrival of the baby he considered the room something of a sanctuary, with his beloved books on the shelves, his favorite lithograph over the mantel, and easy chair in the corner for reading or enjoying a cigar and whiskey in the evenings. He resented Kate's carelessness and regarded her neglect of the baby as inexcusable. Restoring a semblance of order to the room, he listened as the child's crying subsided. After a few minutes Kate descended the stairs, cradling the baby nursing at her breast. Giving her a reproachful look, Barnhill said, "Would you care for a glass of lemonade?" A loud clap of thunder shook the house, causing the baby to wail.

"Would you stop it?" said Kate. "I'm sick of this crying."

"He can't help it," said Barnhill, listening to the wind in the trees outside the window and the hard downpour of rain.

"Well, *I* can't abide it!"

Barnhill felt a flush like the sting from a hard slap and glared at Kate. Bursting into tears, she ran from the room, clutching the bawling child. After a moment he found her cowering in a corner of the kitchen. "I'm sorry, Kate," he said softly. Another crash of thunder rattled the window. She merely nodded, the tears wetting her cheeks. "Why don't you sit down," he suggested, "and nurse the baby. I'll bring you that glass of lemonade."

After a while, greedily suckling at Kate's breast as she lightly stroked his head, the baby quieted and then fell asleep. Barnhill sat in his easy chair, a book open in his lap, listening to the rain dripping from the trees and watching mother and child with a troubled expression.

In the days that followed, he arranged for Dinah to stay with the baby while Kate rested in the afternoon. And each night before going to sleep, Barnhill knelt at his bedside and prayed to God to help his wife learn to care for her child.

Emerging from Dr. Smithers's office a block off the town square, Kate glanced furtively down the sidewalk and patted the hard object in her purse as she started for home. She knew something of the patent medicine from talk among ladies in the store, but her interest had been piqued by an advertisement in a recent issue of *Women at Home,* assuring readers that the nostrum was remarkably effective for the treatment of such diverse ailments as toothache, diarrhea, and melancholia. Dr. Smithers preferred the term "neurasthenia," a common malady, he assured her, among new mothers, and counseled the use of the elixir in small doses when suffering from the "blues." Entering the house by the kitchen door, she spoke briefly with Dinah at the stove and then quietly ascended the stairs, relieved to find the baby asleep in the nursery. With the bedroom door closed firmly behind her, Kate took the brown bottle from her purse and studied the label: "Laudanum, Tincture of Opium." She carefully measured two drops of the amber liquid in a glass of water, as the doctor recommended, swallowed the draught, and lay down on her bed to rest.

Concerned about Kate's fragile condition and leaving the affairs of his clients, not least Addison Parker, unattended for several days, Barnhill reluctantly accepted an invitation to join his old commanding officer, Harry Sellers—now a successful cotton broker in Beaumont—on a hunting trip to the Big Thicket, a large expanse of pine wastes, cypress groves, and swamps with one of the largest concentrations of black bears in North America. Barnhill drew a bead down the open sight of his new Winchester repeating rifle, still redolent of the Cosmoline grease it was packed in. Taking an oily rag, he polished the finely blued barrel and worked the lever action. He placed the rifle in its leather case, slung the pouch filled with boxes of ammunition over his shoulder, and loaded them in the wagon at the back of the house with his tent, bedroll, and lantern. He turned to see Kate standing on the back porch, with seven-month old "little Jim" on her hip, smiling in the bright October sunshine.

"Bye baby bunting," she sang out, "Daddy's gone a-hunting."

"To get a little rabbit skin," Barnhill sang along, "to wrap his baby bunting in." He walked over and gave Kate a peck on the cheek. "You're sure you'll be all right?" he asked, patting the smiling boy's fat thigh.

"I'll be fine," she replied. "Maybe it's the change in the weather, but I feel happier than since I don't know when."

Hearing hoofbeats, Barnhill watched as his cousin Sam Perkins dismounted from a tall black colt at the entrance to the drive. "Well, Kate," he said, "we'd best be on our way."

"Y'all be careful," she said, "and bring home a bearskin for the baby to lie on."

The hunting party consisted of Barnhill, Sam Perkins, Major Sellers, another officer from the old regiment, a cook, three skinners, and one of the regiment's scouts, who owned some of the finest bear hounds in the state. They made the all-day journey on horseback south to the Thicket, where a half-Coushatta Indian guide accompanied them to their campsite deep in the pine forest. Rising at the crack of dawn on clear, cold mornings, they tracked bears in two-man teams, following the hounds, returning to camp for a late lunch and afternoon nap before a final two hours of hunting before sunset. The Thicket was teeming with game, and despite the hardships of hunting in dense undergrowth and miry sloughs, the dogs pursued their quarry, the men were excellent marksmen, and at the end of the second day, the hides of over twenty black bears lay neatly stacked at the campsite.

The men whiled away the evenings on stools around a blazing campfire, drinking copious amounts of Kentucky bourbon and recounting the war, particularly amusing or terrifying anecdotes, and the sorrowful remembrance of the many comrades who perished. Sam Perkins sat quietly, nursing his drink and staring into the embers. Well, Barnhill considered, Sam's celebrated luck had run out, as his young wife had perished in an outbreak of typhoid fever the same week the family cotton gin had been forced into bankruptcy.

On the final night of the outing, a lively discussion ensued over Longstreet's refusal to grant Hood's request to mount an attack on Big Round Top on the second day at Gettysburg, with the former scout narrating his mission to reconnoiter the summit of the hill, unoccupied by Federals, and the Major's riveting account of his ride to Longstreet's headquarters to plead, futilely, for permission for the attack to go forward.

"I'm convinced," said Barnhill as he tossed back the last of his drink, "it was the deciding moment of the war. If we'd taken that tall hill . . ."

"We'd a taken it, by golly," declared the scout.

" . . . we would've rolled up the Federal flank."

"Just," said Major Sellers, "as Marse Robert intended. Goddam Old Pete," he added with a shake of his head. "Stubborn as a mule."

Staring into the fire, rubbing his throbbing shoulder, Barnhill visualized the regiment's pell-mell charge up that boulder-strewn hillside and considered . . . what might have been.

Nearing the end of the long homeward journey, with the mule-drawn wagons carrying the hides and meat creaking under their load, Barnhill parted company with his comrades at a fork in the highway, vowing to return to the Thicket for another bear hunt a year hence. Darkness had fallen as he made his solitary way along the road northeast toward San

Augustine, illuminated by the quarter moon and brilliant stars in the black sky, and both he and his horse were impatient for the meal and familiar beds that awaited them at home. Consulting his pocket watch by the light of a match, Barnhill turned the nervous animal off the road onto a shortcut through the forest, whose towering canopy blotted out all moon and starlight. "Easy girl," he said reassuringly with a pat on the mare's neck as he listened to an owl's screech and struggled to see what lay in their path. "Just a little while, and we'll . . ."

Barnhill brought the horse to a sudden halt with a jerk on the reins. Through the thick trunks of the pines, he could see, perhaps two hundred yards in the distance, a brightly burning bonfire, and the forms of men, many men, silhouetted against the flames. He instinctively reached for the stock of the Winchester in its scabbard at his thigh and checked to make sure it was loaded. With a gentle kick, he started the mare forward again. At a distance of fifty yards from the bonfire he could see that a large number of men were gathered in a clearing, wearing hoods over their heads and many draped in sheets. Loud voices—laughter, catcalls, shouts—filled the night air: the sound of drunken revelry. Curiosity trumping a powerful sense of danger, Barnhill slowly rode forward until he was within yards of the clearing's verge. And then, with a sharp intake of breath and a pounding of his heart, he discovered the object of the spectacle: a black man, facing backward on an unsaddled horse with a noose around his neck.

CHAPTER SIXTEEN

THOUGH HIS HANDS WERE BOUND, the man was not blindfolded, and he stared at the hooded men encircling the horse with abject terror in his wide-open eyes. Barnhill knew those eyes, clearly recognized the face. It was Ernest Wilson, who had spent his first twenty-odd years as a slave on the Barnhill family plantation. Several years younger than Barnhill, they had grown up together on the farm—fishing, swimming, attending Bible classes taught by Mrs. Barnhill—until social convention dictated they part. And, Barnhill knew as he spurred his horse into the clearing, Ernest Wilson was a decent, law-abiding man.

Startled by the sudden appearance of the rider, the men grew quiet and slowly retreated. A tall man, the evident ringleader, pulled a revolver from his waistband, aimed it at Barnhill, and said, "Hold it right there, mister," in a surprisingly high-pitched voice.

Barnhill saw that the rope around Ernest's neck was looped over the bough of a sturdy live oak and estimated the number of men—at least twenty, many brandishing firearms. "What's this all about?" he said as calmly as possible, briefly making eye contact with Ernest, who wisely remained silent.

"Goddam nigger raped a white woman," said the man holding the revolver, eliciting chuckles from many of the others, obviously intoxicated. "Gonna string 'im up," he added sneeringly.

"Put down that gun," said Barnhill as his horse stamped nervously and shook her head.

The man responded by cocking the hammer with a *click* that could be heard above the hiss and crackle of the bonfire.

"I said, put down the gun," repeated Barnhill, keeping the horse on a tight rein.

A man on Barnhill's left suddenly whipped off his hood, drew a pistol from his belt, and trained it on the ringleader. "When Cap'n Barnhill gives an order," he said loudly, "you goddam better obey it!"

Looking from the man—a poor farmer named Kyle who'd served all through the war as a private in the Fifth Texas—to Barnhill, the leader slowly lowered his revolver. "You'd better move along, mister," he said to Barnhill. "This ain't none of your business."

"I know this man," said Barnhill, pointing to Ernest. "Known him all my life. And I'm not about to let you lynch him." In a swift motion, he pulled the Winchester from its scabbard and worked the lever.

"Sorry, Cap'n," said Kyle, still aiming his pistol at the leader.

"Hey," yelled a man from the shadows. "This nigger raped a white gal! You think we're gonna let 'im go free?" The question drew a chorus of groans.

"It's about time," said Barnhill in a firm voice, sitting tall in the saddle, "we had law and order in this county. We've got an honest sheriff now, and a judge elected by the people, *our* people. You say this man's guilty of rape. Well, then, take him to jail, and then let him stand trial."

The lust for violence, at its fever pitch, on a dark night lit by a bonfire, makes ordinary lust seem mild by comparison. It swept over the mob, which surged forward, shouting, "No, goddammit!" and "Hang him!"

Firing a shot that echoed in the still air, Barnhill said, "Take the prisoner's horse, private, and follow me."

With Barnhill aiming his Winchester at the hooded ringleader, Kyle quickly obeyed, unslipping the rope from the bough, yanking the horse's halter from the hands of one of the men, and leading the horse away from the clearing.

"You men go on home," said Barnhill. "I'm taking this man to jail, where he'll be arraigned in the morning on the charge of rape, assuming any of you brave men is willing to come forward without a sack over your head, and press charges." He spurred his horse from the clearing, with Kyle and Ernest Wilson close behind.

Not brave, but impelled by indignation and venom, the ringleader himself—a burly blacksmith by the name of Willoughby, accompanied by two comrades—appeared before the sheriff the following morning and swore out a formal complaint. Within the hour the accused stood before the district judge, was formally charged with aggravated rape, a capital offense, and ordered imprisoned without bail. Barnhill sat across the desk from the new sheriff—John Clark, a native of San Augustine and long-time acquaintance—and draped one long leg over his knee. After lighting a cheroot, Barnhill said, "Seems a trifle odd for an accusation of rape to come from someone other than the victim."

"No more odd than the rest of this case," said Clark, a portly, middle-aged man whose thick, drooping mustache contrasted with his completely bald pate. "Rescuing this Negro from a lynch mob and rousing me in the middle of the night? But as for the victim, these fellers naturally claim to be defending her honor."

"Her honor," muttered Barnhill. "Lucy Grimes, as easy a tumble in the hayloft as any gal in the county."

"But married now," countered Clark, "to Billy Ray Patterson, who's as ornery and hot-tempered as they come."

"Listen, John," said Barnhill, expelling a puff of smoke. "I know Ernest Wilson, known him all my life. And I don't believe this cock-and-bull story that he sneaked into her bedroom. It don't add up."

The sheriff stroked his mustache and then spread his palms on the surface of his oak desk. "Take my advice, Jamie," he said, "and don't get mixed up in this. It'll be nothing but trouble."

"That may be," said Barnhill. He slowly stood up and stubbed out the cigar in a brass ashtray on the corner of the desk. "But I intend, at the very least, to interview Ernest. With your permission," he added.

"Oh, all right," said Clark sourly. "But don't forget I warned you."

Ernest Wilson sat on the hard board cot in the weak light from the small, begrimed window at the top of his cell, resting his back against the wall with his knees pulled up to his chest. When the door to the hallway opened, admitting a slant of light, he squinted and a smile of recognition lit up his face.

"Thank you, sir," said Barnhill as he looked around the cramped space. "If you don't mind, I'd like to interview Mr. Wilson in private."

"Mr. Wilson," grumbled the deputy before letting himself out and firmly closing the door behind him.

"Praise the Lord," said Ernest in an excited whisper.

"Hold on a minute," said Barnhill as he sat on a stool several feet from the cell. Finding a candle on a small table, he struck a match, lit the candle, and then removed a writing tablet and pencil from his leather case. In the flickering light, he looked the black man in the eye and said, "Before we get started, I should warn you that anything you tell me . . . Well, could possibly be used against you, Ernest."

"Why should I tell you anything but the truth?" asked Ernest with a puzzled expression.

"Even the truth," said Barnhill. "Until I decide I can represent you." Ernest blinked at him uncomprehendingly. "Be your lawyer," explained Barnhill.

"You saved my life, Jamie," said Ernest, lowering his legs and resting his arms on the patches on his knees. "That's a fact. A miracle."

"It was a stroke of luck."

"You know better than that," said Ernest, leaning forward so that his face was mere inches from the iron bars. "The good Lord meant it to be, just like Miz Mary taught us."

"I suppose you're right," agreed Barnhill. Ernest was among the brightest and most ambitious black men in the community, having learned not only Bible lessons from Barnhill's mother, but to read and write as well, and was employed as a tradesman, a skilled joiner, at the local mill. "Why don't you begin," said Barnhill, "by telling me how you got into this fix?"

"This lady was a wailin'—I reckon she was scared of her husband – and then these men grabbed me and hauled me off, and then . . ."

"Back up, Ernest," interrupted Barnhill, raising a hand. "Let's start at the beginning. Where were you, and what time was it?"

"Promise you won't tell Pearly?"

"Tell Pearly? Why should I . . ."

"I'd be in a heap of trouble if she knew . . ."

"You *are* in a heap of trouble. Now where were you?"

"Shootin' dice," confessed Ernest, staring morosely at his shoelaces. "Me and some other boys gets together over at Joe's some nights. Just a friendly little dice game. If Pearly knew, she'd skin me . . ."

"Where is Joe's?"

"On the alley behind Travis street. Behind those white folks' shacks."

A rough part of town, thought Barnhill. "What time of night?" he asked.

"Maybe nine o'clock. Anyhow, I heard all this commotion. Door slammin', man shoutin', real angry, and then a woman screamed."

Jotting notes, Barnhill said, "Go on."

"So I went outside to have a look," said Ernest. "I saw some lights in the window of this house oh, maybe fifty yards away. So I kinda wandered over that way and all of a sudden this white man comes runnin' up—it was real dark—and says, 'Hey there!' I think I scared him. And then I saw the lady come runnin' out of the house. I swear, Jamie, she was half naked, nothin' on top, and only them, what-do-you-call-'em, ah, pantaloons underneath. And this big fella, musta been her husband, comes a runnin' after her."

"How could you see them?"

"He was swingin' a lantern. I could make 'em out."

"What happened next?"

"This other fella, the one I spooked, yells, 'Hey! Lookee here! I caught him!' And by jiminy, he grabbed hold of me and started draggin' me."

Barnhill hunched over, writing on his tablet.

"And when the lady sees what's happening, she yells out, 'That's the one! That nigger over yonder!' And I ain't quite sure what happened next."

"Try to remember," said Barnhill patiently.

"Well, these two men grabbed hold of me and threw me on the ground, yellin' at me. I don't know what happened to the lady, but I reckon she went back inside. And they tied a rope around me, and then some other fellas showed up. And they, well . . ." Ernest hesitated, knitting his brow. "I remember this one man said, 'He snuck in the bedroom window and raped her.' 'Cept he didn't use the word rape. And he said, 'Billy Ray came home and by damn they caught the bastard.' I remember that."

Expelling a sigh, Barnhill muttered, "Good God."

"Next thing I knew," said Ernest, "they had me on that horse with my hands tied, and off we went into the woods."

"All right, Ernest," said Barnhill, putting his notes aside. "Is there anything else you can remember? Any little thing?"

Ernest shook his head and then said, "Oh. I do remember this one thing, 'cause it seemed so strange. When I first went outside to see what the ruckus was all about and dang near ran into that fella, I saw he wasn't wearin' shoes. He was barefoot. Now, most folks don't go around barefoot, Jamie, particularly at night."

"Barefoot?" said Barnhill. "You're sure?"

"Yep," said Ernest with a nod.

"Did you get a look at his face?"

"Oh, sure. A good look, though I don't know him."

"One last question," said Barnhill. "You didn't lay a hand on that white woman?"

"No, sir," said Ernest indignantly.

Barnhill stood up, and the prisoner did likewise. Reaching his hand through the bars, Barnhill gave Ernest a firm handshake and said, "I'll take your case, old friend."

"Thank you, Jamie. God bless you."

"I'll do what I can, but it won't be easy."

"Jamie . . . Promise you won't tell Pearly 'bout the dice game?"

Barnhill sat at the table, scanning the day-old Nacogdoches newspaper as he smelled the inviting aromas of frying bacon and baking cornbread wafting from the kitchen. Through the open door he could see Kate, standing over the stove with her apron on, and Little Jim in his highchair, making a mess with his bowl of oatmeal. After a few minutes, Kate appeared, holding a plate with two fried eggs, bacon, and a slice of toasted cornbread, which she wordlessly placed on the table before turning and walking quickly from the room. "Thank you, dear," he called after her, but she ignored the comment and continued into the kitchen. Barnhill tried to concentrate on the newspaper, an article about the efforts of the Democrats in Austin to elect the Speaker of the House, but he couldn't take his mind off Kate and her scathing reaction to the news that he'd agreed to defend Ernest Wilson. Finishing his breakfast and the dregs of his coffee, he rose from the table and started for the kitchen, hesitated, and then called out, "Kate . . . may I please have a word with you?" Barnhill went to the parlor and waited for Kate with his hands resting on the back of a wing chair. When she appeared, wearing a sulking expression, he said, "How long do you intend to keep me in purgatory? Can't we at least talk?"

She narrowed her eyes and said, "Talk? What's there to talk about? I'm utterly mortified. I'll be the laughingstock of the whole town."

"What was I supposed to do?" Barnhill shot back. "Allow that mob to lynch an innocent man I've known all my life?"

"You don't know he's innocent."

"The point is, we need to restore some law and order . . ."

"Well, you didn't have to take his case! You made your point. Why couldn't you leave well enough alone?" Kate muttered something else under her breath and turned to walk out.

"Now just hold on," said Barnhill sharply. "A man's life is at stake here. And I'm convinced he didn't touch that tramp Lucy Grimes."

"You're a fool, Jamie Barnhill," said Kate with her chin thrust forward. "You've worked so hard to make your reputation, and now you're gonna risk it all, throw it away, and why? To represent a *nigger* charged with rapin' a *white woman!*"

"I'd appreciate it," he said sadly, "if you'd not use that word in this house." Briefly remembering the Reverend Bryan's admonishment to the Michigan soldier, he walked from the room.

Barnhill stood before the wizened secretary in the anteroom of Addison Parker's office, nervously twirling his wide-brimmed hat. "You may hang your coat, Mr. Barnhill," said the secretary, pointing a bony finger toward the stand in the corner. "I'm sure Mr. Parker will see you shortly, as soon as he concludes his appointment." Barnhill complied and then sat with legs crossed in the green leather armchair by the warming fire. After a few minutes he heard the sound of heavy footfalls on the stairs, the door to the hall flew open, and a heavyset man wearing a black frock coat and clutching a top hat entered the room with an angry scowl, his thick neck bulging and face red.

"Good day, sir!" he exclaimed to the secretary and let himself out in a huff.

Unperturbed, the secretary smiled faintly and said, "Mr. Barnhill, I believe Mr. Parker will see you now."

Barnhill found Addison Parker standing by the tall windows of his office grasping the lapels of his dove-gray coat as he looked pensively down on the lawn, strewn with brown and yellow leaves. Turning toward his visitor, he gave Barnhill an inscrutable look and said, "Good morning, Jamie. Have a seat."

"Morning, sir," said Barnhill, sitting in one of the chairs facing the broad desk.

"In case you were wondering," said Parker as he lowered his large frame into his leather chair, "that man is an agent of the railroad. The Katy. Had the temerity to demand a bribe for our state legislator to secure passage of a bill that . . . Well, what does it matter? I showed the man the door."

"He seemed . . ." said Barnhill, "disappointed."

"Yes," said Parker with a broad grin. "Very."

"I wanted to meet with you, sir," began Barnhill, "to explain about . . ."

"The case you're handling?"

"You've heard about it?"

"The talk of the town," said Parker. "Why, old Mr. Hennessey downstairs, deaf as a post, commented on it when he brought me my coffee."

"I'd like to explain," said Barnhill, leaning forward in his chair.

"The colored boy is an old acquaintance," said Parker, "as I understand it. Grew up on your family's place. Didn't want to see him . . . ah, killed by a lynch mob?"

"Yes," said Barnhill. "Yes, that's right. But it's more than that. I'm convinced he's innocent."

Parker leaned back in his chair and steepled his fingertips below his goatee. "Black man accused of raping a white woman," he said. "Caught by two white men, one of them the husband, within a stone's throw of the lady's house. Bedroom window wide open, and the lady in question in a state of undress. Am I correct?"

"Yes, sir."

"This would appear," said Parker, leaning forward to rest his elbows on the gleaming surface of his desk, "a poor choice of case to take on. I hardly need tell you that the days of all-black juries are over. It could do great damage to your reputation."

Barnhill nodded and said, "And to yours as well."

"Don't worry about me," said Parker. "I'm an outspoken member of the Republican Party, the supposed friends of the black man. But with your reputation, a Confederate hero . . ."

"If I hadn't chanced on that gathering," said Barnhill, "it would just be another dead black man, and the impression that a lynch mob can get away with murder in this county would be that much stronger."

Addison Parker fixed him in the gaze of his dark, intelligent eyes.

"Sure," continued Barnhill, "I wanted to help an old friend—a decent man, by the way. But this killing has got to end. Now, if I'd insisted—at the point of a gun—on taking that man to jail to stand trial, and then refused to represent him, well, I suppose things would be that much worse, and frankly, I'd consider myself a coward."

Parker slowly nodded and stroked his beard. "I don't suppose," he said, "there's anyone else . . ."

"No, sir. Not another lawyer in the county would touch this case. I'd wager not a single black man accused of raping or murdering a white woman has spent even a night in jail, let alone stood trial."

"I admire your principles," said Parker. "And there's no question of your courage. But I fear, in the end, the man will hang, at the expense of your good name."

"The day is coming, sir," said Barnhill, "when the carpetbaggers and scalawags are gone, just like the Union cavalry. It's in the wind. The people have to learn to trust in . . . well, in the rule of law."

Parker considered. After a moment, he said, "All right. I'm with you. I'll even pay for this man's defense. But promise me one thing."

"Sir?"

"You said the man's innocent."

Barnhill nodded.

"Do your best to make sure he walks free."

Kate paused to gaze out on the courthouse lawn, littered with fallen leaves, her mind filled with an image of the hastily-erected gallows and the limp body of the man who avenged her husband's murder twisting in the cold wind. With a shake of her head, she continued along the sidewalk, pausing to glance through the half-curtained windows into her father's old general store, now owned by a cousin of the hated county judge. Turning the corner to head in the direction of home, she almost collided with Sally Porter, dressed as usual in a fine lilac dress and matching hat with a basket of fruit hooked over her arm, which, in

Sally's surprised reaction, spilled some of its contents. "Sorry," said Kate, reaching down to retrieve the apples and oranges from the sidewalk.

"We missed you," said Sally coolly as Kate returned the fruit to the basket. "At yesterday afternoon's tea."

Responding with a blank look, Kate said, "Tea? I don't seem to recall . . ."

"And cards," said Sally. "At Mrs. Walker's. Hard to play without a fourth."

With utterly no recollection of the invitation, Kate suppressed a cold stab of fear and merely stared.

"What's got into you?" said Sally reproachfully. "You're not yourself. And you're far too thin."

"Well," said Kate, looking away. "I *do* have the baby to look after. I'll . . . try to be less forgetful." She turned and hurried away.

Barnhill stood at the picket fence as Kate wordlessly walked past and let herself in the house. He turned up his coat collar in the cold north wind and resumed his efforts. His shoulders ached from the hours he'd spent with a brush and bucket of whitewash blotting out the words "nigger lover" crudely painted on the boards by one of the untold number of hate-filled townspeople. Even at church he'd been shunned by his fellow congregants, none of whom would condescend to sit in the pew with the Barnhills, with the lone exception of Miss Ellen Graves, who, tall and erect, stood in the center aisle and in a loud voice said, "May I sit with you, Captain?" Nor was there a truce on the home front, as Kate maintained her frosty silence all through the long weekend.

On a clear, cold Monday morning, with a shrug of resignation, Barnhill walked the few blocks to the courthouse and an hour or so later appeared at the jail across the street, inquiring of the deputy if he might have a word with the sheriff. "C'mon back," called out John Clark from his small, cluttered office. "Care for a cup of coffee?" he asked as Barnhill appeared in the doorway.

"Sure," said Barnhill as he dragged back a chair. After the deputy poured him a cup from a steaming pot, Barnhill took a sip and said, "How's the prisoner?"

"Those iron bars and brick walls are all that's keepin' him from being torn limb from limb. I never seen the people of this town so riled up."

"There are at least two of them," said Barnhill, "who undoubtedly have a different feeling about it."

"Oh, really?" said Clark. "And who might they be?"

"Lucy Grimes, or rather Patterson," said Barnhill, "and the man who was in bed with her when Billy Ray unexpectedly turned up."

"Hah," retorted the sheriff. "You'll have mighty hard time provin' anything like that."

"We'll see," said Barnhill. He took another sip of coffee and then said, "I've got something for you, John." The sheriff responded with up-raised eyebrows. Barnhill unfastened his leather case and withdrew a document which he handed across the desk to the sheriff.

"What's this?" said Clark as he slipped on his spectacles and peered at the document, which bore an official seal and elaborate signature.

"A search warrant," replied Barnhill. "Signed by Judge Harper not fifteen minutes ago."

"Don't know as I've ever seen one of these," said Clark. "Says I'm *commanded* to conduct a search of the premises located at 114 South Travis Street."

"That's right," said Barnhill. "The home of one Billy Ray Patterson and his wife Lucy."

"I'll be dad-gummed," said Clark, stroking his mustache with a perplexed expression.

"I suspect your predecessor, Mr. Dinwoody, dispensed with such niceties when he conducted a search. But this has to do with due process, John."

"Due process?"

"Due process of law," said Barnhill. "A lawful search, under court order and your supervision. And whatever evidence it turns up can be used in the trial. In Ernest Wilson's rape trial." Barnhill abruptly stood up. "C'mon, John," he said.

"What, now? I've got other things to tend to."

"Now," said Barnhill. "Like the warrant says. *Without delay.* And bring along your deputy."

"But what if Billy Ray don't go along with it?" protested the sheriff.

"Billy Ray," said Barnhill, "don't have a say in the matter."

CHAPTER SEVENTEEN

BARNHILL, ACCOMPANIED BY THE RELUCTANT SHERIFF and his deputy, stood in a rutted street facing a shotgun shack constructed of weathered boards amid a weed-choked yard with a billy goat tethered to a stake.

"Billy Ray!" yelled the sheriff.

The shack's owner appeared on the front porch, a tall, barrel-chested man with thick red side-whiskers, pulling the straps of his overalls over his broad shoulders.

"Mornin'," said the sheriff. "I need a word with you." He started up the worn path to the porch with the deputy following behind him.

As the sheriff approached him, Billy Ray, with barely controlled fury, said, "What the hell you mean bringin' that goddam nigger-lovin' lawyer 'round my house?"

"Don't have any choice," said Sheriff Clark. "He's got a warrant." Clark removed a folded paper from an inner pocket of his coat and showed it to Patterson, who, illiterate, quickly glanced at the official seal and looked back at the sheriff. "A warrant," said the sheriff, "to search your house."

"Ain't nobody gonna search this house," said Billy Ray, crossing his arms over his chest.

"I'm tellin' you," said Clark, "this warrant was signed by the judge. If you don't let us in, Barnhill will go back and get another 'un. For your arrest."

"You wouldn't arrest me . . ."

"As a matter of fact I would," said Clark hotly. "Now, you and Lucy clear out for a few minutes and let us have a look around."

"Lucy!" bellowed Billy Ray through the screen door. "Git on your shoes! We're takin' a little walk." He disappeared inside. After a few moments he emerged, wearing a red plaid wool coat and clutching his wife by the arm like a rag doll. After a brief word with the sheriff, he walked up to Barnhill, glared at him menacingly, and then spat on the ground and started down the street. Lucy, by no means pretty, was attractive in a cheap, slatternly way, buxom with blond curls and widely curved hips. She made eye contact with Barnhill as she walked past him, a saucy look that betrayed no fear or anger. Joining the sheriff and deputy on the sloping front porch, Barnhill said, "Well, let's get started. Shouldn't take long."

"What is it you're lookin' for?" asked Clark.

"Evidence," replied Barnhill.

"I know," said Clark. "But what kind of evidence?"

Barnhill shrugged and held open the door. Following the two men inside the squalid dwelling, redolent of bacon grease and stale tobacco and lit only by the light filtering in through the windows, he glanced at the threadbare sofa and chair before a crude hearth and various articles of clothing strewn on the bare floorboards. "Why don't you take a look in the kitchen," suggested Barnhill, "while I check the bedroom."

The bedroom, of course, was the object of his visit and the basis for his argument to Judge Harper to issue the warrant. It was dominated by a four-poster bed with a sagging mattress and unmade bedcovers. At the foot of the bed were a pair of Billy Ray's work boots, one of which Barnhill picked up and examined. A very large boot, perhaps size twelve, what you would expect for a man Billy Ray's height and weight, easily six-foot-three and 250 pounds. Dropping the boot, Barnhill walked over to the single window, pushed aside the cheap curtains, and gazed out on the yard, a jumble of tall grass and weeds, unfenced, that extended to a clump of trees and low buildings in the distance. He checked to see if the window was locked. It lacked even a nail latch and opened easily with a light push on the frame. Turning around, he saw the deputy standing in the doorway. "Come over here, Billy," said Barnhill. "I want you to take a look at something."

Eyeing Barnhill suspiciously, the deputy complied. "Look down there under the bed," said Barnhill, pointing to the side of the four-poster where he surmised Lucy slept, the side with a small pillow covered in pink silk. A dirty ruffle skirted the sagging mattress, obscuring the space under the bed. "Bend down and lift up that dust ruffle," said Barnhill. "See if there's anything under the bed."

The deputy did as Barnhill suggested, kneeling on all fours to peer under the bed.

"See anything?" asked Barnhill.

After a few seconds the deputy backed out, glanced over his shoulder and held up a pair of men's shoes. "Just these," he said.

Barnhill nodded. "John!" he called out to the sheriff. "Come take a look."

"Kitchen's a pigsty," said Sheriff Clark as he walked into the bedroom. "Lord, the way some folks live." He stopped to look at his deputy, who was holding up the pair of shoes for his inspection. Clark gave Barnhill a puzzled look.

"They were under the bed," said Barnhill. "Out of sight. Notice anything unusual?"

The sheriff walked over and took a closer look at the scuffed brown brogans, a type of inexpensive shoe worn by common whites. "Nope," said Clark, turning to Barnhill. "Ordinary pair of men's shoes."

"Very ordinary," agreed Barnhill. "But no way they belong to Billy Ray Patterson. About half the size of his foot. I'd like you to put them in your saddlebag."

Standing outside the house in the cold wind, Barnhill visualized the scene: the heavy tread of Billy Ray's boots on the steps to the front porch, affording Lucy's nighttime visitor just enough time to slip on his shirt and trousers, throw open the bedroom window, and flee into the yard toward the safety of the trees in the distance on that dark night. Billy Ray finding his wife half-naked in the bedroom with the window open, bellowing and threatening violence. Her barefoot lover almost colliding with Ernest, who'd left his dice game to investigate the commotion. Barnhill stared toward the clump of trees, perhaps seventy-five yards away.

"Jamie," called the sheriff from the seat of his buckboard with the reins in his lap. "Let's go."

Back in his office at the jail, Sheriff Clark sat at his desk and folded his arms over his chest. "Now, what do you intend to do with those shoes?"

"They're just a piece of the puzzle," said Barnhill. "But I want you to keep them under lock and key in a sack marked 'evidence—Wilson trial.' And promise me, John, not to say a word to another soul."

Sheriff Clark nodded and said, "Fair enough."

The day of the trial dawned bright and cold, with a thin sheet of ice on the water pail at the kitchen doorstep. Barnhill rose early, reviewed his notes over two cups of coffee, shaved, and dressed in a white shirt with a loose black tie and his finest black frock and vest. Gazing in the mirror over the dresser, he considered his graying temples and the fine creases at the corners of his eyes, which gave him an older, more austere appearance than his thirty-four years merited. Satisfied with the knot of his tie, he hurried downstairs, kissed the baby, and bid Kate goodbye, who, unable even to utter "good luck," gave him a look that suggested relief that the terrible business was at last near an end.

Barnhill was determined to arrive at the courthouse—escorting Ernest Wilson, accompanied by the deputy—before the crowds of onlookers, but to his dismay he discovered the corridors lined with townspeople, hissing taunts and imprecations as the three slowly walked past. Barnhill stared straight ahead, not caring to look into the eyes of the same men and women who had hailed him as a hero upon his return from the university. By 10:00 a.m. the courtroom was packed with spectators, including, in the first row directly behind the defense counsel's table, the accused's wife Pearly, who sat with Barnhill's mother and sister and Miss Ellen Graves. Behind them was Addison Parker, conspicuous by his elegant gray morning coat and silk cravat with pearl stickpin, in the midst of a crowd composed largely of farmers and working-class whites clad in homespun, gingham, or overalls. There was a general stir as Ben Wilcox, the district attorney, made his way up the center aisle, pausing to visit with various neighbors and acquaintances. In his midforties, Wilcox had been just too old to volunteer for or be conscripted into the Southern army, but in the war's aftermath he had embraced the lost cause with as much fervor as any man in the county. As he watched Wilcox, a soft-looking man with thinning hair, a double chin, and ample belly, take his seat at the oak table reserved for the prosecution, Barnhill considered that his opponent was an incompetent trial lawyer with almost no experience with a jury, elected to office strictly on the basis of his anti-Republican politics. Waiting for the bailiff to announce the arrival of the judge, Barnhill leaned over to his client and whispered, "Remember, Ernest. Take a good look around and see if you can pick out that man." Ernest nodded silently.

"Oyez, oyez," called the bailiff, silencing the crowd. "All rise." Judge Elwood Harper, a tall, severe-looking man in his black robe, entered from his chambers amid the tramp of feet and strode up the steps to the bench. Ernest Wilson stood beside Barnhill staring straight ahead, clean-shaven and wearing a starched white shirt with his worn, patched trousers and the same shoes, worn down at the heels, he'd had on when he was apprehended.

"Be seated," the judge instructed the crowd, most of whom had never stood before the imposing figure of judicial authority. Taking his place in a high-backed chair, Harper nodded to the bailiff, who briefly exited and then returned with the twelve men of the jury, who nervously took their seats in the oak enclosure to the left of the bench. Barnhill was satisfied with the selection, as the district attorney had squandered his peremptory strikes to eliminate the four blacks on the panel, allowing Barnhill to reject an equal number of poor whites whose sympathies undoubtedly were with the lynch mob. Most of the jurors were personally known to Barnhill: generally decent, hard-working men who respected the law.

Judge Harper put on his eyeglasses, glanced at a paper, and announced, "We will now hear the case of the *State of Texas versus Ernest Wilson*, charged with aggravated rape, a capital offense. Mr. Wilcox, your opening statement."

The district attorney, wearing an expression of bored indifference, addressed his opening remarks to the jurors, a concise narrative of Ernest Wilson's alleged nighttime entry through the bedroom window, rape of the innocent white woman, and apprehension by the outraged husband and neighbors as he attempted to flee. He then called his first witness, Billy Ray Patterson, who squeezed his bulky frame into the witness stand, was duly sworn, and proceeded to elucidate, in his bumbling way, the details of the crime, with the help of Wilcox's leading questions:

"Isn't it a fact, Mr. Patterson, that when you found your wife, her nightgown had been ripped from her body?"

"Why, uh, yessir . . ."

"And the bedroom window was wide open, was it not?"

"I reckon so . . ."

Details that were calculated to outrage the men of the jury, so deeply ingrained was the taboo of sexual intercourse between a black man and white woman.

Wilcox concluded the direct examination with a satisfied smirk, and Barnhill rose from his table and approached the witness. "Tell me, sir," he began, "how long have you and your wife been married?"

Narrowing his eyes, Patterson answered, "'Bout six months."

"I see," said Barnhill. "Newlyweds. Now, what was the weather on the night in question?"

"The weather?"

"Was it warm or cold, wet or dry?"

"Hmm. Cold. Right cold, but dry."

"Now, after you and these other men . . . By the way, who were these other men who helped capture Ernest?"

Patterson furrowed his brow. "I ain't sure," he replied. "Neighbors. It was mighty dark."

"All right," said Barnhill, clasping his hands behind his back. "What did you do with him after you caught him?"

"Tied him up so's he can't escape."

"Then what?"

Patterson glared at Barnhill without answering.

"Isn't it a fact," said Barnhill, "that you and these other men, including Hank Willoughby, rode Ernest Wilson into the woods with the intention of lynching him?"

"Objection!" shouted the district attorney, jumping up from his chair. "The defense is trying to turn this into a trial of the . . . well, of the *victims* of this notorious crime!"

"Mr. Barnhill," said the judge, leaning forward. "You will confine your questions to matters bearing on the guilt . . . or innocence of the accused on the charge of rape."

"All right," said Barnhill equably. "One final question, Mr. Patterson. You're a large man. What size shoe do you wear?"

Wilcox was again on his feet. "Your honor," he said, "what can this possibly . . ."

"You may answer the question," said the judge.

"Well," said Patterson, scratching his chin. "Extry-large. Size twelve I reckon."

"Thank you," said Barnhill. "No more questions."

For his final witness, the district attorney called Lucy Grimes Patterson, dressed for the occasion in virginal white, though unable to resist the temptation, before so many spectators, to rouge her cheeks and paint her lips. She proved a far better witness than her oafish husband, describing the appearance of Ernest Wilson in her darkened bedroom with shopworn phrases—"black as the ace of spades" . . . "could only see the whites of his eyes"—and then, in a torrent of tears under the prosecutor's relentless questioning, melodramatically conceding that "he had his way with me." Barnhill observed that the jurors were on the edge of their chairs, grim-faced with anger as they listened to the salacious account, while certain of the women in the packed courtroom wore decidedly skeptical expressions. And then Wilcox, pacing slowly in front of the jury box, said, "Now, Mrs. Patterson. Would you tell the gentlemen of the jury if the man who, ah, had his way with you is present in the courtroom?" Lucy merely nodded, wiping tears from her eyes. "Can you identify him?" asked Wilcox.

"It's him!" she blurted, pointing a slender finger at Ernest Wilson, who sat immobile, his black face expressionless.

"Thank you," said Wilcox. "No further questions."

"Mr. Barnhill?" said the judge.

"No questions."

"Your honor," said Wilcox as the tearful Lucy was escorted from the courtroom, "the State rests."

"Very well," said Judge Harper. "We'll take a one-hour recess. Mr. Barnhill, we'll resume at one o'clock sharp." He struck his gavel and stood up from his chair.

"Take a good look, Ernest," whispered Barnhill as the large crowd rose from their benches and began to file out of the courtroom. Both he and his client turned in their chairs, scanning the faces of the spectators. He's bound to be here, thought Barnhill. Must have been mighty amused by Lucy's performance on the witness stand.

"Pardon," said the deputy, appearing at the counsel table. "My orders are to take the prisoner back to his cell." Ernest gave Barnhill a knowing look as he rose from his chair before walking with the deputy toward a side exit.

"I'll come by for you at quarter 'til one," said Barnhill.

"Give us a minute, Billy," said Barnhill as the deputy admitted him into the cramped space outside Ernest's cell. When they were alone, Barnhill quietly asked, "Did you see him?"

Ernest nodded and said, "Yep. Sittin' near the back."

"Who is he?"

"Don't know his name, but I think I may have seen him at the livery. But it's the same man. I'm sure of it. Young fella, on the small side, with curly blond hair."

"Mustache or beard?" Ernest shook his head. "All right," said Barnhill, "I need to run by the office. I'll see you back at the courthouse in ten minutes. And Ernest . . . just tell your story exactly the way it happened."

Thankfully, he found his clerk eating a sandwich at his desk. Barnhill dispatched the reliable young man on an errand, told him to hurry, and then returned to the courtroom, arriving at the counsel table just as the clock on the wall struck one. The judge took his place on the bench and, looking out over the large, expectant gallery, said, "Mr. Barnhill. Call your first witness."

Barnhill rose and said, "The defense calls Ernest Wilson."

Ernest walked purposefully to the witness stand, was sworn, and looked directly at Barnhill, who stood before him with his hands clasped behind his black frock. After establishing the details of the accused's personal life, his age, marriage, employment as a skilled tradesman, and spotless criminal record, Barnhill asked, "Would you please tell the court where you were on the evening of October twenty-third?"

"Over at Joe's place with some friends of mine, back behind Travis Street."

"And what were you doing there?"

"We were . . . well, to be honest, shootin' dice." Ernest lowered his gaze as many in the crowd laughed derisively.

"Order!" said the judge with a bang of his gavel.

"And this was what time of night?"

"Nine o'clock or thereabouts."

"Could you tell us, Mr. Wilson," said Barnhill, "what happened next?"

Speaking slowly in a strong voice, Ernest described the commotion that interrupted the dice game, his decision to investigate the cause, and the sight of Mrs. Patterson and her husband as they emerged from the nearby house.

"Can you describe the lady?" asked Barnhill. "What she was wearing?"

"Well, sir, it was pretty dark, but she had nothin' on top and just them frilly, you know, pantaloons." These hitherto undisclosed details elicited gasps from many of the women in the courtroom. "Her husband, least I reckoned it was her husband," explained Ernest, "had a lantern and was kinda, you know, chasin' after her."

"Mr. Wilson," said Barnhill. "Did you ever, at any time, as much as lay a hand on that lady?"

"No, sir."

"After you observed this half-naked woman, and what you presumed was her husband, running from the house, could you tell the court what happened?"

"I dang near run into this fella," replied Ernest. "Actually, he ran into me."

"He was running?"

"Yes, sir. Away from the house where the man and lady came from. I reckon I gave him a start."

"Go on," said Barnhill.

"Well, he looks at me and then yells, 'Hey! Lookee here!' And he grabbed hold of me."

At the sound of the door at the back of the courtroom, Barnhill turned to see his clerk Harrison, whom he motioned to come forward. "Just one moment," said Barnhill to the judge. He briefly conferred with Harrison in an undertone, who then sat at the counsel table. "All right," said Barnhill, resuming his place before the witness. "You say this man grabbed you. And then . . ."

"And then," said Ernest, warming to his story, "he yells, 'I caught him!' And this other man comes runnin' up, and the lady yells, 'That's him! That nigger over there!' And they threw me down on the ground and tied me up and . . ."

"Mr. Wilson," said Barnhill. "Did you get a good look at the man, the first man, the one who ran into you?"

"Yes, sir. I looked him right in the face."

"Could you recognize this man if you saw him?" A sudden silence fell over the packed courtroom.

"Yes, sir."

"And do you see him, seated here today in the gallery?"

"Yes, sir," said Ernest emphatically. "That's him," he added, pointing. "Sittin' near the back." The twelve jurors, and virtually every other man and woman in the courtroom, including the district attorney, strained to make out the man at whom the witness was pointing.

"Your honor," said Barnhill, "let the record reflect that the witness has identified one Robert, or Bobby as he is known, Garfield. Now, Mr. Wilson. One final question, sir. Do you recall anything else about this person that you considered unusual?"

"Yes, sir," said Ernest. "He was barefoot."

"Pass the witness," said Barnhill, returning to his chair.

"Now, Ernest," said Ben Wilcox, walking slowly over to face the witness, "I understand you're a right smart boy." Wilson responded to the prosecutor's sarcastic tone with a blank stare. "Learn to read and write?" asked Wilcox.

"Yes, sir."

"Do sums?"

"A little."

"Learn a trade?"

Ernest nodded.

"And maybe take a fancy to the white women?" Wilcox turned to smile at the packed gallery.

"Objection," said Barnhill, rising from his chair.

"Overruled," said the judge.

"I ain't never," said Ernest in a strong, clear voice, "had a fancy for a white woman. 'Specially not one like her," he added, nodding toward Lucy Patterson, seated next to her husband, a remark that elicited angry grumbles from the gallery, silenced by a rap of the judge's gavel.

Try as he might, Ben Wilcox was unable to shake the witness from his straightforward narrative, replying with a simple, "No, sir," and shake of his head to the prosecutor's inept attempts to entrap or confuse him. Frustrated and unable to think any longer on his feet, Wilcox finally slumped in his chair, and the judge said, "You may step down." With a proud look at his wife on the first row, Ernest returned to his place beside his counsel.

Barnhill rose and said, "Your honor, the defense calls Billy Thornton."

The lanky deputy sheriff, with a tin star on the collar of his vest, approached the witness stand, was sworn by the bailiff, and took his seat.

"Mr. Thornton," said Barnhill, "may I hand you this document and ask you to identify it for the men of the jury?" After showing the paper to the district attorney, he approached the stand and handed it to the witness.

Thornton briefly examined it and then said, "It's a search warrant."

"A search warrant," repeated Barnhill. "To search . . ."

"The premises located at 115 East Travis Street. Billy Ray's house."

"I see," said Barnhill, aware that the jurors were on the edge of their chairs. "And did you participate in a search of this house?"

"Course I did, Jamie," said Thornton with a quizzical expression. "With you and Sheriff John."

"Thank you," said Barnhill. He then reached under the table and produced a small burlap bag with a label attached. "This is defense Exhibit Number One," he said, handing it to Wilcox. "Your honor, I will ask the witness to identify it and move to admit it into evidence." Wilcox examined the label, peered inside the bag, and handed it back to Barnhill, who passed it along to the deputy.

"Would you tell the court," said Barnhill, "what's inside the bag?"

"Sure," said Thornton. "A pair of shoes what we found on the search."

"You have had them in your custody, sir? In this bag, at the jail?"

"Yes, sir."

"Move to admit the exhibit," said Barnhill.

"No objection," muttered Wilcox.

"Would you kindly remove these shoes from the bag, Mr. Thornton," said Barnhill, "and show them to the jury." The deputy did as he was instructed, holding up a shoe in each hand. "And where did you find these shoes?" asked Barnhill.

"Under the bed," said Thornton. "In Billy Ray's bedroom."

"In plain sight?"

"No, sir. Had to crawl down and pull up the ruffle to find 'em."

"Would you say they were hidden under the bed?" The witness nodded. "On whose side of the bed?"

"Lucy's."

"Now, Mr. Thornton," said Barnhill. "Would you please hold up one of these shoes and tell the jury what size it is and any other identifying features."

Holding a shoe in both hands, Thornton said, "Well, it's a man's size seven, and on the inside somebody's wrote the initials B. G."

"B. G." repeated Barnhill. "Bobby Garfield."

"Objection!" shouted Wilcox.

"Granted," said the judge. "The jury will disregard."

"No further questions," said Barnhill. "The defense rests."

By the time he rose for his summation, the wind had gone completely out of the district attorney's sails. After recapitulating the evidence of Ernest's Wilson's guilt—the unrefuted testimony of two eyewitnesses, he closed with an ineffectual appeal to the white man's duty to uphold the honor of the Southern Woman.

Barnhill stood before the jury, looking each man in the eye. "The testimony you've heard today," he began, "clearly indicates that Billy Ray Patterson returned to his home on the night of October twenty-third to find his wife in a state of partial undress, with the bedroom window wide open. It was a cold night, according to Billy Ray. Underneath the bed, out of sight," Barnhill continued, walking over to the counsel table, "were a pair of men's shoes." He picked up one of the shoes and displayed it to the jurors. "Not Billy Ray's, mind you," he said. "Way too small. Now, according to Ernest, the man who almost collided with him was barefoot. Barefoot on a cold night. And it so happens that the initials on the inside of those shoes—B. G.—match the name of the man, Bobby Garfield, Ernest identified as the man he ran into. I submit to you that the only thing Ernest Wilson is guilty of . . ." Barnhill paused and clasped the lapels of his frock. "Is being in the wrong place at the wrong time. Billy Ray surprised another man with his wife that night . . . But it wasn't Ernest Wilson."

A mere thirty minutes after the judge dismissed them, the twelve jurors filed back into the box. Amid the palpable tension within the packed courtroom, Judge Harper asked, "Have you reached a verdict?"

"Yes, sir," said the foreman, a Confederate veteran with a missing forearm. "We find the accused, Ernest Wilson, not guilty."

PART THREE
THE PROMISE OF THE NEW SOUTH

CHAPTER EIGHTEEN

HANGING HIS COAT AND HAT ON THE STAND in the corner of his office, Barnhill walked over to the bookcase and picked up a framed photograph, a portrait of Judge John H. Withers, from whose funeral he'd just returned. Barnhill studied the handsome image, made before the war when the judge was in his late fifties, the silver locks that reached the collar of his coat and clear eyes that seemed china-blue even in the tintype. A fine, dignified gentleman of the old school, of Barnhill's father's generation, who'd come to Texas when it was a primitive frontier, cleared the land, built the towns, and established its public institutions. Hundreds of townspeople had gathered in the warm spring sunshine to pay their respects and to listen, with heads lowered and hats in hand, to the moving valediction Barnhill had offered at the graveside.

Returning the photograph to its place on the shelf, he thought back to the last time Judge Withers had called on him, to offer his congratulations for Barnhill's triumph in the Wilson case. Not long afterward the judge had suffered the stroke that left him confined to a wheelchair. Barnhill sat at the broad oak desk and thought about the advice Withers had given him at that very desk when Barnhill was a young lawyer considering defending Jethro Banks. When you decide to take on the courthouse, he'd counseled, choose to defend an innocent man, wrongly accused. "Well," Withers had said after the Wilson trial, "like everyone else I thought you were a fool to do it, but now you've gotten a black man acquitted by a white jury. Maybe you'll teach the people of this town to respect the law."

If not that, Barnhill considered, they certainly had learned to respect him as a trial lawyer. Scarcely a week passed without some farmer or businessman arriving at the office, seeking redress for a breached contract, damaged or stolen goods, trespass, or clouded title. With the steady stream of work for Addison Parker, Barnhill had to turn much of the business away, though Harrison, the occupant of Barnhill's old office across the hall as a recently admitted member of the bar, was able to take up some of the slack. Kate, Barnhill mused, had been certain that defending Ernest Wilson would destroy his career; now, three years later, his prosperity was such that he'd built her a fine new house near the footbridge on Houston Street.

Mrs. Thomas, a spare widow in her late forties who'd taken Harrison's place at the front desk as both clerk and scrivener for the two lawyers, appeared in the doorway.

"Yes, ma'am," said Barnhill, glancing up.

"I have your mail," she said, walking up to the desk with a small bundle. "Including this one"—she held up an envelope—"that come all the way from Virginia."

"Oh, really?" said Barnhill, reaching across the desk for the envelope and studying the postmark and return address. After she excused herself, gently closing the door, Barnhill slit the envelope with his silver letter opener and extracted three sheets of bond. Beneath the embossed words "Law Offices of Eppa Hunton, 26 Broad Street, Richmond, Virginia," Barnhill read:

April 15, 1875

Dear Jamie,

Three days ago we gathered at the Lee house here to commemorate the tenth anniversary of that fateful day at Appomattox, a solemn and mournful affair. Many of Lee's staff were on hand, proudly wearing their best uniforms, and we were joined by the General's son Rooney, who delivered a stirring encomium to his late father. Listening to the stories, I thought of you, brother, and the sight of the proud remnant of the Texas Brigade surrendering their arms to the Union General Chamberlain.

> I was reminded again of the fondness Lee had for his Texans, whom he regarded as the best fighting men in the army, no doubt due in some measure to the years he spent in your state before the war. I remember the General relating how he learned, while stationed in San Antonio, of the attack on Fort Sumter, how deeply opposed he was to secession and the war, how he vowed "never to lift my sword save in defense." Well, Old Abe gave him that opportunity.
>
> I have heard, through the grapevine of travelers from Texas, that you are prospering in your chosen profession, are married, and have a son. I too have had success through my association with General Hunton, a leading light of our city and state. The General has in fact gotten himself elected to Congress as a member of the new Conservative Party, as sure a sign as could be imagined that the Redeemers have rescued the Old Dominion from the Radicals. These so-called Conservatives are an amalgam of mighty strange bedfellows, unified solely in their determination to rid the state of the Carpetbag regime, consisting in equal parts of old line Whigs, Confederate Democrats, and conservative Republicans, with a few blacks thrown into the bargain! Why, Rooney Lee declared at our reunion that he intends to run for office as one of these newfangled Conservatives (the term "Democrat" being unacceptable to the old Whigs).

Barnhill put aside the letter for a moment, swiveled in his chair, and stared out the open window at the bright new foliage on the oaks and elms. What strange changes the aftermath of defeat and occupation had wrought! Returning to the lines of neat cursive, he continued reading:

> So much for our peculiar politics. I too have found a bride—you may recall that lively belle Harriet Thompson from our dinner dances in '63—but alas, no son as yet. We are thriving and I hope some day to rebuild the old plantation home at Sandy Point, put to the torch by McClellan.
>
> You must write, Jamie, and fill in all the interesting details. And one of these days you must return to dear old Virginia, bring along the missus, and stay as our guests in Richmond. Wishing you all the best, I remain,
>
> > Your affectionate friend,
> > *Edward*

CHAPTER EIGHTEEN

A smile softened Barnhill's features as he visualized Edward Selden in his fine dress uniform, leaning heavily on his crutch as he made his way into the crowded parlor at Mary Chesnut's . . . or in his wheelchair by the fire on that snowy Christmas morn at Mrs. Webb's, so long ago. How he would love to see Richmond and Charlottesville again, he considered with a sigh. Life in San Augustine seemed a drab backwater by comparison, with scarcely another soul who possessed a decent education or appreciation for the finer things. Barnhill ruefully reflected on his life with Kate, who never seemed happy or content no matter how hard he tried to please her, and the difficulty of making a decent living as a country lawyer. What would life have been like if he'd heeded Edward's advice in '68 and stayed in Virginia? Living in a fine old home in Richmond, perhaps. Even the possibility of somehow reuniting with Amelia . . . Barnhill's ruminations were interrupted by a tap on the door. "Yes?" he said, putting the letter from Selden aside.

Opening the door a crack, Mrs. Thomas said, "You have visitors . . ."

"New clients?" said Barnhill with a frown. "Let Mr. Harrison see them . . ."

"No, sir. It's, well, a delegation of gentlemen. A Senator Bell, I believe, and two others."

"Senator Bell?" said Barnhill, rubbing his chin. "From Nacogdoches?"

"Yes, sir."

"Well, then, show 'em in." Walking around the desk, Barnhill reached out to shake hands with the state senator, a great bear of a man, perhaps three hundred pounds, with a round face and long brown beard that obscured his many chins. His two younger companions, by their deference, appeared to be his aides.

"Mr. Barnhill," said Bell in his sleepy drawl. "How good of you to see us."

"Have a seat," said Barnhill, motioning to the chairs facing his desk. Wearing a black string tie and frock, Senator Bell squeezed into an armchair with some difficulty. Returning to his desk, Barnhill said, "What can I do for you gentlemen?"

Glancing around the room, Bell said, "This was old Judge Withers's office if I remember correctly."

Barnhill nodded. "He invited me to join his practice when I came home from the university."

"Good judge, Withers, though a bit too . . . ah, proper." The comment elicited amused smiles from the two young men. "You served under Gen'l Hood, did you not?" said Bell.

"Yes, sir," said Barnhill, folding his hands on his desk.

"My people are from Kentucky. Hood's a distant cousin."

"I see," said Barnhill, wondering when the man would get to the point.

"Well, sir," said the senator, withdrawing a fat cigar from his breast pocket and biting off the tip. Waiting for his aide to strike a match and light it, Bell drew on the cigar, expelled a cloud of smoke, and said, "You've earned a reputation as a mighty fine lawyer."

"Thank you, sir, but I . . ."

"We need good men, Barnhill," said Bell, resting an arm on his ample waistcoat. "In the party." In response to Barnhill's quizzical expression, he added, "the Democratic Party. Or Conservative Democrat, as some prefer. Now y'all have this reprobate here in San Augustine, name of . . ."

"Newton," interjected one of the aides.

"Newton," repeated Senator Bell. "Carpetbagger. In the county courthouse."

"That's correct," said Barnhill.

"We need a good candidate to run him out of office, and out of town," said Bell with another puff that enwreathed his face. "And I think you're just the man, Mr. Barnhill."

"Well," said Barnhill, "there's no one wants Newton out of the courthouse more than I do. But I couldn't possibly neglect my practice . . ."

"Come now, Barnhill," said Bell, stabbing the air with his cigar. "You'd make a fine candidate. Pioneer family, Confederate hero, respected lawyer. Hell, even popular with the Negroes after that celebrated rape trial. And our party is countin' on the colored vote."

And they'd get it, Barnhill considered, with my name on the ballot. His pulse quickened at the thought of replacing the hated Newton as county judge, one of the most prominent positions in the community. Possibly even a springboard for higher office, and there was little question that these new Conservative Democrats would soon be the party in power. Feeling a pang of self-reproach, he said, "From what I gather, you're a former Whig, senator, as are most of the leaders of your party."

"That may be," replied Bell. "But good conservatives, supporting business interests."

"Like the railroads," said Barnhill. "My father was a lifelong Democrat before the war, of the Old Hickory school. I appreciate your stopping by, sir, and I wish you luck in finding a candidate to unseat Archibald Newton, but I'm not your man."

"Very well," said Bell, rising awkwardly from his chair. "But bear in mind, Barnhill, the Democrats are the wave of the future, and we're within an ace of restoring home rule. Come along, boys."

Barnhill had chosen a building site on a slight rise overlooking the creek that wandered through town, spanned by a footbridge almost a hundred yards across that was frequented by neighbors on their way to shops or places of business. The spacious two-story house was constructed of yellow pine and overlooked the moss-draped hardwoods along the creek, with a turret at one end, redbrick fireplace, and wide porch decorated with gingerbread cutouts. Halfway across the footbridge on his way home from work, Barnhill paused to listen to the staccato hammering in the boughs overhead, a pileated woodpecker, with its large black body and bright red crest. As he continued along the bridge, he observed Ernest Wilson, who cheerfully performed odd jobs for the Barnhills, chopping firewood on a stump behind the house, and then glimpsed a flash of motion and color on the lawn—a towheaded boy chasing after a small dog. Reaching the end of the bridge, Barnhill called out: "Little Jim!" The boy stopped abruptly, turned, and with a wide smile raced to his father, who knelt and folded him in his arms.

"Papa," said the boy breathlessly. "I found a puppy!"

"So I see," said Barnhill, standing with the boy on his hip, one small arm encircling his father's neck. Barnhill looked down at the homely little dog, a mix of terrier and hound, eagerly wagging its tail.

"Can I keep him, Papa?"

"Maybe," said Barnhill, continuing on toward the house with the dog at his heels. "I'll ask your mama."

Leaving the dog at the kitchen door, Barnhill let himself in, lowered his son to the floor, and hung his hat on the back of a chair. "What's for supper, Dinah?" he asked the black cook standing at the stove with her back to the door.

"Chicken 'n dumplins," she replied without looking up from her cast-iron skillet. "Just the way you like 'em. And mustard greens."

The boy shot from the kitchen into the parlor with his father close behind. Kate was seated in her favorite armchair, elaborately carved mahogany upholstered in rich green satin, with her sewing in her lap. "Don't run in the house!" she called out sharply.

Slowing to a trot, the four-year-old said, "Mama, I found a puppy and Papa," he hesitated, looking up over his shoulder at his father standing in the doorway, "he, ah, said . . ."

"Evenin', Kate," said Barnhill. "Little Jim found a cute puppy."

"A stray dog?" said Kate. "Goodness only knows where it might have come from."

"Can I keep him, Mama?"

"Of course not." Kate shot a look of disapproval at her husband.

"Why not?" said Barnhill. "Every boy needs a dog."

"Not in my house," said Kate emphatically.

"Our house," said Barnhill. "The dog can sleep in the kitchen, and during the day he'll live outdoors." Glancing out the window, he observed Dinah taking a plate of chicken and dumplings to Ernest for his supper.

"Please, Mama," said the boy, tugging on her sleeve.

"Oh, all right," she conceded. "I can never win against you two."

"Well, then," said Barnhill, walking over and mussing Jim's thick blond locks. "He'll need a name."

"I know!" said the boy. "He's kinda black and brown but his paws are white. Let's call him Whitesocks."

"Whitesocks," said Barnhill with a smile. "Or just plain Socks. I like that."

After the boy had gone upstairs Barnhill stood before the floor-to-ceiling bookshelves in his library, which contained most of the fine books from his father's collection. He'd personally designed it to resemble the library at Mountain Farm. The shelves, as well as the moldings and doorframes, were built of light brown sweet gum and the wide floorboards of cypress, harvested from the nearby forests and milled in town. Lightly fingering the spines of the leather-bound set of Gibbon's *Decline and Fall*, he thought back to the splendid library at Widewater and the hours he'd happily whiled away reading to Amelia. Giving his left shoulder a rub, he reached for the crystal decanter and poured an inch of bourbon into a glass, adding spring water from a small silver pitcher. Taking a sip, he listened to the rhythmic creaking of the rocking chair on the ceiling overhead and the faint sound of singing through the open window—Dinah singing Little Jim a lullaby as she rocked him to sleep. He walked to the window and looked out into the gloaming. Lightning bugs blinked in the gathering darkness by the creek bed. Where, he wondered, was Amelia now? Married, of course, probably with a brood of children, one of whom—assuming she had a son—he'd wager was named Robert. He noticed that the creaking of the rocker and the soft lullaby had ceased; his little boy had gone to bed, no doubt dreaming happily of his new companion Socks. Hearing Dinah's tread on the stairs, he finished his drink in a swig and walked into the parlor.

As the clock on the mantel chimed the half-hour, Kate rose from her chair and said, "Ready for supper?"

"I'm starved," he said with a smile. "And besides, Dinah fixed chicken and dumplings." Following Kate to the dining room, he pulled back her chair and then took his place at the head of the walnut table, which gleamed in the flickering light from the candelabra. The table was set with the blue willow china, the good silver, polished to a bright patina, and linen napkins. As he spread his napkin in his lap, Dinah appeared from the kitchen with a steaming platter and served each of them generous helpings of chicken, home-made dumplings, and greens. When they were alone again, Kate looked to him and Barnhill bowed his head and prayed: "Heavenly Father, we give thanks for these and all thy many blessings. Amen."

"Amen," repeated Kate softly.

"Mmm," said Barnhill after sampling a mouthful of creamy chicken. "That gal cooks almost as well as Hattie. Would you pass the biscuits, darlin'?" Kate handed the plate to him with a wan smile and then took a small bite of chicken. As he buttered his biscuit, Barnhill noticed that her hands were red and lined and her pale cheeks hollow. Always petite, she'd lost weight to the point that her dress hung loose on her shoulders. "Biscuit?" said Barnhill, offering her the plate. Kate shook her head and took another small bite. "Guess who dropped in on me this morning?" he asked. Kate, holding her fork in midair, gave him a questioning look. "Senator Bell," said Barnhill. "From Nacogdoches." After pausing to sample the greens, Barnhill continued: "He's one of the Democrat bosses, and they're hell-bent on taking over the legislature."

"Good," said Kate. "It's high time." She pushed the food around on her plate with her fork. "Why did he call?" she asked.

"They want me to run for county judge."

"Really?" said Kate. "Against Newton?"

Barnhill nodded, taking a mouthful of chicken and dumplings.

"Jamie," she said, brightening. "That's wonderful. With these men behind you, you'd be sure to . . ."

"I told them no," said Barnhill, dabbing his chin with his napkin. "I'm way too busy. And besides . . ."

"You did what? Without even asking my opinion?"

"Kate, I couldn't possibly give up my practice, and I . . ."

"Is that all you care about? Doing the bidding of Addison Parker. What about the poor people of this town?"

Stung, Barnhill stared at her, unsure how to answer. He finally returned to his supper, though he noticed she'd scarcely touched her food. After a long interval of silence, he said, "I'm taking a trip tomorrow down to Jasper, to have a look at the sawmill Mr. Parker is building."

"Fine," muttered Kate, avoiding his eyes.

"I think I'll take Little Jim with me. We'll ride down in Parker's chaise, spend the night, and be back the next day."

"Do as you please," said Kate. "Just take good care of the boy." She abruptly stood up and tossed her napkin on the table. Looking at him with red-rimmed eyes, she said, "I'm getting ready for bed."

Thinking *don't let the sun go down on your anger,* he considered asking her to stay, to work their way through the hurt feelings that so often lurked just beneath the surface. Instead, he merely said, "Goodnight."

The morning was glorious following a late spring norther, with a cool breeze and cloudless sky. Barnhill lifted his boy up onto the rear-facing seat of the carriage and climbed in beside him. Addison Parker's fine chaise was painted dark green, with varnished trim and soft leather upholstery, the top folded down in the warm sunshine. Parker sat comfortably on the back seat, immaculate as usual in a dove-gray coat, old-fashioned shirt and cravat, and kid gloves. "A beautiful pair of animals," said Barnhill, referring to the matched team of tall white horses, over fifteen hands. "Wave to Mama," he added, pointing to Kate standing at the kitchen door. As Little Jim complied, the driver slapped the reins, starting the horses forward with a clatter of hooves, the well-sprung chaise gliding smoothly over the rutted street. "Bye-bye, Socks!" called the boy as the mongrel chased after the carriage.

"Well, sir," said Parker as they rounded the corner. "Couldn't have picked a finer day to make the journey." Barnhill nodded with a smile, holding his son close to him as they passed out of town into the open country. The road was poor but free of dust, since the norther had brought a gentle rain in the night. Traveling due south, they rode for a time in the cool shade of the pines, up and down the gentle hills, through broad fields whose black furrows were planted with early cotton, passing the time with pleasant conversation about the weather, cotton prices, and, of course, politics. Barnhill considered mentioning his interview with Senator Bell but thought better of it, as Addison Parker remained a staunch, though conservative, Republican. Little Jim sat in wide-eyed wonder, taking in the sights along the roadway, his first trip away from the small town.

After several hours had passed, Parker called out, "Stop here for a moment, Sam," at the approach of imposing brick gateposts. The driver halted the horses with a tug on the reins, and both men gazed down a long oak *allée,* at the end of which stood a large neoclassical house, the entrance flanked by thick Doric columns. Even at a distance they could see that the once-imposing building was long since abandoned, with the glass missing from the windows and the broad front porch overgrown with vines and weeds. To the left of the house was a cluster of pitiful shanties, the old slave quarters, now occupied by black sharecroppers. "The old Masterson place," said Barnhill. "One of the finest plantations in the state."

"What happened?" said Parker.

"Lost everything in the war," said Barnhill with a shrug. "Just packed up and left."

After traveling another hour, with the noonday sun at its zenith, Parker opened a wicker basket on the seat beside him and unpacked a bottle of sweetened tea and an assortment of soda crackers, yellow cheese, beef jerky, and oatmeal cookies. After pouring the tea, he fixed each of them a plate, and they rode along in silence, enjoying their simple lunch in the warm sunshine, listening to the clop of hoofbeats and creaking of wheels and springs.

"Whoa," called the driver, reining in the team. Looking over his shoulder, Barnhill observed the approach of a mule-drawn wagon on the narrow road, scarcely wide enough for two vehicles to pass. As it drew nearer, he could see that the wagon was heavily laden with pots, pans, assorted household goods, and five or six children, including a lanky, barefoot youth on the seat with the reins in his lap. Mother and father walked alongside; the man, tall and lean, wearing homespun and a wool hat with a Kentucky long rifle over his shoulder, and the woman, in a calico dress with a sunbonnet, toting a basket filled with provisions and clenching a corncob pipe in her teeth. As they slowly passed by, the man stared sullenly at the handsomely appointed chaise and its finely dressed occupants and then, with a crooked smile, lifted his hat and said, "Howdy-do, gen'lmen. Is this here Texas?"

"It is indeed," replied Parker. "Welcome to the Lone Star state."

"Come all the way from Tennessee," said the woman.

"Good luck to you," said Barnhill, holding Little Jim in his lap. He noticed the letters "GTT" scrawled on the side of the wagon. "Gone to Texas," he commented to Parker once they resumed their journey. "That's what they say when it's time to pack up and move west."

"The only way out of poverty for these people," said Parker, "white as well as black, is to leave the cotton fields and work in industry." Barnhill nodded. "But the ultimate answer," Parker continued, "is education. They must learn to read and do sums."

By four o'clock they had covered some fifty miles south-southeast through the village of Jasper, departing the highway on a logging road into the vast stands of virgin longleaf pine, with Little Jim sound asleep on his father's lap. Scant sunlight reached the park-like forest floor, devoid of underbrush; cool, redolent of pinesap, with the wind singing in the boughs far overhead. Barnhill marveled at the girth and height of the trees, at least four feet in diameter at the base and well over one hundred feet tall. "How many acres," he asked, "have you acquired?"

"Over four hundred thousand," replied Parker, "all contiguous, in the longleaf forest."

"And how will the loggers move the timber to the mill?"

"Teams of oxen or float the logs on the Neches. That's why I chose to locate the mill on the river. But eventually I'll build my own rail spur."

The boy stirred in his father's lap, rubbed his sleepy eyes and said, "How much farther, Daddy?"

With a smile, Parker—who'd never married—said, "We're almost there, son. Just about another mile."

Staring into the primeval forest, teeming with bears, deer, and wild turkeys, Barnhill tried to imagine the landscape denuded of trees, bisected by rail lines, with a sawmill belching black smoke, like those he remembered on the banks of the James River in the Shenandoah. His imagination was soon aided by the sounds of heavy construction—hammering, clanging, men's voices—as the carriage emerged from the dense forest onto a broad clearing at the Neches River, where the spectacle unfolded before his astonished eyes: a large mill pond cut into the muddy riverbank and beside it a great building under construction, at least one hundred yards in length, two stories, with a corrugated tin roof, and hundreds of men, black and white, toiling in the late afternoon sun. As the driver coaxed the weary horses into a trot, they drove past a bull puncher with his team of eight oxen hauling a load of six-foot-diameter logs. Barnhill turned around to face Addison Parker, who was surveying his vast industrial project with a look of satisfaction and determination. What had hitherto been a mere abstraction for Barnhill, drafting documents and pleadings in his law office, was now before his eyes: the undeniable proof of the great changes sweeping over the land.

CHAPTER NINETEEN

KATE WALKED TO THE WINDOW AND GAZED OUT on the lawn and beyond at the creek and footbridge. The curtains hung limp in the stifling humidity. Hearing the peal of a child's laughter, she watched as Little Jim, shirtless and barefoot, raced across the grass, chased by the dog, his inseparable companion. She turned away, feeling faint from the combination of sweltering heat and lack of nourishment, and ran a hand across her moist forehead. Wearing a thin camisole, she considered dressing and going downstairs. Instead, she walked to the dresser and stared into the mirror, turning her chin to study her hollow cheeks, the dark circles under her eyes, the tiny wrinkles at the corners of her mouth. She should go down and look after the boy . . . *No,* an inner voice demanded. The maid could keep an eye on him. Opening the top dresser drawer, she took a small brass key from its hiding place and walked to the cabinet where she kept her jewelry. Unlocking it, she carefully removed a brown bottle and eyedropper. She stared at the label, thinking back to her visit to the doctor who'd recommended the nostrum as a remedy for melancholia, though he'd cautioned her to use it "sparingly." After pouring a glass of water from the pitcher on her bedside table, she uncorked the bottle and, with a trembling hand, added five drops of the amber liquid. Setting it aside, she returned the laudanum to the locked cabinet, hid the key, and slumped on her bed. With a deep sigh, she surrendered to the powerful opiate, downing the mixture in one long swallow, after a few moments slipping into a netherworld of perfect lassitude, eyes closed, insensate, surrounded by silence broken only by a faint rumble of distant thunder.

Hearing the thunder, Barnhill glanced at the western sky roiling with thick, black clouds that suddenly blotted out the sun. For a moment he debated returning to the office for his umbrella and then quickened his pace, thinking he could make it home before the skies opened. As he reached the footbridge, a great rush of wind shook the boughs of the pines and a brilliant bolt of lightning arced across the charcoal sky, followed by an ear-splitting crash. Barnhill began to run, but it was too late. Swept by sheets of wind-driven rain, he was soaked to the skin when he reached the porch. As another crash shook the windowpanes, he stamped his boots and, wiping his eyes, noticed his small son huddled by the kitchen door, clutching the puppy in his lap. "Little Jim," he said, quickly walking over to him. "You shouldn't be out in this storm."

Looking up at his tall father with rain dripping from the brim of his hat, Jim's lower lip trembled and tears welled in his eyes. "I'm sorry, Papa," he said, holding the dog even tighter as the storm lashed the porch.

Barnhill grabbed the knob of the kitchen door. As its top half swung open, he tugged and realized it was latched from inside. "Kate?" he called into the dark kitchen. "Dinah?" Reaching inside, he unfastened the latch and then bent down to take Little Jim by the arm and help him up. "Don't worry," he said as he ushered the boy and dog into the kitchen, closing the door behind them. Once the boy was seated at the table with the puppy in his lap, Barnhill draped a towel over Jim's bare shoulders and then struck a match and lit the oil lamp on the counter, filling the room with a reassuring circle of yellow light. As another clap of thunder reverberated through the house, Barnhill stripped off his coat, dried himself with a cup towel, and then sat next to his son.

"Socks was scared," said Little Jim, softly petting the dog's head.

Barnhill smiled. "You were a brave boy," he said, inwardly furious that he'd been left out in the storm with the door latched. "Where's Mama?" he asked. Jim responded with a shake of his head. "Why don't you and Socks have a sweet," suggested Barnhill, "while I go upstairs and see about her." He walked to the jar on the counter, removed one of Dinah's pecan pralines, and handed it to the boy. After lighting a candle, Barnhill left the boy in the kitchen and walked through the parlor to the stairs, restraining the impulse to call out Kate's name. The sound of the storm was louder upstairs, the rain drumming on the roof and wind swaying the trees outside the open windows. He stood in the entrance to their bedroom, dark and eerie, with the curtains billowing and rain dripping from the sills. Kate lay motionless as death on the four-poster bed, with one thin arm draped over her face. Barnhill walked over, placed the candle on the bedside table, and looked down at her. How could she sleep through such a storm? He bent down and lightly shook her shoulder. As he gave her another shake, she moaned softly and then sat bolt upright, looking at him with terror in her eyes.

"What?" she said. "What is it?" She gaped around the darkened bedroom.

"It's nothing," he said. "Just a storm, and you fell asleep."

"A storm," she murmured. She listened for a moment to the sounds of rain and wind and then cried, "Oh, God. Little Jim!" She swung her legs over the side of the bed and tried to stand but Barnhill held her back.

"He's all right," he said. "A little scared, but fine."

"Thank God."

Barnhill sat beside her. "Kate," he said, looking into her eyes. "How could you?"

She looked away, bowing her head and rubbing her eyes.

"Kate . . ."

With a muffled sob that shook her shoulders, she muttered, "I'm sorry."

"Kate," Barnhill repeated, placing a hand on her arm. "Jim was locked outside in the storm. He could have been . . ."

"Stop," she said, pushing away his hand. "That damned colored girl was supposed to look after him." She glared angrily at him. "I'm not well. I need to rest."

"All right," said Barnhill resignedly. He stood up. "I'll speak to Dinah." He gave Kate a final look, sitting weakly on the bed with her shoulders hunched, staring at her bare feet, and walked quickly from the room. Returning to the kitchen, he found the maid at the stove tying on her apron. He noticed a basket on the counter filled with corn and string beans.

"I sent Little Jim to his room to put on some dry clothes," said Dinah. "He was all wet."

"What did you mean leaving him outside in this storm?" demanded Barnhill.

She stared at him with a bewildered expression. "But I told the missus . . ."

"He could've been struck by lightning. And the poor boy was scared to death, with the kitchen door latched."

"I told the missus," Dinah insisted with her hands on her hips, "I was leavin' for the grocers and she'd have to watch Little Jim. Then I got caught in the rain."

"Are you sure?" said Barnhill.

"Course I'm sure," she replied with an angry flash in her eyes. "Mebbe the missus was havin' one of her spells." She turned her back on Barnhill and reached for a heavy cast-iron skillet.

Sitting down at the table, Barnhill considered Kate's strange behavior, sleeping through such a storm, so deeply asleep she almost seemed . . . drugged. "Well, I'm sorry," he said. "There must have been a misunderstanding."

"Wasn't no misunderstanding. Missus knew darn well I was goin' out, and I told her the boy was playin' outside with his dog."

Little Jim bounded into the kitchen with the puppy at his heels. "Whatcha fixin', Dinah?" he said, tugging on her apron. "Cornbread?"

She turned and smiled at the boy. "Yes, I am," she said. "Hush puppies. And you can help me stir the batter."

As the summer doldrums dragged on, with hot, indolent days and nights filled with the croaking of bullfrogs in the aftermath of late-afternoon downpours, Kate fell deeper and deeper under the grip of the laudanum, a ruthless, pitiless captor, to the point that resistance seemed pointless and her surrender was complete. Leaving the door to the bedroom ajar, she emptied all but the last few ounces of the amber liquid into her water glass, carelessly left the bottle and dropper on the table, tossed down the drink, and slumped on the bedcovers. That was how Dinah, carrying her basket of folded sheets and towels to the upstairs linen closet, found her, half naked and virtually unconscious on the bed. She studied her mistress's pale, limp form and the bottle on the bedside table.

Stepping down from the sidewalk to cross the street, Barnhill heard his name and looked back to see Sally Porter in the doorway of the hardware store, clutching a bolt of cloth. "Hello, Sally," he said, returning to the sidewalk. "Let me give you a hand."

"I can manage," she said in an uncharacteristically subdued tone of voice. Before he could speak, she added, "Could I have a word with you? In private?"

Sally sat in an armchair facing Barnhill's broad desk untying the ribbon of her small hat, which matched her pale-yellow dress. Barnhill noticed approvingly the embroidered satin jacket and flounces at the hem of her skirt, something far more stylish than the simple dresses sewn from patterns by the local dressmaker. "Well," he said expectantly. "A legal problem I can . . ."

"No," she said curtly. "Jamie." She gazed into his eyes. "I'm worried about Kate." Barnhill merely nodded. "I've called on her every week," said Sally with a sigh, "for the past month or so. She won't see me. Your girl says she's feelin' puny or some such excuse. Then I happened to run into her at the store."

"I see," said Barnhill, folding his hands on his desk.

"She's not right, Jamie. Looks like she's wastin' away."

"Yes, I know," said Barnhill, feeling oddly embarrassed.

"Course it's none of my business," said Sally. "But Kate's one of the few friends I've got." An awkward pause followed. "I'm afraid it's the drink," blurted Sally. "Like her poor father." She abruptly rose and said, "I should be going."

Barnhill rose as well and said, "Thank you, Sally. I appreciate it. But it's not what you think."

Arriving home at half past six, Barnhill hung his hat and jacket on the stand in the front hall and walked to the kitchen, whistling softly as he rolled up his sleeves. Dinah was seated at the kitchen table rather than at her usual place stirring a pot on the stove or with a rolling pin on the countertop. "It's late," he said. "Shouldn't you be home?"

"Yassuh," she replied in a somber tone.

Barnhill stopped. "Where's Jim?" he asked.

"I sent him outside to play. So we could talk."

"What is it, Dinah? What's wrong?"

"You been good to me," said Dinah. "And my family. I need this job." Married to one of Hattie's great nephews, a violent man with a weakness for gambling and hard drink, she'd been left to care for their two young sons when her husband suddenly disappeared from town with another young woman. Barnhill had quietly helped Dinah obtain a divorce and discreetly provided her with funds for the children's food and clothing.

"You don't have to worry," he said.

"She'd shoot me if she found out," Dinah interrupted. "But I got to tell you!"

"Tell me what?"

"She's killin' herself with that poison. You got to stop her, Mista James!"

Barnhill felt a cold knot of fear in his gut. "Poison," he repeated. Dinah nodded. "Where is she?"

"On her bed."

Barnhill ascended the stairs, two at a time. Taking a deep breath, he pushed open the door and surveyed the bedroom. Kate was lying on her side, asleep or unconscious, wearing only a nightgown. His eye was immediately drawn to the brown glass medicine bottle on the bedside table. He walked quietly over, glanced down to satisfy himself that Kate was breathing, held up the bottle and read the label. Removing the cork, he held the bottle to his nose and sniffed—a sharp smell of alcohol and something else he couldn't name, like licorice. Of course he knew about laudanum, knew that doctors routinely recommended it to their female patients for all manner of maladies, menstrual cramps, dyspepsia, neuralgia. And an opiate like morphine, but subtler, he was told. He'd seen many a wounded soldier with a craving for morphine so strong that they'd give their last dime for an injection. Placing the bottle on the table, he looked down at Kate. Even in her drug-induced slumber she looked troubled of mind and sick of body; dangerously thin, sallow complexion, and old, though she was only in her midthirties. He resolved not to wake her. Taking the brown bottle and eyedropper, he walked quietly from the room, closing the door behind him.

Seated at the kitchen table with a square of cornbread and glass of buttermilk, Barnhill watched as Dinah ladled clear broth into a bowl and then placed it on a tray with a plate of soda crackers. Turning to look at him over her shoulder, she said, "Ain't no use, Mista James. She ain't gonna touch it."

"We have to keep trying," said Barnhill. "Just leave it at her bedside."

Tightly gripping the tray, Dinah walked to the parlor and slowly ascended the stairs. She hesitated at the top and then made her way to the bedroom, the door slightly ajar. "Miz Kate?" she said, peering into the dimly lit room. Hearing no answer, she pushed open the door and walked to the four-poster bed. Kate lay on her side beneath the covers, facing the wall. "Miz Kate," repeated Dinah.

Turning over, Kate squinted at the black servant and mumbled, "What is it?" Her hair was disarrayed from long hours tossing on the pillows, her complexion pale and cheeks hollow.

Gazing down at her, Dinah imagined she weighed no more than a hundred pounds. "Brought you somethin' to eat," said Dinah. "Some chicken soup and crackers."

Kate merely shook her head and then rolled over on her side with her back to the maid and pulled the covers up to her face.

"I'll just leave it over here," said Dinah, lowering the tray to the bedside table. Casting a final look at Kate's immobile form, she turned and hurried from the room.

Barnhill rose from his chair when Dinah returned to the kitchen. She briefly made eye contact with him, a look of sadness and resignation, before turning away to the stove. "I'll see what I can do," he said, tossing his napkin on the table.

Silently entering the bedroom, he walked to Kate's bedside and looked down at her. After the first few nights, he'd slept in the spare room, unable to share the bed with Kate as she battled withdrawal from the opiate, tossing, sweating, crying out, sobbing, lucky to snatch an hour's sleep before sunup. During the daylight hours she mostly lay in bed, refusing to dress or to eat more than an occasional cracker or piece of toast. One afternoon, Barnhill had found her desperately searching the dresser drawers for the vial of laudanum she'd secreted, which he'd thankfully discovered and disposed of before she could find it. Now, watching her chest rise and fall, not daring to wake her, he felt a powerful wave of remorse and pity, as though her wretched condition was somehow his fault. With a deep sigh, he slumped in the chair by the bed, closing his eyes and crossing his arms over his chest.

"Jamie . . ."

"What?" said Barnhill, startled awake after dozing for an hour. He peered at Kate, who was propped up on an elbow rubbing her eyes. "What is it, darling?" he said.

"Can I have something to eat?" she said softly. "I'm starved."

Barnhill stood, took a step closer to her, and glanced at the tray on the bedside table with the bowl of cold soup and uneaten crackers. Smiling, he said, "Let's get you something special. Dinah baked a pie."

"I'd like that," she said, brushing away a stray wisp of hair. "With a glass of buttermilk."

When Barnhill returned after a few minutes, Kate was bending over the washbasin, wearing a blue flannel robe over her nightgown, splashing water on her face. Drying her face with a towel, she turned to him and said, "I can't bear to look at myself in the mirror. How long has it been?"

"How long since . . ."

"Since I quit taking that medicine," said Kate with tears welling in her eyes.

"Six days," said Barnhill. "And you've hardly touched a bite of food the whole time."

She sat on the side of the bed, and he lowered the tray to her lap. Looking up at him with a faint smile, she helped herself to a forkful of pie, still warm from the oven, and then took a sip of buttermilk. "Oh, Jamie," she said, "I'd forgotten how much I like lemon pie." He sat in the chair and watched with satisfaction as she quickly finished the pie and drank the last of the milk.

"Well," he said, reaching to take the tray from her lap, "why don't you take a little nap, and after a while we'll draw you a nice, hot bath."

For the first time in a week, Kate, wearing her robe and bedroom slippers with her hair combed back and tied with a ribbon, descended the stairs for supper. Barnhill helped her to sit in her accustomed place at the table, with Little Jim at her right elbow. The boy looked at her gaunt form apprehensively, having been told she was suffering from a bout of dyspepsia and strictly enjoined from disturbing her. "Are you all right, Mama?" he said as she spread her napkin in her lap.

Giving him a tender look, she said, "I'm feelin' much better."

Dinah appeared from the kitchen with a platter of fried chicken, rice, and cream gravy. "Yum," said Little Jim. As she served her, Kate looked up over her shoulder and said, "Thank you, Dinah."

"Yes, ma'am."

"For taking such good care of me."

"You're welcome, ma'am."

After they were served, Barnhill reached out to take Jim's hand, bowed his head, and said, "Let's return thanks." Giving Jim's hand a gentle squeeze, he said, "Our heavenly father, we give thanks for these and all thy many blessings, especially this evening for the recovery of thy servant Kate. Give us the strength, dear father, to do what is right and good, and in all things to serve thee. Amen."

"Amen," repeated Kate, releasing her boy's hand and brushing a tear from her eye.

Following the refreshing bath and decent supper, Kate had slept through the night, a good eight hours' rest after months of drug-induced insomnia. And with the restorative rest came the return of appetite, enjoying hearty breakfasts of eggs, bacon, and grits; dinners of country ham, biscuits, and summer vegetables; and Dinah's baked treats: pies, pralines, and cookies. Barnhill arranged for Sally to visit Kate on most afternoons, joining her in rocking chairs on the porch looking out on the footbridge, reading aloud stories and poetry from *Harper's* magazine. By the time a month had passed, Kate had regained her strength and the weight she'd lost and rediscovered an interest in the world around her; in her son's development and precociousness, and in her husband's work. After the first terrible week, nothing was spoken of her months in the thrall of the opiate, a condition they simply referred to as the "blues."

"No more blues," said Kate as they strolled along the footbridge on a fine autumn day, the sky cloudless blue with the temperature in the fifties and the smell of burning leaves in the air. Giving her arm a gentle squeeze, Barnhill glanced down at her and said, "Mother's invited us for dinner tomorrow after church."

"Are you planning to sing?"

Over the course of the summer, with the demands of his work and Kate's deepening despair, they'd often missed church and his participation in the choir. "I sure am," he said with a smile. "Don't know how they've gotten along without me."

"Not very well, I reckon," said Kate, putting her arm through his. "I think I'll gather some pecans from the yard and bake a pie."

"That would be wonderful," said Barnhill. "I doubt mother and sister have tasted pecan pie since Hattie passed."

Sunday was another perfect October day, and with crops laid by, cotton at the gin, and debts, for the time at least, settled with the supply merchants, the inhabitants of the farming community crowded into the Presbyterian church on the outskirts of town: common people grateful for the return of normalcy and the prospect of better days after so many years of war, strife, and destitution. Barnhill parked the buggy on the lawn amid dozens of others and helped Kate and Little Jim down from the seat, listening to the piano notes from the outbuilding behind the small clapboard chapel. Humming the melody of the familiar hymn, Barnhill said, "If you'll take the boy to Sunday school, I'll meet up with you afterward in the family pew."

"I think not, Mr. Barnhill," said Kate, walking along holding her son's hand. "I promised Little Jim he could hear his daddy sing today."

After warmly greeting Miss Ellen Graves, Barnhill assumed his place on the first row of the bass section, facing the rows of altos on the opposite side of the room. Little Jim sat on his mother's lap in the cramped space by the door reserved for non-participants in the singing. At Miss Graves's signal, the men and women rose from their seats. "We'll begin," she said, "with 'Old One Hundred.'" Looking to the pianist for a single chord, the singers opened their songbooks and sang, a capella, the ancient hymn in the peculiar cadence and harmonies of the Sacred Harp tradition. Barnhill was pleased to hear the deep bass voices of the two black men who'd recently joined the choir and observed three gray-haired black women on the back row of the sopranos. After conducting the choir in several hymns, Miss Graves said, "We've missed you lately, Captain Barnhill. Would you care to lead us?"

Barnhill took a step forward, searched the pages of the songbook, and said, "Let's sing Number 125. 'Rock of Ages.'" Briefly making eye contact with Little Jim, who stared at him with a fascinated expression, he waited for the pitch from the pianist and then sang:

> Rock of ages, cleft for me,
> Let me hide myself in Thee;
> Let the water and the blood
> From Thy wounded side which flowed,
> Be of sin the double cure
> Save from wrath and make me pure.

At the hand signal from Miss Ellen, the ensemble joined in, beautifully harmonized, white voices blended with black, the tempo slow, rising to a crescendo in the closing lines:

> While I draw this fleeting breath,
> When my eye-strings break in death,
> Rock of ages, cleft for me,
> Let me hide myself in Thee.

As the voices died away, Barnhill looked at Kate, whose eyes were beginning to well with tears, and then at his son, who beamed proudly.

Following an overlong service, in which the preacher seized on a favorite theme—the rise of the "New South" as a latter day Promised Land for God's chosen people after their years wandering in the figurative desert—Barnhill unhitched the mare and drove the buggy the few miles to Mountain Farm. Arriving within minutes of the buggy transporting his mother Mary and sister Anna, he looped the reins on the hitching post and lifted the boy from the seat. "Why don't you go inside," he said, "and see Grandma." Turning to Kate, who was holding a box with the pie she'd baked, he said, "I'm going to make a quick visit to Hattie's grave." A mockingbird sang brightly, high in the ancient live oak that shaded the family burial plot, which was situated a hundred yards from the house and enclosed by a white picket fence, with a view of the cotton fields bearing the stubble of the recent harvest, and rolling hills in the distance. Barnhill unlatched the gate and walked to his father's headstone.

> Robert H. Barnhill
> Texas Pioneer
> Born September 12, 1796
> Died April 2, 1861

CHAPTER NINETEEN

He tried to visualize his father in his favorite rocker on the porch, remembering his strong voice with the old Virginia accent, his gentle, patient manner, and bedrock Christian convictions. It was a good thing, he considered, that he had not lived to see the devastation wrought by the war and its aftermath. How long would it be, he wondered, before his mother took her place beside his father? With an inward groan, he walked to the place on the other side of the plot where Hattie had been laid to rest, marked by a simple headstone with only the words "'Hattie' Died August 16, 1877." Though, as was generally the case with the former slaves, her surname and date of birth were unknown, she must have lived to her late eighties. After a quick mental calculation, he surmised that she'd been born in the Upper South in the late 1700s, perhaps to first-generation African Americans. Barnhill dropped to his knees on the soft grass, lowered his head, and offered a silent prayer, thanking God for Hattie's life with the hope that her spirit of loving-kindness would remain as a blessing over the family.

Barnhill now occupied his father's old place at the head of the dining-room table; Kate and five-year old Jim were seated on his left, sister Anna and mother Mary on his right. Reaching for the small brass bell to summon the help from the kitchen, Mary said, "Little Jim told me he heard you sing at church."

"He sang right good," interjected the boy, eliciting a laugh from his grandmother.

"Right well," corrected Kate.

Barnhill smiled at Kate as the black servants entered the dining room to clear the table. With her auburn hair tied back with a ribbon, Kate looked pretty again, her cheeks rosy and eyes bright and attentive. "Jamie sang a solo," she said. "'Rock of Ages.'"

"I do love that hymn," said Mary. "It was your father's favorite."

Anna stared at her brother with a down-turned mouth, mildly resentful of the attention and praise he always seemed to receive from their mother. "Jamie says you baked a pie," she said, turning to Kate.

"Here it is," Kate replied as the young black girl entered to serve the first of the dessert plates. "Made with pecans from our backyard."

"My goodness," said Mary. "I haven't had pecan pie in ages."

"Didn't know you could cook," said Anna.

"You'd be surprised," said Kate with a happy smile.

Anna, Barnhill reflected, a spinster now in her thirties, resented not only his position as the presumed favorite, but also his marriage, to a woman Anna no doubt regarded as her inferior.

"Dolly," said Mary to the older servant standing in the corner, "you may serve the coffee now. I don't reckon I'll ever give up coffee," she added, speaking to her son at the head of the table, "after going without all those years during the war."

"Yummy," said Little Jim after taking a large bite of pie.

After sampling the pie and taking a sip of rich coffee from his mother's fine English china, Barnhill looked contentedly around the old, familiar dining room with its pale green paneling and crystal chandelier and smiled at Kate, who seemed at last content with her lot as wife and mother.

Barnhill sat in his favorite chair by the fireplace in the parlor, where the logs hissed and crackled with a cheerful, warming blaze, and reflected on the day: the look on Little Jim's face, sitting in his mother's lap, as Barnhill sang with the church choir; the pride and contentment Kate displayed before his mother and sister at the dinner table, utterly transformed from the broken woman of just a few months ago. Barnhill sipped his glass of diluted bourbon, staring into the fire as he listened to the cold rain that beat against the windows and the wind in the trees. Glancing up, he smiled at Kate who'd silently entered the room wearing a long, diaphanous gown with satin bows at her wrists, barefoot, with her hair untied and lying on her shoulders, the curves of her body silhouetted by the lamplight behind her. "My," said Barnhill, rising from his chair, "you look lovely." Walking over to embrace him, she stood on tiptoe and lightly kissed his lips. He held her close and nuzzled the soft skin of her neck. "Mmm," he said. "What's that fragrance?"

"The French perfume," she whispered, "you gave me for my birthday."

"What about Jim?"

"Fast asleep." After another light kiss, she took his hand and led him to the staircase.

CHAPTER TWENTY

ADDISON PARKER STOOD BEFORE THE FIREPLACE, which radiated warmth from thick pine logs blazing on the andirons. Barnhill, seated before Parker's broad mahogany desk, felt a cold draft seeping through the sill on the unusually frigid February morning. Grasping the lapels of his checked wool jacket, Parker thrust out his goateed chin and declared, "I simply will not stand for it! It's one thing to swindle some poor farmer out of his land and quite another to stand in the way of an enterprise I've invested millions in."

"You're certain," asked Barnhill, "that Gould is behind it?"

"Without a doubt," replied Parker. He walked to the marble-topped stand in the corner and poured a glass of amber liquid from a crystal decanter. "Brandy?" he said.

"No thanks," said Barnhill.

Taking a sip, Parker set the glass down on his desk, opened a burl elm cigar box and removed a slender panatela. He snipped off the end with a silver cutter and struck a match to the tip. "Jay Gould," he said, expelling a cloud of smoke and returning to the fireplace with his glass in one hand and cigar in the other, "is the most unscrupulous manipulator on Wall Street. First it was the Missouri Pacific. Next he wrests control of the Katy from the bondholders, and now, according to my agents, he has his sights on the T&P. Just listen to this." Putting his brandy aside, Parker picked up a week-old issue of the *New York Times* and jabbed a finger at a bold headline: "A Gigantic Combination."

"Gould," he said, "along with that scoundrel Collis Huntington, threw a dinner party at Delmonico's for General Grant."

"Delmonico's?" said Barnhill, leaning forward in his chair to peer at the newspaper headline.

"Fancy New York restaurant," explained Parker. "A favorite of the Wall Street nabobs." He read aloud from the article: "'It is proposed to consolidate the Missouri, Kansas, and Texas with the Missouri Pacific and the Texas Pacific, which would carry the consolidated line to the Gulf of Mexico and the Rio Grande on the south and the Pacific Ocean on the west.' This is Mr. Jay Gould's scheme." Pausing to puff on his cigar, Parker continued reading: "'Another part of the general plan is to make Gen. Grant President of the consolidated company, because of his great ability to direct such a gigantic enterprise.'" He tossed the paper aside with a disgusted expression. "Can you conceive of it?" said Parker. "Ulysses S. Grant as president of the transcontinental railroad?"

Barnhill shook his head, thinking back to Grant's ruthless tenacity in the summer of '64, his willingness to expend Northern lives by the tens of thousands in his relentless pursuit of Lee. "Grant," he said, "should've stayed in the army . . . and out of politics. But I'm not sure I understand what this means for your business?"

"What it means," said Parker, pausing to take a sip of brandy that seemed to add color to his ruddy cheeks, "is monopoly, pure and simple. Look what Rockefeller's managed with Standard Oil. Precisely the same. Gould controls the Missouri Pacific. He grabs the Katy and arranges to lease the Katy's road to the Missouri Pacific, which also takes a lease on the T&P line. Now he plans to combine the whole shooting match with Huntington's Southern Pacific. By God, every mile of trackage in the state will be in the sullied hands of these brigands."

"Yes," agreed Barnhill, "with help from the Democrats in Austin . . ."

"In Gould's hip pocket," interrupted Parker. "Redeemers, Democrats . . . they've delivered the state over to the eastern money interests. All in the name of that shining shibboleth," he added with his penchant for alliteration, stabbing the air with his cigar, "the New South. A mere simulacrum," he concluded with a shake of his large head. "A chimera, disguising the fact that they've sold their souls to Wall Street."

Barnhill nodded and then mildly said, "But isn't it true, sir, that you've financed your mill with Wall Street capital?"

The suggestion of a smile brightened Parker's countenance. "It's a fact that I've borrowed millions from Pierpont Morgan. And also a fact that if these railroad men strangle me, Morgan will step in and foreclose, and own the largest sawmill and more timberland than any man in the South. By God, Barnhill, I'm not about to let that happen!"

Barnhill rose from his chair and walked to the window, gazing out on the bare branches that shook in the cold wind against the dull backdrop of the wintry sky. "How, sir," he said, turning back to face Parker, "do you mean to stop them?"

"My mill is producing eighty thousand board feet of pine lumber a day," replied Parker. "Eighty *thousand.* And the only way to get it to market is downriver to Beaumont or by short line rail to Corrigan and eventually to the Missouri Pacific road en route to St. Louis." Parker tossed the stub of his cigar on the fire. "With Gould in control of the Missouri Pacific, I'm at his mercy."

"The Katy railroad," said Barnhill, slowly pacing with his hands behind his back, "was a creature of the Reconstruction legislature, of dubious legality. And the Missouri Pacific is also a foreign corporation. If we can prove that Gould has control . . ."

"And is setting the rates," added Parker.

Barnhill halted, looked Parker in the eye, and smiled. "You're prepared to take these men to court?"

"Yes, sir. And I believe you're the lawyer to handle the case."

With cat-like tread, Kate, holding a candle on a brass stand, crept on bare feet to the entrance to the library. Clutching her nightgown to her neck, she watched her husband deep in concentration over a thick volume that lay open on his rolltop desk. "Burning the midnight oil?" she said after a moment.

Looking up over his shoulder, Barnhill smiled and said, "Yes, I'm afraid I am." He glanced at the clock on the shelf whose hands showed ten past twelve. "What woke you?"

"I felt the baby kick," said Kate. She walked over and reached for his hand. "Here," she said, placing it lightly on her rounded belly.

He felt the warmth of her skin through the sheer fabric and then a small thump, which filled him with pleasure. With a smile at his six-month pregnant wife, he said, "I wonder if it's a girl?"

"Kicks like a boy," said Kate.

"All that matters to me," said Barnhill, "is that we've got a healthy baby . . . and mama."

Kate put the candle aside and sat down in the easy chair by the desk. "Why are you workin' so late?" she asked.

Marking his place, Barnhill closed the heavy volume, a treatise on constitutional law. "I'm convinced," he said, "that the charter of the Katy railroad was obtained illegally. Which would open the door to challenge the Missouri Pacific."

"It no longer surprises me, Jamie Barnhill," said Kate with a toss of her long auburn hair, "that you'd take on the most powerful men in the state. First it was the carpetbaggers and the cavalry, then the Klan . . . Why not the railroads?"

"Why not?" said Barnhill with a grin. He stood up and doused the oil lamp. "Time to put mama to bed."

Addison Parker stood in Barnhill's law office admiring the buckram-bound books on the shelves. Curious, he reached for a small glass jar and rattled the deformed piece of lead it contained. "What's this?" he asked, turning to Barnhill, who was seated in the swivel chair behind his wide desk.

"The minié ball a surgeon extracted from my chest," Barnhill replied.

"At Gettysburg?"

"No, at Fredericksburg. At Gettysburg I was shot through the shoulder."

Parker returned the jar to its place on the shelf and walked a few paces to examine the faded battle standard of the Fifth Texas that hung next to Barnhill's framed diploma from the University of Virginia. Parker was fascinated with Barnhill's Civil War artifacts, as almost all of their previous meetings had taken place at Parker's office. "Virginia," he said, gazing at the parchment. "Jefferson's university. There were a few Southern boys in my class at Harvard." He turned to face Barnhill. "But none that I knew very well. I understand that most of them died in the war." He pulled back a chair, sat down, and crossed one leg over his knee. "What this state needs," he continued, "even more than industry, is a public university."

"I entirely agree," said Barnhill. "Just as Jefferson envisioned."

"Texas has a unique advantage, shared by none of its sister states," said Parker. "Public lands, by the millions of acres. I intend to enlist the support of the governor for a plan to build a first-class state university in Austin, with the state's public lands providing a perpetual endowment."

"An ingenious idea," said Barnhill, folding his arms across his broad chest. "Texas entered the union under a treaty between sovereign nations. And retained ownership of all of its public lands, an area larger, I reckon, than the entire state of Alabama."

"Well," said Parker, "we're not here to talk about public education. But suing the railroads. Mr. Gould's railroads. I gather you have a recommendation?"

"Yes, sir. I've prepared a synopsis of my research and proposed course of action." Barnhill reached across the desk and handed his client a typewritten memorandum. "Why don't I touch on the main points and you can read it at your leisure?"

"Certainly," said Parker, refolding his reading glasses into his breast pocket.

"To begin with," said Barnhill, resting his elbows on the desk, "the special legislation enacted in 1870 granting the Katy land in Texas for its road and two years' tax abatements is almost certainly unconstitutional. The Katy is a Kansas corporation without authority to do business in Texas. And since the Katy has leased its road to the Missouri Pacific, a finding that the Katy's operating without legal authority would render the lease void."

"Are you suggesting," said Parker, "a suit to invalidate the Katy and Missouri Pacific's authority to operate in Texas?"

"No, sir. As a private citizen, you do not, in my judgment, have standing to challenge the Katy's privileges. The attorney general might, if he had the backbone. But not the Longleaf Pine Lumber Company."

"How, then, do you suggest we proceed?"

Hearing the clamor of men loading a mule-drawn wagon in the street, Barnhill rose from his desk and walked over to close the windows. Turning to Parker he said, "Your mill is a customer of the International and Great Northern Railroad. The I & GN. Now, the I & GN," said Barnhill, pacing slowly before the windows, "was formed by a merger with the Houston and Great Northern in September of '73. First railroad chartered in Texas after the war, in '66. They built the road through East Texas that serves your mill."

"Very interesting," said Parker, "but what does it have to do with the case?"

Barnhill walked back to his desk and rested his palms on its polished oak surface. "I can prove that Jay Gould," he said, "employing his usual scurrilous methods, took control of the I & GN last December and promptly leased its lines to the Katy for ninety-nine years. So that little short-line railroad you've been shipping your lumber on is in fact a part of Gould's vast monopoly."

"I see," said Parker with a satisfied smile.

"And," continued Barnhill, "I've been studying the rates these different roads are charging. Since Gould took control, the I & GN rates on East Texas shippers have been set exactly in conformity with the Katy and Missouri Pacific, the so-called 'Texas differential.'"

"Highway robbery," huffed Parker.

"I recommend we file suit, in the federal district court at Waco, naming as defendants the I & GN, the Katy, and the Missouri Pacific. Seeking damages arising from inflated freight rates on all lumber shipped from your mill, as the direct result"—Barnhill paused and stood erect—"of a conspiracy to stifle competition."

Parker's gaze fell to his hands folded on his lap, seeming to study his finely polished nails. "Sue the railroads," he said in an uncharacteristically soft voice. "Gould, with all his millions." He looked up.

"The federal judge in Waco," said Barnhill, "is a good man, a Democrat of the old school, yet appointed by President Hayes."

"You don't think Gould can buy him?"

"No, sir. Harry Wainwright was a captain in the Fourth Texas."

"I see," said Parker. He rose from his chair and fixed Barnhill with his intelligent gray eyes. "Draft the papers," he said quietly, "and let's get on with it."

"I already have," said Barnhill with a modest smile. "But I'd recommend you consider my memorandum before making a final decision."

Parker briefly studied the document, looked up and said, "I shall." He reached across the desk and shook Barnhill's hand. "How's my favorite boy?" asked Parker. "Little Jim?"

"Growing like a weed."

"And his mother?"

"Very well, thank you. Kate's expecting our second child."

"Oh, really," said Parker. "Congratulations. Now, don't work too hard on this law business. Allow time for your family."

"Yes, sir. I will."

Barnhill flicked the reins, starting the tall roan mare forward along the rutted road at the entrance to Mountain Farm. Kate sat beside him on the pleated leather seat, wearing a sunbonnet with a plaid blanket over her lap. A cool breeze stirred the trees along the roadside, and the cloudless April sky was cobalt blue. In lieu of the Sunday morning church service, they had left Little Jim with Dinah and made an excursion to the farm to visit Barnhill's mother, now in her late seventies and too infirm to rise from her bed. "A remarkable woman, Mother," said Barnhill as they started back toward town, pleased by the smoothness of the ride of the well-sprung buggy, a recent acquisition.

"Yes," said Kate, leaning against his shoulder. "An example of what every woman should be. Not proud, but strong, and charitable to everyone."

"I'm still amazed," said Barnhill as the buggy started down a gentle slope, "how she managed during the war. With my father dead, and me in Virginia, she kept the place going, overseeing the Negroes and raising her own crops."

"With Anna's help," said Kate.

"True," agreed Barnhill, aware that the burden of caring for his mother had fallen almost entirely on Anna, now too old to marry and unfriendly toward Kate to the point of rudeness.

Kate lapsed into silence, lost in her thoughts as she listened to the creaking wheel rims and *clip-clop* of hooves. "I wonder," she said after a while, "if you could admire me as much as you do your mother?"

"Admire you?" said Barnhill, looking briefly in her eyes. "I love you, sweetheart."

"I just wonder if I could measure up."

Barnhill tugged on the reins and brought the buggy slowly to a stop. "You went through a hard spell," he said. "After the baby was born and then with . . . the blues." Kate nodded. "But you got through it. It was hard, but you did it. Do I admire you? You're dang right I do."

"Thank you, Jamie," Kate said softly, finding his hand and giving it a squeeze.

Gazing out over the dark, furrowed soil on both sides of the road, he said, "Cotton's planted. I reckon these poor croppers will try to make it through another season."

Kate nodded and said, "It's different now than when we had the store. Daddy would always help a poor farmer in trouble. But these new men . . ."

"Absentee owners," said Barnhill, starting the horse forward again.

"Yes," said Kate, "and they'll foreclose a crop lien every time they get a chance."

"With the price of cotton so low these farmers will never get out of debt. White or black."

As they passed into the pine forest, the cool air was perfumed with the sweet scent of sap. "Easy girl," said Barnhill, gently pulling on the reins. "Beautiful, isn't it?" he said. The forest understory was thick with white and pink dogwood blossoms and bright green shoots of new fern on the pine straw. As the mare stamped impatiently, Kate looked into her husband's eyes and said, "Do you love me?"

"Of course I do." Barnhill leaned over and lightly kissed her on the lips.

"I've tried to be a good mother. I know I haven't always . . ."

"You *are* a good mother," said Barnhill. "You had a hard time, but that's over."

"I'll do better this time," said Kate earnestly. "I swear."

Reaching an arm around her shoulders, Barnhill closed his eyes, and listening to the songbirds, said, "You'll be fine. Just fine."

It was a courtroom triumph like no other in his career. With no jury, he waged a solitary battle against a battery of railroad lawyers that included a thin dyspeptic who'd traveled all the way from New York to Waco and spoke not a word until the closing arguments; a prodigious struggle whose outcome rested not on oratorical flourishes or the undoing of a key witness but rather on the methodical production of volumes of documentary evidence—stock and bond ledgers, correspondence, memoranda, minutes, freight schedules—the preponderance of which established not only that the International and Great Northern Railroad was but a cog in the great industrial machine controlled by Jay Gould but that the rates charged to its customers far exceeded those in a competitive environment. In a courtroom packed with reporters from the daily newspapers in San Antonio, Dallas, Fort Worth, and Houston, Judge Wainwright held, in *obiter dicta* that nonetheless would have far-reaching consequences, that the act of the Reconstruction legislature granting the Katy exclusive rights to build its road in Texas violated both the state and federal constitutions, rendering the lease of its line to the Missouri Pacific open to attack, and awarded damages of $1,000,000 to the plaintiff, Addison Parker's Longleaf Pine Lumber Company, in recompense for the exorbitant rates charged on the transport of lumber from its East Texas sawmill, the state's largest.

"We're filing an appeal," sneered the railroad's lead counsel as he passed by the plaintiff's table. "That verdict will never stand."

"Fine, but you'll have to supercede it," said Barnhill mildly. "With a bond. And interest will accrue." He began gathering up the piles of papers from the table and packing them in a box.

Addison Parker, clad in a black frock coat and old-fashioned cravat, sat on the first row of the courtroom as it emptied of spectators. When they were alone, Parker stood up and leaned on the oak railing. "Your strategy was brilliant," he said. "No bombast, but a straightforward construction of the facts and analysis of the constitutional law."

"Thank you, sir," said Barnhill. "I seriously doubt that Gould's lawyers can find any reversible error in the court's findings. But that's not to say they won't have influence on the appeals bench."

"I suspect we'll reach a settlement," said Parker, "before a ruling on appeal."

Barnhill nodded. With a glance at the clock on the wall at the back of the courtroom, he said, "If I hurry I can make the two o'clock train to Nacogdoches. I need to get home, as Kate's in her ninth month."

"Go right ahead," said Parker. "Your place is at her side. We'll save the celebration for another day."

There would be no celebration of the great victory over the railroads, notwithstanding the bold headlines that trumpeted the verdict in every major newspaper in the state. Arriving home after a two-hour journey by rail from Waco to Nacogdoches and another three hours by horse and buggy to San Augustine, Barnhill wearily entered the parlor where, to his surprise, he found Dr. Smithers seated in an armchair. "Hello, doc," said Barnhill, slipping off his hat and coat and hanging them on a stand. "Everything all right?"

The doctor, a short, compact man in his early fifties, rose from his chair and hooked his thumbs on his galluses. "Kate's fine," he said. "Resting upstairs as I instructed her." Barnhill made eye contact with him, certain there was more. "The problem," said the doctor, "is that the baby's breach." He paused to make sure Barnhill understood. "And Kate's time could be any day now."

Barnhill nodded, conscious of a sudden dryness in his mouth and the pounding of his heart. There was nothing, he knew, more dangerous in childbirth than an attempted breach delivery. "Well, then," he said, "what can we do?"

"There's always the chance the baby will turn," he replied. "I've seen it before. But the risk is, if we wait and she goes into labor . . ." He hesitated with a frown.

"The risk is," repeated Barnhill, like a lawyer with a reluctant witness.

"To save the mother," said Smithers, "I'd have to perform a craniotomy."

Barnhill signaled his lack of comprehension with a shake of his head.

"A procedure," explained Smithers, "to remove the fetus."

"The fetus," said Barnhill.

The doctor nodded. "The baby would be sacrificed."

"There's no other alternative?"

"Well, there's a cesarean section," said Smithers. "The surgical delivery of the child. I'm certainly not competent to perform it, but more and more often it's being attempted. The risks to the mother, however, are substantial."

"Do you know of someone?" asked Barnhill.

Smithers nodded. "A doctor in Nacogdoches," he said, "by the name of McReynolds. A regimental surgeon in McLaws's Division during the war, with an excellent reputation. And, I understand, experience in performing cesarean deliveries."

Before going upstairs to interview his patient, Dr. Angus McReynolds, a tall, middle-aged man with a long brown beard of the type favored during the war, conferred with Barnhill and Dr. Smithers in the parlor. Even though no decision had been reached, McReynolds had taken the precaution of bringing along his surgical nurse and an assortment of specialized instruments and equipment, including a wooden box that contained a glass sphere and rubber tubing. "And so, Mr. Barnhill," said McReynolds, "you experienced ether during the war?"

"Ether or chloroform," said Barnhill. "Not sure which. When the Yankee surgeons operated on my shoulder at Gettysburg."

"I much prefer ether," said McReynolds. "Induces a deep sleep. The patient won't feel a thing." Barnhill nodded, involuntarily rubbing his shoulder. "Now some physicians," McReynolds continued, "allow the mother to go into labor, to see if the baby might turn, trying a cesarean as a last resort. I believe that's a mistake. By the time surgery is required, the woman's exhausted and far less able to withstand its . . . risks."

"Would you elaborate?" said Barnhill.

McReynolds nodded, briefly exchanging looks with Dr. Smithers. "The risks to the mother are considerable, primarily hemorrhage and postoperative infection, as we are unable to suture the incision to the uterus."

"The womb," added Smithers.

"I just don't know," said Barnhill, rubbing his chin.

"The final decision," said McReynolds, "rests with Mrs. Barnhill. I'll discuss it with her now."

Barnhill knelt at Kate's bedside, which smelled of freshly laundered sheets and carbolic. He lightly brushed the hair at her forehead, leaned over and kissed her, and said, "With the ether, you'll go right to sleep. You won't feel a thing." He glanced at the glass sphere, partially filled with a clear liquid, on the bedside table.

Folding her hands over her large belly, Kate said, "I'm a little scared, Jamie." Faced with the grim alternatives, she'd unhesitatingly opted for surgery, with the promise that it could save her baby.

He nodded as he clasped her hand. "I'll be praying for you and the baby," he said softly. He leaned over and kissed her again.

"It's time," said Dr. McReynolds, standing in the doorway with Dr. Smithers.

"I love you, darlin'," said Barnhill.

"Love you, Jamie," whispered Kate.

Barnhill paced across the Persian carpet in the parlor, smoking a cheroot and pausing now and then to take a sip from his glass of bourbon and water, oblivious to all noise save the rhythmic ticking of the clock on the mantel. He was alone, as Dinah had taken the boy with his dog on a long walk on the mild spring day. He'd left the two doctors and the nurse, clad in a long white dress and starched apron, precisely at one o'clock. The minute hand on the clock now showed twenty past, though it seemed at least an hour had passed. Taking a final draw on the cigar, he stubbed it out and then finished his drink in a swig. Running his hand over his mouth he suddenly heard something from the top of the stairs—a piercing cry. He moved quickly to the stairs and ascended partway. His heart pounding, he heard it again, the unmistakable bawling of a newborn. Dear God, he prayed fervently. Please dear God, spare my wife and child.

"Mr. Barnhill," called the nurse from the top of the stairs.

"Yes," he answered, running the rest of the way up.

"You have a little girl," said the nurse, lifting up the tiny, swaddled child for Barnhill's inspection.

"Thank God," he said. "And my wife?"

"They're working on her," said the nurse in a matter-of-fact way. "You should wait downstairs."

Barnhill sat in his chair by the cold fireplace, his elbows resting on his knees, his collar unfastened, staring at the pattern of the carpet, vainly listening for sounds from the upstairs room. The minutes passed slowly, inexorably, until the clock on the mantel showed five past two. Barnhill suddenly felt a powerful premonition. Looking up, he heard the door to the upstairs bedroom open, heard the tread of shoes on the stairs. Dr. Smithers stopped, gazed dolefully down at Barnhill, and before a word was spoken Barnhill understood. Kate was dead.

CHAPTER TWENTY-ONE

STANDING UNDER THE ANCIENT LIVE OAK that shaded the family plot, James Barnhill held his son's hand as they silently stood before the new granite headstone marking the grave of the boy's mother. Little Jim looked up, wondering whether a grown-up could cry, restraining his own tears by observing his father's impassive mask. After the moment passed, Barnhill walked a few paces to stand before another smooth gray marker, inscribed with the words:

> Mary Sewell Barnhill
> Born October 12, 1804
> Died May 20, 1881
> Gone to her Savior

It was more than Barnhill could bear. A sob caught in his throat, and with tears streaming down his cheeks he knelt down and tightly held his son, patting his back as the boy shook with his own sobs. Pressing his face against his father's scratchy wool coat, Jim raised a hand to his father's face to feel for the tears. Reassured, he quieted and fought back his own. "Daddy," he said softly.

"Yes, son?" Barnhill stroked Jim's hair.

"I think Grandma went to look after Mama."

Barnhill looked into Jim's eyes. He nodded, swallowed hard, and said, "Yes, she did. They're together in heaven now, where there's no more tears. The Bible tells us so." In a sudden gust of wind that nearly lifted his hat, Barnhill stood up and, taking Jim's hand, turned away from the fresh graves and walked to the picket gate. The fields sloping down from the hilltop were lush green from the spring rains and blanketed with blue and yellow wildflowers. The two walked slowly back to the house, their tears drying in the cool breeze. Inside, the old house was silent as death, as the help had finished their chores and retired to their whitewashed cabins. Listening to the tall grandfather clock in the front hall, Barnhill walked with Jim to the kitchen, where he found a pitcher of milk in the icebox and a tin of sugar cookies. They sat at the table, munching the crumbly sweets and sharing a glass of cold milk. Refreshed, Barnhill considered, for the hundredth time, the strange turn of fate that led to his mother's death—a tranquil passing in her sleep—within two weeks of Kate's. He believed in fate, or destiny, in the sense that everything, including his own survival in the war, was destined to be, in God's plan. And though he believed with equal certainty in an afterlife for believers such as his mother and wife, it was almost no consolation to him in the depths of his loss.

He gazed lovingly at the nine-year-old boy, whose laced-up boots almost reached the floor, with a mop of straw-colored hair and clear blue eyes. "I need a word with Aunt Anna," he said, "before we head home to see about the baby."

Barnhill found his sister in their mother's favorite armchair in the parlor with a large book open in her lap. Looking up at him with a pained expression, she said, "Poor Little Jim."

He nodded with a frown and said, "What do you have there?"

"Mama's account book. She kept a record of every little thing." Anna looked down at the neat rows of penciled entries. "She never told me," she said, looking back up at her brother, "that you were providing for us."

"She didn't?"

Anna shook her head and said, "I'm sorry, Jamie. I'm so sorry." He stared at her thoughtfully. "Well," she said, closing the ledger, "I suppose you'll be selling this old place."

"Selling it? Why, the farm belongs to the two of us, in equal shares. Why would we sell it?"

"I assumed she left it to you. And with just me here, all by myself, and all the expenses . . ."

"Don't worry about the expenses," said Barnhill, walking over to the tall window to look out on the sunlit lawn. "I can manage that." He turned back to her and said, "And this is your home."

"Oh, Jamie," said Anna, tears streaming down her cheeks. "I don't know how to thank you. I was so unkind . . ."

"You can thank me," he said, walking over and placing a hand on her shoulder, "by taking care of the farm, like you always have, and helping me with Little Jim and the baby."

"Oh, Jamie, I will," she said, brushing away her tears. "I swear I will."

Barnhill had named his daughter Mary, and even as a weeks' old infant she had Kate's auburn hair and porcelain-fair complexion. Perhaps it was that resemblance, or merely that he was unable to disassociate her birth from her mother's death, that caused him pain to be with her, and so he engaged a black woman to nurse the child and depended on Dinah, who had no daughter of her own, to look after her from dawn till dusk. After the first weeks had passed, he avoided visitors, preferring to be alone with Little Jim and Socks or immersing himself in his work at the office, Saturdays included. In the evenings, after reading to Jim and singing him to sleep, Barnhill frequently retired to his study with a book and a bottle of Kentucky bourbon and pitcher of spring water to ease his torment.

Addison Parker had been naïve to believe that his suit against Jay Gould's railroads would be settled out of court. Gould's well-paid team of lawyers not only filed an appeal to the circuit court but attempted all manner of other procedural gambits, motions for a new trial on the grounds of Parker's alleged "influence" over the trial judge that required Barnhill, aided by his colleague Harrison, to expend countless hours in research, drafting pleadings and briefs, and making courtroom appearances. Returning home at the end of another long day, when the sweltering days of summer had turned to November's cold, dreary rain, Barnhill smiled at his infant daughter when Dinah handed her to him, pink and fragrant of talcum in a soft blue dress, following her evening bath. "Hello, baby girl," he said, balancing her on his knee. Grasping his hands in her chubby fingers, she gazed at him with an expression of curiosity, studying his features and thick brown hair, graying at the temples, and neatly trimmed mustache. A smile curled her bow lips. As Dinah watched from a respectful distance, it dawned on Barnhill with a sharp pang of remorse that his six-month-old child scarcely recognized him.

"She's givin' you the once-over, Mista James," said Dinah playfully. "Wondrin' *who is that fine lookin' man?*"

"I expect you're right," said Barnhill ruefully.

"It ain't just a father," said Dinah in a more serious tone, "that baby needs." She paused and looked Barnhill in the eye. "She needs a momma, too."

Cradling the child in his arms, Barnhill said, "How do you mean, Dinah?"

"I know you ain't over Miz Kate," she replied. "But a man like you . . . well, you shouldn't have any trouble findin' a good woman to care for these chil'ren."

Barnhill sadly shook his head. "I don't know," he said after a moment. "I just don't know."

More than two years had passed since Barnhill's last trip to Addison Parker's sprawling sawmill operation near Jasper, in the heart of the Piney Woods of East Texas. He traveled by train on an early spring day, seated in a first-class compartment reserved for white gentlemen and ladies, provided they abstained from tobacco, as working class whites, most of whom chewed or smoked the weed, were crowded into the second-class coach along with a handful of black passengers. Barnhill scanned the pages of the Nacogdoches newspaper and then glanced out a window filmed with soot pouring from the smokestack, observing the dogwood coming into bloom and, with dismay, great swaths of virgin timber cleared for the cultivation of more cotton. The plight of his countrymen, white and black, had worsened in the years since the war, tenant farmers held in virtual bondage to merchants and absentee landowners. The train rattled on, past furrowed black fields and over trestle bridges spanning muddy creeks. After the lapse of an hour, it slowed perceptibly, and rounding a curve, arrived at the modest Jasper station with a long, piercing whistle and hiss of escaping steam.

Climbing down with his valise, Barnhill was greeted by one of Parker's foremen, a tall, slack-jawed fellow in rough work clothes with a wad of tobacco in his cheek who led the way to the waiting buggy for the two-hour trip to the mill. As they bumped along the red-clay track behind a swayback mare, Barnhill counted no fewer than five "missionary" Baptist churches, tiny whitewashed structures set back in the woods, pastored by some itinerant preacher whose congregants in their overalls and wool hats practiced the old-time religion with evangelical fervor. He considered the ignorance of the people, less than half of whom had attended school or could read or write. And yet they could vote, black as well as white, and they would vote for whomever the ruling Democrats designated. Halting the buggy at a locked gate, the driver climbed down, removed a key on a chain from his pocket, and opened the padlock as Barnhill inspected a sign nailed to a nearby tree: "NO TRESPASSING—By Order of the Longleaf Pine Lumber Co." Returning to his seat, the driver snapped the tip of his buggy whip at the horse's ears, starting her into a trot. After traveling another mile into the dense pines, Barnhill could see bright sunlight streaming into a clearing ahead and hear the sound of shouts and men chanting in unison.

"Loggin' crew," commented the driver laconically as he spat a stream of tobacco juice onto the clay and reined in the horse.

As the buggy came to a stop, Barnhill surveyed a wide clearing that extended a half mile to the far tree line, bare red earth stubbled with the stumps of thousands of fallen trees, and in the foreground a large team of loggers, thirty or forty men, felling the remaining massive pines and preparing the logs for transportation to the mill. Two nearby "flatheads"—lean, powerful men wearing wide-brimmed felt hats, denim shirts, and stained trousers—were working a two-handled saw at the base of an old-growth tree. Other men, so-called choppers and buckers, cleared the logs of branches and sawed them into the desired length to be loaded on big-wheel carts. The crew was divided about equally between white men and black, all dressed alike in slouch hats and overalls, doing identical work under the supervision, according to Barnhill's driver, of the woods boss, one "Pud" Doucette, of French Canadian origin. After a few minutes, the driver flicked the reins and the buggy passed back onto the track through the sun-dappled forest. Sometime later they overtook another mixed-race crew of thirty or more men, mounted on teams of mules hitched to carts laden with twenty-foot logs. The truly massive logs, five-foot diameter old-growth longleaf, were borne on low-slung carts hitched to teams of straining oxen.

After observing another crew laying track for a logging train, the driver turned onto a wider road and passed through a gate beneath a large sign that read:

LONGLEAF PINE LUMBER CO.
Jasper, Texas Mill

An enormous two-story structure stood on the bank of the wide Neches River, with dense smoke billowing from four tall brick stacks. In the foreground was a large millpond, jammed with floating logs, and a row of whitewashed frame buildings to the left of the main street. As they drew closer Barnhill could read the words painted over their entrances: Post Office, Commissary, Hospital, White School, Colored School. A simple church with a tall steeple and stained-glass windows stood apart from the rest. Behind the main street were row upon row of identical shotgun houses for the hundreds of mill employees, white only, as the somewhat inferior housing for the black hands was located a half mile in the distance, farther downriver. The air was filled with the whine of heavy machinery and sweet aroma of fresh sawdust, and the grounds were crowded with mule teams hauling logs from the pond to the mill and wagonloads of finished lumber to the warehouse. "Here we are, mister," said the driver as he brought the buggy to a stop in front of a two-story building with the words "General Office" over the entrance.

"Much obliged," said Barnhill as he reached for his valise. He shook the dust from his coat, stamped his boots on the porch, and let himself in. He entered a large room with the appearance and musty odor of a bank lobby, with gaslights suspended from a high, beaded ceiling, an arrangement of oak tables and chairs and, at one end, a wooden counter with wire caging enclosing men in shirtsleeves seated on stools at the windows. A queue of working folk stood patiently before the windows clutching slips of paper. Slipping off his hat, Barnhill walked to the stairs and ascended to the second floor, a large bullpen with rows of desks occupied by clerks and bookkeepers in green eyeshades. Barnhill approached a prim woman at the reception desk, glanced at the large clock mounted on the wall, and said, "Good afternoon. I'm here to see Mr. Parker."

"You have an appointment?"

"Yes, ma'am. Two o'clock. I'm a shade early."

Running a finger down a line of neat entries in her notebook, she glanced up and said, "Mr. Barnhill?"

"Yes, ma'am."

"Mr. Parker's expecting you. His office is in the far corner."

CHAPTER TWENTY-ONE

Addison Parker's spacious office, paneled in irregular knotty pine with a fine cypress floor covered by faded Persian carpets, commanded a view of the sprawling sawmill complex. As Barnhill entered, Parker was standing at the window, bathed in the bright light from the late afternoon sun as he peered out through the slats of the blinds. Without looking away, he commented, "Magnificent, isn't it?"

"Yes, sir," said Barnhill. "You have virtually your own city, with all the amenities."

Turning to face his lawyer, Parker motioned to an armchair and said, "Company town. But decent housing, medical care, and schools for the children. I insist they attend."

Taking a seat, Barnhill said, "Were the folks downstairs trading their pay for . . ."

"Scrip," said Parker, lowering himself into his reclining chair. "They use it to buy food and provisions at the company store." He was considerably heavier than he'd been on Barnhill's last visit, and his hair had gone completely white.

"How many men do you employ here?"

"Oh, about eight hundred at the mill," replied Parker. "Another hundred or so on the logging crews."

"I happened to notice," said Barnhill, "the blacks working alongside the whites. Ever have a problem?"

Parker shook his head. "It's hard labor, requiring a strong back. The men work in teams and seem to get along well enough, though the blacks take their meals apart and naturally sleep in their own camps."

Barnhill nodded, considering that Parker had managed to create a considerably more progressive society in his city-in-the-woods than in the world surrounding them. "Well, sir," he said, tapping the leather case on his lap, "I've brought along the brief."

"May I see it?"

Barnhill opened the case, withdrew a thick, typewritten document, and handed it across the desk.

Donning tortoiseshell reading glasses, Parker studied the first page and read aloud, "In the United States Court of Appeals for the Fifth Circuit. Missouri Kansas & Texas Railroad Company *et al*, Appellant, and

The Longleaf Pine Lumber Company, Appellee." He scanned the pages and, glancing at Barnhill over the top of his glasses, said, "Appears to be a fine piece of legal work."

"Thank you, sir."

Taking a linen handkerchief from his pocket, Parker removed his glasses and thoughtfully polished the lenses. "I can ill afford," he said, "to have this judgment overturned on appeal. I'm an old man now, Jamie, and have a weak heart."

"I'm confident the trial court's decision was free of reversible error."

"I've put all I have into this mill," said Parker. "To be frank, Gould's representative has approached me with an overture. An offer to settle."

"On what terms?"

"A rebate of freight on past shipments," said Parker with a grimace, "above a certain level, something like $75,000, and an agreement to lower the rates on future shipments."

"That hardly comes close to matching the trial court's judgment . . ."

"I understand," said Parker, raising a hand. "*But*. What assurance can you give me the circuit court will let that judgment stand? How can we avoid Gould's lawyers tampering?"

"None," said Barnhill calmly. "But I believe the circuit court will affirm the decision. Bear in mind, federal judges are appointed for life, and these men were all appointed during Reconstruction, in the Grant administration. I don't believe they're susceptible to Gould's bribes or the blandishments of his New York lawyers."

"Well," said Parker with a sigh, "I hope you're right. I fear we may be heading into another depression, with falling lumber prices. And with the mortgage on this mill . . ."

"It's your decision, of course," said Barnhill. "But I believe the tide is turning against these monopolists. A lawyer from Cherokee County by the name of Hogg is talking of running for attorney general, on the platform of breaking Gould's hold on the railroads." Barnhill rose from his chair and looked his client in the eye. "If it were my decision, sir," he said, "I'd take my chances with the court of appeals."

Having decided the issue, Addison Parker conducted Barnhill on a tour of the cavernous mill, where the four-foot-diameter logs were first hewn by large circular saws, then conveyed on a steam-powered carriage guided by burly men with long cant hooks to the gang saws, and finished by edgers and trimmers. The complex operation, producing thousands of board feet of two-by-six pine lumber by the hour, was directed by sawyers with hand signals, as the ear-splitting noise rendered all other communication impossible. Afterward, Barnhill enjoyed a simple supper with Parker in the dining hall, slept in the company rooming house, and was up at daylight and on his way back to the railroad station. He dozed in the swaying railway carriage with his head against the window, listening to the clack of the wheels on the rails and awakening with a start as the locomotive emitted a shrill whistle at the approach of the Nacogdoches station.

The brief was filed, and after some equivocation on the part of Addison Parker, the appeal was set for oral argument before a three-judge panel in Dallas. In the interim, life resumed its slow, quiet rhythms, celebrating Little Jim's tenth birthday and baby Mary's first. On most Sundays, following church, the family traveled out to the Mountain Farm for dinner with Barnhill's sister Anna, who doted on Jim and little Mary with great affection. With the passing of Miss Ellen Graves, Barnhill's participation in the Sacred Harp choir had come to an end, as had the Sunday school classes for the black children, all of whom now attended the African Methodist or black Baptist churches scattered throughout the county. Though life in the small village of San Augustine had a sense of order and normalcy after the years of tumult and lawlessness during the war and Reconstruction, there was also the sense of diminished opportunity, with steadily falling cotton prices thanks to overplanting, a lack of capital to support new industry, widespread ignorance, and indolence caused by oppressive heat and the scourges of hookworm and pellagra.

Barnhill stood out as an exemplar of the old antebellum order: reasonably prosperous, well educated, and held in the highest esteem by townspeople and farmers, white and black. He was rearing his son as he had been reared, with an emphasis on schooling, reading in particular, piety, and the outdoors. Standing over five feet, young Jim was an excellent marksman with his .22 rifle, bagging squirrels and rabbits that abounded in the woods surrounding their large house by the footbridge. Come October, Barnhill promised the excited boy, he could accompany him and the men of his old regiment on their annual trek to the Big Thicket to hunt black bear. As for his infant daughter, though he still depended on Dinah to look after her, she no longer evoked sad memories of her mother and brought a smile to his face in the evenings as she played with her doll in the parlor or rode the hobbyhorse he'd made for her. Occasionally, on the sidewalk of the courthouse square or on horseback on his way in or out of town, Barnhill encountered Sally Porter, who despite her good looks and relative affluence, remained a widow in a rural community with so few eligible, or desirable, men. It was obvious that she would have welcomed Barnhill's attentions—at the age of five or six he'd declared he'd marry her someday—but he responded to her subtle overtures with courteous, almost chivalrous, aloofness.

On a hot summer morning Barnhill waved goodbye to his son standing at the fence with his hands on the pickets, slapped the rump of his chestnut horse, and started out for Nacogdoches, where he would board the train for the trip to Dallas to argue the most important case of his career. But first he would attend to another duty. He traveled a dusty road deep into the piney woods several miles outside of town, his thoughts turning to the service held for Kate in the austere Presbyterian church, the preacher's solemn words, the mournful hymn sung by the choir. Emerging from the forest in a sunlit clearing, he considered that it was now the turn of his old friend Ernest Wilson, whose wife Pearly had died after a brief illness—cancer, according to Doc Smithers. An assortment of mule-drawn wagons and buggies was parked outside a tiny whitewashed building. As he dismounted, listening to the strains of piano and blended voices from inside, he studied the sign by the entrance: "Mount Zion African Methodist Episcopal Church." After hitching his horse, he followed a young mother holding the hands of daughters wearing matched dresses into the crowded, stifling church, and found an unoccupied space on a pew near the back. The pine casket lay open before the altar, bedecked with sprays of orange and yellow lilies. Barnhill could just make out Ernest, seated in the first pew with his grown sons, over the sea of fancy ladies' hats.

The preacher, a young, clean-shaven man unknown to Barnhill, appeared in his robes, gestured to the congregation to rise, and led them in a gospel hymn, accompanied by a tiny, elderly black woman at the upright piano. As Barnhill sang out he was conscious of the appreciative glances of the men and women standing nearby. The preacher prayed for the family, read his text, a passage from the book of Exodus, and in his sonorous bass voice posed the question: "Are you ready? Are you ready to meet your Savior?" He paused, searching the faces in the pews. "Pearly was ready," he said as he began to pace. "Just as the Lord warned the Israelites at the Passover: *Gird* your loins! Put on your shoes, and *grab* your staff!"

"Amen!" shouted several men in the back.

"Cause the time is a'comin'," declared the preacher. "Any day, any hour. And you *better be ready!*" As his voice rose in timbre, the entire congregation began to sway and moan, men and women calling out: "Holy Jesus! Yes, Brother Jones! We're ready! Amen!" Reaching his crescendo, the young preacher, his face streaming, abruptly slumped in his chair. Accompanied by the tinny piano, the congregation rose and sang a rousing rendition of the old spiritual: "Good news! Chariot's comin', and I don't want it to leave me behind!" At the end of the hour-long service Barnhill waited outside the entrance, politely exchanging greetings with the parishioners, many of whom he knew by name, until at last Ernest appeared, embraced Barnhill, and muttered, "I don't know how I'm gonna get by, Jamie. I honestly don't."

Leaving the tiny church in the woods, Barnhill traveled on horseback to the train station, lost in his thoughts about the power, the raw emotion, of the funeral service, and asking himself the question *Am I ready, truly ready?*

Aboard one of the Katy's passenger trains with intermediate stops at Longview and Tyler, he spent the journey to Dallas largely reviewing his trenchantly argued brief, which cited a recent line of cases upholding a common-law cause of action for business combinations in restraint of trade, especially in the realm of common carriers. Certainly there had been ample, unrefuted evidence at trial of such a combination among Gould's railroads and of the damages suffered by his client as a result of the exorbitant shipping rates it was forced to pay. Putting the brief aside, Barnhill stared out at the telegraph poles flying past and the dipping wire, the gently rolling hills covered with dark green cotton, and the occasional cattle resting in the shade of tall oaks. He silently recited the lines from Shakespeare:

> *When lofty trees I see barren of leaves,*
> *Which erst from heat did canopy the herd*

He trembled with a sharp pang of remembrance, reciting the same sonnet to Amelia as she sat next to him in the upstairs library at Widewater. He could perfectly visualize her face, her sensitive eyes and graceful neck and the simple pendant at her throat. How many years had passed without a word or note? Eighteen. Amelia would be in her forties now. Gazing at the passing countryside he indulged a pleasant daydream, journeying to North Carolina, crossing the wide river at the old colonial town of Edenton, and calling on Amelia; visiting Robert Maxwell's grave.

Barnhill had expected a courtroom without spectators and was accordingly taken aback when two newspapermen, clutching notepads and pencils, accosted him as he arrived in the corridor at the top of the stairway. "You represent the plaintiff?" asked one of the men, clenching an unlit cigar in his teeth.

"That's right," said Barnhill, lowering his heavy briefcase to the marble floor.

"How is it," demanded another, "that your client, Addison Parker, is any different from Jay Gould? Just another Yankee industrialist."

"I'd suggest," said Barnhill, reaching for his briefcase, "you fellows listen to the arguments. Afterwards, I'd be happy to answer any questions." He pushed past them, and as he entered the high-ceilinged courtroom through a heavy oak door, observed another group of reporters seated on the front row. "I'll be dad-gummed," he muttered to himself as he walked down the center aisle, passed through the bar, and placed his case on the counsel table. Gould's retinue of attorneys soon appeared: the ascetic lawyer from New York in a handsomely tailored black suit with finely polished boots, several younger colleagues, and a tall, heavyset man with a neatly trimmed goatee and flowing gray locks that reached his shoulders, wearing a white linen suit with black string tie. The man glanced condescendingly at Barnhill before taking a seat at the nearby table. He struck Barnhill as vaguely familiar; perhaps he'd seen his photograph in the newspaper. The bailiff commanded, "All rise!" and the three-judge panel in their black robes took their places at the high bench. Peering over the top of his spectacles, the senior judge, before whom Barnhill had once tried a contract dispute, said, "Mr. Williams. You may begin." As the tall man with the shoulder-length hair rose from his chair, Barnhill realized he was Lucius Williams, a well-known Conservative Democrat with a reputation as a flowery orator.

Clutching the lapels of his linen suit, Williams smiled indulgently at the panel and then launched into his argument, in a style then popular with Southern politicians of a certain stripe, filled with rhetorical flourishes, larded with sarcasm, and seasoned with quotations from the Old Testament and Shakespeare. Paying scant attention to the relevant case law or the specific findings of the lower court, Williams lavished praise on the builders of the railroads—"great men of destiny"; heaped scorn on the plaintiff—a "little man actuated by greed"; and ridiculed the trial judge—"ignorant of the law and easily influenced."

At the latter comment, one of the judges, hitherto listening with his cheek on his fist, sat upright and said, "Excuse me, counsel. Are you implying that Judge Wainwright was improperly influenced?"

"Well, your honor," responded Williams, "I may have said *easily* influenced."

"All the influence in this case," rejoined the judge with surprising ire, "has been peddled by the railroads. Now I'd be interested to hear what you have to say about the law and the facts."

Lucius Williams, in truth, had little to say about either, and his bombastic argument petered out like a noisy engine running out of steam. As he slumped in his chair, the senior judge said, "Mr. Barnhill?"

Barnhill rose, stood at the lectern arranging his notes and his brief, then looked up at the three judges and said, "May it please the court." For the next twenty minutes, adopting a relaxed but forceful style of argument, he carefully reviewed the evidence admitted by the trial court, the stocks and bonds in each of the railroads held by various Gould-controlled entities, the uniformity of freight rates, the surcharges and other discriminatory pricing practices, and then cogently summarized the case law, in particular a recent decision of the Second Circuit Court of Appeals affirming the common-law cause of action for damages resulting from a combination in restraint of competition. The judges followed the argument closely, occasionally interjecting questions which Barnhill answered without difficulty, and, in the end, nodding in their evident satisfaction with the soundness of his presentation. Gathering his papers, Barnhill thanked the court, turned and looked briefly in the cold eye of Gould's New York lawyer, and then packed his briefcase and hurried from the courtroom.

The reporters were waiting. "Sir," said one loudly, a portly man with bushy side-whiskers and a bowler hat. "Johnson with the *Dallas News*." Barnhill nodded. "Could I have your name?" asked the reporter.

"James Barnhill. From San Augustine."

"Barnhill," repeated another man, jotting on his pad.

"That was a mighty impressive argument," said the red-whiskered reporter. "Do you plan to go into politics?"

"No, sir," said Barnhill with a smile.

"You should," said a third man. "If the court upholds the judgment," he asked, "how much does your client stand to recover?"

"A million," said Barnhill. "Plus interest."

The first man emitted a low whistle. "What do you think are the chances?"

"I believe the facts and the law are clear," said Barnhill. "I expect the court to affirm. Now, if you gentlemen don't mind, I've got a train to catch. In fact, the Katy . . ."

Within a month, as the first cool breeze of September stirred the pine boughs outside his office window, the circuit court rendered its decision, reported to Barnhill via telegram from an associate in Dallas who was in daily contact with the federal courthouse. "Jamie!" blurted the usually reticent Harrison as he burst into the office. "There's news," he said holding up an envelope.

Barnhill reached across his desk to receive it, tore it open, and read aloud: "Circuit court affirms district court decision per curiam opinion full stop." Glancing up at Harrison with a grin, he said, "I'll be damned."

In the weeks that followed, Barnhill was warmly congratulated for his impressive victory, which was widely reported in the major Texas newspapers and richly rewarded by a deeply grateful Addison Parker with a "bonus" fee of $25,000, which Jamie charitably shared with Harrison. On a brisk October morning, his efficient secretary, Mrs. Thomas, returned from the post office with a stack of mail, which she sorted and presented to her employer. "The usual notices regarding the docket," she said, "solicitations, and this." She withdrew a cream-colored envelope from the stack and held it out.

With a glance at the envelope, Barnhill's heart skipped a beat. "Thank you," he said. "You may leave the rest on the desk." When the door closed behind Mrs. Thomas, Barnhill, with racing pulse, studied the neatly written return address: "Mrs. Albert Bondurant, Widewater Plantation, Edenton, North Carolina." Slitting it with a silver letter opener, he removed several sheets of bond and a folded newspaper clipping. He read:

October 2, 1882

Dear Sir,

> I read in the enclosed newspaper article, which appeared in the Raleigh, North Carolina, *Standard*, of an important victory in the federal appeals court in Texas in a case brought against the railroads.

Barnhill unfolded the yellowed clipping and read the headline: "Million Dollar Judgment Affirmed by Federal Court of Appeals". He continued reading:

> I apologize for any imposition, but my attention was drawn to the fact that the attorney who was credited with obtaining this victory was identified as one James Barnhill of San Augustine, whom I presume to be you. I am writing because, during the war, I knew a James Barnhill, a Confederate officer, from Texas, and wondered if possibly the person identified in the newspaper could be the same man, whom I held in very high esteem.

Barnhill put the letter aside and stared out the window, imagining Amelia's face, silently repeating the words, very high esteem. With a sharp intake of breath, he quickly finished her short letter:

> If I am mistaken, please accept my apology. If I am not, I offer my congratulations on your success and hope that you will respond with news of your life to a dear friend from long ago.
>
> Sincerely,
> *Amelia M. Bondurant*

CHAPTER TWENTY-TWO

GLIDING SILENTLY THROUGH STILL WATER filmed in bright-green scum, Barnhill dipped his paddle, stroked, and steered the low-slung pirogue between the wide sloping trunks of two massive cypress trees. The silence was broken by staccato hammering, and Barnhill, pointing skyward, said, "Ivory bill." Little Jim, seated on the thwarts, searched the boughs until he spotted the large black woodpecker with the distinctive white crest. Using the paddle as a rudder, Barnhill angled the dugout away from a partially submerged log, which abruptly disappeared, leaving a telltale trail of bubbles. "Gator," said Barnhill, laying the paddle astride the gunwales and feeling for the revolver holstered at his hip.

"Really?" said Jim, looking back at his father with wide-open eyes.

Barnhill nodded and then cast a look over his shoulder to make sure that Ernest Wilson was following in the other boat with the dogs. Shafts of weak sunlight filtered through the feathery foliage, which stirred in a gentle breeze. Though it was late October, the day was unseasonably warm and overcast, poor conditions for the hounds to track their quarry. Reaching the end of the swamp, Barnhill paddled the pirogue onto the muddy bank, climbed out, and tied the painter to a sapling. He took Jim's hand and helped him from the boat and then knelt and removed the guns and boxes of ammunition. After a few moments, Ernest paddled his dugout onto the bank with the two large bloodhounds bracing in the bow, noses aloft, eyes alert. Barnhill reached out to give Ernest a hand and stood aside as the dogs clambered out.

"This is the spot?" asked Ernest, pushing his red cap back on his forehead. A leather pouch filled with shotgun shells was strapped to his belt next to an eight-inch hunting knife.

"More or less," said Barnhill, searching the impenetrable forest. "So deep into the Thicket I'd wager these bears have never seen a man."

"Well, they's fixin' to see some," said Ernest as he bent down to pat one of the hounds, a bitch named Bessie, with large, sad eyes and reddish-brown fur.

Barnhill handed Jim one of the rifles, a bolt-action thirty-ought-six, and a handful of bullets. "Put a round in the chamber," he instructed him, "and make sure the safety's on." Barnhill picked up his rifle, a '73 Winchester, worked the lever, and carefully inserted seven rounds in the magazine. As Ernest loaded his double-barreled twelve-gauge, Barnhill turned to Jim and said, "We'll let Ernest go ahead with the dogs, and we'll follow behind. But we'll have to keep up, as we don't want to get turned around in these woods."

"Yes, sir," said Jim, shouldering his rifle like a small soldier. Like his father and Ernest, he was wearing a long-sleeved denim shirt as protection from thorns and briars, twill trousers, and tall hunting boots.

Ernest poured a bowl of water for the dogs from a canteen. "Time to go," he instructed them after they drank. "Let's find us Ol' Bruin." The hounds plunged into the undergrowth, noses to the ground, searching for the scent and a pathway through the dense vegetation of the forest. As Ernest and the dogs advanced into the woods, Barnhill slung his carbine over his shoulder, dropped to one knee, and placed a hand on Jim's shoulder. "Remember, son," he said. "We have to be careful." The boy nodded. "A full-grown bear can kill a man with one swipe of his paw. Now, when the dogs find a bear, I'll take the first shot. Just as soon as I fire, you take the next shot. Remember where I told you to aim?" Again Jim nodded. "All right," said Barnhill, standing up. "Let's go." Barnhill could just make out the bobbing of Ernest's red cap as he made his way through the trackless vegetation, pushing aside grapevine and working through the understory of laurel and witch hazel beneath the canopy of oaks, sycamore, and sweet gum. Walking in a semi-crouch, Barnhill listened for the dogs as he kept an eye on the ground for the possible rattlesnake, moccasin, or copperhead camouflaged among the fallen leaves. Detecting motion, he pointed toward a small clearing as four or five turkeys, old gobblers with long black beards, scurried into the undergrowth.

Half an hour passed with no sound from the hounds and no break in the dense forestation. "Let's catch up with Ernest," said Barnhill, quickening his pace.

Once he was within ten yards of the red cap, Barnhill called out, "Ernest! Hold up."

"Hey, there, Bessie!" called Ernest. "Anson!" Standing in the shade of a tall post oak, the men briefly conferred as Jim helped himself to a swig of cool water from his canteen. "There's bears all around us," said Ernest. "Dogs jus' can't find the scent."

Barnhill took off his hat and scratched his head. "Why don't we let Anson work to the east," he suggested, "and we'll follow Bessie to the northwest. It's just so doggone thick in these woods." Ernest sent Anson, a veteran bear hound with a white diamond on his brown forehead, into the brush to the right, waited a few moments, and then started Bessie straight ahead. The three hunters plunged after her. After another hundred yards, the dog stopped abruptly, sniffed the ground furiously, and with a low, throaty growl shot into a tangle of briars and clinging vines. Tearing at the vegetation, Barnhill struggled to catch up. All at once, the dog was on her hind legs, nose in the air, baying at the top of her lungs. Barnhill was conscious of a sudden blur of motion amid the vegetation, dark brown fur and bared teeth. Not more than ten feet from the dog, the bear charged from the brush, swinging a forepaw that lifted Bessie from the ground with a sickening yelp. Barnhill coolly raised his rifle, worked the lever, and in a split second realized the action was jammed. Ernest, standing at his side, fired both barrels of buckshot at the onrushing bear, momentarily staggering it on its back legs. Blood streaming from its angry face, the bear charged again. As Barnhill froze with pounding heart, the loud report of a rifle echoed at his ear, and the bear crumpled and fell, rolling on its side not more than two feet from Barnhill, spattering his boots with blood. He turned toward Jim, standing to his right and rear, the rifle at his shoulder with his cheek pressed tightly to the stock.

"I got him!" shouted the boy with a wide smile.

"I'll say you did," said Barnhill, conscious of the dryness in his mouth and his pounding heart. "That was some shot."

Lowering his rifle, Jim walked over to his father and together they gazed at the bear, terrifying even in death, with wide-open eyes, teeth exposed in a snarl, and blood pouring from the buckshot wounds to its face and neck. Barnhill shoved its shoulder over with his boot, exposing the mortal wound at the center of its massive chest.

Jim's smile vanished as he heard the anguished cry of the bloodhound. Ernest was kneeling over the animal, stroking her head. The bear's swipe had ripped the length of her underside, partially disemboweling her. Standing over the dying dog, Barnhill instructed Jim to look away and then quickly ended her misery with his revolver.

"Poor Bess," said Ernest as a tear spilled down his smooth, black cheek. Looking up, he said, "Little Jim saved the day."

Barnhill put an arm around the boy's shoulder as Jim stared mournfully at the dog. "Y'all go on back to camp," said Ernest. "I'll wait here for the skinners."

Jim's heroics in the face of the bear charging his defenseless father, coolly squeezing off a shot right through the heart, were the talk of the campfire that evening. "Most boys would've turned tail and run," said Harry Sellers, now portly and graying in middle age. "The acorn don't fall far from the tree," he added, a high compliment well understood by the others from Barnhill's old regiment. Barnhill's cousin Sam Perkins had even offered the boy a celebratory tot of whiskey, which Jim promptly spat out with a grimace. "In the war," Sam advised Jim, "they called me lucky, but I say you make your own luck."

Once Jim was asleep in his tent, or at least trying to sleep, the men sat around the campfire swapping tales from their days in Lee's army as they passed a bottle of bourbon and jug of water. Ernest and the other black men sat around their own campfire in the near distance, drinking their own whiskey and, Barnhill supposed, trading their own stories. At last, as the crescent moon rose above the treetops casting silvery light across the canvas and dying embers, Barnhill sat alone in his camp chair, sipping his whiskey and thinking how proud Kate would have been of her son, evoking a wave of longing and melancholy. Before departing on the hunting trip he'd posted a long letter to Amelia, describing his regiment's hardships during the final months of the war, his return to Virginia to study law, his marriage, career, children, and, of course, Kate's death in childbirth, closing with a plea for a long, newsy letter back. Staring at the eerie moonbeams, he tried to remember Amelia, every detail, certain then that he'd never loved anyone as much. Was it possible, he wearily considered as he poured the last of his drink onto the hissing fire, that he still loved her?

At the end of the three-day expedition, Barnhill and Jim returned home riding on horseback, as they'd traded their share of pelts and bear meat with the Coushatta Indian guides and skinners, and Barnhill had no use for another bearskin rug. Though he brought home no trophy of his first bear, the ten-year-old boy would remember the moment and the event for the rest of his life, not only for the pride in what he'd done but also the terror and grisly loss of life. Riding along the dirt road through the pine forest, Barnhill reflected on the quality of courage. From his many experiences in the war he knew it was distinct from physical strength or bravado. Some possessed it, the ability to stand and face terrifying danger, while others were gripped by an overwhelming impulse to turn and run. Jim, he considered with a nod, had courage.

Though he returned home with no bearskins, Barnhill brought a beaded Indian necklace and tiny moccasins for his baby girl and venison back-straps that Dinah could render into her delicious jerky. In his study on cold and often blustery November nights after the children were in bed, Barnhill found himself thinking more and more often of his experiences in the war, perhaps because of the time just spent with old comrades. In a few weeks it would be the twentieth anniversary of the Battle of Fredericksburg. He remembered it as if it were yesterday: the enormous Union army advancing in perfect order across that open field, standards flapping and bayonets glinting in the sun, as the fog slowly lifted; his pell-mell dash with cousin Sam on horseback through the woods as the Confederate center broke in panicked retreat. Wartime recollections invariably evoked feelings of pride and nostalgia, but now, in middle age, Barnhill questioned whether it had been worth the price, perhaps a terrible mistake that had wrecked the South and poisoned relations between the races.

One morning, as Barnhill attended to the usual business at his office before walking over to the courthouse to probate a will, Mrs. Thomas tapped on the door and entered. "I've sorted it," she said, placing a stack of letters on the corner of the desk. "Except for this one." She held up a cream-colored envelope. "Which was marked 'personal.'" Giving him a slightly disapproving look, she handed him the envelope and turned to walk from the office. Barnhill stared at Amelia's blue-black cursive script, removed his letter opener from the drawer and quickly slit open the envelope. Drawing a deep breath, he slowly read:

October 25, 1882
Widewater Plantation

Dear Jamie,

You cannot possibly imagine my pleasure when I received your reply to my note. Surely it was Providence that brought the newspaper article to my attention and led me to you after all these years. Let me first express my deep sorrow and sympathy for the loss of your wife. How tragic for a mother to die in childbirth, leaving you to raise the baby alone. But I was greatly pleased, and not at all surprised, to read that you have enjoyed success in your profession and are blessed with a fine son and daughter.

Years ago, as we were struggling to make ends meet following the end of the war, I thought of you constantly and often wondered where you were and what you would do. I am so proud to learn that you graduated from the University of Virginia and returned to your native state. As for me, I have had my share of life's blessings and sorrows. At the end of the war, Father was a bitter and broken man—in spirit and financially. Forced to sell most of the plantation, he thankfully was able to retain our homestead, but died within a few years of Appomattox.

As I wrote you long ago, I married Albert Bondurant, a good man and younger son of a Tidewater planter who entered business after the war, a successful cotton broker. We have two fine children, a son, Robert, aged twelve, and daughter Charlotte, aged seven. And like you, Jamie, I lost my dear spouse, who died in '78 during an outbreak of typhus.

And so we find ourselves in similar circumstances, widowed, raising a son and daughter alone. I have been able to manage tolerably well, living here in the old house. I am so happy to have reestablished our friendship. I have thought of you often and with great affection over the years, and do hope that you will write again before long.

Sincerely,
Amelia

Barnhill stared at the lines of neat, feminine handwriting. And so Amelia had lost her husband; a possibility that had never occurred to him. A powerful wave of longing suddenly struck him, just as he'd felt with such anguish in the final months of the war, though the moment quickly passed. Yet, like a flicker of guttering candlelight, he continued to feel it. After all the years, he realized with a sigh, it had never left him.

"Mr. Barnhill." Barnhill raised his eyes to the closed door. "Mr. Barnhill," repeated Mrs. Thomas. "Your hearing."

"My goodness," muttered Barnhill with a glance at the clock on the bookcase. "Coming," he said in a louder voice. Carefully folding the sheets of bond, he placed them in a desk drawer, gathered up his papers, and hurried from the office.

In the months that followed he wrote to Amelia with regularity, sometimes a brief note, bidding her happiness and good tidings with the advent of Christmas, but occasionally a long, thoughtful letter, such as the one written late one night by the light of an oil-burning lamp at his rolltop desk, recounting the New Year's celebration at Widewater in the year '64, recalling his despair at the death of Robert, and attempting to explain the convoluted reasons why he could not return for her at the end of war and ask her to marry him. The letters she faithfully wrote in reply, arriving in cream-colored envelopes he eagerly anticipated, covered much of the same territory, the tender area of their mutual feeling that had gone unexplored for almost two decades of separation. "I came to understand," she wrote in one letter, "painfully and bitterly, that your honor would not permit you to violate the oath you'd made to my father, no more than I, sadly, could have defied his absolute prohibition of our marriage."

Christmas came and passed, the first in which little Mary, nearing the age of two, had delighted in the toys, sweets, and festivities, though it was a sad, quiet time for Jim, thinking of his mother. Gazing proudly at the boy on one clear, cold winter day, Barnhill was reminded of the lines of scripture: "And the child grew and became strong; he was filled with wisdom, and the grace of God was upon him." Barnhill no longer felt the compulsion to throw himself into his work but allowed much more time for his family, playing with his infant daughter at the end of the day; singing her to sleep—permitting Dinah to spend her evenings with her own sons, and, increasingly, with the widower Ernest Wilson; outings with Jim in the outdoors; and buggy rides with the children, bundled up against the cold, to Mountain Farm for Sunday dinner with Aunt Anna. Occasionally, he accepted an invitation to dinner or a party, including Addison Parker's New Year's Eve ball, where he'd been surprised to discover that the wealthy bachelor, now in his sixties, was accompanied by the beautiful Sally Porter, wearing a polonaise of blue taffeta elaborately draped over a small bustle in back, with a crocheted fringe and a long strand of pearls at her neck.

In the wake of his celebrated victory over the railroads, his law practice flourished, enabling him to hire a third attorney, a scholarly young man who likewise possessed a college degree. At the approach of the second anniversary of Kate's death, Barnhill confessed he had much to be thankful for, with a deep sense of well-being and contentment that was nevertheless incomplete, and would remain so until he could finally see Amelia again.

Following an overnight thunderstorm that shook the windows, waking the baby, Barnhill strolled across the footbridge beneath bright green foliage and a bowl of Delft-blue sky with a spring in his step and lightness in his chest. Mounting the sidewalk at his office, he glanced at the new gold lettering stenciled on the window—"Barnhill, Harrison, & Gregg, Attorneys-at-Law"—as he let himself in. With a smile at the prim Mrs. Thomas seated at her tidy desk, he tossed his hat on the stand in the corner and said, "Top o' the mornin'."

"Morning, sir," she replied. "That was some gully washer last night."

"Yes, indeed. Creek almost flooded the footbridge."

"After you left the office, Mr. Barnhill," she said, "to watch your boy play in that game . . ."

"Baseball, Mrs. Thomas," said Barnhill. "It's called baseball." He smiled inwardly as he thought of the patient hours Ernest spent with the boy, teaching him to bat and catch fly balls.

"You received this special delivery letter," she continued, handing him an envelope.

Glancing at the return address with upturned eyebrows, Barnhill said, "Thank you, ma'am," and walked to his corner office. Reclining in his chair behind the broad desk, he said, "Edward Selden. I'll be danged." He slit open the envelope and quickly read the letter, typewritten on Selden's embossed law-firm letterhead. The surviving officers of

General Lee's headquarters staff were planning a special commemoration of the twentieth anniversary of the Battle of Gettysburg. "We will gather," Selden wrote, "on the evening of July 1 for an extravagant dinner party in Richmond, to which you are most cordially invited."

> The following day there will be a formal ceremony, no doubt with lofty speeches by the politicians, to commission a monument to Lee in the form of an equestrian statue of the general astride Traveller by a well-known French sculptor. It would do me great honor if you would accept this invitation to participate as a member of our party.

Barnhill put the letter aside and thoughtfully stroked his mustache. The honor was his, of course, to be invited to commemorate the event with the men of Lee's own staff. He rose from his chair and opened the door. "Mrs. Thomas," he said. "Would you come to my office? And bring your tablet. I have a letter to dictate." It was only after composing the letter to Selden, accepting his invitation with heartfelt thanks, that it occurred to Barnhill that, as he would be traveling all the way to Richmond, a stopover at Edenton would be hardly out of his way. He thought back to the trip by rail he and Robert had made from Petersburg, just south of Richmond, to Rocky Mount in North Carolina and on to Widewater. With a pounding heart, he removed several sheets of his personal stationery from the drawer, dipped his pen in the well and wrote:

April 25, 1883

Dear Amelia,

> I have accepted an invitation to travel to Richmond to participate in a tribute to General Lee on the occasion of the 20th anniversary of the Battle of Gettysburg. I will be leaving Richmond on July 2nd, and it would please me beyond measure to continue on to Edenton to visit you at Widewater. For these past months the thought of seeing you again has been constantly on my mind. I will close this brief letter in my haste to post it and eagerly await your reply.

Barnhill lowered his pen to write "Sincerely," hesitated, and then closed with:

Love,
Jamie

CHAPTER TWENTY-TWO

Barnhill folded the brief note into an envelope, quickly addressed and stamped it, and delivered it himself to the post office.

Within days of the invitation from Edward Selden, Barnhill received a letter from his old commanding officer Harry Sellers, proposing that the surviving officers and men of the Fifth Texas regiment travel to Gettysburg for a reunion at the site of their fateful charge on July 2. Seated behind his desk, Barnhill put the letter aside and considered. To return to the battlefield, to see that place again, walk that ground ... Tears welled in his eyes. As he would be in Richmond on the first, of course he would go.

Amelia Bondurant stood before the mirror over the dresser in her upstairs bedroom. In its reflection she could see the morning sun on the pale-yellow wallpaper and the breeze from the open window troubling the lace that hung from the corners of the four-poster bed. Resting her palms on the dresser, she leaned toward the glass for a closer inspection. She studied the tiny crows' feet at the corners of her eyes, even finer wrinkles that accentuated the curves of her cheeks at her lips, and the streaks of gray that silvered her light brown hair. She turned to the side to study her profile; she'd kept her figure with the trim waist, and the soft skin at her neck was firm and supple. At age forty-four she was, she considered with a modicum of vanity, a handsome woman, even pretty. She lowered her eyes to the tintype portrait in its filigreed frame on the dresser: her late husband Albert, posing stiffly in the photographer's studio at about age thirty. Not a particularly handsome man, with a broad face and brow, but as kindly in appearance as he was in his treatment of others. She felt a pang of guilt as her thoughts turned to Jamie, wondering how he would look after all the years; how she would look to him. With a sigh, Amelia brushed back her hair and tied it with a blue satin ribbon, powdered her cheeks, and walked from the sunlit upstairs room, pausing to look in at the library, unchanged from the days she'd sat there with Jamie, reading aloud to her from his beloved books.

Lightly touching the banister, she descended the spiral stairs in a swish of skirt and petticoats and walked back to the kitchen, where the black cook was standing over a kettle with a wooden spoon. "I'm going into town, Betsy," she said.

"Yes, ma'am," replied the cook without looking up from her soup.

"I'll be back before the children are home from school. Do you need anything?"

"No, ma'am."

Exiting through the kitchen door, Amelia walked the short distance to the barn where she asked the groom to saddle her horse. As she waited, she gazed out over the large vegetable garden behind the house, filled with bright green squash, beans, peas, tomatoes, and corn just coming up. Beyond the garden, two milch cows were chewing the thick green grass next to the pigsty and chicken coop. A thin stream of aromatic smoke curled up from the smokehouse attached to the barn. The groom led the horse from the stall and held the reins as Amelia placed a petite shoe in the stirrup and gracefully swung herself up and on the sidesaddle. "Thank you, Johnson," she said as she took the reins and gave them a tug. Turning onto the drive, she rode past the orchard beneath the allée of moss-draped oaks sloping down toward the river, content in the knowledge that her small family lacked for nothing, producing their own vegetables, fresh and canned for the winter, milk, butter, bacon, eggs, ham, and fruit on the self-sustaining farm. Turning at the front gate toward town, the mare trotted briskly along the river road, passing by the dark, furrowed expanse of cotton fields. The cropland belonged to absentee owners, who leased it in fifty-acre tracts to the black sharecroppers, most of whom were former slaves at Widewater who continued to dwell in their old quarters. Reaching the junction, Amelia turned left at the sign that pointed toward the quaint colonial village of Edenton. Located at the mouth of the wide Chowan River, with a half-moon waterfront on Albemarle Sound, a new, thriving form of commerce had taken root since the dark days of Reconstruction: commercial fishing. By late morning the fleet of shallow-bottomed boats hauling their long seining nets was back in the harbor, the crews, mainly black women with heads tied in bright-colored bandannas, were sorting the catch for cleaning, brining, and packing in barrels at the large cannery beyond the waterfront.

She rode along Broad Street with the smell of salty fish in the air, passing by the graceful homes with their well-tended gardens and lawns shaded by towering oaks and magnolias and storefronts largely unchanged since before the war. Arriving at the post office, she gingerly dismounted and tied the horse at the railing. It was her second trip to town in as many weeks, and each time her heart fluttered in anticipation that there might be a letter from Jamie. When her turn came at the worn wooden counter, the clerk gave her a knowing smile and reached for an envelope in one of the slots. "There you are, Mrs. Bondurant," he said as he handed it to her. "Another one from Texas."

Tucking the envelope in her handbag, she said, "Thank you, Mr. Jones," and let herself out. Despite the mare's impatient stamp, Amelia crossed the street and walked a block to the quiet yard of St. Paul's church. There, seated on a wrought-iron bench in the shade of ancient magnolias and the tall steeple, surrounded by weathered headstones, she opened the envelope and quickly read the brief note. Looking up into the pale blue sky and irregular clouds, she wiped away tears. For so long, for so many years, she'd insisted to herself that she would never see him again. He had become a hidden secret, a cherished memory that every so often she would allow herself to bring to conscious thought. And now, she admitted with excitement mixed with trepidation, he was at last coming back as he'd promised.

CHAPTER TWENTY-THREE

AS BARNHILL HAD NEVER VENTURED FROM HOME for more than a few days since returning from the university, and as Jim had never laid eyes on a railroad locomotive, Barnhill had consented to allow the boy to accompany him in the buggy driven by Ernest Wilson as far as the Nacogdoches train depot. Jim's little sister was already ensconced at Mountain Farm with her Aunt Anna, where she would soon be joined by her brother for the duration of their father's trip. It was a hot morning in late June, with a deep blue sky and billowing cumulus clouds edged with gray. While Ernest saw to the horse and buggy, Barnhill took Jim to inspect the I & GN's No. 9 locomotive. Standing on the platform, the boy gaped in stupefaction at the great black monster, with its massive steel wheels, push rods, and a wisp of steam curling up from the whistle behind the tall smokestack. After Barnhill lifted the boy up for a look into the coal compartment, the conductor appeared on the steps and sang out, "All a-booard!"

"Time to go, son," said Barnhill, placing a hand on Jim's shoulder. "You help take care of Mary."

"Yes, sir."

"And Aunt Anna will teach you a thing or two about life on the farm." Barnhill bent down to kiss the boy's cheek, motioned to Ernest, who was standing at a respectful distance, and said, "Goodbye, Jim. I'll send you a postcard from Pennsylvania." He lifted his heavy valise and mounted the steps to the first-class compartment. Finding his seat, he waved out the window at Jim and Ernest as the train groaned, jolted, and started slowly down the tracks. Barnhill stared at the two figures, a black man in overalls and tattered straw hat with his arm around the shoulder of the blond-haired boy, until they were two dim specks in the receding distance. As the train rattled through the piney woods, past wide fields planted in green cotton, he thought back to the letter from Harry Sellers proposing a reunion of the Texas Brigade. His cousin Sam would be making the trip, along with a handful of others scattered among the towns and farms of East Texas. Barnhill read his newspaper, dozed, and then awoke with a start at the piercing whistle as the train approached the station in downtown Houston, a thriving city of some twenty thousand souls.

Barnhill strolled through the impressive Union Station, dedicated three years earlier with an address by former President Grant before a cheering crowd of five thousand. With several hours to kill before the departure to New Orleans, he paid a dime to have his boots shined and took refreshment at the station soda fountain, where he sat at the tiled counter beneath a slowly spinning fan next to a large black woman with a peacock feather in her hat and two little girls in tow, wearing matching dresses with their hair in bright ribbons. Barnhill smiled at the shy girls as he sipped his lemonade. With a quick glance at his fob watch, he lifted his valise and strolled to platform No. 3, crowded with porters pushing carts laden with baggage and sacks of mail and the usual assortment of passengers: well-dressed gentlemen in linen suits and Panamas and their ladies in silk-embroidered long dresses with bustles and wide-brimmed hats, poor whites in overalls or dungarees with rough women in sunbonnets and gingham, and relatively affluent Negroes, as poor blacks seldom traveled on anything but a local. Barnhill stood on the platform admiring the modern carriages in their bright colors behind the big black locomotive with the words:

Texas and New Orleans Railroad Co.
Star & Crescent Route

painted on the tender. The conductors appeared at their stations, and as the engineer gave a blast of the whistle, Barnhill fell in with the other passengers and located his compartment, an airy, comfortable accommodation with upholstered seats he shared with a middle-aged white couple and a gray-haired black clergyman, presumably Episcopal, judging from the purple shirt and stiff collar beneath his black jacket. The seven-hour journey to New Orleans was uneventful, with the clergyman chatting amiably with the married couple or reading his Bible, as Barnhill forced himself to do a bit of legal work, revising a brief on a case before the court of appeals. He found New Orleans to be disagreeably old, dirty, and malodorous in the fetid summer heat, but he passed the night in an adequate hotel in the French Quarter, with dinner at a nearby restaurant serving delicious Creole fare. Barnhill arrived at the station first thing in the morning to board his train for the two-day journey east.

Barnhill had purchased a first-class ticket on the "Southern Express," operated by the Richmond and Danville Railroad Company, offering passenger service from the Crescent City to Lynchburg, Virginia. He boarded the train and made his way to a carriage with comfortable upholstered seats and sleepers, upper and lower berths separated by curtains. Taking his seat by the window, Barnhill was relieved that the place next to him was unoccupied and would remain so for the duration of the trip. He gazed out the window as the train left the station and passed over the long bridge spanning Lake Ponchartrain. It was there, he reflected, that John Bell Hood had died during an outbreak of yellow fever a few years earlier. Hood, who had embodied the beau ideal of the gallant Confederate officer wooing his beautiful South Carolina belle, had ended his days in relative obscurity in New Orleans, crippled by the loss of an arm and a leg and embittered by his public feud with James Longstreet.

By late afternoon, as the train rattled across the Black Belt of south Alabama, Barnhill put his legal work aside and made his way to the club car, paneled in walnut, with overstuffed armchairs and even a potted palm. An older black man clad in a starched white jacket tended the bar, around which were clustered a handful of portly men smoking cigars. Two middle-aged black men, wearing suits and neckties, were playing cards at a table at the back, sipping Pilsner glasses of beer. Barnhill ordered a glass of beer and sat at an empty table. Gazing out at the dipping telegraph wire and at barns with their weathered boards and corrugated tin roofs, his mind wandered to the problem that had vexed him during the darkest days of the war and ever since: the plight of the Negro after the institution of slavery was brought to an abrupt end. The old planter class, with notable exceptions, had a paternal regard for their slaves, an attitude, he believed, that induced a quality of childlike submission on the part of the slaves. But after that moral obligation was severed, what had taken its place? At first, the Radicals, enforcing the rights of blacks at the point of a bayonet. But with the end of Reconstruction, the higher class of whites, men of education and standing—including himself, he conceded uncomfortably—had carried forward the old patronizing attitude toward the blacks. Barnhill took a swallow of beer and watched the two black men at their game of cards. The poor whites, he considered, the upland crackers, wool hats, and rednecks, were determined to crush Negro aspirations and strip them of any vestige of liberty. Thus far, the higher class held sway: the Redeemers, who had brought the hated carpetbag regime to an end, were courting the blacks, seeking their vote in return for a guarantee of basic privileges. Yet why should the blacks accept the dubious patronage of well-to-do conservatives, their former masters, rather than make common cause with the poor white sharecroppers and mill hands trapped, as they were, on the bottom rail of the fence?

These troubled ruminations were interrupted by the appearance at his elbow of a gangly youth in a stained white jacket, who announced, in an accent Barnhill could scarcely understand, "Dinin' cah's open fuh bizness." Barnhill glanced at his homely face, noticing the bad teeth. He finished his beer and made his way along the swaying carriages. Thoughts of the troubled relations between the races had unsettled him. Shortly before he departed on the trip, a delegation of local lawyers had called on him, urging him to allow his name to be placed in nomination as a candidate for district judge. A candidate, of course, of the Democratic Party. He'd taken their suggestion under advisement, though the position paid a mere pittance. Yet he'd earned enough, and saved enough, from his law practice to live comfortably and provide for his children and sister. Staring out the window at the lengthening shadows, he knew it wasn't the pay that concerned him but the difficulty of enforcing laws, statutes passed by the Radical Republicans and constitutional amendments of dubious legality, more honored in the breach than the observance.

He sat alone in the dining car feeling the rocking motion that troubled the surface of his water glass, eating an indifferent supper of ham and mixed vegetables, and thinking about Amelia. How would she look after twenty years? She was frozen in memory: her hair, complexion, the color of her eyes, her voice, her laugh, the delicacy of her hands.... If only he could go back in time. He considered the physical changes that time had wrought on himself, his thinning, graying hair, the mustache he'd worn since university days. Perhaps he should shave it. With a shake of his head, Barnhill dabbed his chin with his napkin, folded it, and rose from his chair to move to the club car for a nightcap. The car was filled with men smoking, drinking, and playing cards in the glare of the gaslights, as darkness had finally fallen on the late June evening. Hitching a boot up on the brass rail at the bar, he rested his arms on its surface and said, "Kentucky bourbon. With a little branch water."

"Yes, sir," said the genial bartender. He mixed the drink and slid the glass across the smooth surface.

Sipping his bourbon, Barnhill closed his eyes, listening to the rhythmic *clack* of the wheels. Tomorrow he'd see Virginia, for the first time since '68. And in another few days . . . Widewater, and Amelia.

The ballroom at Richmond's Spotswood Hotel was resplendent in the light of the chandeliers, with gleaming silverware and china on tablecloths of white and blue and centerpieces of yellow roses. An enlarged photograph of General Lee in his dress uniform was framed on a stand at the front of the room, flanked by both the Bonny Blue and the Stars and Stripes, as both North and South had finally agreed to "bury the bloody shirt." An orchestra in the corner filled the room with martial music as the ballroom began to fill with men in formal dinner attire, some, like Barnhill, vigorous and in their prime, others stooped with white hair and beards. Edward Selden had again come to Barnhill's rescue, with a borrowed cutaway and matching trousers from a local tailor, just as he had provided Barnhill with the fine dress uniform in 1863 to attend Mary Chesnut's dinner party. Leaning heavily on his silver-handled cane, Selden stood beside Barnhill at the entrance to the ballroom, surveying the large crowd. "There's Rooney," he said, motioning to one of the late general's sons. "And old Joe Johnston, standing next to Wade Hampton." Barnhill looked at the spare, elderly gentleman, entirely bald, who had preceded Lee in command of the Army of Northern Virginia, and his stocky, bearded companion who now held the office of Governor of South Carolina. As the gentlemen—no ladies were present—found their assigned tables, the band struck up a rousing rendition of the Confederate anthem, with every man present joining in on the refrain:

Hurrah, hurrah, for Southern rights, hurrah!
Hurrah for the Bonny Blue flag that bears the single star!

This was followed, inevitably, by "Dixie," sung by one of the band members in a clear tenor. Barnhill took his seat, tapping his foot to the lively tune. Waiters poured French champagne, chilled vichyssoise was served, and the first of many speakers appeared at the dais to deliver a tribute to the beloved hero of the Confederacy. Enjoying the four-course banquet and the wine, Barnhill reflected that for all its deficiencies there had been something genuinely noble about the Southern bid for independence, and some of that nobility still shone in the eyes of the proud men seated around the festive ballroom who had served on Lee's staff or commanded his brigades. Barnhill felt at once honored and out of place.

After staying up late into the evening reminiscing about their days together in the war and at the university, the following day Barnhill and Edward Selden attended the large public ceremony where the equestrian statue of Lee was to be erected. It proved a tedious affair whose highlight was a long speech by Virginia Senator William Mahone, who'd served under Lee as a brigadier general, on the importance of industry, the railroads in particular, to the Southern economy. Though General Lee appreciated the value of railroads in a military campaign, Barnhill suspected that the patrician "Marse Robert" would have been a lost soul in Billy Mahone's New South. "Too much speechifyin'," was Selden's succinct assessment at the end of the ceremony. "And too damned hot."

"Remind me to come back," said Barnhill, "for the unveiling of that statue, on a nice autumn day." Selden accompanied Barnhill to the depot, where he boarded the train for the trip to the nation's capital and on to Pennsylvania. As it was the twentieth anniversary of the great battle, large crowds of veterans and their families were converging on Gettysburg, and the railroads had made special arrangements to accommodate them. Barnhill held a ticket on one of these "specials," which pulled into the Gettysburg station just as dusk was falling, enfolding the surrounding hills in a ring of lavender and blue. In the gloaming Barnhill could dimly recognize the cupola of the seminary; otherwise nothing in the town was familiar to him during the brief ride to his hotel. By prearrangement, those veterans of the Fifth Texas who'd made the journey met for supper in the hotel dining room, which led to another late evening of reminiscence over brandy and cigars on the front porch. "We're free to tour the town and cemetery in the mornin'," said Sellers as he rose to go to his room. "Then meet for a picnic lunch with the rest of the brigade. After which those of us who ain't too broken down will see if we can climb that little hill."

Barnhill awoke from a troubled sleep with a violent crash of thunder, and then another with a sound like a ripping sheet followed by a *boom* that shook the windows. Unsure where he was, he rubbed his eyes, searched the darkened room, and then remembered. He'd lain awake for what seemed a long time, listening to the wind and rain with an ache of longing for his children, so far away. The next morning, anxious for strong, black coffee to dispel the woolly-headed feeling from lack of sleep, he dressed in a plain black jacket and brown twill trousers and made his way to the dining room, which was filled with veterans from both armies, some wearing a fragment of uniform, a cap, tunic, or cavalry scarf, others missing an arm or leg, all of them well into middle age. Barnhill found an empty stool at the counter and ordered coffee with bacon and buckwheat cakes. Rather than tour the town and fields with his fellow Texans he was determined to spend the morning alone, avoiding the many gatherings of old comrades, the speeches, and the band music that he could hear already in the streets outside the hotel. Refreshed by the hearty breakfast, he obtained a map of the town and battlefield at the front desk. The air, even at the early hour, was hot and still, with humidity from the overnight storm that beaded his forehead with perspiration and darkened the back of his shirt. Leaving the brick and clapboard buildings clustered in the center of town, he walked south toward the two blue hills in the far distance that rose above the broad swale between Cemetery and Seminary Ridges and entered a residential neighborhood, two-story houses with flower and vegetable gardens in the back, shade trees in front. Barnhill strolled the streets, pausing to study the houses, and to remember. He stopped at a picket gate beneath a trellis overgrown with wild roses and gazed at the house beyond the circular drive: painted white with green shutters and front door, a wide porch, vaguely familiar. Could it be? He opened the gate and walked up the path to the porch. With so many returning veterans about, surely the townspeople expected things like this. He knocked, and within a few moments a young woman answered the door, tall and pretty with blond hair and cornflower blue eyes, drying her hands on an apron. Barnhill slipped off his hat and said, "Pardon me, ma'am."

"Yes," she said, giving him a curious look. "May I help you?"

"I'm looking for a particular house," replied Barnhill. "I was wondering, well, if this might be Reverend Bryan's home?"

She gave him an even more curious look, cocking her head to one side. "Well," she said after a moment, "it *was*. He passed away years ago. Did you know him?"

Barnhill studied her as she nervously clutched her apron. "Might you be Dora?" he asked.

"Why, yes."

"I apologize," he said, "for the intrusion. My name's James Barnhill. Your father did me a great kindness after the battle. In fact, I feel as though I owe my life to him."

"Barnhill," she repeated with a trembling lower lip. "You were the wounded soldier. The nice soldier."

Barnhill nodded. "And you were the sweet little girl. I remember you very well."

Dora invited him in and insisted on bringing him a glass of lemonade. He waited in the parlor, which seemed to have changed very little from the room he remembered, with striped wallpaper, floral carpet, and a tintype portrait of Reverend Bryan on the table in the corner, wearing spectacles and looking rather grim. Dora entered the room carrying a tray with two glasses, which she lowered to the table. Handing Barnhill a glass, she said, "Hot day today."

He nodded and took a sip. "That's delicious," he said. "I remember you brought me lemonade when I first came here."

"I don't remember much," she said. "Except for the battle and the fact that you were here, with the others. I remember the smell. The awful smell." Barnhill sat in an upholstered chair and crossed his legs. "But," she added, "Papa often spoke about it years later." In response to Barnhill's encouraging look she said, "About how brave you were, and kind to the other soldier. That we should always remember there were good and decent men fighting for the South."

Barnhill looked her in the eye and said, "Your father was very kind." He noticed a small blond boy peeking into the room from the hall and smiled. Dora turned and said, "Willie. Come in and say hello." The boy, a virtual replica of the child Barnhill remembered from two decades earlier, entered the parlor and gave Barnhill a diffident handshake.

"Hello, son," said Barnhill. He rose from his chair and said, "I should be going. But it was so good to see you, and this house, again." Dora walked him to the front porch. As he reached for the latch of the picket gate, he turned back to see her holding the boy's hand. He waved goodbye, the child waved back, and Barnhill let himself out, feeling strangely melancholy. He was, he realized, missing Robert Maxwell.

The remnant of the Texas Brigade, perhaps forty men in all from the four regiments that fought at Gettysburg, had agreed to assemble at 1:00 p.m. for a picnic lunch at a place that approximated the site of their brief bivouac on the afternoon of July 2, 1863. A thin stream meandered through a meadow below the shoulder of Seminary Ridge where the southernmost flank of the Confederate line had been positioned, facing, at an acute angle, the Emmitsburg Road. The ground looked vaguely familiar to Barnhill, though the trees were taller and more numerous, but the pale blue hills with their skirt of pines looked no different than on the day he'd slowly driven past them with Robert Maxwell reclining in the back of the carriage. A luncheon of fried chicken, ham sandwiches, and potato salad was laid out on folding tables next to large tubs filled with iced-down bottles of beer. The men formed lines, filled their tin plates, and found a shady spot beneath the oaks and elms to swap stories over lunch and cold beer on the hot July day. Barnhill chose a fallen log next to his cousin "Lucky" Sam Perkins, Major Sellers, and two of the Fifth Texas scouts, men who often accompanied them on Big Thicket bear hunts. The scouts, as they'd done many times before, recounted their ride up to the summit of Round Top on General Hood's direct orders.

"Warn't no Yankees on the big hill," said one as he nibbled on a chicken wing. "Nary a one." The others, middle-aged men in shirtsleeves wearing broad-brimmed black hats, gazed up at the eminence that commanded a view of the entire battlefield, but especially of the smaller hill below it that had been packed with Union infantry and artillery at the time of the Texans' ill-fated advance.

"Hauled us a couple o' six-pounders up that hill," said the other scout, "and we'd a' blown the Yankees all to hell."

"Damned Old Pete," said Sellers as he took a long swallow of beer.

We've been through it all before, thought Barnhill as he gave Sam a knowing look. *Too many times. And now Longstreet had written a book defending his decision to force the division's attack across the Emmitsburg Road, and Hood no longer alive to dispute his account.*

"Longstreet had a bad case of the slows," said another man, a former officer in the Fourth Texas. "And with Stuart's cavalry off God knows where . . . What the hell."

That about summed up the men's view, twenty years after the battle. It had not been meant to be. Barnhill rose from his seat, dusted off his trousers, and took his plate to the mess table. He slipped his watch from his pocket and checked the hour. Another fifteen minutes, and it would be time. At four o'clock the small body of men formed ranks, in the same order as the regiments had formed in '63. Barnhill stood at the head of his column, with Harry Sellers beside him mounted on a rented nag, since his gouty feet prevented him from marching. Out in front, the honor of carrying the brigade's battle standard went to a tall veteran with a drooping mustache and missing left arm, wearing his torn and bloodstained tunic and slouch hat. After briefly consulting his watch, Sellers rose up in his stirrups and called out, "Forward, *march!*" Across the Emmitsburg Road, choked with dust from the many wagons hauling visitors in and out of the battlefield, to the sound of cheerful band music rather than cannon fire from the ridge in the distance, with a peach orchard, filled with ripening fruit in the strong afternoon sun, on their left, the men silently walked. Barnhill was conscious of the carol of songbirds and the tramp of feet, but stared straight ahead, imagining that his sergeant major, the Irishman Dillon, fortified with whiskey, was marching beside him. Dillon, who survived that hellish charge but died of wounds at Chickamauga. . . . There, Barnhill noted, looking toward a tall tree on his far left, was where General Hood had been wounded by an exploding shell. The ground sloped upward and many of the men lagged behind, but Sam stayed up with him. Approaching the trees at the base of the smaller hill, Barnhill quickened his pace, sweating, his breath coming hard. The clearing ahead was strewn with boulders, larger even than he remembered them. The crumbling remains of a stone wall—he remembered Dillon vaulting over it with a shout and fixed bayonet—and beyond it a shallow stream, Plum Creek. They paused for breath at the stream, Barnhill mopping his brow with a handkerchief.

"Devil's Den," said Sam, gazing up the steep slope, the way blocked by boulders amid the tall pines. "Hard to believe our boys charged up that hill."

Barnhill merely nodded and started up again, finding his way between the boulders until he reached a rocky plateau just below the summit. He gazed up at the dense foliage and then down at the smooth slab of granite. Sam, panting, arrived after a moment and said, "Is this the spot?"

"I reckon," said Barnhill. Reaching down to steady himself, he climbed alone the final twenty yards to the summit, obscured by the trees. To his surprise, a man was sitting on a fallen log, one leg crossed over the other, smoking a pipe. "Howdy," said Barnhill, slipping off his hat and wiping his brow. The man grunted and puffed on his pipe.

"Are you, ah . . ."

"The 140th New York," replied the man as he rose from the log. "We held this hill."

"Fifth Texas," said Barnhill. "We tried to take it."

"I seen you stop down there," said the other, pointing down to the rocky plateau. Barnhill nodded. "There was a Rebel officer who fell on that ground. Our boys could scarcely believe he'd made it that far. We hauled him up here when the shootin' stopped, damned near dead."

"Much obliged," said Barnhill, reaching out to give the man a vigorous handshake. "Your men saved my life."

CHAPTER TWENTY-FOUR

AMELIA STOOD IN THE FORMAL LIVING ROOM, listening to the *ticktock* of the grandfather clock in the front hall as she studied her reflection in an oval mirror. She turned and walked absently into the dining room, gazing at the oil portraits of her forbears above the mahogany sideboard. After a moment, she returned to the living room to study her reflection in the mirror, thinking she should apply a bit more powder, and listened again to the clock; how slowly the minutes crept by. The long hand struck the hour, followed by five slow, dolorous chimes. Moving to the tall secretary, she took a slip of yellow paper from a pigeonhole, which a boy riding a pony had delivered the previous day from the telegraph office. Unfolding it, she read: ARRIVING ELIZABETH CITY BY TRAIN NOON JULY 4 PROCEED EDENTON BY CARRIAGE. Tossing the telegram aside, she walked to the front hall and out on the broad portico, pausing with one hand on a fluted column to gaze down the long gravel drive to the gateposts.

A cooling breeze stirred the crowns of the oaks and chestnuts as Amelia strode purposefully down the drive, the wind furling her long cotton skirt, lifting the brim of her straw hat with the bright blue ribbon. She stood at the brick gatepost, looking out beyond the wide river to the slate water of Albemarle Sound in the far distance, remembering that long-ago parting . . . Jamie, so handsome in his uniform, and she in a wide hoop skirt that had long since gone out of fashion. Her gaze fell on the road into town, arrow straight and lined with tall pines. She couldn't remember the last time she'd traveled to Elizabeth City nor the length of the journey. Besides, the train might be late. Across the road was the stump of an old tree, sawn down years ago, a smooth surface where she could sit in the shade and fresh breeze, with a hint of salt from the brackish water. She may have dozed, for when she looked up she could make someone out, a mere speck in the distance, walking down the road. The speck grew larger, a man, judging from his height and the shape of his hat, holding a case. When he drew within a few hundred yards, she slipped from her seat and stood in the road facing him, her heart pounding. He stopped for a moment, staring at her, and then began walking again, faster, almost a trot. She could see his face, his wide smile, and ran to greet him.

Dropping his valise in the road, Barnhill took her outstretched hands and looked into her eyes. "Amelia," he said with a delighted expression, giving her hands a gentle squeeze.

"Jamie," she said. "I can hardly believe it."

"A dream I had, so many times," he said. "And now it's come true." He surveyed the wide sloping lawn with its moss-draped oaks and the graceful white house on the knoll overlooking the river. "Everything looks just the same," he said. "Just like I remember it. Including you."

She blushed slightly and said, "Not really," with a small shake of her head. "You'd be surprised at how much has changed." Barnhill looked into her lively gray eyes and nodded. "You've had a long day," she said. "Let's take your things up to the house and get something cool to drink."

Barnhill sat in a comfortable overstuffed chair in the parlor, one leg draped over the other, admiring the English and Colonial furnishings and the fine oil paintings hung on the robin's-egg-blue walls. He visualized Josiah Maxwell in his black frock with scarlet silk waistcoat before the fireplace, holding forth on the valor of Lee's army and the treachery of his fellow Carolinians who advocated restoration of the Union. He glanced up as Amelia entered the room holding two drinks, one a silver julep cup beaded with condensation, which she handed to him, and the other a glass of iced tea, both garnished with sprigs of mint from the garden. Barnhill held the cup to his lips, inhaled the aroma of mint, and took a sip of sweet, iced bourbon.

"Albert acquired a taste for mint juleps at the Old White," said Amelia. "The Bondurants summered at White Sulphur Springs. Do you know it?"

"Of course. Finest resort in the South."

"Albert taught me how to fix one."

"A right good one," commented Barnhill. "But you're not partaking?"

"I don't touch hard spirits. You may recall . . ."

"I do recall. I may have forgotten . . ."

"Jamie," said Amelia, sitting on the horsehair sofa next to him. "It was a long time ago."

He sipped his drink and looked at her; for all these years he'd had nothing to remember her by, no photograph or drawing. There were subtle changes, of course, from the pretty young woman he remembered: tiny wrinkles at the corners of her eyes and mouth, strands of gray in her light brown hair. But her neck and chin were strong, and she'd kept her trim figure. "Tell me," he said, "about Albert. And the children." The children were away, by design, at the summer cottage near Nags Head on the Outer Banks. Alone in the house, except for the servants, Amelia and Barnhill talked for hours in the old parlor, lighting the oil lamps as shadows fell, Amelia refreshing his julep. She lovingly described her late husband, and Barnhill shared the story of his marriage to Kate, including the murder of her first husband by the Yankee trooper but avoiding mention of her troubles, suggesting, if obliquely, that his devotion to Kate had never equaled his love for Amelia. They compared notes on their sons, both bright, good students and lovers of the outdoors, and Amelia described her tomboy daughter Charlotte, who loved to ride bareback along the river road. The conversation drifted to Barnhill's career; she politely praised his celebrated triumph over the railroads, and finally, over a quiet supper, turned to the events that drove them apart in the last months of the war. To her quiet fascination, he described the terrible suffering the regiment had endured at Petersburg in the winter of '65; how he'd relinquished his last hope of returning for her after reading the letter she'd sent by courier as he huddled in a miserable mud shelter.

"When the end finally came," said Amelia with the light from the candelabra reflecting in her eyes, "the news of Lee's surrender and Jeff Davis's flight from Richmond, Father was too overwrought to leave his study. Some of the poor Negroes wandered up to the house, asking what would become of them. It was then that I learned Father had mortgaged the plantation. And all he had to pay with was worthless Confederate money."

"And so the bank foreclosed?"

Amelia nodded. "We were able to save the house and about five acres. The farmland went to a Yankee speculator; the slaves became sharecroppers, living in the same shanties . . ."

"Same as all over," commented Barnhill. "And the overseer?"

"Mr. O'Grady?" Amelia looked intently into Barnhill's eyes. "The blacks murdered him," she said quietly. "Burned down his house. At all events, Father grew ill, suffered a stroke. I had to care for him and somehow keep the place going. It was terrible, Jamie."

"And then you met Albert."

"Yes. A Godsend. And within two years of the war Father was dead." Barnhill nodded, reflecting on what might have been. Amelia cleared the table and returned after a few minutes with a bottle of vintage port—another indulgence of her late husband—and two wineglasses. They sat side-by-side in rocking chairs on the portico, sipping their port as they watched the three-quarter moon rise over the river, casting a beam of intense white light across the rippled surface, and listened to the mournful song of the whip-poor-wills.

The next morning, following a hearty breakfast of eggs, bacon, and grits in the alcove by the kitchen, they ventured out, strolling down the drive to the road along the river and then walking, arm in arm, in the direction of town. After a quarter mile, they reached a break in the trees near the place where the overseer's house had stood. "Do you mind," said Barnhill, turning to Amelia, "if we take a look?"

"Of course not," she replied. She held his hand and led the way through a narrow stand of pines to the black furrowed fields, some six hundred acres of green cotton shimmering in the midmorning heat. To their right, beside the white board fence enclosing the Widewater property, were the remains of an outbuilding, the boards and beams charred and broken. Barnhill walked over for a closer inspection with Amelia following behind. Apart from a few pieces of blackened timber and a half-buried jar, nothing remained of the house.

Barnhill turned back to Amelia and shook his head. "I'll never forget that day," he said. "It changed my life forever." She came closer and gave him an encouraging look. "I'd gone into town," he continued, "to buy your ring. If I'd only started back sooner . . ."

"If you hadn't come along when you did," said Amelia, "that poor man would have been whipped to death. It was meant to be, Jamie. In God's plan."

He nodded. "Yes," he said, "I suppose you're right," though even after the lapse of twenty years the recollection filled him with bitterness. Staring at the weed-choked ground, an image of the slave came to mind, strapped to the rack with blood streaming down his back, and the overseer, bare to the waist with the coach whip in his hand. He wondered how the blacks had killed O'Grady—probably with a hunting knife—though he wouldn't dare ask Amelia. Turning away, he said, "Could we visit Robert's grave?"

"Of course." Putting her arm through his, they walked back to the road, rather more quickly than they'd come. Entering the Widewater property through a gate at the back, they climbed slowly up the gently sloping hill in silence, each overcome with the power of remembrance. The Maxwell family burial plot was situated at a high point behind the house, enclosed by a wrought-iron fence, shaded by a tall elm, and bordered by a neatly tended flowerbed. Closing the gate behind them, Barnhill gazed at a weathered headstone, mottled and worn away, just able to make out the words "John Sloan Maxwell, born September 16, 1778, died March 19, 1840." Turning to Amelia, he said, "Your grandfather?"

"Yes," she said with a nod. "He built Widewater."

Barnhill glanced briefly at the headstones marking the graves of Josiah Maxwell and his wife and then moved to a lichen-covered stone marker at the back of the enclosure. Listening to the rustling boughs overhead and aware of the cooling shadow of a transient cloud, Barnhill read aloud the inscription:

Robert Sloan Maxwell
Captain, 26th North Carolina, C.S.A.
Born June 12, 1838
Died February 16, 1864

He stared at the words, thinking back to the cold day when they'd lowered Robert's coffin into the ground, rain dripping from the brim of the parson's hat and tears streaming down the cheeks of several house slaves gathered at the gravesite. He turned back to Amelia, who stood behind him with her arms folded at her chest, tears in the corners of her eyes. Barnhill embraced her, holding her close. "He was such a good man," he murmured. "And the best friend I've ever known."

Taking a step back, she held his arms and gazed up at him. "Yes," she said. "And you were so good to him. You brought him home."

He took her hand and led her from the enclosure, strolling down the lawn toward the drive. After a short distance he noticed a particular live oak, with a massive, gnarled trunk and moss-draped boughs. He stopped and asked, "Is that the tree?" Glancing briefly at the old oak, she gave him a puzzled look. "The tree," he explained, "where I asked you to marry me?"

"Oh," she said with a smile of surprise. "I remember now. Let's sit in the shade."

The midsummer sun was well up in the sky, and with their backs against the fissured bark they were thankful for the shade and the breeze from the river. A mockingbird sang overhead and the grass buzzed with insects. Barnhill loosened his collar and rolled up his sleeves, and Amelia kicked off her shoes. "Not very ladylike," he observed, eliciting a happy smile as she leaned her head on his shoulder. He snapped off a shoot of grass and chewed the stem.

"Do you remember the promise you made that day?" she asked.

"Of course," he said. "To marry you."

"No. The other one." Barnhill rubbed his chin and gazed into the distance. Before he could answer, she said, "You promised to go with me over to Nags Head, when the war was over . . ."

"I remember," said Barnhill. "And take a picnic on the beach." She nodded. "With champagne and fried chicken."

"Exactly," said Amelia. "You promised."

"I believe a man should be true to his word," said Barnhill, drawing up his knees and tossing the shoot of grass aside.

"Well," said Amelia, clutching his arm. "I told the cook to fry up some chicken. And I expect there's some decent champagne in the cellar."

"When can we go?" he asked excitedly.

"Tomorrow morning. I promised the children we'd come."

CHAPTER TWENTY-FOUR

"Robert always insisted it was the finest stretch of seashore in the world," said Barnhill. Standing up, he took Amelia's hands and pulled her to her feet and into his arms. Encircling her slender waist, he looked into her eyes and then kissed her, savoring the softness of her skin and her fragrance, thinking, we're falling in love all over again.

Amelia's elegant carriage, painted bright yellow and drawn by a matched pair of grays with a black coachman on the seat, arrived at the Edenton waterfront at 9:00 a.m., just as a flat-bottom fishing scow was docking at the pier. Barnhill watched with fascination as the crew of ten or more black men, chanting in unison, labored to haul in the mile-long seine, filled with the morning's catch of herring and shad from the waters of Albemarle Sound. The *Nanticoke*, a shallow-draft side-wheeler, was moored at the adjoining pier with bright pennants flapping on the halyards in the steady onshore breeze. Barnhill helped the driver to carry the wicker hamper and Amelia's large trunk, packed for an extended stay, up the gangway to the steamer's deck before returning for his valise. He stood beside Amelia at the varnished railing, gazing down at the bright yellow carriage with the red wheel rims, the stamping gray horses, and the quay teeming with workmen and passengers. As black smoke poured from her twin stacks, the *Nanticoke* shuddered and, with the great side-wheel churning the dark water, slipped away from the pier.

Clutching her straw hat, Amelia smiled at Barnhill and said, "Let's go up in the bow. I can point out the sights." As the tall pines and church spires of Edenton receded in the hazy distance, the steamer glided into the open water with the rhythmic rush of the side-wheel. Standing at the railing, Barnhill shielded his eyes and peered at the narrow strip of barrier islands dimly visible across fifty miles of green water. Each summer of Amelia's forty-three years—apart from the summers of '63 and '64 when the Federals had occupied the Outer Banks—had been spent at Nags Head, and over the noise of the water rushing along the sides she reminisced happily of shell collecting, fiery sunsets over the sound, and moonlit strolls on the beach. After two hours had passed, the trees and settlements of Roanoke Island came into view and, with a slight adjustment of course, a conical structure, striped in black and white, appeared on the horizon. "Bodie Island Lighthouse," said Amelia, pointing a slender finger. "I remember the old lighthouse, built when I was a little girl.

To keep away the wreckers."

Resting his arms on the railing with the warm sun on his face, Barnhill said, "The wreckers?"

"That's why they call it Nags Head," said Amelia with the air of someone about to tell an apocryphal story. "The people who settled the Outer Banks," she explained, "had no way of making a living, so they lured ships on to the sandbars and plundered the wrecks."

"How did they manage that?"

"By tying a lantern to a horse's head and walking it down the beach at night. A *nag's* head," she added with a smile. "The ship captains would see the lights and make a wrong turn."

"I'll be," said Barnhill. "Nags Head."

"At least that's the story my grandfather told. And he should have known."

As the coastline grew closer Barnhill could easily see the tall, striped lighthouse and the pale green ribbon of pines and palmetto on the lee shore of the narrow barrier island. With a single blast of the ship's horn, the captain slowed the engines and made a lazy turn to port, bringing the steamer alongside a weathered pier that extended a hundred yards from the shore. With a shout, the deckhands cast their lines to the men waiting below, mooring the vessel to the stanchions as the side-wheel slowed and came to a stop. By the time Barnhill escorted Amelia down the gangway, a handsome black man, wearing faded overalls and a wide-brimmed straw hat, appeared on the pier to greet them. "Mornin', Miss 'melia," he said with an affable smile.

"Hello, Jim," she replied. "This is Mr. Barnhill." The men shook hands and returned to the deck for Amelia's heavy trunk and the wicker basket, which they loaded on a handcart propelled by two barefoot black boys. At the end of the pier, next to the small ticket booth where several enterprising children were selling lemonade for a penny, was a waiting buggy, hitched to a mule with blinders on. After stowing the luggage and helping Amelia onto the seat, Barnhill climbed in beside her and Jim started the buggy forward with a snap of his whip at the animal's long ears. They drove through the tiny settlement of Nags Head, little more than a general store, livery, Baptist church, and icehouse, and continued northward, with mounded dunes and the blue-green Atlantic to their right and views of the sound on their left between stands of pine and scrub oak. After traveling another mile they turned into the drive at a two-story house, painted white with blue storm shutters, with gingerbread cutouts on the broad porch overlooking the beach and ocean. As the driver halted the buggy and climbed down from his seat, Barnhill turned to Amelia and asked, "Was this your family's cottage?"

Amelia nodded and said, "Built by my father before I was born."

Gazing at the quaint cottage with the ocean in the distance, Barnhill smiled and said, "Robert was right. I can't imagine a prettier stretch of seashore." As he walked with Amelia up the oyster-shell path he observed that the house stood on tall stilts and that a large round structure, like an oversized barrel, sat on the roof.

As he studied it, Amelia explained: "It's a cistern. To catch rainwater. There's no fresh water on the island." As they climbed the stairs to the porch Barnhill listened to the crash of the surf and took a deep breath of fresh sea breeze with a tang of salt. Four cane-back rockers lined the screened-in porch in front of tall windows, and next to the front door were a dog's water bowl and a child's toy train. Hearing the sound of footsteps, an elderly maid appeared at the door, which she flung open with a wide smile. "Hello, Aunt Cassie," said Amelia walking up and giving her a hug. "Let me introduce Mr. Barnhill, who's come all the way from Texas."

The maid, who was wearing a starched white dress with her gray hair tied up in a scarf, studied Barnhill for a moment and then said, "I remember the gen'lman from the war, when he was with Marse Robert."

"Hello, Auntie," said Barnhill. "So you remember?"

"Sho do," she said with a smile. "Never could forget how you helped all the poor slaves with that turrble fever." At the mention of the incident all three were silent for a moment, thinking about Robert Maxwell's death. "Come in the house," said Cassie. "There's a pitcher of sweet tea."

The airy living room, paneled in knotty pine with wide plank floors and braided rugs, commanded a view of the beach and ocean, no more than a hundred yards beyond the sand dunes. While Amelia busied herself in the kitchen, Barnhill reclined in a white wicker armchair, contentedly sipping his tea, staring out at the sparkling ocean. Hearing commotion outside, he rose from his seat as a little girl, barefoot and wearing a sundress, threw open the screen door and raced into the house with an older boy in hot pursuit. "Give it back," he yelled and then stopped in his tracks, staring at the six-foot-three stranger. The girl stopped as well, giving Barnhill a frightened look.

"Children!" said Amelia, who appeared in the next moment drying her hands on her apron. "Stop that running and say hello to Mr. Barnhill."

"Hello, sir," said the boy, walking up and giving Barnhill a firm handshake. "I'm Bob." He was tall for his years and wiry, his blond hair sunbleached and his face as brown as a berry.

"And I'm Charlotte," said his sister softly, similarly suntanned but with dark brown hair. Too shy to look Barnhill in the eye, she turned toward her mother.

"You can call me Jamie," said Barnhill with a smile, giving the boy a pat on the shoulder.

"C'mon over, Charlie," Bob scolded his kid sister. "He ain't gonna hurt you."

"Don't say ain't," corrected Amelia.

"Ain't proper," added Barnhill, which caused Charlotte to giggle. Hearing a scratch at the screen door, he walked over and opened it for a large yellow dog, which nuzzled his knee.

"That's Belle," said Bob. "She's a retriever."

"I'd bet there's some fine duck hunting in these waters," said Barnhill. "Could use a good retriever . . ."

"Yes, *sir*," said Bob enthusiastically. "She loves to hunt."

"You children go wash up for lunch," said Amelia. Both mumbled, "Yessum," and hurried into the kitchen.

"Fine-looking children," said Barnhill. "How old . . ."

"Seven and ten," said Amelia. "A bit rambunctious."

"Now about that picnic," said Barnhill, walking over to Amelia and placing a hand on her arm.

"The hamper's all packed and loaded in the cart. And the champagne's on ice."

A small flatbed cart was hitched to a black-and-white pony, surprisingly strong for an animal of its size and impatient to be on its way when Amelia climbed up on the seat. With a flick of the reins, she started the pony down a duckboard path that led from the cottage through the dunes, with Barnhill walking alongside. When they passed through the dunes, Amelia brought the cart to a halt and, shielding her eyes, gazed out on the glittering water and lines of breakers scrolling toward the wide beach. "Let's go north," she said, starting the pony forward again. She steered closer to the water's edge where the wet sand was firm, easing the burden for the small horse. Barnhill, wearing a straw hat with his sleeves rolled up, watched two men standing in the shallows as they snapped their long fishing poles and cast their lines far out into the surf. After passing ten minutes in silence, listening to the breakers and the cries of the gulls dipping overhead, they approached a small wooden structure painted white with red shutters. As they drew closer Barnhill observed a dory, with the letters *U.S.L.S.* stenciled on the bow, and eight long oars leaning against the side of the building. "The Life Saving Service," said Amelia. "They have stations up and down the beach, to rescue ships when they founder on the sandbars." A door at the back of the building swung open and a man with bright red beard appeared, wearing overalls and tall oilskin boots.

"Ahoy, Miss Amelia," he called out with a smile.

"Hello, Mr. Watson," she called back.

Watson strolled up to the pony and patted it on the forelock. "Loovaly day," he remarked in a peculiar accent. "How 'r you todoy, m'lord?" he inquired of Barnhill.

"Very well, thank you," Barnhill replied, giving the man a curious look.

"Enjoy yeerselves," said Watson, turning to go. "Beware the runnin' 'o the toyd," he added over his shoulder.

Once Watson was in the distance, Barnhill said, "What was he saying? I couldn't follow . . ."

"He's what's known as a 'hoy toyder,'" explained Amelia. "For the odd way they pronounce 'high tide.' They've lived out here since Colonial times and still speak the old English dialect. Here," she said, halting the cart with a tug on the reins. "This spot ought to do." As Amelia unhitched the pony, which wandered over to the vegetation in the dunes, Barnhill unloaded the wicker hamper, two folding chairs, a beach umbrella, and a wooden bucket with a bottle of champagne packed in ice. The midsummer sun beat down as Barnhill arranged the chairs in the shadow of the umbrella, uncorked the champagne, and poured two glasses.

Taking the chair next to Amelia, he handed her a glass and, as the steady breeze furled her light brown hair, looked in her eyes and said, "A toast. To the remembrance of departed loved ones, and to life ahead with those we love." She touched the rim of her glass to his and they each took a sip.

"That's mighty good," she said, "though I'm not much of a fancier of champagne. Albert ordered it from Paris."

"It's twenty years late," said Barnhill, taking another sip, "but in a way even better."

Amelia nodded, leaning back in her chair and gazing out at the sparkling ocean and clear blue sky. "At the end of the war," she said after a moment, "there wouldn't have been much to celebrate."

"Amelia," he said, again looking in her eyes. "I've never been happier."

"Nor have I."

"And I never stopped loving you." He leaned over and kissed her softly on the lips.

"Oh, Jamie," she murmured. "I gave up on you loving me a long time ago." He kissed her again. "This seems," she said, leaning back, "like a dream. I have to pinch myself."

"I never stopped believing," he said, "that someday I'd come back."

After enjoying a picnic of cold fried chicken, deviled eggs, ham biscuits, and watermelon, washed down with more champagne, they sat contentedly in their chairs, barefoot, watching the shorebirds—pipers, terns, and gulls—and a formation of brown pelicans flying low over the breakers. "Jamie," said Amelia, placing a hand on his arm.

"Yes?"

"What will you do now? When will I . . ."

"You remember the promise I made to your father," he said. She nodded. "I couldn't have kept it, not then. But," he said, raising himself up on an elbow, "I can now. I'm relatively prosperous, and have a nice home—nothing, mind you, as fine as Widewater. And the local men have asked me to run for judge . . ."

"Jamie," she interrupted. "I have something to show you." She rose, walked over to the wicker hamper, and reached inside. Returning to her chair, she displayed a small velvet box in her palm. Opening it, she removed a gold ring with a garnet stone. "When I accepted this," she said, slipping it on a finger which, Barnhill now realized, bore no wedding band, "it was a promise to be your wife. If you'll still have me . . ."

Barnhill stood up, took Amelia by both hands and lifted her into his arms, holding her in a long embrace.

CHAPTER TWENTY-FIVE

AFTER PAUSING ON THE LANDING TO SPEAK with a young lawyer wearing a sack coat and the new style of shirt collar, Barnhill descended the wide courthouse staircase to the marble foyer, where he purchased a copy of the afternoon paper for a nickel and walked out on the front steps. Standing in the pleasant October breeze that snapped the Lone Star flag over the cupola, he briefly scanned the headlines, noting with curiosity a small notice below the fold.

"Good evenin', Judge," said a portly man of approximately Barnhill's age who passed him on the steps. "Goin' to the meetin' tonight?"

"Evenin', Charlie," said Barnhill. "I just might." With a glance at his old law office across the square, Barnhill proceeded along his accustomed route through the few inhabited blocks of the small town, returning the cheerful greetings of folks he met along the way and crossing the long footbridge just as dusk was beginning to fall. Inhaling the pleasant aroma of a pile of smoldering leaves and pine needles, he entered the kitchen through the back door, where he found the two girls, Mary, now age eleven, and Charlotte, sixteen, at the supper table with the black cook Dinah, whose hair was streaked with gray. Their older brothers were both away at the university in Austin; Jim, now twenty, and Amelia's son Bob, a year younger.

"Hello, sweetie," said Barnhill, walking up to Mary and mussing her auburn hair.

CHAPTER TWENTY-FIVE

"Big Jim," said Charlotte after swallowing an oversize bite of buttered cornbread, "guess what I learned in school today?" Not long after her mother's remarriage and the painful move from North Carolina to Texas, Charlotte had made up her mind to look on Barnhill more like an old family friend than a stepfather and distinguished him from her new stepbrother with the casual appellation "Big Jim." No matter that the son now stood the same height as his six-foot-three father, he was still "Little Jim" to Charlotte.

Pulling back a chair and reaching for a square of cornbread, Barnhill turned to Charlotte and said, "What did you learn?"

"About the Battle of San Jacinto," said Charlotte proudly.

"I know all about that," said Mary, picking at her plate of chicken and string beans.

"Do not," said Charlotte dismissively.

Undeterred, Mary said, "Where Sam Houston whipped the Meskins."

"See there," said Dinah, who thought of Mary as something of her own child.

"That's right," said Barnhill with a smile, aware that every child in Texas knew the fabled history of Texas independence before the age of ten. "And did you know that my father—your granddaddy," he added, looking at Mary "—fought with Sam Houston at San Jacinto?"

"Time to head home and fix supper," called a man out on the porch. It was Ernest Wilson. "Come along, darlin'," he added. After years of looking after Ernest in a hundred small ways, Dinah had finally consented to marry the widower, both of them virtual members of the Barnhill family.

Barnhill smiled at Dinah as she untied her apron. He noticed Amelia standing in the doorway to the dining room. "Hello, sweetheart," he said, rising from his chair and walking over to give her a kiss on the cheek. Though her hair had turned completely gray, she was still pretty, with an unlined face and good figure.

"Guess what came today?" said Amelia. "A letter from Robert." Like many mothers, she used his full Christian name when especially pleased or upset with her son.

"Finish your supper, Mary," said Barnhill, certain that Charlotte, who was growing like a weed, would clean her plate. "Let's go to the parlor," he suggested to Amelia, "and you can tell me all about it."

Barnhill chose his favorite chair in the snug parlor, with its wide plank floor, faded Persian carpet, and an engraving, widely popular in the

South, titled *The Burial of Latane* over the mantel, depicting Southern women, aided by their slaves, presiding over the burial of a fallen Confederate soldier. As Amelia searched for the letter in her sewing basket, he took a thin cheroot from his coat pocket, which he lit with a match struck on the sole of his boot.

"Here it is," she said, seated at one end of the sofa. Scanning the pages filled with Bob's chicken-scratch handwriting, she said, "Reports he's doing well in his classes, though finding chemistry a challenge . . . elected vice president of the junior class . . ."

"A regular college man," interjected Barnhill with a puff of aromatic smoke.

"Yes, but here's the part that should please you. He wrote, 'I've made up my mind to follow Jim's example and apply for admission to the Law Department.'"

"I'll be danged," said Barnhill with a slap on his knee. "Both of them headed for the law school."

"What would you expect," said Amelia with a smile, "of the sons of one of the state's leading judges?"

Later in the evening, with both girls in their upstairs rooms, Barnhill folded his napkin on the dining-room table and said, "There's a political meeting in town tonight. I'm thinking of going."

"Really?" said Amelia with surprise, as her husband generally avoided party politics. "Who's speaking?"

"Cyclone Davis. Should attract quite a gathering."

"Cyclone . . . Oh, that fiery Methodist preacher with the, ah . . ."

"He's no preacher," said Barnhill, "though he can stir up a crowd with the best of the Bible pounders. He's one of the leaders of this newfangled People's Party. I aim to find out what the fuss is all about."

Barnhill stood at the verge of a clearing, just outside of town, unsure whether to continue. A crowd overflowed the large tent, otherwise used for evangelical revivals, whose peaked canvas glowed in the yellow light of flickering torches. Barnhill glanced up at the Milky Way, the bright swath of stars glittering in the black sky, reminding him, as it invariably did, of nights on the cold ground during the war. He listened to the sounds from the tent in the still night air, excited voices, backslaps, and guffaws; common men at a political meeting, passions fueled by strong drink. No,

Barnhill considered, not just common men, but poor, angry white men. Should a respectable figure like himself, an exemplar of the old conservative order, a judge . . . dare to set foot inside that tent?

Drawing closer, he noticed, to his surprise, a number of black men at the fringe of the gathering, farmers, judging by their overalls and patched shirts. Barnhill approached the tent just as the speaker—a tall man standing on a wooden crate—was concluding his introduction of the evening's star attraction: "A giant of a man!" he shouted in a nasal twang. "With the steel backbone to stand up to the ruling class, the bloodsuckin' Yankees! A man of the *people!*" Raucous cheers erupted. "Cyclone . . ." shouted the speaker, "Davis!" Barnhill assumed a place, as inconspicuous as possible, at the back of the tent, a few paces from the black farmers, who appeared equally as ill at ease. As the crowd, almost all poor white farmers, continued to hoot and holler, a tall, impressive man, wearing a simple black suit and white shirt, shook hands with the men standing at the front and then stood up on the crate.

Like many gifted orators, Cyclone Davis warmed to his subject slowly, almost indolently, speaking in calm, measured tones, pausing to make eye contact with various men in the large crowd, a technique that charged the air with a certain electricity, like the unsettled atmosphere preceding a thunderstorm. "I ask you, sir," said Davis, addressing a farmer at the center of the crowd, "what is the price of your cotton today? Compared to the price you were paid five, ten, twenty years ago. A third? A fourth?" he said, jabbing the air as his strong voice rose. "And what of the cost of ginning your crop, shipping those bales to market, let alone the cost of seed and furnish?" Holding a worn volume in the air, Davis rhetorically asked, "What did Mr. Jefferson have to say? The working class," said Davis as he grasped the lapel of his frock, "the poor farmer, the mill hand, has suffered this exploitation at the hands of the men of capital, the railroad tycoons, timber barons, and their eastern bankers, for far too long!" Davis seemed to rise in stature with each hammer phrase. "The time, my friends," said Davis, "has come to *fight!* Not with the *bullet*—not now, at least—but with the *ballot!*" The call to arms was answered with deafening applause and cheers from the gaunt, ill-clothed farmers and laborers.

"You colored boys at the back," said Davis as the cheering died away. "You boys know the meaning of servitude."

"Yassuh!" called out one of the blacks, an older man Barnhill recognized from his days as a field hand on the Lucas plantation.

"Well," said Davis to his curious listeners, "you colored boys gave your allegiance to the carpetbaggers, and what did they do for you? And then the Redeemers came along, the Democrats, and they took your vote, all right . . ."

"Damn right," said a tipsy man in front.

"Oh, yes," said Davis with a smile. "They were happy to take your vote, and your money, and to *hold you down!*" Davis withdrew a handkerchief from his back pocket and wiped his brow. "Well, I'll tell you men something," he continued. "You're *all* in servitude, white as well as black. In servitude to the monied interests, preaching gold over silver, capital over labor. And the time has come," he thundered, raising his fist, "to rise up in rebellion, throw off these shackles, and be free!"

Near pandemonium broke out, blacks cheering along with whites, impelled by the bond of the disadvantaged united against their oppressors, the absentee landowners, merchants, bankers, and worst of all, the hated railroads and mill owners. Conscious of the reek of sweat and alcohol and the palpable threat of the violence of an incited mob, Barnhill slowly retreated into the shadows as the angry men clamored for more. Cyclone Davis, towering over the mass of men, cast a brief, inscrutable look in the direction of Barnhill, who then turned and walked quickly into the chill, dark night.

The elderly secretary at Addison Parker's office on Houston Street was gone now, quietly laid to rest in the cemetery outside town, replaced by an efficient young man recently graduated from Parker's cherished project, the state university in Austin. "Yes, sir, Judge Barnhill," said the secretary, rising from his desk. "Mr. Parker's expecting you." He held open the heavy walnut door to the hallway. Ascending the spiral staircase, Barnhill paused at the top to gaze into Addison Parker's spacious office, thinking back to his first visit as a young lawyer fresh from his modest victory in court over the Katy railroad. For over twenty years Parker had been his most important client, advancing Barnhill's reputation throughout East Texas and paying handsome fees that enabled him to live in relative affluence. Barnhill was relieved to have finally severed his relationship with Parker when he took his place on the bench, ending the duty of loyalty required of an advocate for his client, beholden to no man. He slipped off his hat, straightened his shoulders, and walked into the office, where he found Parker seated in a green leather armchair in the corner, reading the newspaper by the light streaming through the tall windows.

"Good morning, Jamie," said Parker, looking up over the top of his tortoiseshell glasses as he folded his paper.

"Morning, sir."

"Have a seat." Parker rose and moved slowly to the chair behind his desk. In his late seventies, he was stooped and frail, with blue-veined hands and only a wisp of white hair on his crown, and his once-elegant coat was worn and frayed at the cuffs. Slowly lowering himself into his chair, he rested his elbows on the surface of the elaborately carved mahogany. "Now, then," he said with a sigh, "you wanted to see me about these so-called Populists."

Crossing one long leg over his knee, Barnhill said, "Yes, sir."

"Dangerous rabble-rousers," said Parker. "Full of talk of revolution."

Barnhill nodded. "I went to one of their meetings the other night," he said. "Cyclone Davis was speaking. I didn't care for what I heard, and I've been doing some reading about their movement."

"Tell me about it," said Parker, pouring a glass of water from a small pitcher with a trembling hand.

"Well," said Barnhill, "it's an outgrowth of the Farmers Alliance, but far more radical. The mood is angry, even violent. The leaders are promising the poor farmers, black and white, a revolution of sorts. Government control of the railroads and the banks. Price guarantees for cotton and corn."

"Folderol," said Parker. "I was a staunch Republican, as you know. But now I swear allegiance to the Democrats, and we'll put a stop to this riffraff."

"And you should also know . . ." Barnhill hesitated. "They're demanding union rights, including the right to strike."

"By thunder," said Parker, "not at my mills! I could give a damn what these socialists do to the railroads. Serve 'em right. Or empty promises to poor, ignorant farmers. But I've got a hundred Pinkerton men on my payroll, armed with pistols and shotguns. The first union organizer who comes to town . . ."

"Don't forget, Mr. Parker," said Barnhill. "I'm a judge, with a solemn oath to uphold the law. I'll not tolerate violence." He held his long-time client in his steady gaze.

Taking a swallow of water, Parker said, "All right, Jamie. You do your duty, as you see it, and I'll do mine. Besides, I'm an old man, with no one to carry on the business after I'm gone. No one to care for me . . . apart from Sally." Though he'd never married, Parker had maintained an entirely proper relationship with Sally Porter, to whom he was greatly devoted, for many years. Without heirs, he had long since decided to bequeath the bulk of his fortune to the state university, where he had served on the Board of Regents since its founding in 1883.

"How is Sally?" asked Barnhill.

"She's . . . very kind to an old man like me. She deserved much better."

"And business?" asked Barnhill.

"Poor," said Parker with a shake of his head. "The price of lumber keeps falling. And besides, the longleaf is about played out now. Another ten years at most."

Barnhill thought about the magnificent stands of virgin pine, hundreds of thousands of acres teeming with game, now largely reduced to stumpage. "What will you do," he asked, "when the longleaf's gone?"

"We're planting shortleaf and loblolly, the fast-growing pine varieties. Pulpwood rather than sawtimber. But I'm too old to worry about it."

Addison Parker seemed very old indeed, and very tired. He'd blazed a remarkable trail in industry, and used the great fortune he'd made to endow a fine public university, where both Barnhill's son and stepson would soon earn their degrees. "Well," said Barnhill, rising from his chair and slipping on his hat. "It's good to see you, sir."

"Good to see you, Jamie," said Parker, too weak to get up. "And tell that sweet wife of yours I said hello."

"I'll do that," said Barnhill. With a slight nod to the old man, he turned and let himself out.

Judge Barnhill sat at his high-backed chair, resting his black-robed elbows on the long oak bench in the second-floor courtroom. He gazed out at the men and women in the packed rows, most of whom he'd known all his life, his eyes coming to rest on a shabbily dressed man with his lawyers at the table inside the railing. A man by the name of Herman

CHAPTER TWENTY-FIVE

McDougal, the accused, on trial for the premeditated murder of Ben Talbot, Sheriff of San Augustine County, and his deputy, Luther Ellis. McDougal, Barnhill considered, was a typical habitual criminal, with a long career of robberies and assaults, drifting from town to town, in and out of the county jails and the state penitentiary. The deceased sheriff, recently elected to office on the Populist Party ticket, had provoked the wrath of the county's business leaders when he jailed a number of armed guards employed at a local sawmill to break up a union strike. Barnhill studied the accused, with his sallow complexion and scraggly mustache, and his well-dressed attorneys from nearby Nacogdoches, whose fees, Barnhill surmised, were being paid by businessmen, members of the Democratic Party, ruthlessly determined to drive the upstart Populists out of existence. The early summer day was hot; the hum of the slowly turning ceiling fans and call of the songbirds through the open windows filled the otherwise silent courtroom. Barnhill slipped his watch from a vent in his robe and checked the time. Over an hour had passed since he dismissed the jury to deliberate. He briefly made eye contact with his son Jim, seated on the third row next to his stepson Bob, both of whom had followed the trial with great interest as both had been recently admitted to the bar.

In the two years that had elapsed since Addison Parker had died quietly in his sleep, political violence had flared throughout the region, and in each instance the victim was a member of the Populist Party: the lynching of an outspoken black leader, an attack on a newspaper editor and arson of his office, and now this, the sheriff and deputy shot in cold blood by an obviously hired killer. At the sound of footfalls in the hall, Barnhill watched as the side door opened and the bailiff escorted the twelve men of the jury into the box, where they took their seats amid the general murmurs of the excited spectators. It was a predominantly white panel, as the prospective jurors were chosen from the voting records, and blacks were voting in far smaller numbers as the Populist revolt, in full flower in '92, was in rapid decline by the middle of the decade. In the face of determined resistance from the entrenched Democrats, the white Populists, erstwhile friends of the black man, were beginning to question their cross-racial alliance. Well, Barnhill considered as he studied the expressionless faces of the jurors, the Populist revolt had sprung from the lowest class of white farmers, men who had always harbored the greatest contempt for their black countrymen. Barnhill gave his gavel a sharp *rap*, instantly silencing the courtroom. "Mr. Foreman," he said, "has the jury reached a verdict?"

A common-looking man, dressed in the simple garments of a farmer, rose from his chair and, in a loud voice, replied, "We have." Barnhill nodded to him to proceed. "We find the accused, Herman McDougal," said the foreman, "guilty of murder with . . . ah, malice aforethought in the deaths of Sheriff Talbot and Deputy Ellis."

Though Barnhill expected commotion, the packed courtroom remained eerily silent. "A unanimous verdict?" he asked.

"Yes, your honor."

Barnhill looked steadily at the defendant, who affected a look of indifference, and said, "The accused will rise."

After exchanging a quick glance with his lawyer, the man stood. "As the jury has returned a verdict of guilty," said Barnhill, "by the authority vested in me, I hereby sentence the accused, Herman McDougal, to the punishment of death by hanging." The bailiff called out: "All rise!" Barnhill stood, glanced briefly out over the crowded courtroom, and then walked quickly to his chambers.

Wearing shirtsleeves with his collar open, Barnhill sat in his favorite chair on the porch next to Amelia, rocking beside him as a gentle breeze stirred the treetops in the gathering dusk of the late June evening. Both watched with contented expressions as their sons started across the footbridge with their sisters following behind, tall Charlotte with her arm around the shoulder of Mary, now fifteen, on their way into town to attend a church social. Charlotte, following the example of her brothers, had recently completed her second year at the state university, where she was studying literature with the intention of becoming a schoolteacher. "Fine children," said Barnhill as the rocker creaked.

Waiting for the chorus of cicadas to subside, Amelia said, "Yes, Jamie, they are. They're all bright and hard working, with good characters."

Barnhill rocked in silence as the light grew dim and lightning bugs blinked in the darkness beyond the footbridge. After a while he said, "But I worry about the world we've brought them up in." She gave him a questioning look. "I wonder if you remember something you asked me a long time ago, when I was at Widewater during the war."

"Tell me."

"We were upstairs in the library, and you asked me about Carlyle's history of the French Revolution."

"I vaguely remember," said Amelia, visualizing the room with its view of the lawn and river.

"You said, if they destroy our way of life—comparing the Yankees to the French radicals—what will become of us? And who will care for the blacks? Something like that. I thought about it often."

Amelia nodded.

"Well, there was a time," Barnhill continued, "when, after everything we've been through, it looked like things were finally moving in the right direction."

"And they are," she insisted.

He stared into the gloaming. "I'm afraid we've failed," he said at length. "Judging from that man I sentenced to hang today. Men preaching violence and hate, and more violence in return."

Amelia placed a hand on his arm. He placed his hand on hers and smiled. "I take comfort," she said, "that there are men like you. And like Robert and Jim . . ."

"And young ladies like Charlotte," said Barnhill.

"And Mary. Raised to do the right thing."

Barnhill gazed lovingly at Amelia in the pale light of the rising moon. He listened to the mournful call of a whip-poor-will and said, "I love you, sweetheart. And we'll do our best to help them."

"And I love you, Jamie, with all my heart."

EPILOGUE

The Big Thicket
October 1915

The boys awoke in the cold and dark as the first hint of dawn glowed on the tent canvas. Propping himself up on an elbow, Bob, the younger of the two, whispered, "Jimmy? You awake? It's freezin' in here." Staring into the darkness, he listened to the north wind in the boughs overhead.

"Go back to sleep," murmured the other boy, curled up under his blankets.

Bob heard footsteps outside the tent and someone humming, the deep bass voice of Sam, the cook. After a few minutes, the tent grew lighter and the tempting aromas of coffee and bacon penetrated the canvas. Jimmy, hitherto completely hidden in his bedroll, suddenly sat bolt upright. "Dang it," he exclaimed, rubbing sleep from his eyes. "We better git movin'. Grandpa will tan our hides if we're late."

Bob sat Indian-style on his bedroll, rubbing his arms for warmth. It was the first morning of his first hunting trip to the Thicket, and he shivered more with excitement than from the cold. "You reckon we'll find us a bear?"

"Ol' Kil's hounds will find 'em," said Jimmy, "if there's any to be found."

Bob could see his breath clouding before his face and hear the logs crackling on the campfire. "You ever wonder," he said, "what it was like for the soldiers in the Rebel army?"

"I don't know," said Jimmy sleepily. "I suppose."

"Hard to believe," said Bob, "that your Grandpa was fightin' the Yankees at Gettysburg."

"Yep," said Jimmy, kicking off his covers. "But I never can git him to tell about it."

"Well, we better get dressed and get some breakfast."

The boys stood at the back of the line, waiting for the grown men to get their coffee and plates of bacon and cornbread. "Where's the judge?" asked the man standing closest to them.

"Don't know, sir," said Jimmy. "Must still be gettin' ready."

"The judge," said the man with a grin, "is usually up at the crack of dawn for the first cup of coffee, rain or shine."

The boys exchanged uneasy glances. "Let's look in on him," suggested Jimmy. Bob, whose late grandmother had been the judge's second wife, nodded. They walked to the tent, surrounded by pines that blocked the morning sun, and stopped to listen. Jimmy, almost six feet at age fifteen, stooped down and pulled back the tent flap. "Grandpa?" he said, peering at the motionless form lying under the covers. With Bob close behind, he crept inside and knelt beside the still form. "Grandpa?" he repeated. He nervously placed a hand on his grandfather's shoulder and gently shook it. After waiting a moment, he carefully rolled him over and peered at the motionless form.

Tears began to well in the boy's eyes as he gazed at his grandfather's pale, still face, lying peacefully in repose with eyes closed. "He's gone," said Jimmy with his voice breaking, looking up over his shoulder at his cousin. "Grandpa's gone."

ABOUT THE AUTHOR

JOHN KERR, a native of Houston, lives with his wife Susan in San Antonio, Texas. He is a graduate of the University of Texas Law School and of Stanford University, where he studied history, literature, and poetry. *The Silent Shore of Memory* is his fifth published novel, following *Cardigan Bay*, *A Rose in No Man's Land*, *Fell the Angels*, and *Hurricane Hole*. In addition to his writing career, Kerr is actively involved in business and in a number of nonprofit organizations, serving on the boards of the Environmental Defense Action Fund, the Menninger Clinic, Humanities Texas, the Texas Biomedical Research Institute, the Admiral Nimitz Foundation, and the McNay Museum of Art.